MY NAME IS NOT ALEXA PEARCE

Book One Of The Search For Hope Trilogy

KERRI McLOONE

MY NAME IS NOT ALEXA PEARCE

Book One Of The Search For Hope Trilogy

KERRI McLOONE

ISBN-13: 978-1-7323133-0-9   (Kindle)
ISBN-13: 978-1-7323133-2-3   (Paperback)

Cover design by Kerri McLoone
Author photograph courtesy of Kerri McLoone

Contact:
KerriMcLooneBooks@gmail.com

Follow Kerri McLoone on social media:
facebook.com/KerriMcLooneBooks
instagram.com/_kmbooks_
twitter.com/_kmbooks_

DISCLAIMER: This is a work of fiction. Any names, dates, likenesses or events described herein matching actual persons or instances is entirely coincidental.

For My Love,
Without Who I Could Not Have Done This

PROLOGUE

Ever since I was little, my parents would tell me stories about good versus evil. How good was made up of love and light, and evil of hate and darkness. While my friends were hearing bedtime stories about princesses being saved from the tall towers of a nasty queen's castle, I was told stories about a princess who saves the world.

The story went that over twelve hundred years ago, a ferocious demon named Darius, created a small portal from the fiery depths of a hellish world allowing himself and a few other less powerful demons to escape into the human world. He walked the earth leaving nothing but death and destruction in his wake, vowing that he would continue to destroy all forms of good, including magic, and kill anything that got in his way. When he was finished, he would then open the portal forever, allowing demons free reign on the people of earth.

Magical creatures like witches, sorcerers, fairies, gypsies, elves, shamans, and leprechauns came together to figure out what to do. Their strongest leaders pooled their powers and put a curse on Darius. He would be forced to wait until such a time that an all-powerful magical heir was born, one stronger than anyone had ever seen. The heir, a princess of sorts, would be all the best of good magic, a culmination of their collective strengths. If Darius could defeat the princess and steal her powers, only then could he open the portal completely.

My family told me stories of the powers this princess would have: the ability to move things with her mind, to throw fire from her hands, to make anything she thought real, to transport herself wherever she wanted, superior senses, to see the future, and to read other people's minds.

The princess could also change her most trusted friends into her soldiers and bestow her power to move things with her mind on them. They were called Extensios. But the wicked Darius could do that too and with the same power. He could force innocent people or choose the worst of people to be his soldiers, called Victus.

As a child, my grandfather would play out the role of the evil Darius, and my brothers and I would act out the battle scenes from the story. I would lead my older brothers and my army of Extensios to war to defeat Darius and his Victus. Using my "powers" we would triumph, ridding the world of Darius and closing the portal to that infernal place, trapping all demons there permanently.

I didn't know then that it wasn't just a story. I didn't know then that it was both my past and my future.

I didn't know then that I *am* the princess from the story. I *am* the culmination of 1200 years of good magic on earth.

I didn't know then that when I was born my parents bound my powers, cloaking me from Darius to protect both me and my family. I grew up knowing of magic and seeing it was real, but without having any abilities of my own. My grandfather used to say I'd grow into them.

On my eighteenth birthday, my powers were released and my whole world changed. In order to protect my family, I've had to leave my home, using powers I never knew I actually had, and then change my identity and cease to use magic all together, without the assistance of a binding spell.

I have traveled from place to place across America looking for the one thing I need, the key to defeating Darius. I landed in Portland, Oregon fifteen months ago because I now know that the significantly important, essential thing I need is here. Something I have been searching for for the last five years. Something that has been hidden from Darius for centuries.

I must continue to hide until I find it. Until the time is right. Until I am ready.

PART ONE

• 1 •

"ALEXA"

The clock on my nightstand reads 6:59 AM. I open my eyes in time to see it change to 7:00 AM and hear the alarm go off. The new me, "Alexa," is a morning person. The radio is set to a raunchy morning show and today's topic is whether or not it's okay for the interns to all sleep with each other.

A head appears out of a black mound of fur at the foot of my bed. Milo, my six-year-old chow-labrador retriever mix, must've felt me roll over to turn off the alarm. He yawns and sticks out his pink tongue that has blue spots on it, a tell-tale mark of his chow heritage. Milo stands and stretches, first with both front legs stretched out and his rear end in the air, then both hind legs straight out backward, one at a time. He shakes his stocky, sixty-five-pound frame from nose to tail and plops right back down on top of my feet, jostling my whole bed in the process.

Milo was a gift from my grandfather on my seventeenth birthday. "He's a special dog," Grandpa told me. "Always keep him with you no matter what. He will keep you safe."

Milo's had the same collar since he was a puppy, lime green with a red crystal hanging from it. "Never take his collar off, he'll grow into it." Another of my grandfather's instructions.

My grandfather and I trained Milo together. Grandpa actually spent extra time with Milo and taught him some very special and specific commands. Milo has always been a very good dog. Right from a puppy, it's always been as if he can understand every word I say to him — I know now that that's exactly the case.

I pull the warm covers back up to my chin and rub the sleep away from my face. As my eyes clear slightly, I catch a blurry Milo throwing some serious side-eye at me.

"Don't give me that look, Milo, the alarm woke me up too," I laugh at the dog. Regardless of who I've been, I have always been an animal lover. Other than a small box, Milo is the only thing from my previous life that I got to bring with me. Laughing at his expression allows me a rare moment of open freedom from my otherwise heavily guarded existence.

I throw the comforter over my head and say, "You at least have the luxury of curling up and going back to sleep, while I have to go to work."

Hearing my muffled voice say "work" and choosing to hear it as "walk," Milo's beefy frame leaps off of the bed, jostling me around again, and bounds to the bedroom door. His curled tail is waving like a flag in a hurricane. I let out a groan as Milo starts to whimper and scratch at the door to get out.

"I said work, not walk, you fuzzball."

Trying to get any additional sleep before my second alarm is useless now with Milo up. I know he won't stop whining until we go around the block, at least twice, so I grab my glasses from my night table and put on the first pair of sweatpants I see. As I open my bedroom door, Milo bolts to the front door of my apartment, and continues to whimper, turning in circles. He's so excited that he's quivering, I can barely get his harness on. I stand up and take my jacket off its hook; a faded rust color canvas jacket with a plethora of pockets that I've had for what feels like forever. It's actually a little ugly, but it's comfortable and practical.

"We go for two walks every day. Sometimes three! How do you still get this excited?"

"Ah, the pleasures of being a dog with no cares in the world except which tree to pee on and what squeaky toy to chew."

I'm startled by the voice behind me and whip around with one of my arms in its sleeve to see my roommate, Cali Jacobs, sitting cross-legged on our living room coffee table balancing a large bowl of Cap'n Crunch on her left knee while the newspaper and remote sit on her right knee. She's holding the cereal box and a pen, doing one of the mazes on the back.

I didn't even know she was there, I think. *I must be overtired or something. Or I'm getting too comfortable here. Either way, not good "Alexa."*

Cali owns the apartment we live in. Her grandmother bought the top floor apartment of a three-story building thirty years ago. She rented it out when Cali was little, and they lived in a small home. While Cali was in college, her grandmother sold their small house and moved back into the apartment. When she died two years ago, the last of Cali's family, she willed it to her, along with a decent inheritance.

Since it's a two-bedroom, Cali rents out the second bedroom to me for a very reasonable price and lives off of that. She's lucky enough she doesn't have to work right now while figuring out exactly what she wants to do with her life.

Before I know it, Milo has gone over and is eating her cereal right out of the bowl on her knee.

"Milo no! That's not yours!" I stride over and gently tug Milo away from Cali's bowl and peak at the box in her hand. "Using pen? A little adventurous for you, wouldn't you say?" Cali just rolls her eyes in response. I walk back to the door and say "Come on pup, want to go for a walk?"

The upward inflection in my voice and the word "walk" sends him into another tizzy of excitement, and he trots back to me quickly, tail swinging happily. In this moment I could be just any twenty-three-year-old trying to walk their crazy dog before work.

Cali lets out a little cheer as she finishes the maze and picks up her cereal bowl, pours more in to replace what Milo took, and continues eating. I scrunch my nose in disgust, but Cali either doesn't see or doesn't care. I love my dog but would never do that. I've seen what Milo has put in his mouth.

With a mouthful, she says, "Come on Lex, watch Wake Up Portland with me. He can wait, can't you Dog Man?" In a baby voice, she adds, "Who's a good boy!" Milo goes back over and flops down onto his back in front of Cali. "Ooh, he wants a belly rub!"

"I would love to Cal, believe me. But I have to walk him and shower and get to work. That pup ain't cheap you know. And for that matter neither are you." She feigns offense by clutching her chest and we both laugh. "I'm kidding, I'm kidding." *Joking's okay but, you can't let your guard all the way down just yet,* I remind myself.

"Suit yourself," Cali responds.

Tired of the ping pong Milo keeps doing and wanting just to get the day started, I snap my fingers and say, "Milo, side." The black dog is immediately by my side, alert at my left knee. *Thank you, Grandpa.*

"What are your plans today, Cal?" I ask as I clip Milo's leash to his harness.

Around another mouthful of cereal Cali says, "Oh my day is packed. Probably spend most of the day in exactly what I'm wearing right now, may hit the gym, haven't decided yet. But first, I'm going to finish this box of Cap'n Crunch while I watch my show. Players from the Portland Thorns and the new NWSL commissioner are going to be on to talk about the upcoming season."

"Huh, I'm partial to Reign FC," I say to bait her.

"You bite your tongue. This is a Thorns household. Rose City 'til I die, baby!"

"No, ma'am. Fortune favors the bold." We stare each other down for a few seconds before simultaneously throwing our hands up in a silent truce. "So I'm guessing that's why you're awake this early?"

Cali just nods at me while chewing her cereal. A dribble of milk is trailing down the middle of her chin. She wipes it away with the back of her hand.

"I'll probably hit Roast on the way back from Milo's walk, do you want anything?"

"No thanks, I'm going to stop by later. Hey, we should definitely go to a game or two this season."

"Sure that sounds like fun," I voice my agreement as I finally corral Milo out of the door. I hear Cali call after me, but missed what she said, so I catch the door with my foot before it closes.

I stick my head back in and ask, "What'd you say?"

"I said be nice to him on your walk." She pauses, wiggling her eyebrows as she adds, "Maybe the pup can snag you a boyfriend or two."

I know Cali is expecting a response, so I just scoff and say, "I'm always nice, and no thank you."

I close the door behind me and think, *definitely do not need Milo to get me a boyfriend. Milo's job is primarily to keep the wrong people away.*

 **2** ●

It is shaping up to be a beautiful, early April day in Portland. As we're walking, Milo lifts his head and sniffs the still cool breeze that blows in his face. It is such a nice day I decide to walk a little further than usual.

"What do you say, big guy? Another lap around the block?"

Milo turns his head around to me as I talk and gives me a snort in agreement. As he turns to face front, a gust of wind comes by and pushes his floppy ears straight up surprising him. My dog stops in his tracks and shakes himself out from nose to tail. As I watch, I find myself chuckling at him. *This is nice, it almost feels...* Before the thoughtfully forms in my head, I immediately chastise myself. *You and Milo still need to be careful, "Alexa."*

I shake my head and give a command, "Milo, casual."

To anyone watching us, we're just strolling along. But I can tell by Milo's pricked ears and how he's puffed out his chest, that he's now just as alert as I am, taking in every ounce of our surroundings and memorizing it.

Casual is another one of the commands my grandpa taught him. Milo is not only alert to his surroundings, but he's also scanning for any evil person or threat. That special collar of his with the crystal acts as a one-way barrier;

he can sense if evil is around, but evil cannot detect that Milo is himself a magical creature. His magical ability, in combination with his natural dog intuition, has helped me out of a couple jams along our way.

Before going home, Milo and I stop at Roast, a little coffee and pastry shop right around the corner. Dogs usually aren't allowed in but Milo is so well trained, he's one of the few exceptions. Honestly, everyone he hasn't sensed evil from — or been ordered to attack for that matter — loves him. His tail is always wagging and he has a sweet face. Plus he's kind of chunky, which only adds to his appeal.

I get Milo a pup-cup as a treat, which is basically just a dollop of whipped cream in a small cup. For myself, I get a sesame bagel with cream cheese and a hot chocolate. I am not a coffee person, that's something that hasn't changed no matter where, or who, I've been.

As I enter the lobby of my apartment building, I unhook Milo's leash from his harness. Right before we climb the stairs, I say "Milo, side." From the first step to the last, he stays in sync with my left knee. I unlock the door and walk in with Milo still at my side.

I lean down to take off his harness and say "Good job Milo. Good boy, pound it." I hold my fist out and Milo bumps it with his nose. I praise him again as I hang up the leash and harness with my keys next to the door. I take a few bites of my bagel and put the rest down on the counter, pushing it far enough back out of Milo's reach. He may be really well trained, but he's still a dog.

I pour my hot chocolate into a travel mug, rinse the paper cup and plastic top, and put them both in the recycling bin. Milo goes right to his bowls so I give him his own breakfast, fresh water, and pat his head.

I walk back through the living room toward a short hallway that leads to the bedrooms and bathroom.

"Don't eat the rest of my bagel. I'm going to take a shower." I say as I pass Cali who has moved from the coffee table to laying on the couch.

Cali raises her head and asks "You talking to me or Dog Man?"

"Both," I respond. I hear Cali laughing as I go down the hall to my bedroom.

I close and quietly lock my bedroom door. I close the curtains and turn off all the lights. I make it as dark as possible in the room so that no person who is innocently, or intentionally, glancing at my window can see what I'm doing. By feel and memory, I lift the top left corner of my full-size mattress, closest to the nightstand and the door, and feel for the flap in the fabric of the box spring.

I reach my hand in and take out an ornately carved, mahogany box from its hidden spot between the slats. It has a keyhole on the front. The top has an etched saying painted in silver, "Hope will heal the world."

Always keep this box with you, I hear my grandfather's voice say. I also hear the explosions and clashing of bodies from the battle he pulled me away from. *No matter what you have to leave behind from place to place, take Milo and take this box. It has everything you will need until you find what you're looking for.*

What are you talking about? I screamed back at him to be heard over the commotion behind us.

Trust me, sweetheart, everything you need is in this box.

The key is around my neck on a chain as it always is. I unlock the box and add my change from the bagel and two of the eight additional twenties I got from the ATM on my walk. I keep my real license, as well as the letter from my mother explaining everything, a picture of my family, and one new, completely unused identity underneath the money in a false bottom. I never count the money I have in there. I just keep adding to it.

I close, lock and replace the box to its hole. I lower my mattress and put the key back around my neck leaving the lights off while I undress. I wrap a towel around myself, open my curtains and just as quietly unlock my bedroom door.

As I close the bathroom door behind me, I hear my grandfather's voice again, sucking me back into my memory.

"Say these words, sweetheart. Say them three times out loud, and then you need to think about somewhere far away from here and imagine yourself there."

"Was that him? How did he know where we were!? Is this my fault? Grandpa, what about my—"

"Say them!" I remember my spine going rigid. My grandfather has never shouted at me before. He hands me a piece of very old paper, it's yellowed and creased. I look at the words and begin to recite them:

Hear these words that come from me
Hide my family from the evil I flee
Keep them hidden until the time
I am ready to fight and no longer hide

Hear these words that come from me
Hide my family from the evil I flee
Keep them hidden until the time
I am ready to fight and no longer hide

Hear these words that come from me
Hide my family from the evil I flee
Keep them hidden until the time
I am ready to fight and no longer hide

"Good, very good. Grab onto Milo's collar. Now, close your eyes and think of a place and imagine with your entire mind that you are there. When you open your eyes, read the letter in the box."

I have no idea what the old man in front of me is talking about. I search his eyes, I can read him like a book — all I can see is desperation and love. He has never lied to me or gotten cross with me in my life. I trust him implicitly. I close my eyes and say aloud, "Florida." When I open my eyes, my grandfather is gone and I'm on a beach with nothing but Milo and the box...

I get lost in the memory for a moment but quickly snap myself out of it. It's too risky to dwell on my past for too long. I distract myself by making a mental list of things I have to do today as I step into the shower:

One, Milo needs a bath sometime soon.
Two, ask Jeff for more shifts at the library.
Three, get new wraps for kickboxing.
Four, Milo needs a new leash.
Five, Milo also needs more food.
Six, the graphic novels in the teen section are a mess and have to be reorganized.

I add a couple more mundane things and keep checking over my list while going through the motions in the shower.

I shut off the water, pull the curtain back, and step out of the tub. I look at myself in the mirror. Water is dripping from my curly brown hair onto my shoulders and down my back. My mocha skin is smooth from head to toe; joining the gym has made me leaner and stronger, but I still have my curves.

I can see in my reflection a little bit of all of the people, and magical creatures, I come from in every part of me.

I feel a zit brewing on my jawline and put a spot treatment on it before rubbing moisturizer onto my face. Twenty no-muss, no-fuss minutes later I come back into the living room. My still-wet hair is up in a messy bun, my glasses on, face clear of makeup except for mascara which makes my hazel eyes pop. I'm wearing an olive green button down and dark gray slacks with flats. Most of my clothes are dark because Milo sheds like crazy.

I find him and Cali spooning on the couch watching a household cleaner commercial. His solid frame and bushy hair is blocking almost all of Cali's five-foot-five-inch frame.

As I'm grabbing my keys, jacket, and my bag, I pop into the kitchen and snatch my bagel and hot chocolate from the counter, check my watch, 8:33. *Shit, I'm gonna have to jog the whole way to make it to work on time.* Cali pokes her head over the back of the couch, looks me up and down and says, "You look like a librarian."

"Do I? Damn!" I snap fingers and sarcastically add, "Because I was going for cheap daytime stripper."

"Hey! Those people are just trying to make a living!" Cali fires back.

"Whoa, whoa, whoa. No judgment here, kid. No judgment here." I say holding my hands up in front of me.

Cali laughs, "Kid? You're about to turn twenty-three, and I'm only two months younger than you."

"And don't you forget it."

Cali tilts her heard. She looks me up and down again and goes, "Ever thought about getting contacts?"

I nod. "I have, but the thought of having anything that close to my eyes, let alone having to touch them gives me the chills. I have a hard enough time just putting mascara on." I visibly shiver at the thought of it and Cali chuckles.

"Taking the bike today?" Cali has gone back to watching the TV and doesn't realize I've come up behind the couch.

"I was thinking about walking — well, jogging if I want to actually get there on time. You can use the bike if you want. The chain lock is hanging up with Milo's leash."

She jumps slightly at the sound of my voice and responds "Geez you move around so quietly! But thanks, we'll see if I actually move today. I know I said I would go to the gym before, but I bet you five bucks that me and my honey here will be in this exact position when you come back."

"No deal, I need every five bucks I can get. You seeing Mickey today?"

Cali's eye narrow and she purses her lips. "Maybe. She had the audacity to call me childish! Can you believe that?" She looks up at me for my input.

Yeah, I can, I think but outwardly smirk and shrug.

Cali continues, "So I'm ignoring her for a little." She looks up at me and smirks. "I bet you five bucks she caves first!"

"Now that bet I'll take!" I say laughing. "You can leave my winnings with the mail."

Cali laughs with me, "Sure, sure."

Michaela Westin, or Mickey as everyone calls her, is Cali's girlfriend. They started dating a few weeks after I moved in with Cali, which is about eleven months ago or so. She's just over six years older than Cali. Mickey is a personal trainer and owns a small studio where she teaches kickboxing classes and does one on one sessions. It also has a small gym with machines and weights in the back, which is how the two of them met. Cali had signed up for an individual session, but if you hear Mickey tell it, Cali hung around the studio for weeks until a slot opened up just to get her phone number. Cali usually doesn't deny it.

Although they appear as total opposites, they are honestly a perfect match. Cali is five-feet five-inches; Mickey is the same height as me, five-nine. Cali has a bubbly, outgoing, and — dare I say it — childlike personality; whereas Mickey outwardly appears intense and has a seriously intimidating Resting

Bitch Face, although she is a very warm and caring person. Mickey has blue eyes and dark brunette hair with blemish free olive skin; Cali has green eyes and light auburn hair with porcelain skin, her nose and cheeks covered in freckles. Cali is a bundle of constant energy, her movements can appear a bit spastic sometimes; Mickey (unless in a session) is usually calm and there's a fluidity about her.

Each one truly brings out the best in the other, and anyone who looks at them can tell, they were made for each other.

"Hey, you home regular time?" Cali asks.

I nod and bend over the couch to give Milo a scratch behind his ear. "Don't get into trouble," I say as I straighten up.

Cali looks at me slightly confused and says, "He's always good."

"I wasn't talking to the dog," I say ruffling Cali's hair too.

I laugh and jump out of the way of her arm as it comes over the back of the couch to smack me in the leg. Milo starts to get up sensing the playfulness between us. I scratch under his chin settling him back down in front of Cali.

My roommate wraps her arms around Milo again and mumbles, "You ass" into the fur on his neck. Milo must feel the vibration of her voice because he whips his head around and starts licking Cali's face. It makes us both start to laugh again.

It's a brief moment that almost lets me forget how I got here and what I'm here for. Almost. The thought sobers me immediately. I turn away quickly before Cali can sense my change in mood. I shake the thoughts off and check my bag to make sure I have everything I need. I count *one, two, three,* in my head. *Phone, keys, wallet.*

"Alright, later," I say walking to the door.

"Make good choices!" Cali calls after me.

"Okay, mom," I respond. I don't even need to turn around to see the dramatic eye roll I know I'm getting.

● 3 ●

Make good choices...

Cali's voice echoes in my mind as I head down the two flights of stairs to the small lobby of my building. I'm three steps from the ground floor when the voice in my head changes.

The voice now is the same one that soothed me as an infant. It scolded me when I was little and talked to me when I had a fight with a friend. It cheered me on at basketball games and consoled me after my first break up. It encouraged me to always be kind and to treat people with respect no matter who they are or what they look like. I know that voice like the back of my hand. I've heard it every day of my life, except for the past five years.

My mother.

I suddenly feel an intense ache in my heart that burrows into my very soul. I grab the railing and stop dead in my tracks. I never allow myself to just think about her. If I did, it could put everyone at risk. But right now my mother is the single thing filling my mind.

Every synapse of my brain replays movies from my childhood. It repeats her favorite saying over and over. I can see her face as if she is right in front of me. There is nothing else I want more in the world at this very moment than to see—

No! No, I can't.

My vision blurs as tears fill my eyes, but I don't let them fall. I never let them fall. I blink hard to clear my sight and take three deep breaths to steady my heart. I look at my hand still on the railing, the knuckles white from the intensity of my grip, and force myself to let go.

She's safe, I tell myself. *She's safe because she doesn't know where you are. She's safe because he doesn't know anything. It's okay. She's safe. Everyone is safe.*

It's okay, she's safe. They're all safe. It's okay, she's safe. They're all safe. It's okay...

I repeat the mantra to myself a few more times then take a deep, steadying breath, straighten my clothes and glasses, and run my hand over my hair. With a sharp exhale I take the last three steps down, walk through the lobby, and out the door of my apartment building.

I pause just outside under the short awning and look around. I feel vulnerable from my moment on the stairs. I can't be sure if I actually feel someone watching me or if it's just the adrenaline still flowing through my system. I decide on adrenaline, leave the safety of the building's doorway and make a left turn onto SW Jefferson Street.

I'm walking at quite a brisk pace. I tell myself it's only because I'm already running late. I won't admit it, but part of me knows my little episode on the stairs really got to me, and that's why I'm walking quicker than usual.

Before I know it, I'm at the Portland Art Museum and turn right onto SW 10th Avenue. I've got my head down trying to get to the library as quickly as possible, and don't even see Matt until it's too late to stop myself. I ram right into him, knocking us both down in front of Marty's Deli, our go-to lunch place.

Matt lands flat on his back with me right on top of him.

"Oh my god, Matt! I'm so sorry! Are you okay? I didn't even see you."

My cheeks flush with embarrassment, and my breath catches as I realize just how close we are. I have had a crush on the man underneath me since

I first laid eyes on him on my first day working at the library. I scramble to get off of him as quickly as possible.

"That's okay, don't even worry about it," Matt says standing up and dusting himself off. "I should've known better than to get in your way when it's five minutes to nine."

In my stomach, I can feel the butterflies that swarm every time I see the man in front of me start to flutter. I ignore them and scoff as I cross my arms and say, "Nothing wrong with being punctual!"

Matt imitates me and replies, "No, there is not!"

We hold each other's gaze for a second before we break into laughter.

Mathias Moorely is, in the plainest of terms, gorgeous. He's six-two with silky brown hair, light brown eyes, a perpetual tan, and just enough scruff in his beard that it looks intentional, not lazy. Plus he's got the type of body that makes everything he wears look tailor-made for him. And what a body it is — I may or may not have checked him out during one of Mickey's classes. He's funny, charming, insanely smart. Matt checks off every box on the "total package" list. He's also the sweetest guy I've met in the last five years, maybe ever.

He bends over to pick up the messenger bag that I knocked off his shoulder when we collided, giving me a fantastic view of his posterior. *God, he looks good in those jeans,* I think. I shake my head to clear it of that lingering thought.

"Shall we?" Matt holds his elbow out for me to take. I can feel another flush of warmth creeping up my neck and can't hide the shit-eating grin on my face as I hold onto his arm and we cross Taylor Street to the library. Those butterflies start to flap again.

I've worked at the Multnomah County Central Library for the past thirteen months. As soon as I got to Portland fifteen months ago and realized that this library was that same one detailed in my mother's letter, I applied for a job. Luckily, my after school job when I was younger was at the public library at home. Although that probably wasn't luck, it's much more likely it was my mother preparing me for what was to come.

Matt holds the door open for me as we walk in the main entrance. It's a Thursday, so the library doesn't open to the public until 10 A.M., but the staff gets there a little earlier.

I thank him as I walk through. We head over to the Employees Only lounge area. It's really just a back room with a small table, two vending machines, a coffee maker and a couple of computers for staff use. I take off my jacket and promptly log on to the internal network.

Now that I know this library has what I need, I start every workday with a search through the computer archives. It's a slow process because I don't quite know exactly what I'm looking for, I just know it's here, and it's not like I can enlist anyone's help to speed things up.

"Hey, did Cali ask you to go to that taco place tonight with her and Mickey?"

Matt's question brings me back to reality and I look up from the computer.

"She said this morning she was ignoring Mickey," I reply.

Matt rolls his eyes in response.

"I know," I continue. "She bet me five bucks Mickey would cave first. I told her to leave the money with my mail."

Matt laughs and shakes his head.

Matt and Cali have been best friends and inseparable ever since they first met in kindergarten. Their classmates even gave them the nicknames Moose and Squirrel because they were always together. Matt was consistently the tallest in their class, at least until the tenth grade, and Cali was always small with a very animated personality.

Matt was the first person that Cali came out to as lesbian; Cali was the first person Matt called when his parents got divorced. They've supported each other through everything.

Matt introduced me to Cali a couple of months after I started working at the library. He actually is the one who suggested we live together. I had vented to him about having trouble finding a dog-friendly place I could afford, and he knew Cali was looking for a roommate.

When I asked him why he didn't just move in there himself, he replied, "Cali is my best friend in this world, she's like my sister. I love her and there is nothing I wouldn't do for her. But we tried living together summer after freshman year of college..." Matt got very serious, leaned his head closer to mine and dramatically said, "It. Did. Not. Work."

Matt chuckled and then explained that he's very anal retentive and has to have everything in its place, neat and tidy. Cali is almost the exact opposite of that. For their friendship to survive, they both agreed they were better off not living together. Having grown up with two older brothers, I was okay with some mess and I agreed to give it a go.

Cali and I became close almost instantaneously. Or, as close as I am willing to get to anyone right now. One night a few months after we started living together, we were sitting on the roof of our apartment building talking. The conversation became serious once Cali asked about my past. I became silent while I desperately thought of something I could say.

Cali took this to mean I didn't trust her. I frantically explained as much as I could how I had been through a lot, especially in the last few years (without fully elaborating), and had a hard time genuinely trusting anyone.

I told her I trusted her enough to live with her and feel safe with her, and that that was the best I could do right then. Cali being the understanding and loyal friend she is, accepted that and ended the conversation by saying she hoped one day I could trust her, thankfully in an optimistic tone, not a hurt one.

"Well, are you going tonight?" Matt asks again.

"Oh, yeah, I guess so. I'm sure Cali and Mickey will have made up by then."

Matt smiles at me. "Do you want to go together right from work? We can meet them there."

I can feel my heart start to pound in my chest. *Go together? Like, as in a date-together? No, no it can't be a date. If we went as just us it would be a date, right? Or does it technically count as a double date because Cali and Mickey are toget—*

"Alexa?"

Oh right, that's me.

"Right, sorry. Um sure, that sounds great." I smile and nod at Matt, desperately hoping my internal uncertainty and chaos doesn't come through.

"Great," Matt replies. "Then it's a date."

• 4 •

Cali

After Alexa closes the door and leaves for work, Cali absent-mindedly scratches the top of Milo's head and goes back to watching TV. Once the morning show segment with the soccer players is over, she flips through the channels landing on the sitcom Friends.

"Oh, jackpot." She snuggles into the dog's fur, holding him a little tighter. Minutes later, Milo is snoring right next to her. "Hmm, that seems like a good idea, Milo."

She turns the TV off and closes her eyes. Between the warmth and comfort of having the dog so close, Cali falls asleep quickly.

Cali dreams of her girlfriend. Of them working out together. Of them dancing. Of her body pressed against Mickey's. Of Mickey's soft lips trailing down her throat, her chest, her abs, her—

Cali is awoken by her phone buzzing right next to her head.

She opens her eyes and sighs. "Damn, right at the good part."

She checks her phone and sees she has a text from Alexa. "Ooh, Milo look! A text from your mommy!" Milo is startled awake from his own sleep and whips around head-butting Cali right in the nose.

"Ow! Fuck!" Cali yelps. "Jesus, Milo."

Cali rubs her nose and checks to make sure she's not bleeding. Milo jumps off of the couch and sits down facing Cali. He puts his head down on the couch and looks up at her, the globally recognized dog apology. Cali sees his sad puppy eyes and chuckles.

"It's cool, Dog Man. No blood, no foul." Cali holds out her fist and Milo bumps it with his nose.

Cali unlocks her phone and opens the message from Alexa.

> LEX: hiii. did you maybe forget to tell me something?

Cali purses her lips and thinks for a second. She gets another text from her roommate with the taco emoji and a question mark.

"Oh my god! Shit, I forgot to tell her!" Cali yells out loud and smacks herself on the forehead. Seeing Cali's antics, Milo stands up and wags his tail but keeps his head on the couch looking right at her.

> CAL: oh right that. whoops! well we're going to some taco place tonight. you and the 3 m's – me mickey and moose
>
> LEX: yeah that lol matt said that he and i should just meet you and mick there
>
> CAL: oooooo you and moose going together!? like a date?!?
>
> LEX: relax kid. idk about a date
> LEX: wait. did he tell you it was a date?
>
> CAL: no he hasn't said anything to me! do you want me to ask him??
>
> LEX: no!! absolutely not.

Cali rolls her eyes at her phone. "I don't know why they don't just do it already. They so obviously like each other."

She sends the eye roll emoji back to Alexa.

Cali looks at Milo who is still wagging his tail at her. Cali tilts her head and says, "Milo? Do you think mommy and Moose should go on a date together?" Milo barks once and starts to pant, his tail wags even faster.

> **CAL:** look, i asked milo about it and he said that you and moose should go on a date.
>
> **LEX:** oh really?
>
> **CAL:** yes. he also thinks it should be tonight

Cali stares at her phone waiting for a response. She looks at the dog then back to her phone again. She sees the bubbles signaling Alexa typing a response pop up and then disappear.

"Ooh Milo, she's taking a long time to answer! This is so good. I can't wait to tell Mickey."

> **LEX:** it's not a date. it's dinner with friends
>
> **CAL:** ok lex, whatever you say
> **CAL:** listen i'm going to go stop by mickey's studio in a little bit. i'm gonna take milo with me is that ok?
>
> **LEX:** sure. his harness is hanging by the door
> **LEX:** oh and remember to leave me my 5 bucks
>
> **CAL:** yeah yeah yeah
> **CAL:** alright i'll see you later
>
> **LEX:** later

Cali looks up from her phone and sees that Milo has walked away from her. She listens for a second and hears his tags clinking against his water bowl as he drinks.

"Hey, Milo?"

The dog comes bounding around the side of the couch within seconds. He puts his front two paws up on the couch.

"No Dog Man, no more cuddles. Do you want to go see Mickey with me?"

Cali hasn't even gotten the "with me" out before Milo pushes off the couch and bolts to the door of the apartment.

"Hold on there, pup. I have to get dressed first."

Cali walks down the hallway and goes into the bedroom opposite Alexa's. Milo follows her in and jumps up on the bed. Cali goes to her closet and starts talking to herself out loud.

"Do I want to wear work out clothes or regular clothes? Well, whatever it is, it has gotta be skin tight. That'll get Mickey back for calling me childish. Make her drool right in the middle of one of her classes."

She stands still with her chin in her right hand while she thinks. "Let me take a shower first and then I'll decide."

Milo watches as Cali grabs a towel and heads out of the room. He stands up and turns in a circle a few times, finding just the right spot to curl up for a little snooze.

Cali goes into the bathroom and turns the shower on. She checks her face in the mirror, gives herself a wink and a quick finger pistol before hopping into the hot water.

She rinses off and pours some shampoo into her palm. While soaping up her hair she breaks out into her go-to shower song, Wild Cherry's *Play That Funky Music*. She turns around to face the spray of the shower and sings the song's famous hook.

Unfortunately, that's the only part Cali knows, so she keeps repeating it as she finishes showering. She turns off the water and steps out still humming. She wipes the steam from the mirror, dries herself off, then wraps herself in her towel and goes back to her room.

Milo is still on the bed, curled up like before, and is snoring again.

Cali goes back to standing in her closet, looking through her clothes. She pauses for a moment, then says, "Definitely workout clothes."

Cali takes a couple of tanks down looking for just the right top to make Mickey salivate. She scrunches her nose and tosses the shirts onto the bed. Both land on top of Milo, waking him up. As he moves to a sitting position, one of the shirts shifts, settling around his neck. Cali sees this and perks an eyebrow. A mischievous grin spreads across her face.

****

Almost thirty minutes later Cali and Milo, after stopping at Roast for a coffee and another pup-cup, walk into the aptly named Mickey's Kick Boxing and Training Studio. Mickey is right in the middle of a class which is exactly what Cali was hoping for. She chose to wear her tightest black compression leggings with a light blue oversized tank top that shows off both her sports bra and her obliques. She has a bright white hoodie tied around her waist.

Mickey glances toward the door from the head of her class and visibly gulps and stumbles over her words at the sight of Cali. She recovers quickly enough and returns to her instruction, calling out encouragement and the next moves.

Cali looks down at Milo and says, "Mission accomplished Dog Man."

Cali and Milo wait until Mickey's class is done. Mickey talks to a few of the attendees for a couple minutes before coming over to where Cali is standing. She goes to give her girlfriend a kiss. Cali moves her head at the last second so Mickey catches her cheek not her lips.

"Really? You're still upset about the "childish" comment?"

Cali shrugs and says, "Maybe."

"I didn't mean it in a bad way, babe. I find it endearing actually."

Mickey stops and looks Cali up and down. A wolfish grin slowly spreads across her face. She wraps her arms around her girlfriend and presses into the shorter woman a little bit.

"I'm sorry, I really didn't mean it as a bad thing. Why don't you let me show you how sorry I am."

Cali tries to keep her breathing in check wanting to hold the upper hand, but with Mickey so close and pressing up to her like this it's getting difficult. She looks the brunette up and down. Sees her strong arms and legs glistening with sweat, her t-shirt clinging to her stomach. In the mirrored wall behind them, her shorts show off her toned glutes.

Cali looks up again and stares Mickey straight in the eyes. She's aiming for firm but stutters out "I uh, I—"

Mickey's grin grows bigger. She kisses her girlfriend's neck in just the right spot and Cali's knees literally go weak. She stammers again, "I-I uh, I've got Milo here."

"So?" Mickey smirks at Cali. She knows she's beating her girlfriend at her own game right now.

"Well, uh, what if someone comes in and takes him? How could you explain to Lex that someone stole her dog because you couldn't keep your hands off of me?"

Mickey stops and lifts her head to look Cali right in the eyes. "Who said anything about using my hands?" Cali audibly groans at Mickey's tantalizing response.

Cali gathers her resolve and shoots Mickey down. "No, no. Not now. But oh my god, later." With that statement, she finally kisses Mickey on the lips. Both a hello and a promise of what's to come.

When they finally break away from each other, both a little out of breath, Mickey offers Milo a palm to sniff hello. When she actually finally looks at him she turns to her girlfriend in disbelief.

"Is this dog wearing a neon green tank top and sweatbands on his paws?"

"Yes, they match his collar." Cali notes Mickey's exasperated expression and responds with a look of her own. "Well this *is* a workout studio, isn't it?"

• 5 •

DARIUS

Darius is standing at the back corner of a dingy bar in a rundown building in whichever decrepit little town he's currently staying in. After a few hundred years everywhere starts to look the same. He doesn't exactly know where he is, couldn't point himself out on a map, and frankly, he doesn't care.

He's been standing so long at this bar that he doesn't know what day or even month it is. All he knows is that he has been stuck on this world waiting an eternity for his chance to kill the girl, to take her powers and open the doorway to his home to release his demon brothers and sisters.

Then on the day he finally gets his chance, the day his suspicions were ultimately proven correct, those damn witches and sorcerers and the rest of those *good* cretins were there waiting for him and thwarted his entire plan.

He had made the mistake of thinking the girl would know nothing of the magical world, that they would have kept her in the dark to protect her and she'd be vulnerable and ripe for the taking. Now he's being punished for his blunder, and it's back to the constant, insufferable waiting. Waiting for her to slip up. Waiting for her to let her guard down. Waiting for her to use her powers so he can track her and end her.

Waiting, waiting, waiting.

Darius looks down at the empty glass in his hand and feels a surge of rage overtake him. He snarls out, "Fucking waiting!" and heaves the glass against the wall.

The barroom promptly falls silent. Darius scowls and looks around at each person, throws his hands up and yells, "What?!"

No one dares to answer him. They just go back to whatever it is they were doing before. Darius smooths the front of his pristine white button-down shirt and brushes off the arms of his midnight black, tailored suit jacket.

The middle-aged bartender, conditioned and used to these kinds of outbursts from the odd, black-haired man with tattooed hands, just puts another glass on the wooden bar top and refills it with three fingers of whiskey, neat. He never looks directly at the man sitting in the corner of his bar.

Darius sits down on a stool and has just lifted the glass to his lips when the door to the bar swings open. The blinding white light not only informs Darius that it's daytime but obscures the man who walks in. When the door closes behind him, a giant, bear of a man is revealed. The man is pushing seven feet tall, with large muscles and jet black hair, Greek features and beady eyes.

He sweeps his gaze across the room until they land on Darius. As the man walks toward Darius, he makes eye contact with the bartender. The bartender looks down quickly.

The man sits on the barstool to Darius's right. The wood creaks as it takes his considerable weight.

"Well?" Darius growls.

"Nothing. Not a trace. It's as if they never existed in the first place." The man, Viribus, is Darius's strongest and most loyal Victus soldier.

"What do you mean nothing?!" Darius realizes he's shouting by the sudden quiet again filling the bar. He drops his voice and repeats, "What do you mean nothing?"

"I mean nothing, boss," Viribus says. "I've called in every favor I had left, but there's only so much pull a parole officer has to begin with. Ever since that day five years ago, no one has heard from the girl or any member of her family. It's like they've completely vanished."

Viribus downs the pint the bartender had put in front of him in one gulp. As he puts the empty glass mug down, the bartender swaps it out for a full one.

"It's been five fucking years. I've been roaming this decaying rock putting up with its feeble human race for over a thousand years, and you know what's been the longest part of that? Waiting for you to give me some goddamn results! Now, I don't care who you have to talk to, pay off, threaten, kill, whatever. Get me something to go on. She's stayed dark this whole time, so I've got no way of tracking her. That's what I have you for."

He thrusts a finger into Viribus's chest.

"Whatever the old man said to her that day when he pulled her away, she's doing it down to the letter." Darius continues. "He obviously told her what to do to cloak the family. She's not using any of her powers, I would know — I'd sense it — and then I wouldn't need your sorry ass to find her for me.

"You want any chance of surviving, I *have* to get to her before she gets to me." He downs the whiskey in front of him in a single gulp.

"So, you call every officer you can think of, you find any magical creature you can catch and torture something out of them if you have to. Someone has to know something about where she was going."

Darius looks around the bar quickly. No one is paying any attention to him or Viribus anymore. The demon specifically chooses places like this because he knows cash in this kind of Podunk town buys a lot of anonymity, helps people forget he's even there.

Darius leans into Viribus to make absolutely sure no one else can hear him. "Make Julius reach out to his contacts too. Find me anything to go on. I would hate for either one of you to come back to me empty-handed again."

Viribus nods his head and goes to stand up. Darius's right arm shoots out and grabs a bunch of Viribus's shirt. His fist begins to glow amber as his anger rises at being let down again. His hand starts to burn the shirt and singe the flesh of his lieutenant. Viribus knows better than to move or protest against the searing pain rippling right through his chest and stays quiet.

Darius slowly stands from his stool. As he does, Viribus is lifted into the air as easily as if he was a toy bear, rather than the formidable giant he is. He looks Viribus dead in the eyes. Darius opens his mouth and a sound rumbles out, closer to a growl than a voice. Viribus hears and feels the weight of the words regardless.

"If that wasn't clear enough, hear this: if you or Julius don't find me some information about where the girl went, I will make you beg me to vanquish both of your fucking worthless Victus asses."

Viribus gives Darius one sharp nod and the demon releases him. The large man lands on his feet but stumbles. He holds onto the bar to prevent himself from falling to the floor. He straightens up, embarrassed at being disciplined so openly.

The Victus lieutenant turns to the bartender, pulls out a thick envelope from the inside pocket of his jacket, and slaps it down on top of the bar. He turns away without another glance toward his boss. Darius watches Viribus leave, sees the slice of white light pour in then get cut short as the door to the bar is opened and closed.

The bartender picks up the envelope and puts into the front pocket of his apron as he pours the black-haired man another whiskey, neat.

As he turns to check on his other patrons, he can hear the ancient man grunt under his breath, "*Fucking waiting.*"

• 6 •

"ALEXA"

I'm at the counter by the main entrance of the library scanning books being checked out by a young mother holding a little boy on her hip. He looks to be no older than three. The mother is shushing the child saying things like "just a few more minutes" and "we're going home right after this." I smile at the boy but he shyly ducks his head into his mother's neck.

"Did you pick out all of these books yourself?" I cheerfully ask the boy.

He ducks his head more but lets out a tiny, "Yes."

"Well, you made some really great choices here. You even picked out my favorite book in the whole world. Can you guess which one is it?"

This brings the boy out of his shell a little, and he lifts his head looking at me with a smile, the pure kind that little kids can do so effortlessly.

"This one?" He points to *Corduroy* by Don Freeman.

I gasp. "How did you know! Are you a mind reader?"

The little boy laughs and shakes his head, replies with a drawn out "Nooo."

"Can you keep a secret?" I ask him. He nods eagerly. I deliberately look side to side to make sure no one else is nearby, lean over the counter and whisper, "I am. But, shh, don't tell anyone."

The boy's eyes widen and he gasps. He nods his head again vigorously at my secret. I surprise myself that I could so easily share something so profoundly life threatening should it be heard by the wrong person with a three-year-old.

His mother and I both chuckle as I stack the five books and hand them to the mother and say, "April thirteenth is the return date."

She smiles at me and puts the books into her oversized tote bag. She squints and reads my name off my I.D. tag on the lanyard around my neck. "Thank you, Alexa. Can you say thank you to Alexa, Tripp?"

The smile freezes on my face as the boy thanks me. I can only nod for fear of betraying the cold, painful spear that just shot through my chest on hearing the boy's name. Tripp. Not a common name, but the name of someone I wish I knew what happened to and carry guilt over every single day.

I shake it off before that coldness fully overtakes me. I turn to my right and jump when I see Matt leaning against the frame of the doorway to the employee lounge area.

"You startled me. I didn't know you were there."

Matt doesn't answer me right away but continues looking at me with an expression I can't quite get a read on.

"What?" I chuckle nervously.

"Nothing."

"Okay..."

Matt continues to look at me the same way. *God, he looks so good right now,* I think. I realize I've been holding my breath. I turn slightly away and start stacking books that are on the counter while I discreetly exhale. Matt stands up straight and steps over to a spot a few feet from me.

"Just that, that kid was about five seconds away from having a meltdown," he says. "Until you magically charmed his little socks off."

"I don't know about magically." I chuckle again.

"No? I'd say mind reading is pretty magical." He shrugs.

Oh, shit. Play it off, he just thinks you were joking with the boy. Let him keep thinking that. "Oh, that?" I laugh nervously, my mouth suddenly very dry. I have to swallow a couple of times before I can continue. "That was nothing, just trying to make a mother's day a little easier."

"Well, I thought it was very..." He pauses as he thinks for the right word. "Sweet." He finally says. Matt has taken another step along the counter and is less than three feet from me.

"Um, thanks."

Matt takes another step forward, now at an arms length from me. He holds my gaze the whole time. *There goes my pulse again. This man could be the death of me, Darius may not even get a chance.* That thought breaks the spell. I look down clearing my throat and take one step back.

"I um, I have to go put these books away now," I say as I grope around the counter and grab the first stack my hand lands on. *Oh my god, why are you such a dork "Alexa"?*

"Right, okay. I guess I'll see you later."

I turn to my left, walking quickly out from behind the counter. When I look behind me, Matt is still standing at the counter watching me. He's smiling that same smile that's definitely filled with some kind of warmth. I blush at being caught glancing back and whip my head back around straight. I make the first turn I see, desperate to hide within the rows of books.

Smooth, "Alexa." I think. *SO smooth.*

****

I spend the first half hour of my lunch break still hiding from Matt in the employee's lounge while I get over my embarrassment. I'm sitting at the small four-person table in the middle of the room. I have my travel mug of what's now barely-warm chocolate in my hands, and I'm staring blankly at the stainless steel cup.

Cali would have had a field day with that whole mess, I think. *If she catches wind of it at all tonight at dinner, I'm done for. Why am I so insecure around him though? I fumble around him like a baby deer with vertigo learning to walk.*

I'm so lost in replaying my previous bungle with Matt that I don't hear my boss, Jeff, come in.

"Alexa?"

I jump and smack my knee on the leg of the table. "Ow, shit!" I say out loud. *That's the third time today, damn it,* I think. *What is up with me?!*

When the stars in my vision clear and I realize who it is I just cursed at, or cursed near rather, my eyes widen and I immediately apologize. "Oh, Jeff! I'm so sorry! I didn't mean to say that."

"That's alright, Alexa." Jeff Daley is a bland, no-nonsense kind of guy, very straightforward and rarely shows any sort of emotion. Sometimes the rest of the staff here joke that he's probably half robot. "You wanted to talk to me?"

"I did?" For a minute I have no idea what he's talking about. Then I remember — extra shifts. "Oh, right! Yes, I did. I was wondering if there was an extra shift or two available for me to take on?"

Jeff thinks for a minute and says, "Well, I'd have to see if there is anything available, but you're already at forty-five hours a week. Any more than that and you'd have to be paid overtime. In that case, it would need to be authorized by the higher-ups, and I don't see that happening with the current budget."

I deflate a little, I was really hoping for any extra time I could get.

I wonder what he would say if I told him: Well, you don't have to pay me, Jeff. I just need access to the internal network here to find a very particular, important thing that will help me defeat an evil demon named Darius and save the human world as we know it. I don't know what it is exactly I'm looking for, but considering we're in a library, I'm gonna go out on a limb and say it's some kind of book.

Instead I say, "Right, I understand, Jeff. Thanks anyway."

Jeff exits the lounge without further exchange, signaling the end to the conversation.

Could this day get any worse? I internally complain to myself. *First, you run over Matt in the street. Then, he tells you about dinner but you're not entirely sure if it is a date or it isn't a date. Then you go and make a total FOOL of yourself in front of him. And now Jeff has plainly denied any extra shifts. Plus, you're jumpy as all hell. It's only three o'clock "Alexa", what else is going to happen today?*

I sigh and shake away the swirling woe-is-me thoughts from my mind. I don't have time to wallow. I decide to use the last half hour of my break going through the archives searching for the coveted tome I seek. I narrow my search to the oldest books with obscure or no authors. It's not like I'm looking for Shakespeare or anything.

Three hundred and fifty-three results come up. There is no additional way to sort the list, so I just start going through it text by text. In my mother's letter, she was both vague and detailed about what I was being instructed to look for; she went into great detail about what the building looks like that houses what it is I need, but she offered no guidance on what it is I'm actually looking *for*. She wrote that it would be obvious when I found it, that I would just know.

After five years of searching, fifteen months of it in Portland, and thirteen with access to this library's archives, all I'm absolutely sure of is that, based on Mom's letter, whatever it is I am meant to find is definitely at this library. Somewhere in the bowels of this building is the answer to all the questions I have.

I'm scrolling through my results without any expectations when one listing catches my eye. A book is literally called *The Book*, the information attached to it lists no author, and the language is Latin. *The Book* has been at the library since it first opened in the early 1900s, but the age itself is unknown. The hair on the back of my neck stands straight up, and my entire body breaks out into goosebumps.

"Well, if that's not a sign, then I don't know what is," I say out loud.

I read every word included with the listing until I find where in the library *The Book* is located. It's in climate-controlled storage in the basement with all the other old, fragile, and very expensive books; an area that one needs special authorization and a key-card to access.

Holy shit, I think to myself. *Is this it? Is this what I've been looking for? Could this finally, really be something?*

Before I get too excited, I take a deep breath. *Okay, relax, "Alexa."* If this really is the thing I've been searching for, then I have to stay calm and keep my guard up. I have to check it out, make sure it is for real before I do anything else.

The 3:30 P.M. alarm I set on my phone goes off, signaling the end of my break. I print out the section of the list containing information for *The Book*. The hair on the back of my neck is still standing as I take the page from the printer tray and fold it in quarters. I put it in the pocket of my slacks, log off the computer, and gather myself to go back out into the library.

Before I leave the little lounge area, I stop at a small mirror hanging on the wall next to the door. I run my hands over my hair to flatten any flyaways, straighten my glasses and look myself square in the eyes.

"Okay," I say to my reflection. "Time to work."

The rest of my day goes by very quickly after that. I find myself patting my pocket periodically to make sure the paper is still there, that it's real.

I don't see Matt for the rest of the day. Whether that's because of my severe awkwardness with him before or just coincidence, I don't know.

At 5:30 P.M., I begin corralling people toward the main entrance.

"It is now 5:30, the library will be closing at six. If you would like to check out any books, please bring them to one of the check-out counters. If you are logged on to the computers, please finish up and log off."

I repeat that over and over as I walk section to section, floor to floor. No matter how many times I say it, there is always someone who doesn't hear it until the last possible minute.

At 6 P.M., the doors to the library are locked, and the staff goes around the entire building again. Checking the bathrooms, computer labs, media rooms, and all the nooks and crannies for backpacks, stuffed animals, and even a straggler or two who has fallen asleep or is wearing headphones. Anything we find goes into lost and found, books are left on carts to be put back on shelves the next morning.

When the rest of the staff leaves at 6:30, I wait outside for Matt. While I'm waiting I send a text to Cali.

> **LEX:** just got out of work. waiting for matt. still going for tacos?

> **CAL:** oh yeah! i'm still at mickey's studio, been here all afternoon
> **CAL:** we'll meet you there

Cali sends a screenshot from Google maps of the taco restaurant.

> **LEX:** so much for ignoring her, hmm?

> **CAL:** i know. i'm hopeless when it comes to my boo

Cali adds an entire line of the heart eye emoji for emphasis. I smile softly to myself at how sweet they are on each other. Then I suddenly remember something important.

> **LEX:** wait. you've been there all afternoon?

> **CAL:** yeah. why?

> **LEX:** milo??

> **CAL:** oh! he's still here with me. i already called the place. they said service dogs are ok

> **LEX:** milo isn't a service dog

> **CAL:** isn't he though? plus they don't need to know that
> **CAL:** oh and wait until you see him

Her next text is the purple smiling devil emoji.

> **LEX:** why????
> **LEX:** what did you do to my dog?

> **CAL:** you'll see when we get there

I'm mid-eye-roll at the text I've just gotten, when I hear someone next to me say, "I guess you're texting Cali right now."

I look up from my phone to see Matt staring at me as if I wasn't the same awkward monster he encountered before. He's looking at me like I'm the only girl in the world. *Jesus, "Alexa"! Do you even hear yourself? You are literally the only other person waiting outside the library right now so just stop. Snap out of it girl!*

I nod at Matt and show him the text about Milo. He laughs and shakes his head. Most of the time that's the best, if not the only, response when it comes to Cali and the situations she gets herself, and apparently my dog, into.

"The restaurant is pretty close by. Do you want to walk or get a cab?" I ask Matt.

"It's a nice evening, I'd be okay with walking." Matt looks down to check his own phone that's ringing in his hand. "It's my mom. Hold on a second."

"Oh yeah, sure." *Like I'm going anywhere.*

"Hey, ma," Matt answers the phone. "No, no, I just got off work." Matt listens as his mother talks for a couple minutes straight. "I know ma. I talked to Josh just a day ago... Yes. We'll both be there Sunday for dinner... I know, I'm excited to meet her too." Matt listens again. "I don't know if the Squirrel is coming, but I'm actually on my way right now with Alexa to meet her and Mickey for dinner."

Matt looks over to me and mouths "sorry". I wave it off because it's fine.

"I will ask them if they'd like to come Sunday too... Okay, ma. Alright, I gotta go, but I'll call you tomorrow on my break around one. Is that okay?... Alright good, then I'll talk to you tomorrow. Love you, too, ma... Okay, bye."

Matt ends the call and puts his phone into his pocket. I absentmindedly check my own pocket that the folded paper is still there. I decide to take it out and put it in my bag now before I possibly lose it.

"Sorry about that. Moms, ya know?" He looks at me with a soft smile on his perfect face. I feel a well of emotion start to bubble up so I swallow hard and just nod my agreement, hoping he misses the tears gathering in my eyes.

Unfortunately, Matt catches it. He stops walking and reaches for my hand, holds it tight.

"Hey. Are you okay?" He looks my face over, reading the emotion that I'm forcing to stay just below the surface.

"Yeah, yeah I'm okay."

"You sure? Lex, you can talk to me. You can tell me if there is something wrong." I look away and just shake my head. I see him through the corner of my eye look over my face again. "I'm here for you, you can trust me."

Can I really though? Can I trust you, Matt? His light brown eyes never leave my hazel ones. I decide I can trust him, but the entire truth has to wait for another day.

"I'm okay. I am. It's just hearing you talking to your mother reminded me of my own. I lost her about five years ago. It was, uh, very sudden." It's not a complete lie, but it's the best I can manage without revealing too much and possibly letting my guard slip.

It has the desired effect. Matt's face falls as what I've said registers. "Oh, wow. I had no idea, Lex. I'm so sorry." I just nod, it's all I can manage. Before I know it, he's engulfed me into one of the strongest hugs I've ever felt.

As he holds me, I breathe in his scent. A mixture of Old Spice, laundry detergent, and peppermint. When he lets me go, I find myself immediately missing his touch. He doesn't completely let go of me though. His hand finds mine again, and he intertwines our fingers.

We walk the six blocks to the restaurant in a comfortable silence. Just before Cali and Mickey spot us as we walk in, he lets my hand go but not before giving it a squeeze and me a smile. My manic heartbeat and the blood rushing in my ears overwhelms my senses as I understand just how much I liked having Matt so close to me.

And just how dangerous that could be.

• 8 •

"You guys are just in time, they were about to seat us when I saw you two walking up," Mickey says to Matt and me. She raises one eyebrow and grins as she looks at me.

What's that look for? Uh oh, if she tells Cali she saw us holding hands I'll never hear the end of it.

Mickey chuckles and then gestures with her head for me to look down. It's then that I remember Milo is joining us for dinner. He's busy playing with Cali and Matt. Their legs are blocking me from seeing my dog completely. I call for him to come to me as I squat down to his level.

When Milo comes over, curled tail wagging happily, and I finally see him full on, I just stop in shock. I look at him for a moment, proudly showing off his tank top and sweatbands, then I look up at Cali mirroring his proud stance. And I can't help myself. I crack up laughing. Harder than I have in a while. Milo leaps up slightly to put his paws on my chest and knocks me from my squatted position flat onto my ass on the ground.

I continue laughing as he gets riled up and licks my face from top to bottom. Normally I hate when Milo, or any dog, licks my face but I'm laughing too hard to stop him. Cali, Matt, and Mickey are also laughing just as hard.

"Oh, I'm sorry buddy. What'd she do to you?"

"What are you talking about? Dog Man is dressed for success."

"Okay, Milo. Okay, good boy." I calmly pet Milo's head to settle him, which he does quickly. He sits down in between my stretched out legs, facing me, his tail unfurled onto the ground and still wagging. I scratch behind both of his ears at the same time. "That's a good boy, Milo. Now, you have to behave in here, okay?" Milo snorts and ducks his head a bit.

"I swear to god, that dog just nodded his head at you," Cali says, reminding me that the three of them are waiting on my boy and me.

Matt leans over offering a hand to help me up. I feel a jolt of electricity as I grab it. He pulls a little too hard, and I pop up off the ground ending up nose to nose with him. He holds my body and my eye contact for an extra second before releasing me.

Cali claps her hands twice, effectively ending whatever moment Matt and I were possibly having. "Well, now that we're all here, how about some food?"

The hostess seats us toward the back of the restaurant, whether it's because of Milo, or that she can tell we'll be a loud group, I'm not sure. It's probably both.

We sit down at a four-person table. Cali to my left, Mickey across from me, and Matt on my right. Milo lays down under the table across my feet.

Within two minutes of sitting down, our waitress comes over to introduce herself. She asks for our drink order and if we would like guacamole and chips to start. We all declare a resounding yes to my personal favorite snack before putting in our drink orders; Cali orders a margarita, Matt orders a bottle of Modelo, and Mickey and I both order seltzer with lemon.

When the waitress leaves I see Cali take Mickey's hand that is resting on the table.

"I see you two have gotten past whatever little tiff it is you had?" I ask with a smirk.

"Yeah, she can't resist me," Mickey replies with a sly smile, raising her eyebrow again.

Cali scoffs. "I can too resist you."

"No, you can't," Matt and I say in unison.

"Can too." Cali reiterates letting go of Mickey's hand.

"Is that so?" Mickey asks. Cali stubbornly nods her head. "Well, what about..." Mickey trails off as she leans in to whisper something into Cali's ear. Whatever she says, it makes Cali's eyes widen and causes her to blush so deep, her ever apparent freckles all but disappear. Cali squirms in her chair slightly and bites the side of her lower lip.

"Okay!" Matt laughs. "Before you two run off to have sex in the bathroom, let's change the subject. Oh, this'll help keep it in your pants. Mom wants to know if you're coming to dinner on Sunday." He directs his question to Cali, but swings his head to both Mickey and myself adding, "You are both also invited."

Mickey leans back over to sit entirely on her chair, while Cali responds, "I'm good for Sunday. Mick?" She turns to look at her girlfriend.

Mickey pulls out her phone from her bag to check her schedule for Sunday. "I have a few classes from mid-morning to early afternoon, but they're all done before three." She adds, "So if dinner is after that, then sure, I'd love to."

The three of them turn simultaneously to me for my answer about Sunday. How do I tell them that I would go but Sunday, a day I'm not working, is already earmarked to be spent in the place where I do work to try and get access to a specific publication that has been hidden, possibly for centuries?

I'm searching my brain for a solid enough excuse when I'm saved by our drinks arriving and a man in a chef's jacket wheeling a cart up to the table with a mortar and pestle and the makings for guacamole.

I turn to Matt and say quietly, "I'll let you know about Sunday, okay?" He nods. I can see his smile falter a little bit, but he recovers quickly enough.

I hear Cali ask that no onions be put in the guacamole. The chef responds with an, "Of course." When it's done being mixed, the chef leaves the mortar, sans pestle, in the middle of the table and places a bowl of red, blue, and yellow corn chips next to it.

Cali is the first to take a chip and some dip. She puts it on the small plate in front of me. I'm slightly confused by this but pick up the chip anyway.

"Uhh, thanks, Cal."

As I'm bringing the chip to my mouth, Cali says, "Whoa, whoa! That's not for you."

Now I'm really confused. "Um, what?" I ask her. She looks at me as if the answer is obvious.

"It's for Dog Man."

Matt rolls his eyes at Cali while Mickey just retakes her girlfriend's hand and brings it to her lips. I shrug rather than argue and lean down to present the chip to Milo. "Take it nice, Milo." My dog sniffs the chip once and gently takes it from my hand. "Good boy, Milo."

When I sit up straight again, there are three more chips on the plate.

"Are these mine now, or still for the pup?" Cali's stare tells me all I need to know. "Okay, then."

I feed Milo his chips while dipping some of my own. As the first chip touches my tongue, I close my eyes at the taste of it. It might be the best guacamole I've ever had. Or maybe it's because in my foolish hiding from Matt earlier, I sort of skipped lunch. I quickly eat four more chips and then decide to cool it so I can enjoy my meal.

Our waitress comes back to take our order for dinner. I choose the fish tacos platter, but rather than have half my meal go to Milo under the glare of Cali, I also order a grilled chicken breast plain with no seasoning, no tortilla. I see out the corner of my eye that Cali gives me a satisfied nod at hearing my order.

Matt orders the carne asada tacos, and Mickey orders chicken tacos. The waitress then turns to Cali for her order. I can tell by the look on Cali's face that she is about to make a strange request.

"I'll have what they're having."

The waitress looks confused, so she clarifies, "You want fish tacos, carne asada tacos, *and* chicken tacos?"

"Yes, please. But without the rice or beans, just the tacos please."

The waitress pauses for a second and looks at the rest of us. We all shrug so the waitress says resignedly, "Okay." She puts her order pad in her apron, collects our menus and goes back to the kitchen.

We all stare at Cali for a minute. She merely continues to eat the chips and guacamole from the plate in front of her. Matt snickers and says, "Oh my god, Squirrel."

With a mouth of chips and dip, Cali looks perplexed and asks, "What, Moose? I'm small, but I burn at least half of my calories just trying to keep up with this one."

Mickey chokes a bit on the chip that she's chewing and reaches for her seltzer. Her blush of embarrassment at Cali's statement makes us all crack up again.

"Maybe that's true," Matt says. "But also, some things don't change." Matt explains that Cali has always been able to eat more than anyone else ever since they were little. He launches into a story of how she challenged the captain of their high school wrestling team to a tater-tot eating contest and absolutely demolished him.

Sitting at the table, us all laughing, I feel lighter than I have in a while. *It's so nice to just have a good night,* I think. *A good meal with good friends. I really needed this.*

When our food comes, Matt is in the middle of a story about someone at the library today who was looking for erotic novels of a highly specific nature. He's got the rest of us, especially me, cackling so hard we're gasping for air. I have to take off my glasses and wipe tears from the corners of my eyes with my napkin.

Mickey, Matt and I are each presented a platter of four tacos with a side of black beans and yellow rice, plus the chicken breast I ordered for Milo. Cali is presented with two giant plates, each with six tacos on it.

I cut up the chicken breast into small cubes and lay the plate down on the floor in front of Milo. He's being so good and quiet that if it weren't for the weight of him across my feet I would forget he's even here. I make a mental note to give him a couple of crunchy bones with his scoop of food when we get home.

I scarf down my first taco, barely tasting it just wanting food in my stomach. I eat the second one much slower. The conversation has all but stopped as the four of us chow down on our meals. I finish my second taco, and as I scoop up some rice, I ask Mickey how things are at the studio.

"Things are great. Really busy, but really great." Her blue eyes sparkle as she gets excited talking about her business, her passion. "This is my busiest time of year. In January, you know, everyone comes in with their resolutions but it usually doesn't last. When it starts to get warm out, I guess people are like 'oh shit, it's almost summer,' and then I'm their first stop. Usually, almost every class throughout April and May is full."

"That's awesome! So then do those people stay on?" I can see Cali in the corner of my eye looking at her girlfriend while she talks with a soft smile. Mickey nods as she swallows her bite of food to answers my question.

"Yeah, mostly. I think people come in initially because *they* think they need to look a certain way when it gets hotter out, or whatever. But I don't like to perpetuate unrealistic standards or shame anyone for not looking a certain way. I tell everyone when they first sign up that my place is not about losing weight or fitting a mold of who you *think* you're supposed to be; it's about improving what you already have and that there is no one set way to do it — mentally, physically, spiritually, emotionally. That's why I have that sign posted up: Be Better Today Than Yesterday."

"I love that sign." Matt chimes in.

"Me too," Cali adds. "And I love how passionate you are about it." She reaches over to lightly rub Mickey's upper arm. Mickey smiles and leans in to kiss her girlfriend. *They are so good together,* I can't help but think, and for a moment — longer than I'm willing to admit to myself — I'm jealous.

My eyes widen as a thought comes to me. "You know, you should have t-shirts made with the Be Better saying on them," I suggest. "You could sell them at the studio."

"That's such a good idea!" Cali exclaims. "I could design them for you, babe!"

Mickey raises her eyebrows and nods as she thinks it over. "Yeah, that could work."

"That really is a good idea," Matt says to me with a genuine, easy smile, looking me straight in the eyes.

I duck my head back to my meal before I hold his stare for too long, trying to calm the severe blush I can feel rising up my neck. I take a final bite of food finishing my whole plate and lean back stuffed. I say to Mickey, "Well after this meal, I think I'll definitely be in class tomorrow."

Matt and Cali bob their heads in agreement, cheeks comically bulging with food.

• 9 •

DARIUS

Over two thousand five hundred and ninety miles away from Alexa's joyous dinner with friends, just outside of Atlanta, Georgia, Darius still stands at the bar. His foot is tapping the ground persistently. He grips his glass of whiskey hard enough that the clear crystal starts to splinter under the pressure. He drains what's left in one gulp and slams the glass onto the bar.

He spins away from the bar and heads toward the door at the back of the room that leads to the grease caked kitchen. He walks through, never breaking his stride and exits to the deserted alleyway behind the building. He paces for a few minutes, his anger rising until his eyes land on the crates of empty bottles ready to go back to the beer distributor.

With a wave of his hand, his telekinesis power takes three wooden palates from the ground and leans them at an angle against the brick wall at the end of the alleyway. Another wave and three full crates of empty bottles zip through the air, clanging down one on each palate.

Darius walks ten paces away from the crates. With each step, his anger at his ceaseless waiting rises higher. By the time he turns back around, his right fist hanging at his hip is glowing a bright yellow. With his left arm out to the side for balance, he thrusts his right arm straight out in front of him. A ball of fire launches from his hand. It slams into the crate causing the bottles to explode and sets the wooden palate on fire.

As pieces of glass rain down onto the ground, Darius jerks his right arm out again and another glowing ball crashes into the second crate. It meets the same fate as the first.

Darius is about to hurl a third flaming orb when a door opposite the one he exited bursts open. Darius has only seen this guy in passing but knows it's the owner of the pawn shop next to the bar the demon has set up camp in.

"What the hell is going on out here?!" the man shouts.

Darius looks at the man and sizes him up.

The pawn broker's sweat-stained white tank top strains against his substantial beer belly; the thick, gaudy gold chains around his neck meant to look fancy are downright tacky; his thinning hair is styled in a comb-over, slick with grease from his scalp; black three stripe joggers cover toothpick-skinny legs; his feet, concealed in dirty socks with a hole in the left big toe, sit in slide sandals.

The whole ensemble presents a clear picture to Darius: this guy is a through and through sleaze ball. And Darius likes sleazy guys. But right now Darius doesn't have the patience for anyone, or anything.

Darius lets his hand fall back down to his hip flesh-colored again. He turns to face the man head on and scowls through furrowed eyebrows.

Darius speaks very slowly and enunciates every word. "Get the fuck back inside your hole."

The man bristles at some random guy in *his* alley telling him what to do.

"Look, buddy, I don't know who you think you are, but—"

Darius interrupts him and repeats his command even slower. "Get, the fuck. Back inside. Your. Hole."

With each word his fist is beginning to glow again, brighter and brighter. The pawn shop owner's eyes go directly to the demon's hand. He doesn't know what the glow means and has no plans to stick around and find out. He scrambles to open the door he came out of, but his palms are slick with sweat from fear and he can't get a grip on the handle.

Darius's hand glows brighter and brighter as it heats up ready to discharge more flames. Darius fires the instant before the man gets his door open.

The man jumps through into the safety of his pawn shop just as the third crate of beer bottles explodes, shooting glass shards against the door as it slams shut behind him.

Darius's anger has not changed after the three crates of bottles and palettes are obliterated. He waves his arm again and this time stacks a half dozen boxes in three piles.

****

Viribus enters the bar again, his vision sweeping across the room. When he does not locate Darius in his customary spot at the end of the bar, he looks at the bartender. The man looks five years older than when Viribus saw him earlier today. The lines on his face more profound, the gray hair at his temples more pronounced.

The barkeep holds Viribus's gaze this time and nods his head toward the door leading to the kitchen. Viribus nods knowing where his boss has gone to.

He makes his way through the kitchen that reeks of cooking oil and stops at the door to the alley. He opens the door cautiously to see what Darius is taking his anger out on, sees there are six crates of empty beer bottles stacked in three piles. He will wait until his boss has exhausted some of his rage before showing himself.

He hears a crash as the fire thrown from Darius's hand reaches the first stack, followed by a whoosh as what's left is set ablaze. He calmly waits. He's seen what Darius's firepower can do and has no plans of being caught in its crosshairs.

Viribus hears two more bangs in quick succession and decides the coast is clear enough to present himself to his boss. When he steps out into the alley, Darius is facing away from him.

"Boss," Viribus calls out.

Darius doesn't turn around but replies to his lieutenant. "You have something for me?"

"Actually, I think I might."

At that, Darius faces the mammoth man. He grits his teeth, impatience already bubbling that Viribus isn't speaking faster. "Well?" he barks out.

"Julius put out word along the pipeline that if anyone had seen a young girl age eighteen to twenty-three, alone, no friends, no connections, new in town, to let him know. Asked people to send information along quietly, that it's all off the books."

"Get to the fucking point already!" Darius shrieks. His desperation at finding the girl overpowering his typically cold demeanor.

"He got a call from Blue in New Orleans. He asked each of his parolees about the girl. Made it sound like she had skipped out of her own parole from up north. He gave them a description and one his guys remembered something from around the public library of all places. Turns out it wasn't who we're looking for, but Blue had someone follow up just to be sure, and he found out that three years ago, some random young girl was staking out the library. She was asking questions about when it was built and if it always looked the way it looked now or if it had been changed at some point. Didn't want to know anything about the books inside, just the building."

"A library in New Orleans from three years ago?" Darius clarifies.

Viribus nods eagerly, believing he's given his boss a lead they can pursue.

Darius sweeps his left arm out, and Viribus flies into the air slamming into the brick wall still scorched and smoking from its previous assault.

"What the fuck can I do with information from three years ago?!" he shouts as his anger increases tenfold. Darius freezes his left arm where it is while his right hand flares to life.

"Darius, please. Don't. I'll keep searching. I'll get you what you need. I swear, boss. I swear." Viribus begs him, saying anything he can think of to get his boss to spare his life. Darius's left hand now starts to form into a fist, Viribus can instantly feel a vice closing on his throat.

Viribus chokes out, "I'll go to New Orleans myself and get you more information. I'll do anything... please." His face is turning purple and his eyes bulge, black dots are starting to form in his peripheral vision. Darius launches an orb of blazing energy from his right hand. At the same instant he opens his left, dropping Viribus back onto the ground in a heap, gasping for air. The ball of flames hits the brick wall exactly where Viribus's heart was seconds ago. Bits of mortar and red dust rains down on the lieutenant from the crater left behind on the wall.

"No more chances, Viribus. You go where you have to and only come back when you can tell me what I need. Nothing less. Do you fucking understand?"

Viribus is still on the ground coughing, trying to suck in as much oxygen as possible. He nods, never once looking up at the demon.

"Good. Now go."

Viribus staggers to his feet, his large frame unsteady as he walks down the alley, not bothering to go back through the bar. He walks past where Darius is standing, head down, one hand rubbing his throat.

"Oh, and Viribus?" Darius calls out. The lieutenant freezes and slowly turns around, looking slightly to the left of his boss's head, not brave enough to chance looking him in the eye.

"I won't miss next time."

• 1 0 •

"ALEXA"

I'm jostled out of a deep, dreamless sleep Friday morning by Milo pawing at me. I keep my eyes closed and ignore him until I feel him licking my face and whimpering. I finally open my eyes when he lets out a little yelp-like bark. The clock on my nightstand shines a blurry 7:30 A.M. at me.

I groan, "Ah, shit."

I must have forgotten to turn the alarm on last night. I have to hustle, or I'm going to be late for work. I throw off my covers, grab the same sweatpants from yesterday morning and my glasses, and open my bedroom door. I stop dead in my tracks outside the door because something just feels off, the apartment is completely silent. I cautiously walk down the hall toward the living room. I peek my head and see nothing different from yesterday, except no Cali. *Cali,* I realize.

I sigh and roll my neck and shoulders a few times to relax a little as I remember that she stayed at Mickey's last night. Plus, Milo showed no signs of there being anything wrong, so I got worked up for nothing.

"Come on, Milo. No time to waste today." He follows me obediently to the door and doesn't move too much as I put his harness on. I grab his leash and keys from their hook and unlock my apartment door. I decide to put his

leash on downstairs. "Milo, side," I say. He's instantly at my left knee. As I'm about to open the door, I feel a vibration at my knee as Milo lets out a growl.

I stop cold. Milo's growls only mean one thing and it's never something good.

I quickly throw the deadbolt back into its slot to lock the door and check the peephole. Through the small glass lens, I see a warped picture of the short, well-lit hallway and the top of the stairs to the right of my door. I angle my head back and forth to try and get the full picture. I see my bike against the wall where it usually is, but don't see anything else out of place, which is strangely more unsettling than relieving.

Milo growls again from his spot at my knee. My heart starts to race as my mind spirals with all the possible threats that could be on the other side of the door: *Is it Darius? Has he found me? But how? I've been so careful! I could get ready to deflect any fire or demons who might be hiding... No! If it's not Darius, that'll give me away! Maybe it's a burglar just waiting for someone to open the door. Could it be Cali playing a prank trying to scare me? But Milo wouldn't growl if it was her.*

Milo presses into my leg and takes a small step forward, putting himself between me and the door now entirely in protection mode. I trust my dog more than my own eyes but decide to look again anyway. I go up on my toes to see if there is something, or someone, directly beneath the peephole. This time I see it.

It looks like an ordinary, medium-sized, brown cardboard box. Normally an utterly harmless thing. But if Milo is on alert then I am too. My entire body breaks out into a cold sweat as I rack my brain trying to remember if Cali or I ordered anything. *But it's not even eight in the morning, no one delivers yet. Plus it definitely wasn't there when I got home last night which was after ten. It has to be a trap. But from who? Or what?*

I don't know what to do. Do I open the door? Do I call Cali and ask her about it? Do I call out sick?

But I finally have something of a lead, I yell in my head. *I* have *to go to work today!*

I realize the only thing I can do is open the door and give Milo the command I've only ever had to use three times.

My palms are slick with sweat. I wipe both hands on my sweatpants and slowly reach out, putting one hand on the doorknob, the other is on the deadbolt. I look down at Milo who is staring intensely at the door and say, "Milo, set."

He takes a few steps back, positioning himself to be in the direct path of the door as I open it. I take a deep breath, say, "Milo, seek," throw the bolt and yank the door open.

"Seek" is the command I use when I want Milo to attack. He's been trained by my grandfather and me to go after whatever object or person I'm looking at and use his power to sense if there is a direct threat. If there is, Milo attacks. If it's a false alarm, he circles whatever it is twice and then comes back and sits next to me. "Seek" is a more conspicuous command than "attack" which gives both Milo and I a break if it is a false alarm. It's pretty difficult to explain to someone why you gave your dog a command to attack them, especially if it turns out there is nothing wrong.

Milo bolts through the opening and barrels right into the box, no hesitation at all. The box topples over and I see a piece of paper go flying off of it. Milo bites into the cardboard in a couple places and then just stops. He doesn't circle twice and return, but he doesn't continue to attack it either. It's like he's confused.

Unsure of what I should do in this situation, I tentatively step into the hallway. My eyes dart everywhere, above me and side to side, checking to see what has my dog stymied.

Could Milo have smelled or heard something through the door and that's why he growled? I go to pick up the piece of paper and see a handwritten note: This came to my place instead-Ty.

That explains why he went so nuts. But ugh, I think. *I would've too.*

Ty is Tyler Pentz. He lives in the apartment directly below mine. Tyler is an appalling person, sleazy and vulgar at every turn. The first time I met him, Milo immediately growled and put himself between us, which was all I needed to know about the guy but unfortunately I know more. Tyler is the type of guy who catcalls women and then gets insulted when they don't fawn all over him for it. He has no concept of personal space whatsoever. He doesn't believe women can be gay. In fact, I've heard him say to Mickey and Cali that they "just haven't been fucked by the right man yet" — the gross insinuation being that he's the *right man*. Tyler also believes his opinion is the only opinion.

The multiple times I've rebuffed his advances I've heard him use a racial slur and call me a stuck-up bitch. He is just the worst kind of person. He makes my skin crawl every time I see him.

I crumple the note and throw it over the railing. I watch it fall through the air onto the landing in front of Tyler's door. I turn back to the box and Milo, he's sitting next to it still unsure what to do.

"Good boy, Milo. You did real good, pup." I scratch his ears as I kneel down and look at the box. It's from one of those giant online warehouse stores and is addressed to Cali. I lift it to bring it inside and put it on the coffee table. I hope whatever is inside didn't get wrecked or anything from Milo.

I check the clock on the cable box, 7:53 glows bright green back at me.

"Shit!" I cry. If I want to shower before work, I only have time to take Milo around the block once. I put his leash on now instead of downstairs and race out the still open door, slamming it behind me.

"Sorry big guy, no pup-cup this morning," I tell Milo as we head out of the building. He shakes himself out from head to toe and promptly sits down. I don't realize he's not moving until I get tugged back a little by his weight and strength. I turn around and give a gentle tug on his leash. "Come on, Milo." He turns his head away with his nose up refusing to move or look at me.

"The fuck?" I mumble. "Milo, don't you want to go for a walk?" I use my sweetest voice to entice him with no luck. I rewind the last few minutes in my head to see what changed from the top of the stairs to now. I roll my eyes as I realize what's going on.

"Seriously? Okay, listen. No pup-cup right now, but I promise when I get home later I will bring you a double pup-cup, okay?" Milo finally stands and wags his tail. "Okay then, let's go," I say nodding my head and coaxing him along with each word.

We've just turned the corner at the block when I look down at him and chuckle to myself. This dog just basically threw a temper tantrum over some whipped cream. *He must've learned that from Cali,* I think. Realizing I should probably give Cali a heads up about that box, I pull out my phone to text her.

> **LEX:** you got a package here. it was outside the door when milo and i left for our walk. he may have attacked it a little. sorry!

I don't expect her to be awake to text me back but I quickly see the bubble pop up signaling she's typing back.

> **CAL:** i'm sure it's fine! just a couple of books and
> some scarves
> **CAL:** they were on clearance!

For someone who honestly doesn't have much of anything to worry about financially, Cali is one of the thriftiest shoppers I've ever met. She will wait until something is on sale, or it's the seasonal change when stores are trying to clear out their stock or visit three different sites to find the best deal on something. There's only one thing I know of for sure that she's paid full price for since I've known her: a multi-year platinum membership to Mickey's Kick Boxing and Training Studio.

> **LEX:** oh, ok then i'm sure they're ok. i left the box on
> the coffee table for you
>
> **CAL:** thanks
> **CAL:** sooooo how was the rest of your night????

I know what she's aiming at, but I play dumb.

> **LEX:** what ever do you mean my dear roommate?
>
> **CAL:** don't play coy with me!
> **CAL:** moose: do you want me to walk you home?
> **CAL:** lex: yeah that'd be great....... (cue hair flip
> and giggle)
>
> **LEX:** lol he only offered because YOU went to mickey's
>
> **CAL:** sure lex. sure. moose may be a gentleman, but you
> my friend are blind
> **CAL:** did he kiss you goodnight?

I don't answer right away. Instead, I let the memory of last night wash over me as Milo and I round the last corner and head back to our building.

Milo, Matt, and I slowly walked the nine blocks from the restaurant to my apartment. Our languid pace was only half due to the amount of food we had consumed. He was following my lead, and I was definitely going slower trying to prolonging our time together. I couldn't tell if the ever-present butterflies were excited at him being so close, or if I just had indigestion, but my stomach was in knots. Our arms brushed together when we moved over to let a group of people pass us. His hand easily slid into mine after that.

I decide to tell Cali the truth about my feelings for Matt. *They are best friends,* I think. *She wouldn't egg me on if he was interested or hadn't said something to her, right?*

    LEX: `he kissed my cheek`
    LEX: `i just about died`

I followed those texts up with a line of heart-eyed emojis.

As Milo and I walked up the stairs to our apartment I couldn't keep the smile off my face. I ignored the chime of my phone alerting me that Cali has responded to my text. I open the door and we walk into our home together. Milo goes to his bowls, as is customary after a walk. I give him some food and fresh water then grab a couple granola bars for myself and throw them into my bag.

I put my phone on the counter with my keys and trot to my room. I have exactly ten minutes before I have to leave for work. Not enough time to shower so I'll have to just wash up and get dressed. I style my hair in a low ponytail, letting my long curly hair trail down my back, and pay extra attention to my mascara. I grab a loose black tunic blouse and dark gray leggings from my closet and put on the same flats from yesterday.

I pick up my bag from the counter, check that I have my wallet, phone, keys; check that the granola bars are still there and haven't been stolen by a certain canine. I have the feeling that I'm forgetting something but I shake it off. I don't have time to figure it out right now.

I check to see that the printout from yesterday is still in there too. My heart skips a beat as I touch the page. *This could really be it,* I think.

I check the clock on my phone and see I have two minutes to spare. I go to one of the cabinets in the kitchen and pull down the airtight container I keep Milo's treats in. I open it and grab two crunchy bone cookies for Milo. After I put the container away, I turn ready to whistle for Milo but he's of course already at my feet, seated nicely with his gaze zeroed in on his treats.

I stack the cookies one on top of the other turn to Milo and say, "Milo, pound it." He bumps my fist with his nose. "Good boy. Take it nice," I say as I hold out the bones. Milo takes them both in his mouth gently and quickly scurries over to eat them underneath the coffee table.

"Okay, Milo I'm going to work," I call out to him as I grab my bag and jacket and head toward the door. "Be a good boy today!"

I take my phone out from my bag as I hear another text message notification. I check the screen and see I have five messages waiting from Cali. I let out a tiny snicker and think, *she can wait a little longer.* I smirk as I head to the stairs.

I walk out of the building and head left toward the library, head up, smirk still firmly in place.

• 1 1 •

I finally give Cali some relief and read her messages as I'm waiting to cross the street.

    CAL: what?!? oh my god that is so sweet!!
    CAL: was it like a quick peck or did he linger a little
    bit? tell me everything
    CAL: lex come on you can't just say that and then not
    tell me more!!
    CAL: lex!!!!!!
    CAL: LEX COME ON!!!

This kid is going to give herself an aneurysm if I don't answer her soon, I laugh to myself.

    LEX: alright alright! i was getting ready for work
    jeez!
    LEX: it was very sweet. it wasn't as short as a peck
    but he didn't linger too long. it's was just right

    CAL: awww omg like goldilocks!

    LEX: haha sure
    LEX: i really like him cal. i'm just so nervous about
    screwing it up or ruining it. i don't even know if he

likes me too. plus we work together. i mean how awkward
would that be if it didn't work out??

CAL: lex he SO likes you!!
CAL: believe me
CAL: and don't worry about it getting screwed up because it won't. just relax and let things happen like
they're supposed to. i've known moose forever, i can
tell he definitely likes you too

I feel like such a middle schooler right now. "Okay, I'm asking you, to ask him, to tell you, so you can tell me if he likes me." *Why does it feel so complicated, it's not like I've never had a boyfriend before.*

I don't need to wait to give me an answer. I know what's holding me back. It's because Matt is the first guy I've really liked since my eighteenth birthday, since my life was simpler. I'm also hiding a huge part of who I am from everybody I know. How can I start a romantic or sexual relationship with someone while carrying around this giant secret?

I know Cali is waiting for a response, so I decide to go with the truth again. Well, part of the truth.

LEX: uuugh i feel like i'm in middle school right now!

CAL: don't sweat it
CAL: i got you.

LEX: what does that mean??

CAL: it means i got you
CAL: i gotchu

LEX: cali.

The text bubble comes up and disappears a few times. I lose my patience after a few seconds and text Cali back right away.

LEX: what does that mean?

Still no response from my roommate.

LEX: tell me what that really means or i'll tell mickey
you told milo he is a better kisser

CAL: you wouldn't!!

LEX: i would

CAL: man that's cold
CAL: what i meant was i'll be very subtle and ask moose how he feels about you

LEX: NO!! no you will not!

CAL: the game's afoot i say! soooo, i gotchu

LEX: cal, i love you, but subtlety is not your forte

CAL: hey i take offense to that!

I'm in the middle of typing my response when my phone rings in my hand. I see Cali's face come up on the screen.

"Hey," I answer.

Cali doesn't waste time with pleasantries, she just jumps right in. "Mickey was getting annoyed with the constant alerts, so she said to just call you."

"You also say each word out loud as you type," I hear Mickey add from the background.

"Oh yeah, you definitely do that, kid. Tell Mickey I understand."

"What is this, gang up on Cali time?" I have no mature response to that so I just stay quiet. "Anyway. Look, Moose definitely, definitely has the hots for you. We could see it last night, right babe? He kept looking at you when you weren't watching."

I hear some sounds that must be the phone changing hands because the next voice I hear is Mickey's.

"It's true, Lex. He had this small, soft smile on his face all night like he was just happy being near you or something. It was really sweet. Plus, don't forget I saw you two holding hands walking up to the restaurant."

"WHAT?!" I hear Cali yell in the background.

"That's not what you think it was though. It was—"

Mickey cuts me off. "Whatever it was, it was cute. You guys are a match. You fit. Just relax and let it happen naturally like I told Cali to tell you before. 'Cause it's gonna happen."

"Yeah, he obviously already likes you as you are, so don't worry. Just if he flirts with you, now you can flirt back!" Cali's voice is a little echoey, she must have put the call on speakerphone.

"Flirt with him? I am SO awkward at flirting!" I can already feel my face heating up at just the thought of flirting with Matt.

"Relax Lex, don't focus on flirting with him," I hear Mickey chime in. "Just continue doing whatever you're already doing, because it's working."

"My love is right. Just keep being yourself."

I feel a bit childish at needing to be reassured so much that the guy actually likes me.

I've continued walking toward work while talking to the couple. At this point, I'm across the street from the library stopped at a corner waiting for the light to change. I can see Matt with his head down waiting near the entrance, checking his phone.

"Oh my god, he's outside the library! You think he's waiting for me?" I whisper-yell into my phone as if Matt could hear me from across the street.

Mickey and Cali respond at the same time with a long, "Awwww."

Mickey continues talking. "Alexa, you'll be fine. Look, I'll talk to him after my class tonight, feel him out, see what he's feeling. I'll tell you what he says."

"Okay," I sigh. Her voice is so calm and soothing.

"Hey! How come Mickey can talk to Moose about it but I can't?" Cali's voice on the other hand is a tad indignant.

Mickey's even voice answers, "Because subtlety is really not your forte, babe."

"I take offense to that," Cali replies without any bite. "Alright, Lex, Mickey will talk to him tonight after class and then you'll know for sure, okay?"

Damn, that's what I forgot! My bag with my workout clothes to change into.

"Shit. Cali, I forgot my bag, are you going to stop back at the apartment before tonight?"

"Yup," Cali answers, popping the P at the end.

"Can you grab it for me? It's on the chair at the end of my bed."

"Oh, yeah. I gotchu."

"Stop saying that!" Mickey scolds the younger woman. I can hear her laughing so I know she isn't really annoyed. I can now hear loud kissing noises as Mickey continues laughing with Cali repeating "I gotchu" over and over in between them.

"Okay, I gotta go but thanks, guys. I'll see you later tonight."

"Bye!" They both say at the same time.

I step off the curb just after the light changes, walking with my head down. I can't help thinking again that I want what Cali and Mickey have. They are so right for each other. They're meant for each other.

I also can't help but stumble over the secret I'm hiding and how my regular life, not just my love life, could implode when it's revealed.

I look up and Matt has moved over and is now at the corner waiting for me. He smiles when our eyes connect.

Are you right for me? I think while smiling back at him and holding his gaze. I keep walking right toward him. *Are you my match Matt Moorely?*

• 1 2 •

Cali

After hanging up the phone call with Alexa, Cali continues to pepper obnoxious kisses all over Mickey's face who is still laughing at the younger woman. Cali is kneeling next to Mickey on the couch in the living room of the older woman's one bedroom apartment. Cali realizes she has a bit of an upper hand right now and decides to take advantage of it. She slows down her kisses, making them softer and longer, and moves her lips down to the brunette's jaw.

Mickey feels the change. She knows what Cali is doing, and tilts her head a little to the side to give Cali access to her neck. Cali doesn't waste time and brings her lips down to Mickey's pulse point, a spot she knows is a weakness for the trainer. The younger woman kisses and nips her girlfriend's neck, then sucks the skin into her mouth a little, gently at first, then a little harder. Mickey's breath becomes shallow, her heartbeat beginning to speed up.

Cali releases her girlfriend's neck and moves her mouth to Mickey's ear lobe and gives it a little nibble. She then brings her mouth to Mickey's and gives her a long, lingering kiss. She sits back slightly to look into Mickey's eyes. Cali sees that the blue eyes of the woman in front of her are almost black, the pupils blown wide with the same desire Cali now feels building in herself.

Mickey draws Cali forward by her shirt and captures the woman's lips in a bruising kiss. Cali uses her leverage to push Mickey onto her back on the couch. The younger woman settles on top of her girlfriend in between her legs without breaking the kiss. The couple can feel the intensity and hunger between them, their mouths moving together with want.

Mickey pulls the shorter woman's bottom lip into her mouth and swipes her tongue across it. Cali instantly responds by opening her mouth. When their tongues meet, Mickey lets out a soft moan that resonates through Cali's body and settles deep within her.

Mickey continues kissing Cali greedily. Cali runs her left hand through long, dark hair, cradling Mickey's head while her right moves to the bottom of her girlfriend's shirt. Cali slides her right hand up Mickey's torso, over abs that tighten at the touch, and up to her chest, her hand stopping just before it reaches where she knows Mickey wants it.

Mickey lets out a whimper and arches her back, rolling her hips up into Cali. The movement causes some tantalizing friction for both women and this time it's Cali that moans. Mickey grips Cali's shirt, giving it a quick tug. Cali sits up, breaking her mouth away, already missing the contact. She rips her own shirt off and tosses it to the side, then does the same to Mickey's.

Cali lays back down on top of her girlfriend, their bare, braless chests pressing together. Mickey runs her hands up and down Cali's back. Her hands are just about to settle on Cali's ass when the younger woman sits up quickly and pins both of Mickey's hands above her head. She looks Mickey deep in the eyes, an impish grin on her face.

"Uh-uh. No touching right now," she says. Cali knows this drives Mickey wild, making the buildup more tantalizing and her climaxes that much more intense.

When the older woman nods, agreeing to her rule, Cali begins to slowly rock her hips against the taller woman; not enough contact to give either woman a release, just enough to work them both up even more. Cali's lips return to Mickey's pulse point. Her girlfriend's mouth and hips are driving the older woman mad.

"Bedroom," Mickey pants. Her ordinarily soft voice is low and rough, deepened by her craving for the woman on top of her.

Cali lifts her head from Mickey's neck. Her green eyes lock onto blue ones. "No," she says. "I want you here."

Cali is taking full control right now, which turns Mickey on even more. She dips her head again but this time her mouth takes in Mickey's breast instead of her neck, her tongue moving at a slow, tortuous pace. The older woman gasps at the new connection, her hips involuntarily jerking up, searching for more contact at her center. Her hands, still pinned above her head, grip the arm of the couch behind her.

Cali uses her body weight to hold Mickey's hips in place while her hand moves along the top of her boyshorts underwear. She dips the tip of one finger just under the elastic band and lightly slides it across from hip bone to hip bone.

Cali removes her hand bringing it back up to her girlfriend's hair as her mouth moves to Mickey's other breast. The younger woman continues her painfully slow movements on top of her lover's body. Mickey feels the tension building in her lower abdomen and lets out a soft whimper in response to Cali's diligent attention to her body.

"Please, baby," Mickey whispers. She gasps sharply as she feels Cali bite down on her sensitive nipple. "Please...I need more."

"What do you need?" Cali asks releasing Mickey's breast. She wants to hear her girlfriend say it.

"I need..." Mickey's breath is uneven. "I need..." She's cut off by Cali wildly capturing her mouth again.

Mickey groans as she feels both of Cali's hands move underneath her to massage her ass for a minute before moving to her waist, thumbs pressing down on her hips. Cali runs her tongue over the woman's stomach stopping to leave a dark hickey next to her belly button.

"Tell me, baby," Cali whispers into Mickey's soft skin.

Mickey swallows and says, "I need you to fuck me."

Cali moans loudly at finally hearing Mickey give herself over to the younger woman. The placement of her mouth makes the sound send a vibration straight to Mickey's center, causing her to let out her own moan in response. Cali moves her head down Mickey's body, one hand following to where the brunette needs her most, her other hand resting in the shallow between Mickey's breasts. She gives her love the release she craves, over and over and over again.

****

Cali is standing at one of the counters in Mickey's kitchen pouring herself a glass of water. She opens the fridge and leans in to return the water pitcher. When she stands up, she feels Mickey's strong arms wrap around her from behind.

Mickey kisses the back of Cali's head, hair still damp from their shared shower, and asks, "What do you want for lunch, baby?"

Cali closes the refrigerator door and turns in Mickey's arms to face the taller woman. With a cheeky grin, she answers, "Well I just ate, multiple times, so I'm not very hungry right now."

She takes a slow, deliberate sip of cold water and smiles. Mickey takes the glass from her hands and puts it on the counter next to them then quickly presses the younger woman's back up against the fridge.

"Mmm, so did I, but I'm still a bit hungry."

Mickey leans in with her own face sporting a mischievous grin. She sees Cali close her eyes, anticipating her lips feeling Mickey's own in a moment. Just before their mouths meet, she pulls back holding a take-out menu she grabbed from a stack on top of the fridge.

"I'm going to order a sandwich from Marty's. Do you want anything?"

Cali scoffs and mutters, "Way to get a girl's hopes up."

She gives Mickey a pout that the older woman immediately kisses off of her face in the same obnoxious way Cali did earlier this morning. Laughing now, Cali takes the menu from Mickey and goes back to the couch in the living room.

"What time is it?" she calls over her shoulder to the brunette still in the kitchen.

Mickey checks the clock on the microwave. "Almost noon."

"Really? Damn, baby, that was like three hours." Cali wiggles her eyebrows at Mickey as she sits down next to her on the couch.

"Anything worth doing is worth doing right, right?"

Cali chuckles at the woman's response and gives her a quick peck on the lips. "What are you gonna have?"

Mickey puts her chin in her hand as she thinks. "Hmm, probably a chicken sandwich." Mickey sees that Cali mouths the words "chicken sandwich" with her. "What?" she asks as her girlfriend rolls her eyes.

"You *always* get a chicken sandwich." Cali states.

"Yes, and you always get roast beef with cheddar, tomato, and mayo," Mickey fires back. "At least I change what goes on the sandwich."

"Yeah, that's true," Cali concedes. It's Mickey's turn to roll her eyes.

"Do you want to go there or have it delivered?" the older woman asks.

Cali pauses before answering and looks Mickey up and down. With a devilish smirk, she answers, "Have it delivered."

She puts her hand on Mickey's knee, her index finger lightly drawing random patterns as she slowly moves her hand up to her thigh. Mickey raises an eyebrow at her girlfriend's calculated movements.

"Delivered? And what do you propose we do in the meantime?"

Cali shrugs, "I may have an idea or two."

Mickey grins and answers with an "mm-hmm." She gets up to get her phone from the kitchen counter and call in the order. Cali stands and walks around the couch when she hears Mickey end the call.

"They said a half hour." Mickey walks over and wraps Cali up in her arms, presses herself completely against the shorter woman. "What can we do in half an hour?" she asks with a coy smile.

Cali takes a few steps backward pulling Mickey with her. "I know what I want."

"Oh? And what is that?" Mickey replies playing along.

Cali doesn't answer. She just continues to walk backward with the blue-eyed woman, kissing her lips slowly while moving them toward the bedroom. She doesn't say anything until she feels the bed hit the backs of her knees, she falls onto it dragging Mickey down on top of her.

"I want you," Cali says into Mickey's ear.

Mickey pulls back, about to ask Cali what she means to draw out their flirtation a little more. But her mouth goes dry and her heart rate jumps when she sees Cali reaching over to open the drawer of the night table, her hand disappearing inside. When Cali's hand reappears, she knows what the green-eyed woman wants, and Mickey wants nothing more right now than to be the one to give it to her.

• 1 3 •

"ALEXA"

For a Friday in early April, the library was busier today than I expected. Not only had I barely had any time to talk to Matt except when we first came in, but I haven't even had time really to sit down. What I wanted to be doing is going through the computer archives one more time to make sure what I found yesterday wasn't a fluke, that it was really real.

Instead, I'm squatting down, just about finished with sorting through the piles of returned books on one of the carts we keep behind the counter. I hear a noise and I look up to see Matt leaning over the counter. Today he has on a bright blue button down shirt with the sleeves rolled up and very dark washed jeans. *God, it's like he just walked off the page of a magazine.*

"Jeez, can you believe today?" he asks dropping his head so his forehead gently thuds onto the artificial wood surface. His voice is slightly muffled as he speaks again with his head still down. "It's been non-stop all morning!"

"I know," I say standing up. "I've been back here all day. This is the third cart I've filled just this morning." I push the cart out and around the counter, careful not to bump anything. I have to use my bodyweight to counteract the cart's momentum to be able to stop it. "I may not even need to go to Mickey's class tonight if this keeps up."

Matt lifts his head and asks almost nervously, "But you're still going tonight, right?"

"Oh yeah, of course," I answer. *I've got Mickey all lined up to cross-examine you,* I silently add. "We should walk there together." I give him a hesitant smile. Before he can even answer me though, I quickly add, "I mean, we're both going there, and we get off work at the same time." *Man, you are so smooth "Alexa,"* I internally berate myself.

Matt lets a slow, easy smile spread across his face. "Sure." It's a one-word answer, but somehow when he says it, it has meaning.

I move around to the front of the cart to pull it into the rows of shelves. I nod my head to the side as I walk backward indicating to Matt I want him to follow me. He stands and walks toward me, a curious expression on his face.

I stop at the first section and as I'm scanning the shelves to put the books back in their proper place, I speak.

"So I thought more about what you said last night, and if the offer still stands, I'd love to come to dinner on Sunday."

His eyes brighten. "Of course!" I see his smile falter a little as he asks, "You sure you can make it?"

It's like a role reversal, I muse. *He's suddenly acting insecure whereas I seem to have unexpectedly uncovered some secret confidence I never knew about.*

"Yes, definitely. I have some errands and laundry and stuff like that, but I can do it all tomorrow."

"Okay, cool," he replies.

Our conversation halts there as we both just look at each other. It's surprisingly not awkward, it's actually kind of nice. *Comfortable,* I tell myself. The thought both warms me and terrifies me.

Comfort means unguarded, which could jeopardize everything.

But I really, really like Matt!. But I also might actually finally be close to something. You can't do anything to risk that "Alexa."

The thoughts war in my head and I can feel myself starting to panic. I'm racking my brain for an excuse to leave when I hear a woman clear her throat behind me.

"Excuse me, I'm sorry. Do you know where I can find books on earth science?" The woman appears to be middle-aged, with short blonde, perfectly styled hair. She's wearing a long, billowy maxi dress that fits her considerable frame quite nicely. She has an exasperated expression on her face and is holding a piece of paper with printed words on it. I briefly catch the word "ASSIGNMENT" at the top.

"Of course, miss. They would be in the Reference section," I politely answer.

"Thank you. My son has had two months to do this project and tells me this morning that it's due Monday and he hasn't done any of it. Thank god his teacher put some suggested books on his assignment sheet." She vents her frustration and sighs, then turns to Matt laughing as she asks, "Do boys ever grow up?"

Matt looks between me and the woman shrugs and responds with a good-natured, "Nope."

The woman lets out a loud cackle and says, "Oh good, so it's not just my son. Oh, lord." She sighs again. "So now, honey," she puts her hand on my arm and asks, "where is the Reference section?"

"It's upstairs," I answer. "If you take the elevator it's to the left, but if you take the stairs it's to the right."

"Okay, elevator and to the left," she laughs that loud cackle again. "And the elevator?"

Matt smiles and points her in the direction of the elevator. "And if you need any help finding the books you're looking for, Jackie should be behind the counter upstairs. She'll be able to help you."

The woman calls her thanks over her shoulder as she makes her way to the elevator bank.

Matt whistles as he exhales, slightly shaking his head. "She is the sixth mom I've had today ask me about earth science books. Either a bunch of schools are doing the same project, or an entire grade of kids from the same school forgot about it."

I chuckle. "I'd say it's the second one. That's only the third mom for me though. But all day I've had people returning books. Every time I turn around the return bin is full again."

I gesture at the cart. "This is literally all I've been doing today."

When what I would rather be doing instead is checking on a particular book for myself.

We continue pushing and pulling the cart through the shelves. A very easy silence settles over us as we work in tandem — me handing the books to Matt and him shelving them. We take the elevator to the second floor to continue putting the books away. Matt spots some of the mothers we've sent to the Reference section, and he deliberately steers the cart in the opposite direction.

As Matt is reaching up to put away the last few books on a top shelf, his untucked shirt rides up a little and I get a glimpse of his ass in his jeans. *Damn,* is all I can think. Then I berate myself, *I need to stop, it's so inappropriate that I check him out every chance I get.*

I shake my head to clear the thought and check my watch to distract myself. "Well, at least this day is going quickly," I say out loud. "It's almost one. Have you had lunch yet?"

Matt brings his arms down and adjusts his shirt. He shakes his head no. "Not yet. Do you want to get something?"

"Yes!" I answer quickly. I clear my throat and add, "I woke up late so I didn't get a chance to eat breakfast. Marty's?"

"Sure." It's the same one-word answer, but Matt still has that same easy smile on his face.

"Great. Let me bring the cart back down and grab my bag, then we can go?" Matt nods and walks with me back to the elevator. As the doors open and we step in, I recount the story of Milo waking me up this morning. I have Matt cracking up at the tantrum he threw about the pup-cup. I make sure to leave out the scene of me cowering behind the door to my apartment and my entire conversation with Cali and Mickey.

As the doors open, Matt and I step out pushing the cart with us. In front of me, I see Jeff.

"Oh, Alexa, good. I've been looking for you."

"Hey, Jeff," Matt greets him.

"Matt," Jeff says. Did I mention he's a straight-forward, no-nonsense kind of guy?

"Hi, Jeff. What's up?" I join in.

"Well, I've just gotten off the phone with Samantha. She's come down with a bad cold and won't be in tomorrow or Sunday." He has a clipboard in his hands and looks down at it as he says, "I have coverage for tomorrow, but I'll need you to come in on Sunday." He looks up at me. "Okay?"

My stomach drops. *I just told Matt before that I would come to dinner on Sunday at his mother's house and now Jeff is saying I have to cover a shift here?* Half of me is devastated, but the other half is excited to have an opportunity to possibly do some snooping to find *The Book*.

I look at Matt. I see my own disappointment mirrored on his face and the first half of me wins out. I turn to Jeff, "Um, I actually just made plans for Sunday. Is there someone else who would be able to do it?"

Jeff looks surprised. "I'm sorry, I thought you wanted extra shifts here."

"Well, yes that's true. But—"

"Filling in for others is the best I can offer right now," Jeff says flatly.

"I understand tha—"

"Well, then great," Jeff cuts me off again. "I'll see you on Sunday."

He nods at us both and then walks away. I let out a long exhale to calm the annoyance I feel. What an ass, I think.

"What an ass." Matt mumbles.

I respond with "Mm-hmm, my thoughts exactly."

I pinch the bridge of my nose then look at Matt. He looks deflated like someone just took the wind out of his sails. I realize then just how excited I had been about the prospect of going to dinner on Sunday.

"I'm sorry." It's all I can say.

Matt waves his hand and says, "Don't worry about it. Not your fault." It's obvious though that he's still a bit upset. He says after a beat, "Anyway, lunch?"

"Yes, please. Let's get out of here." I walk briskly to the counter and return the cart to its original place then step into the lounge to grab my bag. Jeff is sitting there at the small table in the middle of the room. I ignore him as I pick up my bag and leave, careful not to slam the door and make any loud noises, I'm still in a library after all.

Matt is waiting for me by the door. He opens it for me, allowing me to walk through first. We head to the corner and wait for the crosswalk signal. When the light changes, he takes my hand and interlaces our fingers. I can't help the smile spreading across my face and can see in my peripherals that Matt is looking at me and smiling too. I internally swoon.

I give his hand a short squeeze as we walk the short distance to Marty's Deli. We don't say anything, just continue to hold on to each other enjoying the warm spring Portland sun.

• 1 4 •

As we step up to the counter to order our lunches, Marty himself greets us.

"Moose! Lexi! How ya been?"

Marty is the only person that knows me as Alexa to ever call me Lexi. I don't really like it, but seeing as it's not really my name, I don't let it bother me too much.

Marty is "fifty-eight-years young" as he likes to say and is originally from Brooklyn, New York. He moved out to Portland twenty years ago when his wife was offered a very lucrative job opportunity with an international athletic brand. Cali and Matt grew up with Marty's son Martin, Jr.

"We're good," I answer for the both of us. "Been a crazy day so far."

Marty chuckles. "Oh yeah? A crazy day at the library, huh? Who'd've thought."

Matt tells Marty about the procrastination epidemic that is currently sweeping one of the area's schools while I grab us each a bottle of soda from one of the coolers at the back of the store; grape for Matt, orange for myself. I pick up a bag of cheddar and sour cream chips and place them near the cash register just as Matt finishes his account of our unusual day.

I see Marty shaking his head and says, "Boys. We just don't grow up do we, Moose?"

Matt offers the same shrug and "nope" as he did to the mother at the library before. Marty lets out a hearty laugh and asks us what we're having today. I order the chicken salad on a roll with lettuce and tomato. Matt orders a Reuben: corned beef, Swiss cheese, sauerkraut, and thousand island dressing on rye bread.

"Two usuals coming right up." Marty nods his head. "You two have a seat, I'll bring it out to ya."

Matt and I snag a table in the middle of the big glass window at the front of the deli. I drape my bag across the back of the seat and am about to sit down when I remember the sodas and bag of chips I left at the register. I grab them and sit down.

Matt picks up his bottle of soda, takes a long sip and lets out a content "ahhh." He sees my bottle of orange soda and cocks his head to the side. "Orange?" he asks.

"Yeah," I respond taking a sip of my own.

"You usually get seltzer though."

"I know, but today I need the sugar to make it through the rest of this day."

"Tell me about it," he says rolling his eyes. "I mean what was that with Jeff? He was so..." Matt pauses searching for the right word.

"Rigid?" I suggest.

"Yes! That's exactly it. Rigid." Matt huffs and bites down on a chip. I explain the conversation I had with Jeff yesterday about extra shifts, obviously leaving out the reason I was asking for them.

"Here ya go!" Marty comes over and places two shallow, red plastic wicker baskets in front of us. Our sandwiches are sitting on top of red and white checkered parchment paper. Practically as soon as my lunch is in front of me, I grab it and take a large bite.

"Ya know," Marty adds, "My guy just came back from a delivery to Mickey's not twenty minutes ago. Our little Squirrel must be there cause the order was for two. My guy said he had to knock a few times though because there was a lot of yelling. Those kids aren't fightin' are they?"

Matt starts coughing on his sip of soda. I almost choke on my food, but recover quickly and reply to Marty, "No, no. They definitely are not fighting." Marty quirks an eyebrow at my response. "I mean, I just spoke with Cali this morning, and she would've told me if something was up," I hastily add.

Matt swallows a bite of his sandwich and asks, "How's MJ doing?" effectively changing the subject.

"Ah, yeah, he's doing real good. Still over in New York, you know. He stayed there after college. Been living with my brother Walter the last year, but should be gettin' his own place soon. But he'll be coming home for Passover in a couple weeks. Janice said he's been seeing someone and that he'll be bringing them when he comes."

"Yeah? Good for him. Tell MJ to call me. Hopefully I can see him when he's here."

"Yeah, I'll do that." Marty claps his hands once and rubs them together slightly. "Alright, I'll leave ya to it. Lexi, give that mutt of yours a good hug for me."

I laugh, "I will, Marty."

As soon as Marty is out of earshot, Matt leans in and asks in a whisper, "So what do you think Squirrel and Mick were *really* doing?"

I giggle and lean in myself to respond. "I don't need to know the details, but I'd guess it was probably something that would make even Hugh Hefner blush."

Matt gasps, "Alexa Pearce!"

I can't help but snicker at how scandalized Matt looks. Our faces are just inches apart right now. I can see the crumbs on the side of his mouth, the small flecks of green in his eyes. *It would be so easy to just lean over and kiss him,* I think. Matt licks his lips the same moment that the thought crosses my mind. I smile at him and slowly lean back in my chair.

Soon, I tell myself. *Not now, but very soon.*

• 1 5 •

The rest of the work day went by relatively uneventfully compared to the morning. At four o'clock I texted Cali to remind her to bring my bag with my workout clothes to Mickey's studio tonight.

LEX: hey kid. you back at the apartment?

CAL: yeah, got here a couple hours ago
CAL: chillin with dog man

LEX: did you open that box? i hope nothing was ruined!

CAL: no it's ok! no damage done
CAL: but damn, milo really went after this box!

LEX: yeah i guess i forgot to tell you, but tyler left a note on it. apparently went to his door by mistake. milo must've smelled him on it or something

CAL: no wonder

Cali adds the eye roll emoji to her response.

CAL: that guy is a pig. he's the only person i've ever heard dog man growl at

LEX: i think pig is putting it too nicely
LEX: i gotta get back to work. but you'll bring my bag for me tonight?

CAL: yeah no problem. i already put it on the coffee table so i won't forget.

LEX: thank you!

I send another text of alternating thumbs up and heart emojis.

CAL: haha you're welcome
CAL: i'm gonna take dog man for a walk and then we're going to take a nap

LEX: ok sounds good. i'll see you later

Cali saying she'll take Milo for a walk reminds me of his dog attitude this morning. Also, how I promised I'd bring a double pup-cup for him when I got home. I'll have to stop at Roast on the way to Mickey's. I laugh to myself. *I can't wait to tell Cali all the great tricks she's teaching my dog.*

As I'm putting my phone back into its spot under the counter, I see the return bin is full again. I sigh and load up the cart for the fourth time, dragging it behind me to weave my way around the library replacing the books. It's monotonous work, but it frees my mind up somewhat to think about *The Book.*

I haven't had a chance today to check the computer. I put my hand on the piece of paper I've kept in my pocket all day. I don't even need to look at it as I go over the information in my head for what feels like the hundredth time in less than a day. *No author, title is simply* The Book, *language Latin, it's been in this building since the early 1900s, but the exact origin date is unknown.*

I'm lost in my thoughts, so I don't hear or see Jeff coming up to me. It wasn't until he was right next to me that I finally noticed him.

"Hi, Alexa," he says. He's still holding the clipboard from before.

"Hey, Jeff," I say back making sure I remain polite regardless of still feeling a bit irked at having to work on Sunday. I pick up a couple more books to put on the shelf.

"I wanted to talk to you about Sunday," Jeff continues.

"Oh sure, of course," I calmly reply. He is, after all, my boss. I put the book currently in my hand in its correct place on the shelf. I turn to give him my full attention.

"I wanted to tell you that Samantha is working on a special project for me. We're updating our online presence, especially regarding our rare book collection. So what you'll be doing on Sunday is you'll be downstairs in the climate-controlled storage room in the basement looking over the books to catalog them in a fashion more detailed than our current internal files. You'll also need to photograph the cover and first few pages of the book to add to the online database."

My heart rate started to speed up when he said "rare book collection" and it skyrocketed when he added "climate-controlled storage." That is exactly where I need to be. *I must be imagining this.*

"So, just to be clear, you want me to scan through each of the books, give a synopsis of what it's about, the author, the year it was printed and its approximate age, genre, et cetera, and then photograph it and upload that onto our internal servers which will eventually be part of an accessible online database?" I ask Jeff. I need him to make this as plain to me as possible. I cannot jump to any conclusions, especially when I've possibly just gotten that much closer to *The Book.*

"Yes, that's correct," Jeff replies. "Now, it is a very involved process, and you'll need to be careful handling the books, so I understand it will be quite time-consuming. It could take you all day to catalog two or three books. I would not expect you'd be able to get more than three done."

"Alright. You know, it actually sounds very interesting." I try to keep my voice as neutral as possible even though internally I am pretty much jumping for joy.

"Yes, that was Samantha's response as well." He looks down at his clipboard and picks something up. "You need authorization to access the rare book room, so I've made you a new I.D. tag. It has a magnetic strip on it that you'll need to swipe to enter." He hands me the tag on a Central Library lanyard. "Be sure not to lose that card, it grants access to the entire library, even after hours."

I look at it quickly and then wrap the lanyard around the card and put it into my pocket. *Oh, Jeff, I could kiss you! I cannot believe what I am hearing!* I slowly breathe in and out to calm myself.

"Thank you, Jeff," I look at his serious expression, but I think I can see a small glint in his eyes. "I understand you are placing a lot of trust in me with this project and I appreciate that very much."

Jeff nods before replying, "I will be here Sunday, so if you run into any problems or have any questions, you may ask me."

"That sounds great." I pause after answering. I can't help the downward turn my brain takes. It's been my defense mechanism for the last five years.

Could this be too good to be true? This literally just fell into my lap, it's pretty serendipitous. What if this is actually a trap of some kind? Could Jeff be a demon or a Victus reporting to Darius about me? Oh no, what if that spark I felt when I saw the computer listing for The Book *sent out some sort of signal to Darius? No, no. I would know if that were the case. Wouldn't I?*

Jeff breaks me out of my spell by clearing his throat to get my attention again. "Alexa, it is now 5:15. Please finish shelving these books and go around letting our members know the library will be closing."

"Right, of course," I nod and return my attention to the cart of books.

He turns and walks abruptly away, I watch him leave. I don't want to believe that Jeff is a Victus and that I am being lured into a trap, but decide it's better to be safe than sorry. I will go through the box under my bed tomorrow and reread my mother's letter and my grandpa's instructions. I want to be as prepared as possible if I finally come face to face with *The Book* after all this time.

I finish replacing the books and put the cart behind a counter. I walk around the library saying the same words over and over that I do every day at closing time:

"It is now 5:30, the library will be closing at six. If you would like to check out any books, please bring them to one of the check out counters. If you are logged on to the computers, please finish up and log off."

I go through the motions of preparing the library for closing mechanically. I go area to area asking people to log off the computers, to bring the books they'd like to check out up to a counter all on autopilot. My mind is occupied by the possibilities that Sunday could bring, what it could mean.

I'm still running scenarios through my mind as I gather my things together; I collect my phone from under the front counter, grab my bag from the lounge, check that my keys and wallet are still in place, put on my jacket.

I see Matt come into the lounge but it doesn't register in my brain that he's waiting for me until he speaks, "You ready to go?"

I smile and answer in what I hope is a bright voice, "Yes, definitely."

My mind, however, is still focused on *The Book. Stop it,* I tell myself. *You have all day tomorrow to check the box and prepare for Sunday. You still don't even know if this book is what you're looking for.* I nod in agreement to what my inner voice has said.

"Oh, I have to stop at Roast on the way and get Milo his double pup-cup."

Matt laughs, "Yeah, we don't want him throwing another puppy tantrum like before."

"I swear he must've learned that from Cali," I chuckle.

We leave the library and make our way toward Roast. Matt adjusts his bag on his shoulder, when he puts his arm down, it's me who reaches for his hand this time. He interlaces our fingers like before and holds it the whole way to the coffee shop. As we walk, he narrates for me how the rest of his day went, that he had three more frazzled mothers and two fathers approach him, each one asking about those damn earth science books.

• 1 6 •

DARIUS

On the other side of the country, the derelict bar that the demon has set up his current base in is full with the local townsfolk. Seeing as it's 9:30 on a Friday night, the bar has been loaded for the past four hours, since quitting time, the parking lot filled with dented and scratched pickup trucks, some old enough to drink themselves.

Darius is perched in his corner, glass of whiskey in hand. He watches as the bartender looks after his customers with fluid movements, rarely pausing to hear an order before producing drinks.

The black-haired man puts his glass down and turns to scope out tonight's prospects. He sees a tall, bald African-American man playing pool that shows promise. He looks like a football player; broad chest, flat stomach, thick arms — probably a tight end. He's surrounded by four men who most likely were his teammates back in the day but are now very far past their prime.

The demon's eyes move across the rest of the bar. Other than the couple of women he might take to his bed later, there is nothing else promising from this crowd. Darius puts a mental bookmark on the football player and turns back to the bar, his glass full again.

As the main entrance to the bar opens, Darius hears a large group of loud and rowdy halfwits come in. This group is younger than the rest of the crowd filling the bar and none of them look familiar. *Excellent,* Darius thinks.

The black-haired brute enjoys watching people, especially people he's never seen before. He's been observing humans for centuries, studying them, learning their weaknesses. New masses inevitably lead to conflict in some form; maybe an advance by a man is rebuffed by a woman, or someone bumps into another person who's having a bad day and is looking to fight, or someone gets looked at wrong, or people who are just inherently violent are looking for trouble. All these interactions can be found in a crummy, dilapidated bar in any of the decaying towns across this earth. All Darius has to do is sit back and wait.

Darius wipes his mouth with one of his tattooed hands, watching as a woman from the new group breaks away to head to the bar. She's young, probably in her twenties, short, has blonde hair, and a curvy body being shown off in clothes at least a size too small. She has to pass the table the former footballer is playing pool at to make her way the bar. Darius sees the man follow her with his eyes the whole way. This catches the attention of one of the guys in the woman's group, a scrawny guy with shaggy, greasy hair wearing a flannel shirt with arms cut off displaying his severe lack of muscle.

And so it begins, Darius thinks as the former tight end approaches the woman at the bar.

"Hey there, sugar," the muscled man says in a smooth baritone, tapping the woman lightly on the shoulder. "I'm Damon. Can I buy you a drink?"

Across the room Darius sees the shaggy guy shoot up out of his chair to get a better view of what's happening at the bar.

"Um, no thanks." The woman has a high pitched, almost squeaky voice. It instantly irritates the demon.

"Oh, come on now, honey. Just one drink?" *Ooh, nice touch Damon,* Darius considers. *Why don't you give her a little tap on that round ass, while you're at it?*

"I said no thank you," the young woman says with a bit more bite. She goes to move away from Damon but there isn't much room around her.

"Darling, why don't you just let me buy you a drink. I won't ask nicely again." Damon steps into the shorter woman's space, crowding her.

The door to the bar opens again, and Darius sees that it's his number three, Julius. The short, squat man makes a beeline right to where Darius is located.

"Boss," he says a bit out of breath.

Darius shushes the man. "I'm watching my program," he says. "And it's just getting to the good part," he adds seeing the unkempt skinny guy coming over to the duo at the bar.

"Hey! We got a problem here, buddy?" He pulls on the footballer's shoulder, trying to clear some space between him and the girl. Up close the guy looks like a child standing next to Damon.

The exponentially bigger man chuckles, leans his elbow onto the bar and says patronizingly, "No, no problem here pal. I just offered this fine looking woman a drink, and she turned me down twice. Can you believe that?"

The face and neck of the shorter guy turn dark red. He puffs out his chest and practically screeches, "Yeah, I can believe it. 'Cause she's here with me. You got that?"

"Bobby, stop. Come on, let's just go." The woman puts her hands on the flannel covered shoulders in front of her.

Damon laughs, "Bubba? Of course your name would be Bubba!"

Bobby's face gets even darker as his anger rises. He reaches a hand behind him and pulls a hunting knife out of his pocket. "You want to say that to me again?" He aims for slow and intimidating but his voice cracks at the end.

Damon laughs at the man again. "Oh, sugar. You should put that away before you hurt yourself." Damon leans in, his voice dropping to an even deeper register. "Or before someone takes it from you and shows you how to really use it."

Sold!

Darius is just about giddy, or as giddy as a demon can get, watching the man who he will make his next Victus put the little loser in his place.

Bobby's face loses a little of its color. He puts his knife away slowly and turns to the woman behind him, "Come on, Janey, let's just go."

Damon watches the couple walk back to their table, gathering their friends to leave. "Bye-bye, Janey!" he calls out. The woman stops just inside the doorway, looking back upon hearing her name. "I'll see you later, honey."

Darius is chuckling to himself swinging back around in his seat to face the bar. He holds up his empty glass getting the bartender's attention. It isn't until the whiskey has been poured and he's taken a big sip of it that he sees Julius out of the corner of his eye.

"Julius! Did you like that episode? I think we will have to keep an eye on Damon. I like his style."

"Sure thing, boss." Julius rarely makes direct eye contact with Darius but right now he is practically staring the man down.

Darius views this as a challenge. He stands ready to knock Julius back down to his place. "You got a problem?" he growls at the portly shorter man.

"N-n-no, no sir," Julius stutters out casting his eyes back down at the floor.

"Well, then what?" Darius is losing his patience at the blubbery man currently ruining his good mood.

Julius takes a deep breath and looks up again.

"I think we've got something."

• 1 7 •

"ALEXA"

Matt and I arrive at Mickey's studio just before seven, right as her previous class is about to end. We give a small wave to Mickey, she nods her head slightly in acknowledgement without breaking stride. We spot Cali waiting off to the side sitting on the floor with her knees up, phone in hand.

"Five bucks says she's playing the game with the squirrel finding nuts," Matt says to me under his breath as we approach her.

I look at him and smirk, "You're on." I know that Cali recently discovered a new solitaire app that has a squirrel deck and that it's her current game of choice. Which is only technically cheating.

As we approach Cali, I notice something missing: my gym bag. Cali lifts her head from her phone as Matt and I plop down on the floor beside her. When she sees me her eyes widen.

"Ah, shit, Lex. I saw the bag, I even had it in front of me and I meant to bring it, I swear. Shit, I'm sorry. Do you want me to go back and get it, 'cause I can. I will." Cali spews out the string of words without breathing.

I try to hold a stern look on my face, but I break when Cali raises her eyebrows and pouts. "Please don't be mad," she says.

I laugh and tell her not to worry about it, that I'll borrow some of Mickey's extra clothes she keeps in her office.

Cali lets out a long "whew" before noticing the cup from Roast in my hand. She tilts her head to the side and asks, "You got a hot chocolate before kickboxing? Won't that make you sick?"

She's spending too much time with Milo, I laugh to myself. *They are even adopting each other's mannerisms.*

"No, this isn't a hot chocolate," I answer her. "This is a double pup-cup for Milo that I promised I would bring him because we didn't have time this morning on our walk to get one. He made it very clear that that wasn't going to fly when he plopped himself down and wouldn't budge until I said I'd bring him home a double tonight."

Cali shapes her mouth into an O and cracks up. "Dog Man is a bit of a diva!"

"Uh-huh. And I wonder where he's learning it from?" I give her a soft elbow jab in the side.

"I have no idea what you're talking about," Cali deadpans.

"Sure," I drawl.

Matt laughs at the little performance between us then gets up and heads to the men's locker room, presumably to change into his own workout gear.

Mickey finishes up the class she was teaching and the group applauds having made it through. Cali and I are still sitting on the floor talking when she comes over.

"Hey, Lex," she says wiping her brow with a towel.

"Hey, Mick," I respond standing myself up. "Listen, your girlfriend here forgot my bag, so is it okay if I borrow some clothes and sneakers from your extras in your office?"

Mickey chuckles and says to Cali, "I thought you had her bag."

"I did! I had it in front of me, I saw it there. I just forgot to actually bring it with me." Cali shrugs from her spot on the floor.

Mickey turns to me. "The extras are in the metal cabinet next to the mini-fridge."

"Thanks. Okay if I put this in the fridge, too?"

"Of course, but I think your hot chocolate will taste weird after sitting for too long."

"Oh, it's not hot chocolate. Cali can fill you in."

We look down at Cali still sitting on the floor. She's got a guilty look on her face and is biting her lip. I roll my eyes and laugh then make my way toward Mickey's office to grab a t-shirt, sports bra, socks, and sneakers.

Good thing Mickey and I wear the same size, I think. I pick up a pair of shorts, *Good thing I shaved my legs the other day, too.*

****

Mickey stands at the head of the room just in front of a wall of mirrors. Above her mounted in brackets are two large speakers in either corner; dead center is a large digital clock controlled by Mickey's watch.

She greets her class. Besides Matt, Cali, and myself, twelve other men and women are in tonight's class. Most of them are around my age, but there are two badass ladies who look they are in their mid fifties but proudly boast being seventy-two and seventy-three respectively.

Each of us are standing at stations that are evenly spaced out. At our feet we each have a yoga mat laid flat, boxing gloves, sparring pads, a towel, and a jump rope. On the mirror at dead center on the wall, Mickey has written in a paint pen what's on tap for tonight's class. She reads it out to us before we get started.

"Okay guys, here's what's on for tonight. We'll start with a warmup of jumping jacks, burpees, butt kicks, and jumping lunges. Thirty seconds each for a total of two minutes.

"Then we'll move right into our strength circuit. Thirty slow push-ups, a sixty-second plank, then thirty slow squats. We're gonna do that twice, total of six minutes.

"Round three is cardio. Sixty-second jump rope, thirty-second air punches, thirty-second burpees, thirty-second air punches. That happens twice, total of five minutes.

"After that, the real fun starts." Mickey pauses her speech with a devilish smile. I hear the group around me let out a nervous laugh. "I'll demo the kickboxing sequences and then you'll pair off.

"Remember, if you need to, take a five- or ten-second break and then jump back into it. If it's too intense you can reign it in, don't go as deep into the movement. Try and keep up as much as possible, but if anything hurts or doesn't feel right, stop immediately.

"Everybody ready?"

She gets a resounding cheer from us. Mickey hits play on her stereo. Loud, thumping dance music blares from the speakers filling the room with sound. She holds up her wrist ready to start the clock. The class around me, myself included, are each bouncing lightly on the balls of our feet.

Mickey counts down, "Three, two, one, go!"

Mickey's classes are no joke. She typically likes to combine a bunch of styles together, especially the advanced one that we're taking tonight.

We're less than fifteen minutes into the forty-minute class, and my legs and lungs are already burning. My heart rate is up, my body is coated in a sheen of sweat, and my breathing is heavy. The room is pulsing with the music flowing from the wall-mounted speakers. Mickey's normally soft and gentle voice rings out over the music calling out the next item loud and commanding. The class follows along in complete synchronization.

With the warmup, strength, and cardio circuits done, Mickey pauses the music and tells us all to catch our breath, get some water if we need it. She then calls Matt up to the front to hold the pads while Mickey demonstrates the sequence she wants us to follow.

"Okay, we're going to start with a jab, jab, cross, jab, knee. We're going to put our non-dominant foot in front, so for the righties it's left foot slightly forward. You're going to face your partner at more of a diagonal than head-on. Jab with your non-dominant hand, cross and knee with dominant. Matt and I will show it once slowly, and then we're all going to do it."

I watch as Mickey jabs twice with her left hand, crosses with her right. She displays the next jab and then puts both of her hands on Matt's shoulders, moves her body weight onto her left leg and brings her right knee up into the part of the pad at Matt's navel. She calls out each movement as she does it.

How is she not even out of breath? I'm dying over here, I pant. *Even my thoughts are breathing heavy!*

"Five times with your non-dominant foot forward, then switch your stance and another five. Then switch with your partner." We all bend down to pick up our pads and gloves. I see Cali pick up her gloves, so I grab the pad.

"Remember," Mickey continues, "when you're holding the pad try to keep your core engaged and your feet shoulder width apart one slightly in front of the other. No injuries tonight, people."

I get myself set up as I watch Cali check her stance, right foot forward, and ready herself. I hear the music come back on and Mickey's voice over it.

"Okay, here we go! Jab! Jab! Cross! Jab! Knee!"

Cali grunts with each hit as Mickey continues calling out the moves at the front of the class. I take a quick peek and see that Mickey's concentrating on her form and keeping her tempo steady.

"Do you think... she'll be able... to ask Matt... about anything?" I time my words between the thumps on the pad from Cali's strikes.

"What?" Cali doesn't pause for a moment, just keeps connecting her gloves to the pad before bringing up her knee.

"Do you think... she'll be able... to ask Matt about... anything?" I ask again absorbing the blows.

"Switch your stance!" Mickey calls out. "Dominant foot forward and dominant hand jabs."

Cali looks down at her feet and does a couple quick air jabs before getting ready again. She glances over at Mickey and smiles. I look over and see Mickey wink at us.

"Yeah, I think she'll find time to talk to him," Cali says to me with a smirk.

I let out a heavy exhale and get ready for the next set. "Trust us," Cali breathes out. "We gotchu." A broad smile spreads across Cali's face.

I hear Mickey yell in the background, "And, go!"

• 1 8 •

I'm toweling off and chugging a bottle of water trying to bring my heart rate back down and trying to be as discreet as possible watching Mickey and Matt chatting after class finished.

"Stop it," Cali hisses next to me.

I turn my head quickly toward her. "Stop what?"

"Staring," she says. "You're practically ogling the guy."

I scoff, "I am not." I look back at the two. "Do you think she's talking to him about me?"

Cali laughs, "Oh my god, Lex. You're smitten with Moose!"

"Shhh!! They are literally right there."

Jesus, Cali. I roll my eyes in exasperation. I return my attention to Matt and Mickey. *What if he's telling her that we're just buds and he really isn't inter-ested in me romantically? But if that's the case, then what happened at lunch today? We definitely almost kissed! Right?* This teenage-like insecurity is driving me nuts. I bite my lip as my brain runs through the possible options of what's being said.

"Lex," Cali puts her hand on my arm and moves to block my view. "Trust Mickey, she'll figure it out for sure. But I say Moose is definitely into you. I've known the guy forever, and I've never seen him look at anyone the way he looks at you. Seriously, trust me."

I smile and duck my head, and answer with a breathy, "Thanks." But inside my head is a different story. *Trust them. That's at least the third time in two days I've heard that, but can I really, truly trust them? All of them? Cali, Mickey, and Matt?*

I'm knocked out of my thoughts by Cali poking a sharp elbow into my side. I blink a few times to clear my mind and see Mickey and Matt walking toward my roommate and myself. They look happy, they're laughing. *Maybe that's a good sign. Maybe we should all go out for a drink, I bet Cali would go for that. Oh, the bet!*

As Mickey and Matt reach us, I turn to Cali and ask, "Oh, by the way, what game were you playing on your phone before class?" I catch Matt's eye and raise my eyebrow, he smirks back at me.

"Oh my god," Cali gushes excitedly. "It's this brand new app I found, I don't remember the name but, you have a board with nuts and leaves and twigs and berries and stuff. You have like twenty moves or whatever to get the three nuts in a row, and when you do a squirrel comes across the screen and eats them! The point is to fatten the little guy up for winter."

"Man, you are really taking this whole squirrel thing to the max," Matt chimes in.

Cali crosses her arms and says, "Need I remind you, *Moose,* that you are currently wearing Bullwinkle socks?"

Matt looks down at his socks and goes, "Oh, hey, look at that." The three of us all laugh at his concession while he just shrugs.

"So," Mickey cuts in. "It's Friday night, classes are done, and Jack is staying 'til closing to lock up the gym for me." She looks at each of us before adding, "Kris's?"

Kris's Tavern is one of the local bars near my apartment. It's housed in what used to be a bank, and still has the giant metal vault complete with the huge round door which they use now for private parties. It's more of a sports bar, but there is sometimes live music, darts tournaments, and the bartenders know their regulars.

"That sounds like a great idea!" Cali exclaims. "We should all go home and shower then meet at our apartment, right Lex?"

She turns to me, so I nod. "Definitely."

Mickey puts her arm around Cali who tucks into her girlfriend's side. She turns her head to her left and says, "Matt?" A silent look passes between the two, but it's gone before I can decipher what it could mean.

Matt looks at us three girls and smiles. "Absolutely."

"Good then it's settled," Cali says, taking charge and stepping out of Mickey's embrace. "Babe, you go home and shower and change because you're kinda stinky."

"Like you're a spring meadow," Mickey retorts, crossing her arms.

Cali ignores Mickey and turns to her best friend, "Same for you Moose."

Matt snaps to attention and salutes her. "Aye-aye Captain Squirrel."

Cali turns to address me but pauses and directs her attention back to Matt. "Captain Squirrel. I like it! Well done Major Moose," she throws up a salute of her own.

"As I was saying, Lex and I will go home, walk Dog Man and get ready ourselves. You two meet us there in like, what, an hour? Then we can all go to Kris's together. I'm excited, this is going to be fun! Who's ready for an awesome night?"

The rest of us just shrug and reply at the same time with minimally enthusiastic "yeah," "sure," and "sounds good." Frustrated, Cali tries again.

"You don't sound very excited people. I said, who's ready for an awesome night!?"

We all look at each other before offering Cali the same response of shrugs and "yeah, sure, sounds good."

"That's the spirit!" Cali laughs.

I laugh at Cali's antics as I go to Mickey's office to pick up my clothes and bag. I'm about to leave the room when I remember Milo's pup-cup in the fridge and turn back for it. I come out of Mickey's office at the same time that Matt exits the men's locker room.

"So I guess I owe you five bucks then," he says.

"Why don't you buy me a drink at Kris's and we'll call it even."

"Definitely."

Cali and Mickey are just waiting for us near the door. Once we reach them, we all leave Mickey's studio together.

Matt flags a taxi for himself and Mickey since they live roughly in the same neighborhood. He waits to get in while Mickey and Cali kiss goodbye. Matt looks over at me with an expression I can't quite read. *Is that longing? Apprehension? Both?? I don't know!*

I pull my eyes from the gorgeous man in front of me and look to the couple still saying goodbye. A Cali and Mickey kiss is never just a peck, it is always deliberate and with meaning. I clear my throat to get their attention, but it doesn't work. I try again. Finally, the cabbie honks his horn. It startles the two women from their embrace.

Matt steps away from the car and guides Mickey into the cab, saying, "Okay, you'll see her in an hour, let's go."

I laugh and turn to my roommate, "Jesus, Cali. If that's how you say goodbye when you'll see her again in sixty minutes, what will you do if you have to leave town or something?"

Cali gives me a devilish smile and wiggles her eyebrows. "Well," she begins.

I cut her off laughing, "Scratch that. I don't want to know."

****

I can hear Milo's tags jingling and his nails clicking on the floor as I put the key in to unlock the door. As I open it and step into the apartment, he's standing right there, tail wagging a mile a minute, little black paws stomping in place.

"Dog Man!" Cali shrieks coming in behind me.

Milo's excitement spikes and he spins in two tight circles. He jumps up on his hind legs with his paws landing on Cali's chest. He licks her face while she scratches his floppy ears.

"Oh, he's such a good boy! Such a good puppy!" Cali continues saying sweet nothings in her baby voice saved especially for dogs while I close and lock the door.

Milo gets down off of Cali and comes to me, tail still swiftly wagging, and sticks his head in between my knees. He lightly presses some of his body weight into me and I get the same welcoming feeling that comes every time he does this: I'm safe. He sits down and pulls his head back to look up at me.

I squat down to his level and scratch under his chin. "You are a good boy," I say quite seriously, giving Milo a strong hug. "In fact, I believe I promised to bring this good boy something."

Milo's normally floppy ears perk up as straight as they can go. He stays seated, but his tail sways quickly across the hardwood floor. As I produce the pup-cup from my shoulder bag, Milo starts stomping his front paws again but doesn't get up. I take off the to-go cover and hold the cup just out of his reach.

"A double pup-cup," I say. "As promised." I sit down on the floor with my legs out straight, and Milo lays down in between them. My dog leans forward to sniff the cup even though I'm sure he knows exactly what it is. "Take it nice," I tell him.

My big, silly, ferocious, furry, sweet, protective, loyal dog crawls a few inches closer to me to put his black snout into the cup and lap up the whipped cream. I count to ten in my head and pull the cup away so he doesn't eat the whole thing at once. Milo's nose comes out bright white, and he has dabs of white on his whiskers.

"Okay, big guy, that's enough for now," I say standing up. I go into the kitchen and put the cup on the counter. I turn around from the counter as I ask Cali, "Do you want to come with me—" I stop because there is no Cali in the living room.

"Cal?" I call out.

"In my room!" I hear from the back of the apartment. I walk through the main room to the small hallway with the doors to each bedroom and the bathroom. I reach Cali's door, it's mostly open but I knock anyway.

"Yeah?" I hear her say.

I open the door all the way and step into the room. Cali is standing next to her bed which has more clothes strewn about it than hanging in the closet behind her. She has a towel wrapped around her body and her hands on her hips scrutinizing her clothing options.

"Well, I guess that answers my question," I chuckle.

Cali finally looks up. "Huh?" she asks.

"I was going to ask if you wanted to come with Milo and me on our walk, but I think I already know the answer."

"Oh," Cali snickers and adds, "Well I guess I could go like this, but I don't think that's socially accepted." I shake my head no. "You take Dog Man on a nice walk and I'll shower in the meantime."

"Good idea," I respond. Cali starts rummaging through the clothes on her bed, so I turn to leave her bedroom. I pause and turn back. "Umm, what should I wear tonight?" I ask nervously.

Cali looks up. It's obvious she's about to crack a joke but she stops. I guess how nervous I'm feeling is showing through clear as day.

"Don't worry about it just yet," she says to me gently. "Just take that pup for a good walk, and I'll help you pick something out after you shower."

I nod only slightly reassured. "Right, okay." I feel so vulnerable right now, this may be the most real Cali has ever seen me.

I readjust myself and say to her, "Okay, I'm going to take Milo. I'll be back in like, twenty minutes tops, so we can work on beautifying me then." I hope the joke will mask my insecurity.

"Sure."

Just like her best friend earlier in the day, Cali gives me a one-word answer. And just like before, it also has meaning. Cali smiles sincerely at me and adds, "I got you."

I must've heard Cali say that phrase over a dozen times today, but this one is different. She's not being facetious or playful, she's completely serious and sincere.

My brain then scrolls back to an early memory of Cali and myself, us sitting on the roof and me telling her I have trust issues without really elaborating as to why. I remember how accepting she was of that. She's never been offended by it or forced the issue these last eleven months.

I realize then that she's right. She's there for me, she has my back, she's proven it time and time again every day that we've lived together. She's got me.

I know at that moment that I can trust Cali with my secret and I know, as long as I convince her I'm telling the truth and not having a mental break-down, she would do everything she can to help me.

I move fully into Cali's room and make my way around her desk chair, the pile of books next to her bed, and the mound of dirty laundry overflowing from the hamper. Careful not to bump into her easel with her current mas-terpiece propped on it, I step right up to her and hug her. Cali immediately hugs me back very tightly.

I'm not one to shy away from physical contact, but I rarely will initiate it. Even with a roommate as snuggly a person as Cali is, she's always re-spected my need for personal space. So for me to come to her, it makes her know I mean it.

"What was that for?" she asks.

"Just thank you, Cali," I say. I lean back without completely letting go of her and look her square in the eyes. "I trust you."

As soon as I say the words, it feels like some of the oppressive weight pushing down on my shoulders is lifted a bit.

Cali's face displays shock and happiness and exultation all at once. "You're welcome."

I can hear in her voice that Cali is touched. I pull back farther to look her straight in the eyes. "I trust you, Cali. I really do." I tell her again, trying to convey through those few words exactly how much I mean it.

Cali's eyes fill with tears, and she pulls me in for another hug. As she hugs me, I feel my own eyes filling with tears. I finally feel like maybe I can let just a few of them fall, but still, I hold them back. She gives me a quick squeeze and then I feel her snuggle into my neck, a very Cali move.

One of the things my mother put in her note is that once I found what I was looking for, I would need to enlist people to help me. She said I would know them when I found them. *Well, I think I finally found one, Mom.*

• 1 9 •

Milo and I round the corner two blocks away from home, both of us with our heads held high. I gave Milo the casual command as soon as we left the building so I could be in my head.

I've replayed my hug with Cali a few times. Each time becoming more and more sure that trusting Cali is right. It may be a gut feeling, but so far my gut hasn't steered me wrong.

My mother was right, I can't do all of this alone. And I don't know for sure yet, but I am ninety-nine percent certain — again a gut feeling — that *The Book* listing I saw on the library archives search and the very thing I've been looking for are one and the same. Sunday will tell me for sure, but until then, at the very least I know I can trust Cali.

What trusting her may mean going forward, I can't think about right now.

Milo and I round the next corner and walk four blocks in the opposite direction. I tell him, "Easy Milo," and as he relaxes out of his casual command, I quiet my mind long enough to allow Milo time to just be a dog on a walk rather than my magical protector.

I watch him become playful with a young puppy on one of her first walks. The owner apologizes when his little pup starts jumping all over Milo, but I tell him not to worry about it, that Milo is very gentle. *Unless, of course, you happen to be a demon, puppy man.*

Milo spends the last block before turning back toward home chasing a page of newspaper blowing down the sidewalk in a breeze, pulling me along with him. Sometimes a dog just needs to be a dog.

We make the turn onto SW Jefferson and are one block away from our building when something just doesn't feel right. As I get closer and closer the odd feeling increases, something is just off. But I can't put my finger on what's different or if there is a threat and where it could be coming from.

Then it hits me. The streetlights are out. I scan the rest of the block and it seems the lights are out in only one section.

Could be nothing, "Alexa." Or this could be a planned attack set to ambush you. My mind battles between being paranoid and being smart.

Usually, the streets are very well lit in my neighborhood, and I rarely if ever feel unsafe. But tonight there is about a fifty-foot long stretch leading up to my door that is almost pitch black; the only light coming from passing cars and first-floor windows. It's spring so it's is getting darker later, but at 8:30 at night it's still basically midnight outside.

I take my phone out of my pocket and turn on the flashlight app. I give Milo his casual command again, just to be on the safe side, and we walk with purposeful strides to the door. Milo never indicates a threat and we make it home in one piece.

See? Nothing to worry about. I exhale and relax then suddenly stop and remind myself, *Right now at least.*

I look down at Milo who is looking up at me slowly wagging his tail just waiting for what's next. *Hmm,* I think. *Let's let the boy have some fun.*

"Hey, Milo. Want to race?"

Again, sometimes a dog just needs to be a dog. But sometimes I just need to be a twenty-three-year-old.

Milo immediately drops his chest and front paws to the ground leaving his back legs straight and his tail whipping back and forth. Universal dog body language for "let's play."

I unhook his leash from his harness and get myself ready. Milo waits next to me but is clearly becoming impatient. He actually whines and stands to circle me a few times.

"Ready?" Milo drops his chest back to the ground, eyes locked on me.

"Go!"

I take off running up the stairs two at a time. At the top of the first flight, we're tied. I'm pretty fast, but Milo is faster plus he has the advantage of two extra legs. He flies past me on the landing and reaches the top of the second flight a solid three seconds before me.

We're both panting but I'm the only one who feels the need to put their hands on their knees to catch their breath.

"Good job, Milo," I hold out my fist for a pound which my guy dutifully gives me. "Although, I think you cheated. Unfair advantage: extra legs. Let's see you take one of Mickey's classes and then walk eight blocks and then..." I inhale deeply "...I want a rematch."

Milo has the good sense to flop over onto his back, still panting at my feet, and goad me into giving him a belly rub. I bend to give him a quick rub and then unlock the apartment door.

He goes immediately to his bowls and laps up all the water that's there. I pick it up and run the water at the kitchen sink while offering Milo the rest of his pup-cup. He finishes the same time the bowl is done filling. I put down his fresh water and add a scoop of his food in his other bowl.

I fill a cup of my own with water and drink it all in one go. I put it on the side of the sink and turn around to see Cali coming into the living room wearing only black skinny-jeans and a bra.

"Oh, good, you're back. I know exactly what you should wear tonight! I already took it out of your closet and laid it on your bed. Come look!"

She dashes back down the short hallway and goes into my room. I follow her hoping I like what she chose. I walk into my room and see Cali has put a shirt and jacket on and is sitting on the floor pulling on ankle boots. She stands and I see her completed ensemble: A loose white v-neck t-shirt half-tucked into the black jeans, a bright cerulean blue denim jacket with cuffed sleeves, and black leather ankle boots. Her hair is pulled back into a tight bun accenting her jawline and cheekbones.

"Oh, I love that jacket," I tell her. *That is a very Cali jacket,* I think.

"Right!? It's so bright and how great is this color?" She spins in a circle with her arms out, silently asking how she looks.

"You look hot, kid. Mickey is going to drool when she sees you."

"That's the idea," Cali wiggles her eyebrows at me. "Just you wait until Moose sees you. Now you get in the shower, we're already running late."

"Yes ma'am," I reply.

I grab my towel from the hook behind my door and hurry to the bathroom. I rush through my shower and walk back into my bedroom ten minutes later with my towel wrapped around me. Cali is still in there tweaking my outfit.

"Okay," she says. "I think you will look great in this. And better yet I think it'll make Moose's jaw drop."

She holds up white skinny-jeans, a medium wash denim button-down shirt, a light gray suede jacket, and bright gray Converse sneakers.

"Where did you find these?" *Maybe Cali has some powers of her own,* I think to myself.

Cali rolls her eyes. "The shirt was mine. I got it on clearance online but it was too big, so I gave it to you. Still has the tags on it, by the way."

"Oh, yeah, I remember that now."

"The pants are yours. We got them at that sale last October? They were like, sixty percent off. That whole white after Labor Day crap. Again though, tags still on."

"That I don't remember at all. The only thing I remember buying is that jacket. And I've had those shoes forever. But it looks good all together."

"And that's what counts," Cali chimes in.

Cali instructs me to go blow dry my hair while she cuts the tags off the clothes. I jump back into the bathroom and see the blow dryer already plugged in ready to go. *Thank you, Cali!*

I flip my hair this way and that making sure I get my thick hair as dry as I possibly can. I go back into my room and kick Cali out so I can have some privacy while I get dressed. Cali grumbles something about hurrying up. When I open the door, Cali is standing there with a flat iron in one hand and my mascara in the other.

"You'll be wearing your hair down tonight," she says. Now it's my turn to grumble. I rarely wear my hair down and when I do, I end up putting it up anyway.

She sits me down on the closed toilet with a small mirror so I can put on some mascara. She tells me not to drop the mascara wand on my jeans but drapes a towel over my lap anyway. Cali stands behind me with the straightener, humming while doing my hair.

Cali finishes and unplugs the flat iron. I stand up to look in the bathroom mirror, and my jaw drops at what I see.

"Holy shit, kid." My mascara is perfectly even — first time ever that that's happened — but my hair is flawless. Cali straightened it just enough so that my normally curly hair is soft and smooth. Plus my zit from yesterday has gone away.

"I feel like I'm in a shampoo commercial," I laugh. "I just want to bend over and flip my hair up dramatically."

"Don't you dare," Cali laughs. "We have maybe ten seconds before they get here. Not enough time to get it like this again."

I feel guilty for leaving Milo alone so much today, so I give him a rawhide bone I know he'll chew on for a few hours. He takes it from me happily and settles underneath the coffee table (his customary chewing spot) and starts gnawing on it immediately.

Cali and I are standing at a counter in the kitchen gathering our respective keys, phones, and wallets into each of our bags when Cali gets a text from Mickey saying she and Matt are waiting in the lobby.

"Right on time," she says.

I tell Milo to be a good boy as Cali ushers me out of the apartment and closes the door behind us. I practically skip down the first set of stairs, with her a few steps behind.

I slow my pace on the second flight, so as not to appear too eager. When I get my first glimpse of Matt, I almost miss the last step. He's wearing a red t-shirt with the Portland Thorns team logo on it under a dark gray canvas jacket, and jeans with red sneakers.

He looks literally perfect, I think. *How does he do that?* I greet the two of them as I come off the stairs with a shy, "Hey."

Matt's eyes widen as I come toward him. "Wow. You look really great," he says, the smile never leaving his face.

I can feel the blush shoot up my neck and spread over my entire face.

"Thank you," I reply with a smile and check over my clothes. When I look back at him, his expression hasn't changed at all. *You look really fucking hot,* is what I would like to say back, but instead, I look him in the eyes and add a, "So do you," as sincerely as I can. His eyes stay locked onto my own and I realize how close we're standing to each other, but I don't dare move.

We're broken out of our loaded staring match by a loud squeal behind us. Mickey has scooped up Cali and is spinning her around. She stops still holding the shorter woman.

"Damn, babe," Mickey says. "Maybe we should just go back upstairs and forget the bar."

"Hmm," Cali responds. "Or..." Cali's voice trails off as she whispers something into the taller woman's ear. Mickey closes her eyes and gives the slightest of nods. She kisses her girlfriend then puts her down.

When Cali's feet touch the ground again, she steps back to admire her love, nodding approvingly as she looks her up and down from head to toe. The brunette is wearing faded skinny jeans with a black tank top and an olive green leather jacket. Between Cali's heeled boots and her flat three-stripe sneakers, when Cali steps back in to give Mickey another kiss, they are almost the same height.

Cali pulls away slightly and takes Mickey's arm to put it around her shoulders. Her own arm wraps around Mickey's waist. She looks to Matt and me standing by the door waiting on the two of them. I can feel Matt still looking at me out of the corner of my eye. I fight the urge to look at him and keep my gaze trained at Cali and Mickey.

Cali's eyes dart back and forth between us then deliberately land on me. There is mischief swirling in her green eyes.

"Okay," she says with a small smirk. "Shall we go?"

• 2 0 •

Cali

Cali takes Mickey's hand as they exit the building. She takes a quick peek over her shoulder at Alexa and Matt walking less than ten feet behind. Cali watches as her best friend takes hold of her roommate's hand, she sees the smiles that spread across both of their faces.

Cali leans in to give Mickey a kiss on the cheek. When the older woman looks at her, she asks, "What did Moose say after class?"

"Well," Mickey begins, pausing for a long minute to build suspense. "He's crazy about her."

Cali's eyes immediately widen and her jaw drops. "I fucking *knew* it," she says under her breath.

"I know!" Mickey exclaims quietly. "I asked him if he planned on asking her out or anything and he said, 'the next chance I get'."

"Awww! Oh my god, Lex and Moose!"

"Shh!" Mickey puts a finger to her lips to quiet the smaller woman.

"Oh, right." Cali covers her mouth with her free hand, but her excitement is still evident by the glint in her eyes. Mickey unclasps their hands and puts her arm around Cali's shoulder.

"He actually seemed pretty nervous about it," Mickey continues in a hushed voice. "He even asked if I thought she'd say no. What's with those two? They clearly really like each other but both of them are so nervous that the other one doesn't."

"I don't know, but maybe some alcohol will help them get over it," Cali says sending a devilish grin in her girlfriend's direction.

"Uh-oh. What does that mean?"

Cali just covers her mouth again and shakes her head.

"Cali," Mickey tries again. "Don't get in the middle of it." Cali lowers her hand, but her expression hasn't changed. "Just let them do what they're gonna do."

"Okay," Cali concedes. "Or..." She takes in a deep breath and Mickey can tell she's ready to yell something. Mickey takes her own hand and quickly covers the shorter woman's mouth with it. Cali promptly licks her palm.

Mickey stops walking and uses the arm still around Cali's shoulders to pull her in as close as she can, leaving her hand in place over the other woman's mouth. She puts her lips up to Cali's ear and says, "I've felt your tongue on every inch of my body. Do you think I care if you lick my palm?"

Cali slowly shakes her head no. Mickey removes her hand.

"Well," she whispers quietly to the brunette still holding her close, "would you care if when we got to the bar I pulled you into a dark corner, got down on my knees right there and licked you from sl—"

"Hey, why'd you guys stop walking?" Matt's voice right behind them jolts the couple from their sidewalk moment.

"Oh, uh," Mickey clears her throat. "We, uh—"

"I was just telling her what I want to do to her and she got a little weak in the knees, so we had to stop for a second."

"Cali!" Mickey cries.

"What? He asked."

"And he wishes he hadn't," Matt sighs. He chuckles and uses his left hand to pinch the bridge of his nose. Cali sees that his right hand is still holding Alexa's but before she can say something about it, a pinch on her elbow and a look from Mickey silences her.

Instead, she says, "Come on, Moose. The bar is right around the corner. Loser has to buy the other two shots. Ready? Go!" Cali takes off as fast as her heeled boots will allow.

"I'm not racing you, Squirrel!" Matt calls after her. When she turns around to jog backward and gives him the finger as she rounds the corner, she sees him let go of Alexa's hand and take off after her.

Matt and Cali reach the front door of the bar at the exact same time, yet Cali immediately throws her arms in the air and declares herself the winner.

"No way!" Matt argues. "You cheated and I still got here first. So, I win."

"You do not!" Cali maintains. She turns to the bouncer sitting on a stool at the side of the door. "Jorge," she huffs and crosses her arms. "Who won?"

Matt turns his attention to the man, "Ignore her, please." He turns back to his short friend and says, "Because you so did not win."

"Alright, that's enough children!" Alexa's voice cuts through their juvenile arguments. "Let's just go inside and have a good time, yeah?"

They each take out their IDs and one by one go inside. They stand just inside the entrance putting their licenses away. As the door is closing behind them, they hear Jorge say, "Matt won."

"What?!" Cali cries.

Matt raises his arms straight in the air and throws his head back in victory. Cali whips around ready to go back outside and present her case but is tugged into the bar by the collar of her jacket by Mickey.

****

Cali and Alexa are seated at the table the foursome had grabbed once they came in. They are watching Mickey and Matt waiting to catch the bartender,

Ricki's, attention to order another round. Alexa starts pushing the smattering of empty glasses scattered across the table toward the center.

Cali turns to her roommate and sees a peculiar expression on Alexa's face. She can't tell if it's eagerness or nervousness, she assumes it's most likely both.

"You having a good time, Lex?" she asks.

Alexa nods. "I am," she says with a smile.

"Good," she replies. "When they get back, I say we do a darts tournament. Two versus two." Cali points two fingers at Alexa and continues, "You and Moose against me and Mickey."

"That sounds like a good idea," Alexa agrees.

"What sounds like a good idea?" Mickey asks putting down four fresh glasses and a pitcher of beer.

"A darts tournament," Alexa answers.

Cali explains, "You and me versus her and him." Cali looks around and doesn't see Matt. "Where is him?"

"He went to the bathroom," Mickey replies.

"Well then maybe now that he's gone for a second, it's a good time for a status report?" Cali suggests.

"Yes, I agree" Mickey turns in her chair to face Alexa who has an honest, hopeful expression on her face. "He's crazy about you."

Cali sees Alexa visibly relax once she hears that.

"Really?" Alexa asks with a huge smile.

"Really," Mickey repeats.

"That's..." Alexa pauses for a moment. "Fantastic," she finishes.

"So now you know!" Cali is getting excited, but Mickey puts a hand on her arm to settle her. "And now you don't have to worry about it," Cali says in a normal voice.

"Exactly," Mickey adds. "You know he likes you, so you don't have to question anything. And you can just relax and be yourself around him."

Cali brushes some of Mickey's hair back behind her ear and sees in her peripheral that Matt is making his way back to their table.

"Moose!" she calls out, deliberately loud enough so Mickey and Alexa hear her. "We're having a darts tournament."

"Are we?" he asks with a smirk.

"Yup," Cali says popping the P. "Me and Mick versus you and her." She punctuates her statement by pointing at Alexa.

"Okay, I'm in," Matt says with a brilliant smile directed straight at the girl with glasses.

"Me too," Alexa adds with a brilliant smile of her own.

"Cal, do you know the rules of the game?" Mickey asks.

"Well, no," Cali responds.

"And are you any good at darts?"

"Nope," Cali offers with a shrug.

"Okay, then," Matt chimes in rubbing his hands together. "Let's play some darts."

• 2 1 •

"ALEXA"

I'm sitting with Cali at the table we claimed upon coming in three hours ago. I'm openly staring at Matt who's standing at the bar with Mickey getting our next round of drinks. To prevent my mind from wandering too much about Matt and what he and Mickey talked about or how he feels, I busy myself by pushing the empty glasses on the table into its center.

"You having a good time, Lex?" I hear Cali ask

I really am, I think. "I am," I answer her with a genuine smile.

Cali mentions something about having a dart tournament and I agree with her that it sounds like a good idea.

"What sounds like a good idea?" Mickey asks. I watch her put down a pitcher and fresh glasses.

"A darts tournament," I tell her. I frown a little realizing that Matt hasn't come back to the table. Before I can ask about him, Cali beats me to the punch.

"He went to the bathroom," Mickey explains.

This is a perfect moment for Mickey to tell me what Matt said after her class. I don't want to sound too desperate so I silently will Cali to ask the question for me. When she does, I have to pause for a minute and make sure I didn't actually cause that. As soon as Mickey responds, I know I'm in the clear.

The next words I hear build a warmth in my chest and sends my heart rate into overdrive.

"He's crazy about you," Mickey says.

It's like getting a breath of fresh air after being underwater too long, and I can feel my body physically relax.

I can't wipe the smile from my face as I ask, "Really?"

Mickey answers me back, "Really."

"That's..." I have a million adjectives floating through my head all at one time. *Amazing, awesome, wonderful, marvelous, excellent, fantastic.* I say the last one out loud, "Fantastic."

I hear Cali and Mickey keep talking but I don't listen to what they are saying. Matt likes me too. In fact, he's crazy about me. I'm thinking about the possibilities that come with finding out someone's interested in you. I'm so focused on the good that I'm blindsided by the next thought that enters my head.

What will he say when he finds out who I really am? How hurt will he be that I've been lying to him constantly? What will he do when he knows the truth?

"Moose! We're having a darts tournament!" Cali's excited voice brings me back to the present.

When Matt says that he's in, I make the decision to just enjoy the present that's in front of me. I can't get any closer to anything until Sunday, so for now, I'm going to be just a twenty-three-year-old woman playing darts with my friends and a guy I am very much attracted to. I allow my face to mirror the actual way I feel for once and say, "Me too."

****

The four of us are gathered around the middle of three dart boards hanging on a wall to the side of the vault door in the bar. I did a quick Google search to find the rules for darts and we all decide that the 501 game seems to be the easiest.

Each team starts with five-hundred-and-one points and you subtract the number value of whatever section your dart lands on, three darts a piece per round. The first team to get exactly zero points, or the team closest to zero after twenty rounds, wins.

When I went to get the darts from Ricki behind the bar, she gave me a warning to keep an eye on Cali. Her exact words were: "I don't need anyone leaving here with more holes than they came in with. A dart wielding squirrel is not covered by my insurance."

After ten rounds, Matt and I, or The Overdue Late Fees, are decisively in the lead over Cali and Mickey, or The Flying Squirrels. My roommate, of course, chose both team names and wouldn't budge on altering them.

It's a good thing no other people were playing darts because Cali and Mickey have been all over the place. On Cali's last turn, she had one dart in the ceiling, another in the wall underneath the board, and the third was the only one to actually hit the board. On Mickey's turn before that, she had two darts on our board, and her third got a bullseye on the board directly to our left. None of us could quite figure out exactly how that happened.

We had moved our drinks and jackets to a table near the boards and had ordered some typical bar food: nachos, chicken wings, and fries. Out of the corner of my eye, I see Ricki coming out from behind the bar to bring us another pitcher.

"Thanks, Ric," I said to the woman. Even with some food in my stomach, after four beers I am feeling looser than I have in months. *I think I'm done drinking for tonight though,* my inner monologue tells me, so I decide to cut myself off.

"No problem," Ricki responds.

"Hey, Ricki!" Cali's words are a little jumbled together as she asks, "You want a cameo shot?"

"Sure," Ricki replies easily. She takes a glance at the chalkboard scorecard on the wall and smirks. "I think you two could use all the help you can get," she says in Mickey and Cali's general direction. Ricki throws the three darts in quick succession and they all land on the twenty point section, two of them on a double.

Cali whoops excitedly about the one hundred points just scored for her team. Matt and I immediately start protesting about how unfair that is and that now Ricki needs to do a cameo shot for our team. The bartender shrugs, pulls the three darts out the cork and launches them again. She repeats her performance and gets all three in the twenty spot, two again on a double.

We all throw our hands up with a drawn-out chorus of, "Ohh!"

"Damn, Ricki," Matt drawls. "Are you a pro or something?"

Ricki only offers a shrug and a non-committal, "Or something," as a response as she heads back to resume her bartending duties.

I go with her and get myself a seltzer. While she's pouring it from the soda gun, I see behind her a plaque with a framed picture of her and Jorge, the bouncer. The brass plate has the words Pacific Northwest Darts Tournament on it. Apparently they made it to the semi-finals.

She sees me looking at the plaque and gives me that same shrug. "Well played, Ric," I tell her. She smirks as she pushes my drink across the bar to me.

The big jump in points allows Matt and me to win the game in five more rounds. He and I slap hands in a double high five. He doesn't let go of my hands right away but instead pulls me into a hug. I'm surrounded by his scent: Old Spice, laundry detergent, and peppermint. *I could get lost in this smell forever.* I hug him back and hold on a little longer than I normally would.

When I let go, I turn to see Cali staring at us with crossed arms and frowning. I offer my hand for a shake and say, "Good game."

"I demand a rematch," she says ignoring my hand.

"Absolutely not," Mickey says before Matt or I can answer. "Babe, let's face it..." she pulls her in close and says in a stage whisper "...we suck at darts."

"I take offense to that," Cali deadpans.

We spend another couple of hours at Kris's Tavern talking and joking. Matt and Cali have me cracking up retelling the pranks they used to play on their teachers. Matt has moved his chair right next to mine and has his hand on my knee while talking.

After their story about air horns, duct tape, and the creative places they scattered them, I get a glimpse of Mickey trying to discretely hide a yawn. Yawns are proven to be contagious so of course, I yawn in response. I check the time on my phone and see it's almost two in the morning.

"Oh, man," I say. "It's almost two. Milo's going to wake me up in six hours to go for a walk."

Mickey puts her hand over her mouth, yawning again. She turns to Cali and says, "Baby, I'm beat. You ready to go?"

"Yeah, you had a busy day," Cali says. "You staying over tonight?"

Mickey nods and lets out an "mm-hmm" around another yawn. Her eyes are starting to tear from yawning multiple times. I see her blink quickly to clear them. Every time Mickey opens her mouth, I follow suit three seconds later.

"Wow, you really are tired," Cali says. "Okay let's go."

We all stand up and put on our jackets, checking our pockets and wallets to make sure that we didn't leave anything behind.

"Are you going to grab a cab?" Cali asks turning to Matt.

"No, no," Matt says stifling a yawn of his own now. "I'll walk you guys back, and then catch a cab from there."

"Such a gentle-moose, Moose," Cali replies with a wink. She seems to be the only one of us still with energy.

We go as a group up to the bar to for Ricki to have a moment to close our tabs. The bar has quieted some over the last half hour so we don't have to wait long. We say goodnight to her and to Jorge on our way out.

Matt and I are lagging about fifteen feet behind Cali and Mickey on the way back to my apartment. Instead of holding hands, Matt has his arm around my shoulder and I have mine around his waist. Every time he looks at me, his eyes dip to my mouth. I want so badly for him to kiss me. After the third time of him staring at my mouth, I decide to just go for it myself.

No more wishy-washy ifs and buts "Alexa." It's time to woman up.

I stop walking and slightly pull on Matt to stop him too. I put my hand on his cheek and search his face for uncertainty or any apprehension. *Here goes nothing.* I lick my lips and tilt my head up so our mouths meet lightly in a tentative kiss.

I've barely pulled away before I feel his mouth on mine again, firmer this time, more purposeful. He pulls me into him, the arm still around my shoulder moves to around to the back of my neck, the other snaking its way across my lower back under my jacket. His mouth moves against mine perfectly, no hesitation. I tilt my head to get better access to him.

Before I know it, both of his hands are sliding through my hair and I have my hands on his chest, his jacket bunched up in my fists. I pull my lips from his only when the need to breathe overrides my need for Matt.

I don't move an inch of my body except to open my eyes. I inhale sharply to catch my breath. I see Matt's face so close to mine, his eyes hooded with the same hunger I feel in my own depths. I feel his heart pounding beneath his jacket that I'm still holding, as hard as my own.

Wow, I think.

"Wow," he says out loud.

"My thoughts exactly."

• 2 2 •

DARIUS

"Are you sure?" the demon asks his Victus soldier.

"Y-y-yes. Ahem, I'm positive," Julius replies. "I followed up with Blue in New Orleans, and he sent me everything the person at the library said. The questions the girl was asking about the building matches the description of the library in Portland, Oregon."

"And how the fuck would this person know what a library in Oregon looks like?" Darius has no tolerance to be hampered by yet another dead end.

"Apparently the guy is some sort of historian or something. I don't know exactly, but I thought it was worth telling you and having someone check out."

Darius raises his eyebrows at this unusually confident reply from such a typically timid, little man.

"I see," the ancient man says. "And who do you propose we send on this field trip? Hmm?"

At this Julius returns to the stuttering wimp Darius is used to. "Uh, well I-I-I don't know. I could go if you want, boss. Or I-I-I could send someone there."

Darius considers his options. He turns away from his Victus as his eyes scan the room. They land again on Damon who is still hanging around the pool table.

"Go over to that man, Julius," Darius says his stare fixed on Damon. "Tell him I'd like to discuss a "business opportunity" with him."

Julius follows his boss's gaze and scurries over after a quiet, "Yes, sir."

Darius watches as Julius goes over and taps Damon on the shoulder. The former footballer turns around holding the pool cue across his body with both hands. Julius gestures back toward the end of the bar, but Darius can tell he's having trouble convincing the man to come over. His arm movements become more frantic, and Darius feels his chest fill with ire at the obvious incompetence of his number three.

He gives it another minute before Damon pushes Julius away, possibly breaking the cue over his head. Darius would let him too, except Julius is the one who has most of the connections throughout the pipeline of parole officers across the country. That pipeline is vital to Darius getting information and getting it fast.

When Julius grabs Damon by the arm, the stumpy man gets shoved away, falling to the floor. Darius internally debates how involved he wants to get in the ass-kicking that's about to come Julius's way. The demon sees his Victus stand up and shove Damon back. It's clear by how far Damon flies and how hard he hits the wall behind him, that Julius used his telekinesis power. The tall bald man's friends are too shocked by what they just saw to come to Damon's aide.

Damon stays flat against the wall as Julius walks up to him. He must explain himself this time in a way that gets through to the muscular man. Damon glances over to where Darius is sitting and nods. Julius turns around and begins walking back to his boss, Damon following behind him.

About time he grew a fucking set of balls, Darius thinks.

"Boss," Julius says as he approaches the end corner of the bar top. "This is Damon. I believe he is ready now to hear your proposition."

Darius claps Julius on the shoulder and gives him a short nod. It's the most approval the Victus has ever gotten and it makes him stand a little taller, satisfied with himself.

"Hello, Damon," Darius says, reaching out a hand for a shake while taking a sip of his whiskey. Damon grips it and shakes it once before letting go. "It's a bit loud in here, how about we move to a quieter spot?"

"I'm not a fucking idiot," Damon fires back. "This fatass said you got a job offer for me, and I'm not going anywhere with you until I hear it."

Julius steps in. "This fatass just laid you flat against a wall, and he," he quirks his head toward the demon "can do worse. So why don't you just shut up and listen."

Darius can see the anger start to rise in Damon's eyes. "Alright listen," he says stepping in. "Let's just go outside and talk. I guarantee what I'm about to offer you, Damon, no has ever been able to before. If it makes you feel better, you can bring your friends over there with you. You don't like what I have to say, you walk away. Sound good?"

Damon looks at his linebacker buddies who are intently staring at him, then back to the two men standing to his left and right. He sizes them up and thinks five against two gives him good odds. He waves his buddies over.

"Okay," Damon says. "I'll hear what you gotta say."

"Excellent," Darius says with a flat affect. "Let's all of us go out to the alley in the back, and you and I can discuss what I have to offer."

Darius leads the way through the kitchen and out the back door. He has a nefarious grin on his face as he thinks, *It's so easy to lure these dumb humans into a false sense of security.*

Although still early in April, the warm night hints at the hot Georgia summer to come. Darius walks halfway down the alley, resuming the same spot he stood before when destroying the beer crates. He hears the five humans file out, and the slam of the door as Julius closes it. He waves Damon over to him so they can continue talking.

"So, my friend," the demon begins. "This job I have for you requires you to travel a little and gather some information for me. You'll be going with Julius. You know, the man who shoved you into the wall inside? You have a very specific and simple task that should you fail, it will make me very disappointed."

"Seriously?" Damon scoffs. "That's it? That's the opportunity no one else has ever given me?"

"Ah, ah, ah," Darius waves a finger. "Don't get ahead of yourself now, son."

Darius takes a pack of cigarettes out of his jacket pocket, takes one out and puts it in his mouth. The tip of the index finger on his right hand glows a bright amber color. When Darius touches his finger to the cigarette, it lights.

Damon's eyes bulge. He's definitely never seen anything like this before. He tries to hide his surprise and recover his previous unflustered demeanor.

"Nice trick," he says nervously. "Now tell me something that I haven't heard before, or I'm outta here."

Darius looks over Damon's shoulder at his long-time soldier, Julius. A silent communication passes between them and the Victus moves away from the four men standing by the door.

Darius returns his eyes to the man in front of him. His voice drops an octave as he growls out, "How about I show you instead?"

Before Damon has a chance to understand what's happening, both of Darius's hands shine with white light. With two flicks of each wrist, four spheres of fire shoot from his fingertips and slam into Damon's comrades. The men are devoured by enormous flames; reduced to skeletons in three seconds, piles of smoking ash in five.

Damon, unable to fully understand what just happened, falls to his knees in shock. He breathes heavily before retching. Darius kneels and flicks some ash from his cigarette into the puddle of bile on the ground.

"Now," the demon says. "Normally, I would charm you, possibly trick you into giving me what I need. But you see, I am running low on patience. Very low. In fact, I'd say I might even be out of it entirely. So, would you like to end up like your friends over there, or will you be traveling with Julius to Portland?"

Damon turns his head to look at the man kneeling next to him, his breath still coming in gasps as he finally understands that he just witnessed four of his friends be killed. His stomach heaves again making him empty all of what's left in it.

"Prove to me that you are worth more than that," Darius says flicking his cigarette toward one of the steaming piles of ash. "You come back with something useful, and I will give you power like you've never dreamed of, and money you've never seen before."

Darius stands and brushes off his pant leg. He walks to the door that leads into the kitchen of the bar. Before opening it, he turns back around to Julius and says, "Leave first thing in the morning. Go to New Orleans and meet with Blue. Have him take you to whoever he spoke with before. Then fly to San Francisco and rent a car and drive up. If she is in Portland, I don't want you to use any magic or potions that could possibly alert her. You've got a week to bring me something."

Darius yanks open the door to the bar. "Don't disappoint me boys," he calls out down the alley before stepping inside. "You've both see what will happen if you do."

PART TWO

• 2 3 •

"ALEXA"

Waking up this morning, I can't be sure if I had dreamt last night or if it actually happened. With my luck, it was probably a dream, so I want to stay in bed as long as possible and relive it over and over. I'm pulling the covers back over my head to try and lull myself back to sleep when I hear a knock at my bedroom door.

"Yeah?" My voice is groggy and doesn't carry. I clear my throat and try again, "Come in."

The door opens but I don't have my glasses on and can only see a blurry outline. By the dark hair I realize it's Mickey standing there.

"I'm making eggs," she says. "Do you want some?"

"Definitely. Thanks." I sit up and put my glasses on.

"Where's Milo?" I ask after not seeing him at the foot of my bed.

"Oh, he's in the living room," Mickey replies. "He must have heard me when I got up a couple hours ago. He was whining at your door, so I let him out. We just got back from a walk, actually."

"Thank you for that," I say. "I'm surprised I didn't hear him. Or that he didn't wake me up himself. What time is it anyway?"

"It's almost ten. I told him to let his mommy sleep," Cali says coming in and plopping herself down next to me on my bed. "After all, you had a big night last night." She wiggles her eyebrows suggestively at me.

So it wasn't a dream, I think. *Thank god.*

I can feel my neck and cheeks warming as I blush. I'm saved from having to answer Cali by Milo trotting in and jumping onto me. His momentum and weight knock me down onto my back, and he promptly lays down across my chest.

"Cali, leave her alone," Mickey says from her place still in my doorway.

"Why? She asked me all about our first kiss, said something about how it's her right as the roommate to know. So," Cali then turns to me with her chin in her hand, index finger vertical against her lips, a serious expression on her face. "How was it?"

I hug Milo and bury my face in his fur trying to hide the enormous smile on my face. "It was," I pause wanting to pick the right word. "It was wow."

"Wow?" Mickey asks. She comes and sits at the foot of my bed.

"Yes, definitely wow." I tap Milo's paw and he instinctively knows I want him to move off of me. He shifts himself and is now laying in between Cali and myself. "It's what I was thinking, and what he said."

Cali squeals with excitement, but Mickeys beats her to the next question, "Did he initiate or you?"

"I did." I tell them how as we were walking, whenever he looked at me his eyes went to my lips. "I don't know where this surge of confidence came from, but I stopped walking and kissed him." I sigh as I relive the tentative first touch of our lips and then Matt's more desire filled kiss. "It was just a light kiss, but then he kissed me a second time, harder."

"And that was the wow?" Cali asks.

"It was all wow," I say.

****

I didn't have a chance for the rest of the morning to grab the box under my mattress and reread the letter from my mother like I wanted to. After the three of us ate the eggs Mickey made (the fluffiest I think I've ever had), I told them I had some laundry to do, hoping that would give me a window. But Cali chimed in that it reminded her she had a ton of laundry to do too and that she'd join me. Mickey had to go to her studio to do payroll and expenses and to prepare for her afternoon classes and sessions.

So now I am sitting in the row of chairs across the back wall of the laundromat, with Milo at my feet — same arrangement as Roast, dogs are not usually allowed but Milo is the exception. Cali is at one of the tables nearby sorting the mountain of laundry she brought. We're the only two people here, which is surprising since it's a Saturday.

I have a red leather notebook in my lap and I'm trying to jot down what I remember from the stories I was told as a child:

The demon was cursed to wait until he defeats his magical equal to fully open the portal; his powers are similar to the princess, but not exactly the same, the heir should have at least two he doesn't; he has Victus, she has Extensios — both get telekinesis; he has to recover after creating a Victus, princess does not; he can force humans into being Victus; if he dies, his Victus die also except for the Forced; if the princess dies, her Extensios revert back to human. She can use her projection power to heal herself, he has to rest and wait to heal naturally...

I have about five pages worth of notes about the princess and the demon. I'm reading them over to see if I forgot anything when I feel a detergent packet bounce off my forehead and land in my lap. I glance up surprised and see a nervous look on Cali's face.

"Whoops," she says. "I was trying to juggle, and one got away. Sorry."

I look at the floor around Cali and there are six other packets on the floor. I laugh and say, "I think a few got away." I toss the pod back to her.

Cali shrugs and starts picking up the rest of the detergent packs. As she stands up, the wash cycle for my clothes ends. I stand up to change the load to the dryer.

I give a command to my dog before moving, "Milo, watch." Milo will stand guard now over me and everything I left on the chair, not allowing anyone near either.

I'm leaning into the machine to get the last of my clothes at the bottom when I hear Milo let out a growl. I spring back upright and whip around to see what's going on. My mood instantly sours as I see that Tyler Pentz has walked into the laundromat. He doesn't have any laundry with him and no other clothes are being washed, which means he must've seen us in here and came in.

Cali and I make eye contact. She turns her back to him and sticks a finger in her mouth while rolling her eyes up into her head.

"Ladies," I hear him say. *Ugh, even the sound of his voice turns my stomach.*

"Tyler," I say back, but my eye is on Milo who has slowly moved away from the chairs, placing himself as a physical barrier between Tyler and Cali and myself.

"Milo, back," I command. Milo backs up, even slower than he approached. As much as I don't like Tyler, it's obvious Milo likes him even less. I may think Tyler is worse than the scum on a garbage truck, but I do not feel physically threatened by him, so I don't want or need Milo to be in protection mode ready to strike.

I pick up my basket of wet clothes and move around to the chain of dryers. From here I don't have a clear view of the room, but I don't need one to know that Tyler has come over to me; I can smell his overwhelmingly noxious cologne trying to mask the fact that he hasn't showered in a few days before I hear him speak, plus Milo has tracked me and is again by my side.

"Hey, Lex," he drawls. Tyler braces himself with one arm against the dryer next to mine, he's aiming for suave but as usual, comes off as piggish.

I don't look at him as I load my clothes into the dryer, but again say, "Tyler."

"Listen," he says as he runs his hand through his grimy, unwashed hair. "I was thinking that you and me should go out sometime."

Yeah, that is never *going to happen,* I think.

"Umm, no," I say, trying to keep the disgust off my face. "I don't think that's a good idea."

"Come on," he presses. "We'll get some drinks, go back to my place, and then I'll show you a real good time."

My nose scrunches up at the thought of spending another second near this creep. I clear my throat and say, "Tyler, that's not going to happen. I'm seeing someone. And even if I wasn't, I am completely not interested."

Tyler's features immediately change as anger settles onto his face at being rejected. "Now, that's a mistake." He takes a step closer to me. With Milo pressed to my leg, the only thing separating us now is the door to the dryer.

"Tyler, you need to back off. I said I'm not interested. At all." I can feel Milo pressing harder into my leg, just waiting for me to give him the green light to attack.

Tyler doesn't move back but does put both of his arms on the chest-high open door of the dryer I'm using. He leans in slightly.

I smile at him and say, "Milo, set."

I take a step back allowing Milo to position himself directly in front of me, teeth bared, growling loudly. I am not afraid of Tyler, I know that I could defend myself against him, but I have bigger things to worry about right now than this asshole.

Tyler looks down at Milo and then back up at me. I can see he's weighing his options, but it's not fast enough for me.

Bye-bye, Tyler, I think as I say, "Milo...."

Milo barks once and picks up a paw, ready to launch. Tyler throws his hands up from the dryer door. "Okay, okay. I get it." He takes a few steps backward. "I'll see you later, honey."

"No, Tyler. You won't."

My face hardens as I say it. He sneers at me as he leaves the laundromat.

"That guy is such a piece of shit." I jump hearing Cali's voice, I was so focused on making sure Tyler left I didn't even realize she was behind me.

I look down at Milo and see he's still in a state of alert ready to pounce on anything. "I know," I say to Cali before I add, "Good boy Milo, it's okay now." He looks back at me but doesn't fully relax. "It's okay, pup. Really."

Milo comes over and circles Cali and myself, his ears are still up and his tail stiff. He sniffs us both, then presses his head in between my knees. I scratch both of his ears and tell him that everything's okay, until his tail starts to wag.

"I've never seen him like that. Milo must really not like that guy," Cali says stepping over to pet Milo too.

"The feeling is mutual," I say. I load the rest of my clothes into the dryer and start it. Milo sits down in front of the machine, content to watch the clothes inside spin.

"Can I ask you a question, Lex?"

"Of course."

"What does that command you gave him mean?" Cali looks nervous as she asks it.

I told Cali last night that I trust her, so I don't hesitate to tell her what "set" means. "Set is the command I give if I feel threatened or uncertain and want Milo on alert. There is a second command, seek, that tells him to go. If he feels the threat too, he attacks, if not he circles the person twice and returns to me."

"And he can tell the difference, whether to attack or not?" Cali asks.

"Yeah," I say simply.

I don't add the part about Milo having some magical help in telling the difference. I have a feeling Cali will find that out soon enough.

Cali looks down at Milo, then squats to be face to face with him. She reaches out with both hands to give his ears a deep scratch. He licks her face just before she says, "Very good boy, Milo."

• 2 4 •

The past few hours of my Saturday afternoon, following my laundromat run-in with Tyler, were spent at Waterfront Park. Cali and I stopped back at the apartment to drop off our clothes before going to the park. After I put my notebook away in the drawer of my nightstand, I grabbed Milo's favorite tennis ball — the one with a squeaker in it — his collapsable travel bowl and a couple of water bottles. Cali got an old blanket from her closet for us to sit on.

Matt had called me at close to two in the afternoon, I was still at the laundromat waiting on the end of a dryer cycle when I answered. He asked what I was up to and I told him what I had planned after my laundry was done. When he asked if it would be okay if he joined me at the park, I had to bite my tongue before the, "Oh, hell yeah!" that zipped through my brain flew out of my mouth.

When Matt got to the park just after three, Cali was laying on the blanket reading a book, and I was throwing the ball for Milo. Matt came right up to me and kissed me hello, I responded without a second thought. I sighed happily when our lips parted. Matt held me for an extra beat until Milo bumped my leg, impatient at my not throwing his ball again right away.

The next time Milo trotted back to where I was, he dropped the ball at Matt's feet. Every time my dog does something that displays his trust for Cali, or for Mickey, or for Matt, it reaffirms to me that I'm surrounded by good people. That I can trust these people too.

We stayed at the park for only a couple of hours. It's still early April, and the weather in the Pacific Northwest hasn't fully lost its winter chill, plus dusk arrives early. I invited Matt over for dinner and told Cali to tell Mickey to come when she was done at work too.

So now I'm standing next to the stove in my apartment cutting up some chicken breasts for a stir fry. Matt is next to me slicing carrots, broccoli, and red pepper; Cali is on the couch flipping through channels on the TV and snuggling with Milo.

I turn when I hear Milo's tags jingle as he hops off of the couch and goes to the door, tail wagging. A few seconds later I hear the deadbolt slide then see Mickey walk in. She's wearing capri length leggings and a baggy, scoop neck t-shirt with her gym bag and purse slung over one shoulder.

"Hey baby," Cali gets up and greets Mickey at the door. She takes the bags from her girlfriend and asks, "How was work?"

"Long," Mickey answers. "My computer froze right after I finished the payroll. I didn't know if I should restart it or if that would cancel the payroll, then if I did the payroll again would it go through twice."

She sighs as she grabs a glass of water from the pitcher in the refrigerator. Mickey leans against it as she continues, "So I spent over an hour on the phone, most of it on hold, with the payroll software people to see if it went through. Jack had to run my 1:30 *and* my 2:30 classes."

Cali comes over and cuddles up under Mickey's arm. "So I restart the computer while I've got the person on the phone with me, and of course the payroll goes through a second time. So they're like 'oh, no problem, we can cancel it for you.... but there's a fee'."

"Of course there is," Matt says.

"Right?" Mickey says exasperatedly. "By the time that was finished, I was so mentally exhausted that I was glad I only had two one-on-one sessions on my calendar, instead of group classes."

"So who's closing up the studio tonight?" I ask putting the raw chicken into a pan on the stove.

"Melanie."

From her spot under Mickey's arm, I see Cali make a face at the name. When Mickey and Cali first got together, Melanie was a relatively new hire at the studio. She pursued Mickey hard, but it was clear to everyone around them — including Melanie — that once Cali and Mickey went on their first date, they were it for each other. Melanie backed off after that and has a steady girlfriend of her own now.

Cali holds a bit of a grudge over Melanie, saying that she still flirts with Mickey constantly. But I've met her a handful of times and Melanie just has a very outgoing personality that can be mistaken as flirty.

Mickey sees Cali's reaction to hearing the name. I can tell she understands Cali's feelings and instead of downplaying them, she squeezes Cali tighter and gives her a sweet kiss. She says something into Cali's ear that I don't quite catch, but based on the warm smile that fills Cali's face, I don't have to.

I take the chicken off the stove and scoop it onto a plate, leaving the hot oil in the pan. I throw diced garlic and onion in and sauté it a bit. Matt is right next to me ready to toss in the vegetables on my cue.

"I'm going to go take a quick shower, wash today off of me," Mickey says. "Thank you for cooking dinner, Lex. Cali and I will do the dishes later."

"We will?" Cali asks.

Mickey bends over to kiss Cali, who has sat back down on the couch, and says, "Yes, we will."

I tell Matt to add the veggies and grab the last few things I need; minced ginger and hoisin sauce from the fridge, and water chestnuts and microwave rice from the pantry cabinet. I put the chestnuts and ginger in the pan and then put the chicken back in. I drizzle everything with the hoisin sauce, stirring it together while it finishes cooking.

When Mickey returns to the living room with a towel around her head wearing big baggy sweatpants and a tank top, I put the rice in the microwave. She sits down on the couch next to Cali, who immediately wraps her arms around the woman. Milo jumps on the sofa and nestles down on the other side of Mickey.

"Good boy, Milo," Matt says quietly reaching into the cabinet to get four plates. He turns to me smiling and says, "I love that dog. It's like he knows Mickey had a rough day and needs some extra TLC."

"He's definitely a good boy," I say smiling.

The microwave beeps and I take out the rice, fluff it with a fork and put it in a bowl. I take out a new serving spoon from a drawer and pour the contents of the pan on the stove onto an oversized plate. Matt takes the dishes he took down before, some forks, and the rice and brings them over to the coffee table. I bring over the stir fry as Cali and Mickey pass out the plates.

"Milo, down," I say as I sit cross-legged on the floor. My pup comes over to me and lays down with his head in my lap. "Good boy, Milo," I tell him, scratching his ears.

Matt sits down on the floor next to me and starts dishing out the food. He hands me the first plate which I give to Cali, and the second I pass to Mickey. Cali gets up quickly to get napkins, glasses and the water pitcher from the fridge.

I look at the people around me, see them eating and joking with each other, and I feel warm contentment fill me. I glance down at Milo who is completely relaxed next to me and can't help but finally feel like just a regular, run-of-the-mill twenty-three-year-old.

For the first time in the past five years, I feel completely happy and my worries are quieted.

For now.

• 2 5 •

I'm already awake Sunday morning when my alarm goes off, the anticipation for the day is almost overwhelming. I've really never been a morning person, like ever, but between how great the past forty-eight hours have been — I've kissed Matt four times now, but who's counting? — and the possibility of getting my hands on *The Book* and seeing if it is what I've been looking for, I spring out of bed fully awake and ready to go. In fact, it's me who wakes up Milo today instead of the other way around.

We're out the door on our walk by 7:06 A.M., earlier than we've been all week. It's another gorgeous spring morning and the sun is shining. Milo and I take the long way to Roast, and since I'm in such a good mood, I get him a pup cup along with my hot chocolate and bagel.

Walking back to my apartment, I'm in a state of serenity. It's early so our street is awash in typical morning scenes; some people are jogging, some are getting in their cars (maybe they got stuck with a Sunday shift too), and others are just sitting on their stoops enjoying the brisk start of the day.

Milo and I are half a block from my door when a stiff breeze gusts by us. I pull my rust colored jacket a little tighter around me to ward off the chill. A stray leaf blows by catching my canine companion's attention. He goes to follow it and being in such a good mood this morning with time to spare, I follow it too. It blows down our sidewalk, zigzagging in front of Milo. The leaf brings us right to the entrance to our building. Milo wants to go after it more, but I direct him into the lobby.

I take off Milo's leash at the base of the stairs and ask, "Want to race, pup?" His tail starts wagging so hard that his butt is shaking too. "Alright," I say. "First one to the door wins. But no cheating this time, got it?"

Milo spins a circle once to acknowledge the rules.

"Ready—" I put his leash in my coat pocket and Milo drops his chest to the floor, tail raised high.

"Set—" I put one foot on the bottom step, Milo's tail starts up again. I cheat and run up a couple of stairs before I say, "Go!"

Milo barks at me once, as if to voice his outrage that I jumped the gun when I just told him no cheating. He lets me know what he thinks of that by flying past me on the first landing and reaching our door before I'm even a quarter way up the second flight.

Shit, I've gotten my endurance up but I still need to work on my speed. I make a mental note to ask Mickey about what I can do to build speed.

"Damn, Milo. You smoked me." I hold up my hand for a high five and Milo jumps up to smack my palm with his paw.

I check the time on my phone as we enter the apartment, 7:38. Plenty of time for a nice, hot shower *after* I eat my breakfast. I give Milo fresh water and a scoop of food, then sit down on the couch and open a solitaire app on my phone. I start a new hand and take a few bites of my bagel.

Milo comes around the side of the couch after finishing his own breakfast, jumps up on the couch next to me and puts his head on my thigh.

"You're kind of stinky," I say to him. "I think today might be a bath day, dog." Milo whines and looks up at me with sad puppy eyes. For a dog that could just as easily snuggle with someone or rip their throat out, the bathtub has always been his kryptonite.

I shake my head at him and say, "Sorry, Milo. It is what it is, pup."

I take a few more bites of my bagel and give the last of it to Milo as a peace offering. I give him a few big smooches on his head before I get up to take a shower.

I'm cognizant of the fact that Mickey and Cali are still asleep, so I refrain from singing my go-to song, *(You Make Me Feel Like) A Natural Woman* written by Carole King for the queen of soul, Aretha Franklin. I hum it as I go through my routine; shampoo, conditioner, body wash, towel dry, tweeze, mascara. I wrap my towel around my chest and go into my bedroom to get dressed.

I walk back into the living room at 8:23 to see Milo sprawled out on the couch, laying on his back and snoring. *My fearsome protector, ladies and gentlemen.*

My mind is buzzing with all the possibilities today could hold as I quietly gather my bag, keys, and phone from the counter in the kitchen. I open the fridge and take out the container of left-overs from last night to bring for lunch. Before I leave the apartment, I grab my bike helmet off its hook by the front door thinking, *This could be the day that makes the past eighteen-hundred-plus days worth it.*

****

Jeff was waiting for me outside the library when I got here this morning. He came over to me as I was locking up my bike surprising me with pleas- antries which aren't often Jeff's style. He walked in with me, saying he wanted to make sure my new ID worked properly and to make sure I got all settled in downstairs.

Jeff and I make our way through each locked door without Issue. We go down two long flights of stairs and when I open the last door, I'm in awe of what I see.

The climate-controlled storage of the library is housed in a well-lit sub-basement the size of an American football field. The room is cavernous, the walls made of concrete cinderblock, the ceiling must be thirty to thirty-five feet high. Multiple thick metal beams span its width. It's broken into six sep- arate, glass-walled cubes with metal framework laid out straight down the room in a single row. One side of each cube is up against the wall to my left creating a walkway down the right side of the room where the door to each cube is.

The cubes are quite large. I'd guess they measure twenty feet tall by thirty feet wide, and there is at least ten to fifteen feet in between each one. The center of each cube's glass ceiling is attached to an HVAC duct that extends upward to the high ceiling of the sub-basement.

They each have their own temperature and humidity control with a digital display next to an electric lock that is only accessible with a keycard. The floor inside the cube is hardwood, but the floor of the makeshift hallway and walkway between each cube is covered in thick carpet. Each room is equipped with a small, chest-high table to use when examining the books.

Jeff showed me the first room, CCR1, closest to the basement entrance. It has a digital camera attached to the laptop that I'll be using, and Jeff demoed for me how to create a new entry in the database software. He pointed out a notepad that Samantha had left behind, on it her own handwritten notes on the instructions. He said that unless I had any questions he would leave me to it. I didn't, so he promptly left me to my project.

As soon as Jeff left, I scanned every book in the room. CCR1 has eight, back to back bookcases made of sturdy oak shelves that are fifteen feet tall. The books are spaced out so the covers are not touching one another. There is a ladder on wheels that can be moved from one bookcase to the next attached to a track installed at the top of each shelf. Not one of them was titled *The Book*, nor did I have any kind of physical response like when I saw the computer listing. The closest I've come to the tome I'm seeking is still the crumpled print out tucked away in my pocket.

After not finding *my* book, I picked up where Sam left off indicated by a piece of lined paper stuck underneath the spine of a book. Even though I knew pretty much what to do, I read over the instructions she wrote out on the pad next to the computer just to be sure.

In the bright white cloth gloves Jeff had sternly instructed me to wear, I archived the next three books on the shelf in quick succession. A first edition copy of *Treasure Island* by Robert Louis Stevenson, from 1883; a first edition of *Strange Case of Dr. Jekyll and Mr. Hide* also by Robert Louis Stevenson, from 1886; and a leather-bound copy of *A Midsummer Night's Dream* by Shakespeare, stamped with a date of 1830.

I photographed the covers of each book and the first fifteen pages. The camera was plugged directly into the laptop so the photos loaded to the database seamlessly. I entered the title, author, publication date, and other pertinent information about the book itself before writing a quick but detailed synopsis. The gloves made using the trackpad on the laptop impossible, so thankfully there was a mouse.

It was quite surreal to hold books that were so old and so well known, especially the first editions of books I had read as a teenager. And although I was really disappointed not to have found *The Book* right off the bat, I had to admit to myself that so far I was at least enjoying this project.

Now at 12:30, over three hours after Jeff "left me to it," I decide to stop for lunch only because my growling stomach has become louder than I can ignore.

It's such a nice day that I choose to eat outside on one of the benches near the library. I don't even bother to heat up my food before exiting the building.

Even though what I have been doing in the sub-basement is interesting, I can't help but think of the morning as a total bust. *What if the entire day goes by and I don't get my hands on The Book at all?* I roll my eyes at myself and my internal whining. *Well, then I just convince Jeff to let me continue working on this project,* I answer myself.

I finish my food while finishing the round of solitaire from this morning on my phone. The sun is warm on my shoulders as it cuts through the budding trees lining the library. It reminds me of springs from my childhood. How the air felt when getting to finally play outside again at recess after long cold winters. Although, early April at home could still threaten a snowstorm or two.

I close my eyes at the memory. I ache so much for it that I can almost smell it. *Home.*

I shake my head to jostle the thought of home quickly away. I've gone too long, and I'm too close to something to make a mistake now.

I go back inside the library and make my way down to the sub-basement. I use my ID card to unlock CCR1 and get ready to get back to work. I feel oddly compelled to look over Sam's instructions one more time and this time see something I missed before. In her smooth, loopy handwriting, I see Sam wrote: **Jeff only expecting 2-3 books per day.**

My eyes widen as a realization comes to me. *I've already done three books today.* I look down at the ID tag hanging around my neck. I know it will open rooms CCR2 through CCR6, and any other locked door inside or outside the library.

I exit room one and stand in the makeshift hallway created by the layout of the six cubes. I know that *The Book*, what I believe to be *my* book, has to be in one of the other five rooms. I've got a computer print out that says so.

I mentally put an X through CCR1 and move to the door of CCR2. I swipe my card through the slot. The red light above the handle turns green and I hear the electric lock slide in its casing.

Let's see what's behind door number two.

• 2 6 •

JULIUS

At noon local time, three hours before Alexa takes her lunch break in Portland, Julius and Damon are entering the New Orleans Parole Office. The pair had gone straight from the alley behind the bar to Damon's house. Julius had stood by and watched as the man packed a bag. From there, they took Julius's car and drove to the longterm parking lot at the Hartsfield-Jackson Atlanta International Airport.

Julius pulled his own go-bag from the trunk, and the pair boarded the airport shuttle headed to the terminal. They had to wait around until 9:30 A.M. for an available flight out of Atlanta. Julius had called their contact as soon as they were wheels down in NOLA.

Damon has kept a wary eye on the shorter man currently walking in front of him ever since leaving the bar last night. He doesn't know if Julius has the same abilities as Darius, but after seeing what happened to his friends, he's not eager to experience it himself. He absolutely does not trust the guy. He stays a half-step behind, on his toes ready to defend himself against an attack from his... partner, for lack of a better term.

Julius walks up to the counter just inside the main entrance to the building and sees a young man sitting behind it staring at his phone. The peach fuzz on his chin and the acne on his face make him look more like a boy than a man.

"Hi there, son," Julius says. "We're here to see Rodger Blusseau. He's expecting us."

The young man lazily raises his eyes from the phone in his hand. Skipping all pleasantries, he asks, "Names?"

"I'm Julius Togan. And this is Damon Jennings."

The kid drags a finger down a printed list of names. He taps his finger a few times when he reaches the bottom and scans the sheet again.

"I don't have either of you down with check-ins for today. Who's your parole officer again?"

"Oh, no. You misunderstand, son," Julius chuckles. He's aiming for light and amused, but it comes out gruff and tense. "You see, I'm an old friend of Officer Blusseau. I called him to let him know I'd be in town for business and he said to come by." Julius's continued attempt at an informal tone comes out sounding patronizing.

"Uh-huh. Well, let me just check on that for you," the young man replies adopting his own condescending tone. Julius's eyebrows furrow at the boy's response. Behind his back, Damon's mouth twitches into a quick smile but he swiftly erases it.

At the desk, the young man picks up the office phone and dials a four-digit number. He listens for a beat then says, "Officer Blusseau, there are two men here to see you. A Julius Toboggan and a Damon Jennings."

"*Togan*," Julius hisses at the kid.

The boy rolls his eyes and mouths, "whatever," in response as he listens to the officer's response.

"Yes, sir. Okay, thank you." He hangs up the phone and smiles sweetly at the men in front of him. "Officer Blusseau will be down in a minute. You can have a seat," he says dismissing the men.

Damon smirks at the deepening color on his comrade's face as Julius turns away from the counter. The duo goes over to sit on one of the hard plastic chairs lining the walls. Damon pops a piece of gum in his mouth and pulls out his own phone to play a game while they wait.

"Let me do the talking," Julius says in a low volume.

"Sure," Damon responds, his gaze remaining on his phone. Then taking a bolder approach, adds, "You know, 'cause I have no fucking idea what is going on."

"Just shut up. You're here because the boss wants you to be."

"No," Damon says through gritted teeth looking up at Julius. "I'm here so that that monster fuck freak of nature doesn't kill me or turn me into a god-damn pile of ash like he did my boys." Damon's throat tightens at the mention of his friends.

"Well then, do what you're told and there won't be a problem," Julius explains with zero empathy.

Damon's attention returns to his phone for the next few minutes the pair waits. Julius busies himself brushing away some lint from his suit pants. They both look up as the heavy, metal door behind the kid at the counter buzzes then opens. A man even shorter than Julius walks out wearing a tailored dress shirt and black pants. Whereas Julius has a generous girth around his middle, the man walking toward them now is trim and muscular.

"Blue!" Julius exclaims.

"Jules!" Blusseau replies with equal enthusiasm.

Julius grunts as he stands up to hug the man. They give each other a few rough claps on the back in greeting. Damon also stands and towers over the other two. He actually has to tilt his head down in order to see the men in front of him.

"Rodger Blusseau, meet Damon Jennings," Julius says facilitating the introductions.

"Dear god, don't call me Rodger unless you happen to be my granny in disguise. Name's Blue," the officer says with a soft, southern twang.

Damon nods as he grips the man's outstretched hand. He notices that Blue's hand is dwarfed by, and all but disappears into, his own.

"I don't know about you guys," Blue continues. "But I'm starving. Why don't we grab something to eat and we can catch up."

He raises an eyebrow and gives Julius a brief, meaningful look.

"Right, right," Julius replies, easily catching on. "Where to?"

****

Blue's compact silver sedan pulls into the parking lot of a local dive and stops. Damon had to practically fold himself in half to fit in the small back seat. His kneecaps were on the verge of touching his cheekbones the whole ride. So as soon as the car stops he's opening the door eager, to get out quickly.

The two old friends up front paid no attention to Damon's cramped quarters while they comfortably caught up on tedious things. Nothing they've discussed so far has anything to do with the reason why Julius and Damon are in New Orleans.

When they walk in the restaurant, they bypass the host stand and sit themselves down in a booth near the front entrance. Blue and Damon are on one side, with Julius across from them. Within minutes, the waitress comes by and Blue orders for the three of them.

Damon is becoming quite impatient with Blue's lackadaisical personality. He thinks that maybe if Blue had seen his own buddies reduced to ashes in seconds, his attitude would be a little more industrious right now. He's squirming in his seat and tapping his foot on the floor. With a cold look, Julius silently reminds Damon of his earlier instruction to keep quiet. The large man settles down and for the next ten minutes, the old friends continue to shoot the breeze.

As soon as the food comes, Damon demolishes his sandwich in three massive bites. He drains his glass of water and is again just waiting on the two men. He's tapping his thumbnail on the empty glass and is about to ask some questions himself, when after two big bites of his shrimp po'boy, Blue finally says something of worth.

"Alright, so here's the situation," he begins. "I asked all of my parolees about the girl. Made it sound like she skipped out on something up north and told them there is a reward for any information that produces a solid lead. My guys know people practically across the entire Bayou, so I hoped when I mentioned there was a reward they'd ask around and I'd at least get something."

Blue pauses his story to take another bite and washes it down with a huge gulp of sweet tea.

The waitress comes to their table again, an older woman with tightly curled, short white hair. She's wearing an apron and is carrying a coffee pot. A web of raised veins shows through the wrinkled, ashy skin on her arms.

"You boys needing anything?" she asks in a Southern lilt.

"Uh, yes actually," Damon answers. "Could I get another two shrimp sandwiches and some more water, please?"

"Sure thing, darling. How about you two?"

Blue and Julius shake their heads.

"No, I think we're all set, Irma," Blue says.

"Alright, honey. I'll put that order in for you, darling," she says looking at Damon. The waitress moves on from their table and makes her way toward the kitchen.

"What was I saying?" Blue asks.

"You were offering a reward," Julius tells him.

"Right, right," Blue wipes his mouth with his napkin and continues.

"So I ask 'em all about her, and I get a lot of shrugs and 'that could be anyone' type responses. But one guy, Collin Kings, tells me he was at the library the other day to use the computer since it's free, and he thinks he might've seen her."

Blue takes another swig of his tea. He clears his throat and continues, "I told him good, and I'd see him next week. I sent one of my guys over to follow up on it, but wasn't expecting much."

Blue goes silent when a busboy comes and refills the water glasses at the table. When he leaves, Blue speaks again.

"He comes back and says that the librarian there didn't remember seeing anyone the other day, but there was a girl there a couple of years ago that fit the same description."

"Which library?" Julius asks.

"Hang on now, I wrote it down so I wouldn't forget." Blue pulls out a black leather notepad from his back pocket and opens it to the last used page. "The Cita Dennis Hubbell Library over on Pelican Ave across the river."

"That library have anything special about it? Any affiliations or... leanings?" Julius inquires.

"It's not connected with any of yours as far as I can tell."

Damon's eyes narrow. "What does 'any of yours' mean?" he asks stiffly.

"Nothing that you need to know yet," Julius quickly retorts. "Go 'head, Blue."

"Right. The librarian there, a uhh..." he looks at his notepad again, "Smith, Alton Smith, retired architect, he works there part-time now. Something of a building historian actually. Told my guy that about three years ago, a young woman no more than twenty came in and started asking questions about the building."

"And he remembered a girl from three years ago?" Julius asks skeptically.

"That's right. Mr. Smith said he remembers her distinctly because no one before or since has ever asked about the building itself rather than the books inside, and how prime he was to give her all the information she wanted."

"A building historian," Julius repeats.

"Everyone's got their interests, Jules," he says pointedly.

"Right. Well, I believe I'd like to meet this Alton Smith. Hear more of what he has to say."

Irma returns right then with Damon's food. "Here you go, darling," she says putting the plate down in front of him.

"Thanks," Damon says before picking up his second sandwich and biting half of it off at once.

"Y'all want anything else?" Irma asks looking between Blue and Julius.

"No, thank you, sweetheart," Blue says. "I think when my friend here finishes eating we'll be on our way, so just the check whenever you have a moment, Miss Irma."

Irma smiles at the men and moves on to check her other tables.

As soon as she's out of earshot, Julius centers his dark eyes on Damon who is mid-chew and says, "Eat fast."

• 2 7 •

"ALEXA"

Stepping out of CCR2 I put another mental X on my list. I move down the line to the next room and swipe my keycard. The light turns green and I open the door.

Holy fuck.

That's all I can think the second I step into CCR3. I feel an intense pull toward the last set of shelves in the room. It's as if an invisible hand is reaching out and grasping my own, leading me.

My heart starts to pound as I inch closer to the last shelf. I'm in the back corner of the cube, facing the glass wall that's up against the cinderblock walls of the building's foundation. The only sound I hear right now is the blood rushing in my ears. I close my eyes and turn around to face the shelves.

I never got the chance to check my mother's letter in my box, but I don't have to. Before I even open my eyes, I know. *It's here. It's right here.*

I look at the shelf in front of me. I'm about to search it top to bottom, but my eyes are drawn to a tall, thick book that is dark maroon in color. There is no writing or markings of any kind on the spine. It looks ancient, much older than any of the other books surrounding it but sturdy and strong.

I reach out my hand to touch it but stop myself inches away. *What if when I hold it, my powers are released in a way I can't contain or hide anymore? What if I touch it and that instantly lets Darius know where it is?*

It seems like another thousand *what ifs* run through my head while my hand hovers right above the shelf in front of me.

"Okay, *'Alexa'*, " I say out loud to myself emphasizing my current name. "You've waited a very long time to come face to face with this thing. So you're either brave or you're scared. You can be both later, I guess, or whatever, but right now you have to pick one."

It's a horrible pep talk, so I try again: "Pick up the damn thing!"

My arms stretch out in front of my chest. They both tremble until they finally fall to my side. I step away from the shelf, my back pressing against the glass wall. I sigh and drop my head into my hands. *I have waited five years for this,* I think. *I have lost too much, and I have missed too much, and I have spent too much time searching to just do nothing now that I've actually found it.*

I straighten up and step back up to the shelf. I reach out and take the books on either side off the shelf; an early printing of *Don Quixote* by Cervantes, and *A Tale Of Two Cities* by Charles Dickens. I place both books gently onto the assessment table with bare hands. Another part of this I won't be telling Jeff about.

In this cube the table is next to the door, so I check the rest of the hallway outside to make sure I'm still alone. I grab my phone from my pocket to check the time, almost three o'clock. That gives me a solid two hours to look at *The Book*. What i know now is *my* book.

As soon as I gather the courage to actually touch it.

With plenty of space on either side of it, and having confirmed I'm still alone, there is nothing else I can use to stall. It's time. If it sends out a signal to Darius, at least I'll have *The Book* with me and I can project Milo and the box to me then transport us away.

As my hands get closer to *The Book*, my body starts to tingle before I even touch it. I let the fingertips on my right hand lightly brush the spine. Even from that light of a touch, I immediately get a feeling of strength and resiliency, there is quite literally nothing I can't do right now.

I yank my hands back. *Did I just use my powers? How could I have felt so much through such a minor touch? Does Darius know where I am now!?* I pause and inventory my powers, I haven't used any of them.

I don't realize that I'm holding my breath until black dots start to form in my vision and I gasp for air. Panting, I now remind myself of the way every story began when I was little:

Power is neither good nor bad, it's how you use it that creates light or dark. Darius uses his power for evil to bring great darkness to the world. But the princess, the princess uses hers only for decency, kindness, and light. Except for the effort it takes to defeat Darius, she never uses her powers forcefully on others. If she ever does, she'll be just as bad as him.

I shake my head quickly, roll my neck, and wring out my hands. I fill my mind with only the purest of intentions, remind myself that the absolute only reason I need *The Book* is to vanquish Darius and close the portal to his world.

I exhale sharply and put both of my hands fully on the front and back covers of *The Book*. I feel the strength and resiliency wash over me again. While touching it, I repeat to myself the differences between me and Darius.

I lift *The Book* off of the shelf and turn it so the front cover is facing up. Just like the spine, there is no writing, no title or author, no symbols on its maroon surface. I open it and see an inscription inside the front cover.

Possessor ex hereditate possidebitis in hoc libro historia ac maxime in key vincere semper tenebris ambulant in hoc mundo.

I don't know the language but my computer printout says Latin, so I take out my phone and download a translator app. I type in the inscription, careful not to miss or misspell any of the words. I press the speaker button to hear the translation out loud. The robotic voice recites:

"The holder of this book possesses the history of and key to defeat the greatest darkness to ever walk this world."

Well, that at least explains why Darius wants this thing so bad. It's basically a how-to on how to end him. But if this whole thing is in Latin, it's going to take me a very long time to get through it.

I sit down on the floor with my legs crossed and balance *The Book* on my lap. I flip through the first few pages. They are thick, closer to vellum than paper. I run my fingers over the words that are impeccably handwritten. There are intricate drawings on every other page that clearly depict Darius creating a portal from his world to ours and the destruction he was generating. It makes me realize that my magical ancestors took a lot of time in creating this and it's my responsibility to use it right and to make sure nothing happens to it.

I hear my phone chime and check it to see what the alert is. It's just a notification from an app, but I see the time is 4:25 P.M.. I absolutely have to talk to Jeff before I go home and convince him to allow me to continue working on this project.

I stand up and reluctantly put *The Book* back on its shelf. I grab Dickens and Cervantes from the table and gently return them to their places. I check to make sure I haven't left anything behind and exit CCR3. I use my card to grant access again to CCR1 to get my bag, make sure my entries are saved in the database.

I'm about to close the database software when I hear the electric lock of the room click open.

"Alexa," I hear Jeff's voice behind me. I turn around and greet him.

"Hi, Jeff," I say. "I just finished my third entry. I was about to come up and get you to double check I did everything correctly." *A little fib in this case won't hurt.*

"Wonderful," Jeff says without any actual excitement. "That's exactly the reason I came down. May I?"

He gestures to the laptop on the table. I move away from the computer as I wave him over. "Please."

"This all looks great. Photos are clear, synopsis is detailed but not too long. Very impressive." Again, said with barely any inflection.

"Listen, Jeff," I begin. "I wanted to ask if I could continue working on this? I've really enjoyed today. And I was thinking if it's alright with you that I could work on it in during the mornings of my shifts. And if you needed additional help on the weekends, I can check if I'd be available."

I may be rambling but I think I've made my point.

"It's as if you read my mind, Alexa." Jeff actually smiles at me. "I was going to ask you if you'd like to continue, but after seeing your work, I'm requesting for you to."

My stomach flips at how much time with *The Book* that would award me. "That sounds great," I say trying not to pounce immediately and create suspicion. "Maybe we can discuss logistics tomorrow morning?"

"That sounds fine to me." Jeff checks his watch then and says, "Look at the time. Please pack up your belongings and make sure all the doors are securely closed behind you. Then you may go."

"Of course," I respond. "And thank you again, Jeff."

He nods and exits without another word. As always, a very Jeff-like exit.

• 2 8 •

The entire bike ride home, I relived the little time I'd had with *The Book*. I felt ownership and protectiveness over it now — it's *mine*. I'm not going to let Darius, or anyone, take it. The same way it can be used to take down Darius, in essence, it can be used to take me down too. And I'm not about to let that happen.

When I unlock my apartment door, Milo is sitting there waiting for me, his tail wagging happily. I scratch his ears before I hang up my bag up on a hook by the door. I put my helmet on the floor, take off my jacket and put it on top of my bag. Then I squat down and give my boy a big hug.

"Today was a good day, Milo," I say. I cradle his fluffy face in my hands and drop my voice to a whisper before I say, "I finally found it. I finally found what we've been looking for!" I squeeze Milo again before standing up.

Milo trots after me as I go to my bedroom. I change into old, comfy yoga leggings and an oversized sweatshirt. I go back to the front door and pick up Milo's leash and harness.

"How about a nice jog, big guy?"

Milo barks once in agreement. I bend over to put on my running shoes and strap my pup in. I stand up and bounce on my toes a few times. Coming across *The Book* today after searching so long for it has left me with abundant energy. I take my phone and wallet out of my bag and put them into the front zippered pocket of my sweatshirt. I take out my keys, and then Milo and I step out of the door.

I lock up my apartment and do some dynamic stretching on the landing outside my door to get my body warm. It's not a Mickey workout but it serves its purpose.

Milo and I exit our building and make a quick right on SW Fourth Avenue. We go straight for three blocks and then make a left onto SW Salmon Street. After another three blocks, Milo and I go left again, this time on SW Broadway. Our third left puts us back on SW Jefferson Street.

We pass our apartment and go all the way down to SW First Avenue, the block right before the park we went to yesterday. We go right on First and over three blocks to SW Market Street. We make a right and head up three blocks which brings us back to SW Fourth. We finish our figure eight route once we come back to Jefferson. Then we repeat the loop one more time.

Milo and I had kept up a relatively steady pace throughout and we finish the almost two-mile long jog in just under twenty minutes.

Once we are back on Jefferson, Milo and I walk back to our apartment. When we get into the building, up the stairs, and in the door, Milo puts his head between my knees and presses in with a bit of pressure. Like always, a feeling of safety washes over me as he does this. I bend down to his level and take off his harness and leash.

"Okay, Milo," I say scratching under his chin. "It's bath time."

The moment the words are out of my mouth, Milo turns tail and bolts. He dives under the coffee table facing away from me.

"Come on, Milo," I say standing up. I get a whiney bark in response. "It'll take twenty minutes tops pup, then we can snuggle and watch a movie." It's a small bribe, but that's usually what it takes to get Milo into the tub.

I go into my room and grab the Milo-specific bath towels and his oatmeal shampoo I keep in my closet. I left the medicated anti-flee shampoo treatment in the shower once soon after I moved in and Cali accidentally picked up the wrong bottle. It didn't hurt her scalp or make her hair fall out or anything, but for half the day the smell made her nauseous. So now I keep all of Milo's bath items in my closet, just in case.

I put his stuff in the bathroom and then make my way back into the living room. The only part of Milo that's visible is his tail sticking out from under the table.

"Milo, please." I get down on my hands and knees and crawl around the coffee table. I peek under the corner to face him. "You need a bath 'cause you're stinky." He doesn't look directly at me but does give me some serious side-eye.

I try my stern voice: "Alright, that's it. It's bath time, mister. No more games." Milo doesn't budge.

"Come here, pup. Who's a good boy? Oh, he's such a good boy!" The baby voice doesn't do it either.

I gasp and lift my head up quickly trying to spark his curiosity.

"Oh my god, Milo! What's that noise?" But, alas, trickery does not work either.

"Okay, okay," I lay flat on my stomach with my nose inches from his. I decide to sweeten the deal from before hoping it'll do the trick.

"You drive a hard bargain, I'll give you that. How about this? You come out and take your bath, and I will not only go down to the corner store and get that peanut butter ice cream we both like," I see his ears perk up at this. "But we can watch Beethoven's Second while we eat it. Will you take a bath for that?

"Come on, pup. What do you say?" He slowly crawls out from under the coffee table, comes to me inch by inch. "There's my good boy!"

I point to the short hallway leading to the bathroom and Milo trudges along slowly toward it. I get him into the bathroom and close the door. I turn on the tap for the tub and check the temperature with one hand as the other pets Milo. He's looking at me with his "sad eyes" trying to guilt me out of this.

I give him a bunch of kisses on his head and say, "Okay, Milo. In."

His stocky body climbs at a snail's pace into the tub. I switch the tap to the shower head and take the handheld hose down and wet him from head to toe. I brace myself behind the shower curtain expecting Milo to shake head to tail.

He doesn't, so I open the curtain and pick up his bottle of shampoo. I get Milo good and soapy, and that's when he chooses to shake, covering me in soap suds and water.

"Real nice, Milo," I say frowning. He starts panting. It looks like he's smiling at me.

I scrub Milo down and rinse him off thoroughly. Milo moves to jump out of the tub but I stop him.

"Uh-uh. Not done yet, dog." I douse him again in shampoo and start scrubbing again already reaching for his conditioner knowing I have to act fast.

Milo looks at me with the saddest eyes I've ever seen. I don't need to use my powers and read his mind to know that there's only one thing that's playing on repeat: *This sucks.*

****

Milo may not be able to stand taking a bath, but he loves getting blown dry. I towel him off as much as I can, but his thick, silky black hair stays wet so long that I have to get out the blow dryer.

He puts his puppy-like face right up to the dryer and turns it side to side, enjoying the warm faux wind rushing through his hair. He rolls onto his back to expose his belly. I give him a belly rub as I dry him and tell him what a good boy he is.

Once Milo is dry, I brush him from head to toe. "Oh, look how handsome you are!" He spins in a circle and poses proudly at the compliment.

I open the bathroom door and he dashes out as if he's just been released from captivity. He runs two circles around the couch and coffee table in the living room and then jumps onto the couch, rolling onto his back and squirming from one end to the other.

After I hang Milo's towel up over the shower curtain, I get a glimpse of myself in the mirror. My mascara is running, I have droplets of water all over my face, there are soap suds on my head, I've got clumps of Milo's fur that he shed stuck to my neck and shirt. In short, I look like a drowned rat. Status quo when Milo gets a bath — I usually come out more soaked than him.

I get Milo a treat from the kitchen and give it to him before grabbing my towel from my bedroom. Even though I showered this morning, after my run and Milo's bath, I'm in desperate need of another. I bust out into my second go-to shower song, *Lady Marmalade*, the early 2000s version. I'm in and out in ten minutes.

I get dressed in purple camo-print capri sweats and a white long sleeved thermal shirt, put my thick, curly hair up in a messy bun, and put on black sneakers. When I walk into the living room, Milo is in the kitchen drinking water. I bend down and take his almost empty bowl from him and refill it from the sink.

I open the fridge to see if there's anything Cali and I need that I can get at the corner store since I'm going for ice cream. We're a little low on milk. Probably from when Cali ate that whole box of cereal. *Oh, cereal!* I think.

I check the cabinet above the fridge and the cereal boxes that usually fill it are gone. I take a pad of paper out of a drawer near the sink and start a list for the store: milk, cereal, peanut butter ice cream. I check our bread and jelly situation and both are good.

"Okay, Milo," I call out walking to the door. "Ice cream time."

I take his leash and harness off its hook and strap him in. I check that I've got my phone, keys, and wallet, and we head out.

The little store is literally right around the corner so we get back to the apartment quickly. I put the three boxes of cereal in the cabinet above the fridge and put the milk and ice cream away.

I make myself a PB&J sandwich with smooth peanut butter and strawberry jelly, and leave it on the counter out of reach from my pup. I go Into my bedroom and grab a blanket from my clean laundry pile. I toss it onto the couch and grab my sandwich and a can of seltzer from the kitchen. I plop down and drape the blanket over me.

"Come on, Milo," I say. Milo jumps onto the couch and settles on the blanket next to me. I turn on the TV and go through the menu options to play the movie on demand.

At the opening credits, Milo snuggles closer to me and puts his head on my knee. He lets out a deep sigh as he relaxes next to me comfortably. I can't help but let one out myself.

A very good day, I think.

• 2 9 •

I'm kissing Matt. My breathing is ragged. My back is against a wall and Matt is pressing his entire body into mine. I can feel how much he wants me.

My tongue manipulates his. One of his hands is on the side of my neck, his thumb on my jaw. The other hand is moving under my shirt from my hip up to my breast. My hands are tucked into his belt, pulling him even closer to me.

His fingers ghost up my side making goosebumps appear all over my skin. He increases the pressure of his touch as his hand gets closer and closer to my chest. His palm closes on my breast and starts massaging it.

My heartbeat is rising. My breath is coming faster.

I pull his bottom lip into my mouth. He sucks in a breath when I move my hands under his shirt. I play with the tuft of hair just beneath his belly button. I drag my nails down his tight abs and slide my hands over his skin back to his belt and unbuckle it.

His lips move from my mouth to my cheek, to my jaw, to my neck, and back to my mouth. I pop the button on his jeans. He moves my bra and clasps the bare skin of my breast. I gasp at the contact.

His scent is encompassing me. I feel my arousal drastically increase with every deft touch of his fingers and mouth.

His other hand slides down my thigh. When he trails his hand back to my hip, he pulls my skirt up with it exposing my skin. He moves his hand across my hip bone around to my ass and grabs.

He bites my lip as I slowly lower his zipper. He slips his hand down again to my knee, pulls it up to his hip. I move one hand from his jeans to grab his shirt and pull him impossibly closer to me. His lips still on my mouth, he gasps again as I reach under the elastic band of his boxers and grab his—

The brassy chime of Cali's keys jingling in the deadbolt wakes me from one of the greatest dreams I've ever had. My arousal carries into my conscious-ness, and I take a few deep breaths to quiet the pulsing between my legs. *Damn, right at the good part too,* I think.

When Cali walks into the apartment, she finds me and Milo on the couch. Beethoven's Second is nearing its cinematic climax with the puppies climb-ing the mountain looking for their parents. I yawn with a gaping mouth and smile sleepily at her as she comes in.

"What's this?" she asks laughing. She points first at the TV, then at the emp-ty bowls in front of Milo and myself; mine has just a spoon in it, Milo's is licked clean.

"Well, we went for a run when I got home from work, and then someone had a bath." I jerk my head toward Milo a couple of times.

"And then I'm sure you needed a bath of your own after Dog Man was through with you," Cali says.

"You're absolutely right," I laugh. "And now we're having a movie night com-plete with some snuggles and peanut butter ice cream." I see her eyes widen and I grin.

"There's some left in the pint for you. I also got some more milk and cereal."

"Thank you," she mouths while dropping her head back and looking at the ceiling.

Cali comes around the back of the couch and kisses the top of my head be-fore she plops down next to Milo scratching his back a little. He lifts his head from my knee and faces Cali. He wags his tail a few times before putting his head back down and returning his attention to the TV screen — Beethoven's Second is his favorite movie after all.

"How was dinner?" I ask.

She tilts her head slightly and gives me a closed mouth smile. She knows how much I had wanted to go.

"It was good. Mom made pot roast with carrots and potatoes. She gave me a container with extra for you." Cali holds up a plastic container the size of a hardcover book. "'Just a little taste.' Mom's words."

"Thank you, or I guess thank you to Mom," I say as I take the container from Cali. Milo's nose twitches a bit but he doesn't lift his head to investigate.

"Josh was there with Sheila."

"Sheila?" I feel a deep twinge in my heart at the name. *Make good choices* echoes in my head.

"His new girlfriend," she says. "She's very nice, helped Mom with the dishes and brought a homemade pie for dessert. She's way outta Josh's league though, for sure."

"Cali!" I scold with a laugh.

"What?" she asks innocently. "Even Mickey said the same thing!" She pauses for a moment before continuing. "She asked about you."

"Who? Mickey?" Cali rolls her eyes in response. "Oh," I say understanding. "Matt's mom, you mean."

"Yup," Cali says popping the P. "She asked how come you couldn't make it, and I explained you had to work. Then she asked Moose if he had made a move yet." Cali cracks up laughing.

"What?!" I can feel my cheeks instantly burn as I flush with embarrassment. I cover my face with the hand not holding Mom's leftovers.

"I know! Josh and Sheila, and Mickey and me all choked on our wine." Cali laughs even harder before she says, "Moose turned so red. It was awe-some."

So he's talked to his mother about me. He must have it bad, I think. *Good to know.*

"Sooo?" I ask, drawing out the sound.

"Sooo what?" Cali asks back.

"What did he say!?" My voice squeaks as I ask. I raise my eyebrows and put a hand to my throat. I try again more calmly, "What did he say?"

Cali looks at me and grins. "Well, first he said 'Mom!' Then he got all smiley and said, 'We kissed.' And then he said..." She stops suddenly before finishing, "Oh, right, I'm not supposed to tell you that part."

"What the hell does that mean, Cal?" She laughs as I reach over Milo and lightly smack her thigh. Cali, smirk still firmly in place, swipes her thumb and index finger across her lips and mimes turning a key and throwing it away. "Seriously, you can't tell me?"

"Apparently, you'll find out soon."

I level a glare at her but she holds her hands up, palms out.

"That's all I can say! Moose *and* Mickey made me swear on celibacy that I wouldn't say anything. Celibacy, Lex. So one set of my lips, for the sake of the other, is sealed right now."

We both start cracking up at Cali's crude joke.

"Come on, you know you're going to tell me," I say trying to goad her into spilling the beans.

Cali laughs and says, "I take offense to that!"

"Well, what if I guess?" I say. "Then you would be in the clear. Or you could tell me and just not tell them that you to—"

"No way, Lex!" Cali cuts me off and laughs. "I'm not risking my sex life on a technicality or secret. All I'm allowed to say is you'll find out soon."

She deliberately turns her attention to the movie that is now almost over. We watch the end of Beethoven's Second, and as the credits roll, Milo drags himself off the couch and stretches out. He shakes from head to toe then puts his head back in my lap and raises his eyes to look at me.

I pick up the remote and exit the on-demand menu. I flip through the channels until I land on a home renovation show. Milo whines a little when I don't look at him right away. I drop my eyes to him, he takes a few steps backward and lightly stomps his front paws. I check the time on the cable box and see it's almost ten.

"Oh, I'm sorry pup! Didn't realize it was this late. It's time for Milo's nighttime walk." I turn to Cali. "Do you want to come with us?"

Cali stands up and stretches herself. "Nah, I'm gonna head to bed. I can't afford to have you pry what Moose said out of me."

A frown settles on my face as I look at her. I cross my arms and say, "You saw through my plan."

"I know your tricks! You can't keep anything from me, Lex." Cali calls over her shoulder, chuckling as she heads to her bedroom.

The words cut straight through to my heart as I stand up and put the leftovers in the fridge. I rinse out our ice cream bowls and notice my hands are shaking slightly as I turn off the tap.

I hook Milo into his harness and attach his leash. I throw on my rust-colored jacket and put my phone and keys in the pockets. As I walk down the stairs, I think about the last thing Cali said.

I know I've made the right choice in trusting her. She's proven to me time and again that she's a solid friend, I'm confident she'll be there when I need her. However, I can't help but wonder exactly how Cali will react when she finds out just how much I am actually keeping from her.

The gust of chilly Portland air that greets me when I open the building's door clears my head. I tell myself I'll worry about the spectrum of Cali's possible reactions when the time comes. Since there is absolutely nothing I can do about it until then.

• 3 0 •

JULIUS

"I know that, Viribus. I'm just telling you what I've found out so far."

Julius listens to the demon's number two for a minute. He's sitting on one of the two double beds in the decent motel room the men are holed up in. They are now in Emeryville near UC Berkley, just outside of San Francisco, California. They had stayed in Louisiana overnight into Monday and got a flight out midday.

Damon is laying down on the other bed on top of the comforter, fully clothed, staring at his phone. Julius hasn't told him how long they'll be staying, so he's left his clothes and shoes on for the moment.

"I understand that the boss doesn't care how Blue is doing and that we spoke to an old guy who likes buildings," Julius says into the phone. "What I'm saying is... Will you just shut up for a fucking second?!"

He gets up and starts to pace at the foot of the two beds.

"This is what I'm saying," he continues with his voice still loud and agitated. "I'm saying to tell the boss that we're already in California. That we're going to drive to Portland tomorrow. We'll get another motel room, and then on Wednesday we'll check out the library and ask around about the girl."

Damon keeps his eyes on his phone, not wanting to draw any of Julius's current ire toward himself. He does a Google search for a nearby diner to get some food, but before he taps the magnifying glass icon, he changes the text in the bar to "Portland library." His first results show up in Maine, so he adds Oregon to the search bar and hits enter again.

The top three results are all for Multnomah County. The public library has Central, Belmont, and Midland locations. He pulls up the Wikipedia page for the first one, Central Library. He scrolls through it while Julius paces and grumbles some more. On the right side of the page is a picture of what the library looks like.

Damon notices that there is a resemblance between it and the Hubble library they went to in New Orleans. Seems to fit what the old guy, Smith, told them about the buildings. He glances up at Julius who is getting more frustrated with his call and then back down to his phone.

Damon thinks for a moment before he closes the browser window and puts his phone in his pocket and turns on the small TV perched on top of a mini-fridge. He's been told many times to keep his mouth shut on this trip of theirs, so he decides that's exactly what he's going to do.

Julius suddenly stands and shouts into his phone. "Goddammit Viribus! If the boss asks, tell him what I just told you. If he doesn't ask, then don't tell him anything. If you absolutely have to tell him something and you don't like what I've told you, then fucking make something up." Julius ends the call and throws his phone onto the bed.

"That fucker is only higher up than me because of his gigantor size," he grumbles. He sits on the side of the bed, the old springs in the mattress squeaking as they take his hefty frame.

"I need a drink," Julius says. "Come on, let's go."

Damon looks away from the TV and stares at the man on the bed next to his. He raises his eyebrows and stares at Julius.

"Stare all you want little man," Julius taunts. "Wherever I go, you go."

Damon doesn't move. He doesn't shift his gaze or appear to even breathe. He stays still for a long minute before looking Julius up and down.

"You think I'm intimidated by you?" he asks.

"I think if you were smart, you'd think twice about me," Julius responds. He leans forward slightly, adding, "And I think you're just a dumb fuck."

Damon has had enough of Julius's posturing. He sits up to face the shorter man. He faints like he's going to launch himself at the Victus. He expects the shorter man to flinch, but Julius stays as still as a statue.

The second Damon settles his weight back onto the bed, Julius's arm flings forward and Damon is hurled through the air across the room. He slams into the wall, his head snaps backward and makes his vision spin. The sheetrock behind him crunches from the impact of his solid body against it. He's pinned there, his feet dangling off the ground.

"You know why you're a dumb fuck?" Julius asks as he stands up. His arm is locked in a straight out position, keeping Damon frozen on the wall. He's seen the demon do this before and it always has the desired effect of obedience.

"Because you forget who you're dealing with."

He walks around the bed and comes to stand in front of the footballer. He looks up at Damon's face, luxuriating in the fear he sees in the taller man's eyes.

"You've seen a glimpse of what the boss can do. You don't know what *I* can do, yet you continue to test my patience, minuscule as it is already."

He lowers his arm and Damon immediate drops to the floor. His legs crumple underneath him not ready for the impact, and he lands hard on his hip. A concave spiraled web is left on the wall in his place. Julius leans in close to Damon's face.

"Don't test me again."

Damon stays still as Julius steps away from him and moves toward the door of their motel room. He checks himself in the mirror and adjusts his shirt collar. Damon watches as Julius sighs at his reflection and rolls out his shoulders. He turns back to Damon with an almost friendly expression as if the last few minutes hadn't even happened.

"I could really use a drink right now," Julius says. "So get your ass up off the floor, man. Let's go."

It takes a moment for Damon to get his legs under him. His vision is slow to clear. When he finally stands, he keeps his hand on the wall to ground himself. He shakes his head roughly and straightens up. He rolls out his own shoulders and dust and bits of wall fall off his back.

Damon doesn't say anything to Julius but glares at him with open hostility. The Victus patronizes the man by giving him a thumbs up with an overly cheerful smile before throwing open the door of their motel room.

They leave the room and walk down the block to a bar. They're in a college town so the place is filled with men and women in their late teens and early twenties. Damon's eyes narrow as his gaze locks onto a busty blonde. He sneers as he watches her cross the room to the bar. Julius notices and laughs gruffly.

"Well, no wonder the boss took such a shining to you," he says. Damon's stare leaves the young woman and his eyes harden as he looks at Julius.

Julius looks his associate up and down before he says, "You're a predator."

****

After a night spent at the nearby college bar, drinking and leering at coeds, the demon's number three and his human tagalong get into their rental car at noon to head out for Portland. Damon starts the engine and adjusts the driver's seat to his long legs. Julius pulls up the GPS app on his phone and directs Damon to the on-ramp for Interstate 580 West.

They follow the road running parallel to the California coast bypassing Richmond, Vallejo, Fairfield, and Red Bluff, merging from I-580 W to I-80 E, from there to the 505 N and ultimately to I-5 N. The men make their first stop three hours later in Redding, California. They pull off the highway at a rest stop.

After gassing up the car, they pull around and park right out front of the small building. Julius reaches over and takes the key out of the ignition before the two men enter the building.

Damon goes to the bathroom and when he comes out, Julius is holding two coffees, two bottles of water, a handful of Slim Jims, some peanuts, and a book of crosswords. He doesn't say anything to Damon before turning on his heel and going back to the car.

Julius drives the next leg of their trip. They get back on Interstate 5 North and follow it all the way through California into Oregon. After passing Ashland, Medford, and Canyonville, the men pull off at Roseburg. The two have spent the last four hours in almost total silence. The gas tank of their V-8 rental is again close to empty, plus it's dark and nearly eight o'clock so both men are hungry.

They find a diner not too far from Interstate 5 and plop down in a booth for dinner. They quickly scan the menus and place their order as soon as a waiter comes by. Julius is studying his phone, trying to determine their next stop and only looks up once their food arrives.

"From here it's only another couple hours to Salem. We'll get a motel there or somewhere around it for the night," he says around the cheesesteak panini in his mouth.

"It's only about an hour to Portland from there, so we can leave first thing."

Damon swallows the bite of his gyro before tentatively asking, "Do we have anyone we're meeting in Portland to... show us around?"

"No," Julius pauses before answering further, considering how much to tell the man. Eventually, he says, "My contacts don't reach this far. The boss has people out here who know of him, but they aren't... on his payroll. We're on our own."

"So how then, exactly, do you plan on finding which library we're supposed to look for?"

Julius looks at Damon as if he's an idiot and mutters, "Dumb fuck," before he says, "It's a large city so it'll have a public library, and probably more than one. So we'll start at the biggest and work our way down if need be."

He turns his phone toward Damon to show him the information he's pulled up on the browser. The bright, backlit screen shows the home page for the Multnomah County Central Library.

• 3 1 •

Cali

Wednesday morning Cali's first alarm goes off at nine. She shuts it off and falls back asleep quickly. When her second alarm goes off at ten, she sleeps right through it until it shuts off itself. Finally, when her third alarm goes off at eleven, Cali slams her hand down on the large off button on the clock, stretches her body and picks up her phone to put on some music, all while not quite fully awake.

The soft sheets glide smoothly over her naked body as she rolls to her side and reaches her arm out for Mickey, looking for some morning cuddles. The side of the bed is cool to the touch, and her hand lands on a piece of paper instead of the equally naked body of her girlfriend. The crinkling sound it makes as her hand closes around it wakes her fully.

The note says: Forgot I had an early session today. I'll see you later for lunch. Love you!

Cali's mouth turns up, forming a soft smile. She yawns and gets up out of bed. She stretches again before putting on some pajama boxers and a t-shirt that smells like her girlfriend. She tucks her phone into the elastic band of the shorts, music still playing.

She opens her bedroom door and walks to the small kitchen. As she hums along with her playlist, Cali grabs a big bowl from the cabinet and a spoon from the drawer. She takes the milk out of the fridge and jumps as she feels Milo brush up against her leg.

"Hey, Dog Man, way to stealth. I didn't even hear you coming," Cali says through a yawn. She bends down to ruffle Milo's fur and says, "Man, I can't seem to wake up today, dude."

Cali settles onto the couch after grabbing one of the boxes of cereal Alexa had picked up on Sunday. She pours herself a bowl and turns on the TV. Before it powers on entirely, she gets a glimpse of her auburn hair in her reflection on the screen. It's an unruly combo of bed-head and sex hair. Milo sits in front of her waiting patiently for any pieces that drop from Cali's bowl or mouth.

The still half-asleep woman flips through the channels and doesn't find anything she feels like watching so she goes through the On Demand menu. She scans through the options and can't decide on something to watch, so she scrolls back to her recently played options, finds Milo's favorite movie and hits play.

"Check it out, Milo," Cali points with her spoon to the TV. Milo turns and gets up panting as he sees the St. Bernard dog come onto the screen. He jumps up onto the couch next to Cali and lays down, for the moment forgetting the food Cali is eating.

Cali smirks and says to herself, "My, my, my. How convenient."

At a quarter to one, Cali sends a text to Alexa asking her if they are still on for lunch together today. As soon as she hits send, she remembers that her roommate said she's doing some project for her boss in the basement of the library in the mornings and service is spotty. So she's surprised when she gets a text back almost immediately.

LEX: yes please!

CAL: yay! do you want to go to Marty's?

LEX: definitely
LEX: want me to meet you there? or you could meet me here? then we can walk there together

CAL: i'll come to you. i'm going to bring dog man with me. we could both use some fresh air

Cali throws a blanket over her and Milo so only their heads are visible and takes a selfie of them. She edits the photo on her phone to add some sleepy ZZZs and sends it Alexa.

> **LEX:** milo could use some fresh air for sure. that pup is getting soft!
>
> **CAL:** he is not! you're just jealous because i get to spend more time with dog man than you
>
> **LEX:** .....soft

Cali scoffs then laughs as she says to the pup next to her, "Can you believe what your mother just said to me, Milo?"

The dog gives her a sideways glance but doesn't move his face away from his movie. She types out her response and says each word out loud as she does.

> **CAL:** i take offense to that!
>
> **LEX:** hahaha
>
> **CAL:** i'm gonna get dressed real quick so what time should i come?
>
> **LEX:** i'm still in the basement and probably won't be finished for another half hour maybe?
>
> **CAL:** ok. i'll meet you outside the main entrance at 139
>
> **LEX:** 139? that's an oddly specific time lol
>
> **CAL:** haha shut up i meant to hit the 0
>
> **LEX:** ok i'll see you then

Cali gets up, rinses her empty bowl and spoon in the sink, and puts the cereal box away above the fridge. Shooting a quick text to Mickey letting her know what time and where they are meeting, she goes back through the living room and bypasses her bedroom. Cali heads right to the bathroom to wash up.

She exits the bathroom in a towel and heads into her bedroom to rummage through her closet for something comfy to wear. Five minutes later she's back in the living room wearing olive green jeggings and a waffle knit gray long sleeve shirt with a hood.

Cali steps over to the couch that Milo hasn't budged from and turns off the cable box and TV. Milo's head shoots up and he immediately starts to whine.

"Sorry, dude, we got to go," Cali says to the dog. "We're going to grab some lunch at Marty's."

Milo, still whining, rolls onto his side on the couch and buries his head under the blanket. Cali takes his harness and leash off the hook and clicks the clasp a few times. That's all it takes for Milo to forget about his movie. The prospect of going for a walk to a dog is always exciting.

Before they know it, Cali and Milo are walking down SW Tenth, closing in on the library. A couple of men walk past Cali and Milo and the taller of the two bumps into Cali. The force whips her around and she stumbles. If not for the arms of the man darting out to steady her, she would've fallen to the ground.

"Excuse us," the man says still holding onto Cali. The fur on the back of Milo's neck rises, he presses himself into Cali's leg as he growls at the two men in front of them.

"Whoa. Easy there, Fluffy," the shorter of the pair says taking half a step back. He glares at Cali with cold black eyes and says aggressively, "You might want to put a muzzle on your mutt there."

The taller man who caught Cali still hasn't let her go. His grip is slowly becoming tighter on both of her forearms. Milo maneuvers himself in between them and growls again. The man ignores the dog and starts talking to Cali.

"Hey there, sugar," he says. "I'm Damon."

He towers over her and smiles at her. It's not a friendly greeting though. His eyes look closer to a lion's when it's about to go in for the kill. Milo's growling becomes louder, but without being told any command the rumbling in his chest is as much as he's allowed to do.

"Let go of me," Cali says calmly but forcefully. Damon doesn't release her but instead squeezes a little more. She tries to pull her arms out of his grasp, but Damon holds tighter and pulls her in a little closer to him.

"Let go!" Cali yells loudly. She takes a full step backward, able to finally disentangle herself from him with a strong yank. Rubbing her arms that are sore from his grip, she takes another large step backward and turns around to keep walking toward the library.

"Hey, where you going, honey?" Damon says sweetly. She's stopped again as she bumps into the shorter man that she hadn't realized had moved behind her. Damon takes a few quick steps to come and stand next to the other man blocking Cali. Milo growls louder as he again moves between Cali and the men in front of them.

"You didn't tell me your name, sugar."

"Intentionally," Cali replies stepping to the side to move around him. Damon steps with her.

"Come on now, don't be like that," Damon says. "How about you tell me your name then you and I go get a drink."

"No," Cali firmly replies.

Damon goes to take a step toward her and reaches out again as if to grab her. Milo has had enough and barks loudly at the two men drawing some attention to them. He lunges slightly forward with each bark. Cali tightens her grip on his leash as she holds him back.

She suddenly remembers the command that Alexa told her about over the weekend, but she sees something directly behind the two men that makes her realize she doesn't need it. A broad grin forms on her face. The menacing smiles on both of the men in front of her quickly change to perplexed frowns.

"Do we have a problem here?" Mickey's voice is steelier and more forceful than Cali has ever heard, but still music to her ears and especially right now.

Cali uses the mild surprise both men exhibit at the voice coming from behind them to her advantage. As they turn around to face whoever is butting into their business, she gently tugs Milo and moves to stand behind Mickey. Milo pulls on his leash to step in front of Mickey and put himself in between the pairs.

Damon smirks at the two women in front of him and says, "No, no problem. I was just offering to take sugar here for a drink."

"And what did she say?" Mickey asks. The sound coming out of her mouth is frigid, her anger at someone disrespecting her girlfriend hardly concealed.

"She said no, but—"

"Well then you've got your answer," Mickey cuts Damon off.

"No, I don't think so, sweetie. I think she needs to think about it a little before she just says no, you know?"

Damon takes a slight step forward and Milo promptly blocks his way. Mickey looks down at the dog and then back up and smiles at the man with zero warmth.

"Well, sugar," Mickey says patronizingly. "No means no. Both of you walk away now or I'm calling the police. Okay, darling?"

"Alright, that's enough Damon," the shorter man says, stepping in to push Damon back a little. "Move it."

Damon doesn't budge. He just stares at Cali hungrily. When he licks his lips, the shorter man puts two hands on his chest and shoves him more forcefully and says, "Damon, now."

Again the taller man doesn't move. The short, fat man shakes his head and puts the fingertips of one hand on Damon's chest. The bald man stumbles backward, catching himself before he falls.

"Let's go."

Damon finally starts backpedaling away from the women. He calls out over the shoulder of the shorter man, "Bye-bye, baby, I'll see you again, soon."

Mickey turns around to Cali and tucks her girlfriend under her arm. The two women hear the shorter guy growl something that sounds like, "We're not here for this, you dumb fuck."

"You okay, baby?" Mickey asks.

In the safety of her girlfriend's arms, Cali begins to tremble slightly as her adrenaline starts to recede. She looks down first at Milo stock still on alert watching the men walk away, then up to Mickey and says, "Y-Yeah."

She makes some kissing sounds and calls Milo over to settle him. He doesn't budge at first but Cali remembers what Alexa said at the laundromat to calm him down.

"What was that guy's problem?" Mickey asks. She pulls Cali into her even tighter. Her eyes are narrowed and zeroed in on the two men who are strolling down the block as if without a care in the world. As if they hadn't just hurt Cali.

Cali gives her girlfriend a kiss, her body still buzzing. She tucks her face into Mickey's neck and says, "I don't know. But, let's go catch up with Lex. She's probably waiting for us."

• 3 2 •

"ALEXA"

"What's wrong!?"

Matt's tense voice cuts through the daydream I was having, imagining what I could accomplish this afternoon in CCR3 with *The Book*. Even though the library didn't technically open today until about a half hour ago, I had come in at ten to work on my project. Matt only works half a day today but came in early for us to all go to lunch. I had spent the last few hours with Samantha in CCR1 cataloging the next five books together as a team.

I look up to where I heard the sound and see him coming down the cement steps in front of the library. I'm ready to ask what he means, but I follow his gaze and realize he's not looking at me, he's looking at Mickey and Cali stepping onto the curb from the crosswalk.

My roommate is secured next to her girlfriend's body. Cali's face is pale, she's clearly shaken up by something. The couple is trying to calm Milo down without success. I see the fur along his spine is raised and he's on full alert. His lip is curled, barring his teeth and his eyes are constantly roaming, ready to attack anyone who gets too close.

I'm briefly paralyzed as I watch my dog come closer to me. I've only ever seen this extreme of a reaction from Milo once before. *Milo acting like this can mean only one thing,* I think. *There is evil nearby. Supernatural evil.* I'm unable to think of anything else at the moment as I get up and quickly go over to the women, right on Matt's heels.

"What's going on?" I ask. Milo immediately pulls against his leash to get to me as quick as possible. As soon as he's by my side, he puts his head between my knees and presses in tight, nearly knocking me over. His tail is down and motionless.

"What happened?" I ask again.

"Some jerk grabbed me, and then he and his lardo crony blocked my path," Cali says. She's tucked under Mickey's arm and I have a feeling she's going to stay like that for a while. "I thought Milo was literally going to bite his leg off."

"Where are these assholes now?" Matt asks. His face hardens with anger. He looks over the women's shoulders searching for the culprits. Mickey stops him with a hand to his chest.

"I watched them walk away," she says.

Cali looks me right in the eyes and says, "He was way more riled up than when we saw Tyler at the laundromat. I was pretty freaked out by those guys, but Milo was, like, instantly on guard. I even thought about giving him one of those commands you told me, but I didn't have to."

She looks down at my dog, who is still pressing his head between my knees. Cali pats her hand on Mickey's stomach before squatting down and calling Milo to her. I tell him everything's okay and he goes over to her. Cali hugs Milo tightly and holds onto him, the tip of his tail starts to wag slightly. It's a long moment before she speaks again.

"Thank you, Dog Man," she says. "It's like you knew those guys were bad news before they even bumped into us."

Cali stands up and curls herself into Mickey again. She buries her face into her girlfriend's neck. When she moves her face to look at us again, her eyes are shiny with tears.

"That guy really grabbed me," she says clearly shaken and overwhelmed by all of her emotions. "I mean, he bumped into me accidentally and then grabbed me to stop me from falling. But then he held on too tight for too long.

"I know self-defense," she looks around at the three of us, we nod to confirm we know that too. "And I usually don't feel threatened by anything. But this was different. It's like I was so shocked I was paralyzed."

Cali looks down at Milo. "And nobody said anything. There were people on the street, but nobody did anything. If Milo wasn't with me," she pauses and looks up into Mickey's eyes. "Or if you didn't show up when you did, I don't know what might've happened. He could've..."

Her voices cracks as the seriousness of what just happened settles over her. Mickey hugs her tight and directs her to one of the benches around the library. The two sit down holding onto each other. Cali puts her face in the crook of Mickey's neck. The older woman kisses the top of her head and rubs her back.

"It's okay, you're safe now. I've got you."

Mickey repeats that a few times while slightly rocking with Cali. I can feel Milo pressing into my leg and hear him whining softly. I reach down without looking to pat his head but Matt's hand is already there comforting my pup.

At this moment I wish I could read Milo's mind and find out exactly who those men were. But, it doesn't even really matter. His reaction leaves little doubt about their identities. If there are demons in Portland, or at the very least Victus, it means that they are most likely here for one thing — me.

It also means that someone I care about has gotten hurt because of me again.

The guilt that I have repeatedly buried over these last five years compresses and settles like a stone in my stomach. I've left my family to fend for itself. I don't even know for sure what happened to one of my brothers. Darius, evil incarnate, is still out there. *Who knows how many other people have been hurt or killed while I've been running scared,* I think. I can feel my eyes burn as they start to fill with tears.

No, I internally scold myself. *I am the one who will stop all of this!* I look at Cali and silently vow that I won't let any demon, or any Victus, or any jerk ever hurt her again. I soundlessly promise the same to Mickey and Matt.

At the same time, I make my vow of protection, my mind flashes like a neon sign that I'm running out of time. I need to learn more, I need to study *my* book inside and out. I'm going to have to find a way to either stay in the library after hours or smuggle *The Book* out with me one day. If I get caught stealing, that could create more problems. *Better to say I lost track of time while working,* I think. *I'll start tonight.*

"Do you still want to go to lunch?" I hear Mickey ask, breaking me out of my thoughts and returning me to the reality at hand. "I can take the rest of the day off and take you and Milo back to your place. We can just order something."

"No, I want to go to Marty's," Cali answers. "I haven't seen him in a while. Plus, those guys are gone, right?"

"Yes, baby," Mickey answers softly. "I watched them walk away. They're gone."

"Maybe we should call the cops," Matt says. He's squatting down in front of Cali next to Milo. My sweet dog has inched his way over to put his head in Cali's lap to comfort her.

"And say what?" Cali asks. "A big, tall guy was walking with a fat guy and one of them grabbed me?"

"Cal, you were assaulted so, yes, exactly that," Matt answers. I've never heard him call her by anything other than Squirrel. It's odd to hear, but it tells me how deeply Matt cares for his friend and how unsettled he is. He stops for a minute, observing his friend before speaking again.

"You keep rubbing your arms," he says. Then, softer than before, "Are you hurt?"

"I don't know."

Cali pulls up the sleeves of her shirt and reveals a large red blotch encircling each forearm. The four of us stare at the marks. All of us are shocked into silence.

"Holy shit, Cali!" Matt exclaims, the first to talk. "That's it, I'm calling the cops."

Matt pulls his phone out of his pocket and stands up to make the call. His best friend puts her hand out to cover the screen.

"Okay, we'll call and report it," Cali asks. "But can we do it at Marty's?"

"Whatever you want to do, baby," Mickey says in a soothing tone from her spot on the bench next to Cali.

The couple stands up together, neither one letting go of the other. Matt reluctantly puts his phone back into his pocket while keeping his eyes on his friend. He looks nervous and tense like Cali could shatter into pieces in front of him if he even touches her.

Cali takes Milo's leash from me, and the three of them — plus my pup — walk to the corner of the street. I'm rooted to my spot, my brain not entirely quieted, analyzing everything that has happened within the last few minutes and what it all means.

"Lex, you coming?"

For a moment I almost say no to my roommate. I'm itching to get back inside and hole up in CCR3 for the next week. But I smile warmly at her instead and say, "Of course."

While we're all waiting for the light to change to cross the street, Mickey starts murmuring something quietly to Cali, getting her to smile a few times. She still has her arm protectively around her girlfriend, the younger woman still holding tightly to Milo's leash. Matt takes my hand and brings it to his lips, placing a soft kiss on the back of it just below my knuckles. He lets go of my hand but quickly replaces the contact with his arm around my shoulders.

The light changes and the large group of people waiting at the crosswalk begin to move as a single mass. It doesn't take magical abilities to sense that the five of us, including Milo, are still a bit shaken up, Cali most of all. None of us shift or change our grip on our partners, nor do we say much the entirety of the brief walk to Marty's.

● 3 3 ●

Matt and I are sitting at one of the small tables inside of Marty's Deli, Milo is under the table laying across my feet. There are four of the red plastic baskets on the table, a few bags of chips, and four bottles of water. The baskets where Cali and Mickey were sitting are empty; Matt's is almost empty, with just a few crusts left. My sandwich has barely been touched.

My appetite vanished as soon as I realized who the men that bumped into and then grabbed Cali are. In fifteen months, in crisscrossing this entire city, I have never run into anyone that Milo has sensed is supernatural. He's reacted to some unsavory characters, but never like this. Not since my eighteenth birthday. That means that something led those men here. That means they are tracking something or someone. More precisely, me.

Cali and Mickey are standing close by, talking to the two female officers that quickly arrived, Officers Garcia and Lang. Marty was beside himself when Matt told him what had happened. He insisted that Cali call right away after wrapping her in a tight hug.

I'm pushing my sandwich around trying to appear as if I'm eating it while listening intently to Cali explain to the officers what took place.

"I was walking down Tenth on my way to the library," I hear Cali say. "Two guys were walking toward me, a short and fat white guy, and a tall, muscular black guy. The tall guy bumped into me hard enough to spin me around. He caught me to keep me from falling to the ground. But then he held on to me."

She stops here to roll up the sleeves of her shirt again to show the officers the red marks on her arms that are quickly turning purple on her pale skin.

"He didn't let go of me and his grip was getting tighter. He wouldn't let go, but instead called me sugar and introduced himself as Damon."

"And where was the shorter guy standing during this?" Officer Lang asks looking up from the pad she's taking notes on. She and her partner both have sympathetic eyes. They are diligently paying attention to Cali and what she's telling them.

"He was standing behind the guy at first, then he moved to behind me. Damon asked me to get a drink, and I said no, but that didn't make him let me go."

"Okay," Officer Garcia says. "What happened then?"

"Well, I was able to finally pull my arms out of Damon's grip and I turned around to continue walking away. I bumped into the other guy, the fat one, and was stopped again. The first guy, Damon, hopped around me to block my way, too. They both blocked me completely."

"Now, what did you see happen?" Garcia asks Mickey.

"I was across the street on the other side of Tenth, also going toward the library," Mickey says. "I heard a dog bark that sounded like Milo, so I looked around to see if it was him and Cali. I was closer to the corner but I turned toward the sound and I saw two men blocking her way."

"Did you confront the men?"

"I crossed the street and came up behind them. I think I said something like, 'Is there a problem here' and both of them turned around to face me."

"That's when I moved away from the guys and went to stand behind Mickey."

"Right," Mickey continues. "The tall guy was saying how Cali wouldn't tell him her name, and that she said no to a drink but he thought she should think it over a little more. I cut him off, I don't know exactly what I said, but that's when the shorter one started tugging the taller one away."

"You said 'no means no,' and then you called him darling." Cali smiles as she says it, but it quickly evaporates.

"The shorter guy had to shove the tall one a few times before he got him to walk away."

"Yeah, he wouldn't budge. But then the shorter guy, like, barely touched him with one hand and the guy went stumbling backward."

Officers Lang and Garcia nod approvingly at Mickey's gall before Lang asks, "Did anything else happen? Did they say anything to you as they walked away?"

"Or to each other?" Garcia adds.

"Damon said something like 'bye-bye sugar,' and then the shorter one called him a dumb fuck."

"I heard that too," Mickey says. "I also heard the short one say that they weren't here for this, whatever that means."

"Would either or both of you be willing to sit down with a sketch artist to help create a rendering of their appearances?" Lang looks between Mickey and Cali for their answer. The couple nod.

Lang checks her watch before saying, "Are you both available to come to the precinct in a couple hours, say four o'clock?"

"Yes," Cali answers. "My day is completely open."

"I'll be there, too," Mickey says. "I just have to call the studio and reschedule some things."

"Well, if you'll both write down your contact information for us here, please," Lang holds out her notepad and pen to the women. Cali and Mickey write down their names and phone numbers and give back the pad to the officer.

"Here's our card," Garcia says handing over a business card. "If you think of anything else in the meantime, please don't hesitate to call. But unless something changes, we'll see you at the precinct at four. Ask for either of us at the main desk and we'll go from there."

Cali and Mickey nod and thank the officers. The female cops turn to leave but Marty stops them. He quickly packs a paper bag with two wrapped sandwiches, a large bag of chips and a handful of napkins. He tells them it's on the house and to grab whichever drinks they want from the coolers as he hands them the bag. They thank him and grab some water bottles before taking their leave.

As Mickey and Cali sit down at the table again, I go over what I learned from their conversation with the officers:

The men are obviously supernatural. I guess they are Victus, but I don't know for sure. One of them definitely had powers and used it out in the open. And if they are Victus then had to have been sent here by Darius. It sounds like the shorter one was in charge, telling the taller one what to do. They also were clearly in Portland for a specific reason, so they definitely are not locals. Milo could sense them, but they couldn't sense him.

I've been here for fifteen months, so what brought them here now? Why not before? What's changed? My throat closes, I can feel the bile churning in my stomach as I realize the answer. I found *The Book*. That's the only thing different from when I arrived over a year ago.

I have to get back to the library and get back into CCR3 and figure out what to do. I check my watch discretely and then tune back into the conversation going on at the table.

"You should call a cab and go home for a bit," Matt says to Cali. He's sitting in such a way that he's able to drape one of his arms on the back of Cali's chair and has his other hand on my thigh.

"Yeah, babe," Mickey chimes in. "We can take Milo home and just hang out there for a bit before we go to the station. I'll call Jack to cover for me this afternoon."

"Lex and I have to get to work," Matt says. He looks down at his watch, his eyes widen as he sees the time. "We're already twenty minutes late."

He gets up to throw out our trash and put the red baskets in the return bin on the counter. Mickey takes out her phone to call a cab that is animal-friendly to pick them up. Marty sees us all get up, and he comes around to give each of us a hug.

"You need anything, my little Squirrel," he says. "You just call me. Any time." He turns to Mickey and adds, "Take care of her, Michaela."

Usually, Mickey would flinch a bit when someone who isn't her mother uses her full name, but this time coming from Marty she just nods and says, "Yes, sir."

The fours of us step outside and I hand Milo's leash somewhat reluctantly to Cali. I have a strong desire to keep him as near me as possible based on the day's events. With one more hug for each of us, and last check-ins that Cali is okay right now, Matt and I head back to the library leaving her and Mickey and Milo waiting outside Marty's for the cab.

• 3 4 •

"Hey, Sam," I say letting myself back into CCR1.

"Hey, Lex," she replies not looking up from the laptop she's typing away on. "I'm just finishing up this last synopsis and then I'll be out of your hair."

We usually both work on Wednesdays, but Jeff asked us to come in early to work on the project in the morning for some overtime. We flipped a coin — Sam lost — so she has to spend her actual shift upstairs while I thankfully get to stay down here.

Samantha Stavros is a quarter Native American, a quarter Chinese, and half Greek. She's in her late forties but looks like she's in her early twenties. Good genes, she'd tell you. Her short brown hair is styled in a faux-hawk today and she's wearing a fitted, light gray, cotton dress. Sam is quite simply beautiful with a capital B.

"Okay. I'm sorry I took so long at lunch, there was a bit of an emergency."

The clacking of the keyboard ceases. Sam finally looks up at me and her face shows immense concern.

"Is everything okay?" she asks pushing the sky blue frames of her glasses higher up on her nose.

I don't know how much to tell her. I don't know if Cali would be upset about me sharing with Sam, if it would add to her distress. Or if she would be okay with it as a way of making others aware of these guys. I decide to go with the latter and will apologize profusely to Cali if it ends up being the wrong choice.

I push up my own glasses and say, "Uh, not really. My roommate Cali was on her way here with my dog, Milo, to meet me for lunch. And some really tall guy bumped into her and then grabbed her and wouldn't let go."

"Oh, my god!" Sam exclaims.

"Yeah. She's got bruises on her arms. Her girlfriend Mickey was on her way here too and saw them. She was able to get the guys to walk away, but it definitely shook Cali up."

I sigh and rub my forehead and pinch the bridge of my nose under my glasses.

"You should be careful when leaving later. I mean, Mickey got them to leave, but I don't know if they're actually gone. Maybe call someone to meet you here or take a cab or something."

"I'll be careful. Is Cali okay though, really?"

"I think so. She called the police and filed a report, and she and Mickey are going to the station in a bit to sit with a sketch artist. It was a tall and muscular black guy that actually grabbed her, but he had a short and heavy white guy with him."

Sam's brow furrows, "Hmm."

"What?"

"It could be a coincidence, but I think I might've seen those guys."

"You did? Where?"

"Here before when I went upstairs to get a cup of coffee right before you went to lunch," she says.

I don't know if it's possible to feel the color drain from your face, but based on my sudden lightheadedness, I'm going to say you can.

"They were talking to Jeff," Sam keeps talking unaware of my current unease. "He did not look happy with them. You know Jeff, his emotions can be a little flat, but he actually looked... angry. Huh, that's probably why I took notice because it was such an unusual reaction from him."

My vision starts to swirl in tandem with the thoughts running through my head. *Oh, no. No, no, no, no, no. Could Jeff be a Victus and I've missed it this entire time?!* A cold fear is creeping up my spine as I fully comprehend how much danger I am in if Jeff turns out to actually be against me. My voice roars in my head: *How could this have happened?!*

"Could you hear anything Jeff was saying? Do you think he knows who they are?" To me, the tremble in my voice is clearly audible, but if Sam hears it she doesn't acknowledge it.

"Only a little. It sounded like Jeff was saying that he wasn't going to confirm or deny who his employees are without being given an excellent reason. Whatever that means."

"Weird," I say outwardly. Internally I think, *Oh, fuck. I know exactly what that means.* Sam nods her agreement with her eyebrows raised.

"Anyway," I continue. "You should go. Jeff wants one of us upstairs for our shift, and I've already made you late enough."

"Yeah, okay," Sam says.

She saves her entry in the database, returns the book to the shelf, and grabs her lanyard with her key card from the table draping it around her neck. She takes off the white gloves and hands them to me. She gently squeezes my shoulder as she moves toward the door.

"You be careful too, Lex, okay?"

I count to two-hundred in my head after Sam leaves before I exit CCR1 and use my card to unlock the door of CCR3. Between the two of us, Sam and I have made six entries, so I don't think Jeff will mind too much if another one isn't added for today.

I beeline to the back corner and grab *The Book*. I push down the powerful feeling of strength and resiliency before it can go to my head and open it. I take out my phone and open the camera app. I start flipping through *The Book*, taking a picture of each page. When I get to the end, I check the photos.

"Dammit," I curse. Every single one is blurry to the point of being indiscernible.

I go back to the beginning and steady my phone far enough away to get the whole page, but close enough to catch all the detail. I tap on the screen to trigger the focus and then touch the shutter icon. I press on the thumbnail of the picture and it's still blurry.

"Dammit!"

I slide my thumb across the screen of my phone changing it from photo to video. I steady my hand above *The Book* and touch "record". I leave my hand hovering in the air, count to five and turn the page. I count to five again and end the recording. The video is just as blurry as the images.

I grab a different book from the shelves in front of me and take a few pictures and seconds of video just to check that there isn't something wrong with my phone. Everything comes out completely clear, nothing out of focus even slightly.

There must be some charm or spell on *The Book* protecting it somehow. So short of taking it out of CCR3 and bringing it upstairs to photocopy it, or actually stealing it — which I haven't completely ruled out — I'll have to study these pages here in person.

The library closes today at eight, and I shouldn't be expecting Sam for the rest of the day. I debate staying right there in CCR3 but if Jeff comes down to check on things or to ask me something, it would be better if I at least appeared to be doing the project he assigned to me.

I close *The Book*, pick up my phone and my lanyard, and go back to CCR1. I take the last book Sam was entering into the database back off the shelf and place in on the table next to the laptop. I arrange everything in a way that if Jeff opens the door, the computer will block *The Book* from view and it will look like I'm making another entry. I leave the door of CCR1 cracked slightly so I'll be able to hear if anyone comes into the sub-basement.

The same lined notepad with Sam's instructions is still next to the laptop so I flip to a fresh page and draw a line vertically down the center. I write Latin on top of the left column and English on the right. I open *The Book* and starting with the inscription inside the cover, I begin copying it out by hand.

I've written down the first few pages when a thought about today races through my head that I can't seem to shake off. *If the Victus were asking Jeff about who works here, then they somehow must have connected me to this place. If they've linked me to here, they know it's because* The Book *is here. And if they know it's here, it won't be long until Darius is here too.*

I check the time on my phone and do the closing-time math in my head. I have at minimum three more hours down here. I check what I've written down so far to make sure I haven't misspelled any of the Latin or missed any words. I'm about to continue copying out *The Book* when I hear a click echo outside of CCR1.

I scramble to close *The Book* and put the notepad on top of it. I shift my stool over slightly so I'm in front of the laptop screen and slide on the white gloves, pretending to read over my entry. The door of CCR1 opens outward toward the hallway and drags over the thick carpet, making a swish sound. "Alexa."

I don't need to turn to know who it is, but I turn around anyway and face my boss. "Hello, Jeff," I say politely. "What can I do for you?"

"I think it's something I might be able to do for you," he answers.

"Oh?" I ask. *I don't like the sound of that.*

"It seems that the two men that injured your friend Cali may be the same who were in the library this morning."

"How do you know about that?" I ask.

My fight or flight sensors are sparking to life and I discretely edge my seat back closer to *The Book*.

"Matt," Jeff answers. "He's very upset by the whole thing. I find that I am also."

I can't shake the gut feeling that this could still be some sort of trap. My muscles tense ready to spring into action if necessary.

"If these men are one and the same, then they came in here asking some very... intruding questions about the female employees. Personal questions about their backgrounds, appearances, and ages."

He pauses there and hesitates almost as if he doesn't know exactly how to proceed. "I'm telling all of the people working today about this, both women and men, and I'll be sending an email out about it so that everyone not here is aware. I refused to answer their questions, but based on the nature of them, I believe these two men may show up again."

I don't know exactly what to say, so I nod along with Jeff.

"I would like to ask you to do something," he continues. I nod again.

"There is footage from this morning from the cameras upstairs. I don't know for sure, but I hope there will be an image or two of the men that the police can use. I was wondering if you would bring a thumb drive with the video to the station."

"Uhh, s-s-sure," I stammer. "Of course. I can bring it on my way home later."

I'm confused now. If Jeff is in cahoots with the two men, sending me to the police station with footage that could identify them doesn't seem like a smart move. Unless they came here to tell him to hurry up and find *The Book* himself, and now he's trying to get me out of the way. But if that's the case, why assign me here in the first place? That suggests Jeff doesn't know exactly who I am and is maybe just outsourcing the grunt work to find *The Book*. Of course, that's assuming he actually is a Victus and knows *all* of this to begin with.

And if Jeff *isn't* a Victus and has absolutely no idea about anything supernatural going on in his library, then he's just a good guy who wouldn't give out information without cause and wants two scummy men to be caught.

Of course, he could be the first option and is only pretending to be the second to escape suspicion.

My head is starting to hurt.

"There are only a couple hours left for the day anyway so I'd like you to go now," Jeff says. The inkling of a trap creeps up in my mind again but is chased away as he adds, "I've asked Matt to go with you, and I'll be telling everyone to leave in pairs or groups today."

"Okay, I can do that," I say. "I'm just about done with this entry, I'm just proofreading."

"Very good," Jeff answers. "When you are finished, you may find Matt and leave. I've already given him the thumb drive."

"Okay, great," I answer. I go to turn back to the computer but Jeff clears his throat. He must have more to say.

"Alexa," he starts. "Since you and Sam have been doing such a great job and it's moving along so well, I was hoping you'd be able to stay late tomorrow and Friday to get a couple more entries done? Sam will be here this weekend so you won't be required to come, but do you think you'll be able to stay the next two days?"

More time in here is exactly what I need right now. It solves that small hiccup of whether or not to steal *The Book*. Without sounding too eager about it, I answer with a good-natured, "Oh, no problem."

"Good," Jeff says. "Well, like I said, once you're finished with that entry, you may go."

"Thanks, Jeff." He nods and leaves, pulling the door to CCR1 fully closed behind him.

I save and close the entry in the database before exiting out of the software program. I return the first edition to its shelf, and take off the white gloves.

I flip ahead in *The Book* until I see the word "Extensios" and write down everything I see with it. I may need to learn how to do that sooner than anything else. Once I finish copying what I believe is everything, I tear off the sheets of paper I used from the notepad and stuff them into my pocket. I scan CCR1 quickly making sure nothing is left behind before picking up *The Book* to return it to its current home.

I reluctantly put it back on the shelf in CCR3. If I linger down here, it may cause Jeff or Matt to come down to get me, inadvertently bringing direct attention to *The Book*. *I'll have all day tomorrow*, I remind myself. I make sure the doors to cubes one and three are securely closed before I exit through the heavy sub-basement door.

• 3 5 •

DARIUS

The incessant knocking on the door and the calls of his name rouse Darius from his Zen-like state. Demons don't ever sleep, but the oldest ones have taught themselves a type of meditation that essentially allows them to shut down for short periods. Darius growls as his awareness languidly comes back to the world.

"Boss?" he hears through the door.

He shakes his head a few times to clear his vision. He's in one of the rooms above the bar. The shades are drawn, preventing the day's falling sunlight from entering. The single bulb in the ceiling throws out a dim light. The walls are stained yellow from decades of cigarette smoke, the wooden floor scratched and discolored from hundreds of shoes and spills.

He's laying on a dingy full sized mattress propped up in the middle of the floor on the same kind of wooden palettes that litter the alleyway out back. Unwashed sheets are bunched up by his feet, his head is resting on a soiled pillow. The only other furniture in the room is a small, lopsided table with one chair shoved over in a corner. His jacket is draped over the back of the chair.

Darius sits up as the knock comes again.

"What!?" he yells. The door inches open and Viribus ducks his watermelon-sized head in.

"Sorry, boss," he says in his deep baritone voice. "But I just got off the phone with Julius and he told me to tell you something."

"About fucking time. What'd he say?" Darius rubs a hand up and down his face to clear his vision. He stands and motions for Viribus to fully enter the room.

"He and the guy you sent with him are in Portland, Oregon. They went to New Orleans and met up with Blue. He took them to the library, they spoke with the old man who remembered the girl. He told them about the library in Portland, so Julius—"

"I don't want a history lesson Viribus," Darius says, sternly cutting the giant off. "Just give me the bottom line: do they have her or not?"

"They don't have her." Darius starts to grumble but Viribus quickly continues, "But they are convinced that she's in Portland."

A look of curiosity momentarily breaks through the anger on Darius's face. "Talk faster."

"Julius is almost completely positive that they bumped into someone who was walking the dog."

"The dog? What the hell are you talking about?"

"The dog. *The* dog, boss. The girl's dog."

Darius remains quiet, trying to understand what his Victus is talking about. Slowly, a millennia of memories sort through his head and a movie of that day five years ago plays in his mind. When he arrived, people began running all over the place. Darius freezes on a snapshot of the girl's grandfather whisking her away quickly, a black dog practically glued to her leg.

"The black dog," he says out loud.

"Right, boss," Viribus says. "Julius thinks that it was either a dog walker or a friend, he's definitely sure it's not the girl — skin color wasn't right. But someone was walking the dog and they bumped into her. A happy accident, he said. The dog immediately started growling and barking at Julius and the other guy."

"Promising. When will Julius be back?"

"Tomorrow. They booked a flight for first thing in the morning," Viribus an-swers. He's standing straighter now, stretched to his full height at the de-mon's positive reaction to what Julius has found out.

"Tomorrow. What day is it now?" Time doesn't mean much to a demon un-less he's waiting on something important. Such as finding the girl who has the power to eradicate him from this world.

"It's Wednesday evening, boss."

"Good."

Darius begins to pace around the small room making a mental list of what he'll have to do to get to the girl now that he knows where she is. He walks over to his Victus and grabs him on the back of the neck. Darius pulls him down so that their foreheads touch.

"You did good, Viribus," he says. He claps his hand on the back of the sol-dier's head twice. "This is very good."

Viribus sighs in relief before asking, "What do you need now, boss?"

"When Julius gets back, we have to facilitate the transition to Victus. We'll need transport potions, six total. Three to get there and three to go the por-tal after. I want you to stay here Viribus." The Titan-sized man's face falls and his shoulders start to sag.

"Listen to me," Darius continues. "Listen. You are my strongest Victus, and I will need you to help me open the portal fully. I can't risk you getting lost. I don't expect she'll be able to put up much of a fight, but I won't take that chance."

Viribus nods obediently, but he's not happy with being left behind. "Yes, boss," he says begrudgingly.

"After Damon's transition, I'll need you to watch over me while I recover. You know that's when I'm in my most vulnerable state. I don't trust anyone else to do that."

"Yes, boss," Viribus says again, his pride re-inflating a bit.

Darius can see he's placated the giant. He goes to the chair in the corner and puts on his jacket. He comes back over to his soldier and punches him on the shoulder.

"Let's go downstairs and find some people to... celebrate this new turn of events with."

A smile covers Darius's face, but the joy that is there is tainted with the malicious intent behind his statement. He's convinced that the girl is finally within his reach. He salivates at the thought of being rid of her and the maddening curse she represents.

A sneer graces Viribus's face, he understands completely what the demon means. He takes a step to the side to allow Darius to exit the room first.

"Won't be long now, Viribus," Darius says walking down the narrow, dark hallway to the staircase that will bring them into the grimy kitchen of the bar. "Soon the real fun starts."

• 3 6 •

"ALEXA"

After stopping at the police station, Matt and I grabbed a cab back to my apartment. I texted Mickey to let her know we were on our way so that we wouldn't startle her or Cali. We got to my door at the same time as the delivery guy holding two pizza boxes. While Matt paid, I took the food and unlocked the door of my apartment.

I'm met by a black blur as Milo barrels into me, knocking me to the floor. Thankfully the pizzas land right side up and dinner isn't ruined. He doesn't squander a minute before hopping into my lap, whipping me with his tail, and slobbering all over my face.

"Okay, Milo," I say trying to calm him down. I rub his ears and kiss him between his eyes.

"He's kind of been like this all day," Mickey tells me as she picks up the pizza boxes. "This is actually the first time he's left Cali's side."

Cali wastes no time opening the boxes and taking out her preferred slice of black olive. "He even waited outside the bathroom door for me," she says around a mouthful. "It ended up being a cute picture though."

Mickey hands me her phone open to the picture she took. Milo is sitting in front of the closed bathroom door, his ears pricked and his eyes locked on the doorknob. Mickey swipes her finger across the screen and the next picture is of Milo in the same spot, door still closed, but his head is twisted back to face Mickey with his mouth open and his tongue hanging out.

I smile at the picture then go over to my roommate and give her a hug. She doesn't hesitate to hug me back tightly. I hold her at arm's length and look her in the eyes. We stare at each other a minute, and I rub her arm satisfied that she's feeling okay. Matt hands me a plate with a piece of plain pizza and the four of us settle around the coffee table like we did four nights ago.

How much can change in just a few days, I think. I slightly shake my head and ask, "Did everything go okay at the police station?"

Cali and Mickey begin to tell Matt and me how things went; that the artist was very personable and made them both feel very comfortable, how he and Cali discussed technique and talked shop when he finished, and how it turns out that the artist's wife is a member at Mickey's studio. Half of my mind is listening, the other half is planning out my day for tomorrow and Friday. I have a long night ahead of me — I want to translate as much of *The Book* as possible, starting with the part on Extensios.

I swallow the last bite of my slice and get up to get another. I ask if anyone wants more and Mickey and Cali both say yes. As I'm putting three pieces onto my plate, I feel Matt come up behind me and wrap his arms around my waist. He kisses the back of my neck and then rests his chin on my shoulder.

"You okay?" he asks. "You seem a little out of it."

"Yeah," I answer, turning to face him. I put my arms around his neck. "Long day," I say as I pull him in for a kiss. It's a sweet kiss, I take comfort in him being so strong and so close to me. I feel some of the stress of the day melt away a little.

"And the next couple days will be more of the same. Jeff asked me to stay late tomorrow and Friday, see if I can get more of this project done."

"Oh," Matt seems disappointed. Then slightly hopeful, he asks, "What about Saturday night? Are you working then?"

"No," I say missing his point. "Sam's got the weekend shift."

"So then you're free Saturday?"

Ohhhh. "Yes," it comes out a squeak. I clear my throat, all hopes of being suave gone, and try again. "Yes, I am."

"In that case," Matt smirks. He opens his mouth to continue, but he's interrupted before he even begins.

"Hey lovebirds!" Cali calls. "Can we get our pizza over here already?"

"Oh my god, Cali," Mickey laughs. "Way to ruin their moment."

"But I'm hungry," Cali whines in response.

I hold a finger to Matt and bring Mickey and Cali their slices of pizza making sure to bow obnoxiously to my roommate. I come back to the kitchen and wrap my arms around his neck again. His fingers interlock at the small of my back. Our bodies are flush to each other.

"I believe you were saying something about Saturday?" I ask coyly.

"I was," he replies. "I was wondering if I could take you out."

I don't hesitate for a second before I answer, "Definitely."

The smile that lights up Matt's face is the best thing that has happened all day. His eyes twinkle and he nods his head once. "Great, then it's a date."

"Definitely," I say again.

****

It's three in the morning. Milo is sound asleep, snoring at the foot of my bed. I'm sitting up, my pillows stacked behind me, and I have the pages from the notepad spread around me. I numbered them so I wouldn't lose the order they're in. I borrowed Cali's tablet and have the browser open to a page that will translate from one language to another. I would use my phone but the screen obviously isn't as big. I'm fighting off sleep as it is, so I need all the help I can get.

It's sitting on top of the notebook I had brought to the laundromat that I used to write down what I could remember about the princess and the demon. The box with my mother's letter is safely tucked away under my mattress.

Matt had gone home shortly after the pizza was finished, but not without an invigorating make-out session just outside my front door. An hour later,

Mickey got a call from Jack at her studio that one of the pipes in the ceiling was leaking. She left to handle it but came back when it was fixed.

While Mickey was out, Cali asked if I would snuggle with her on the couch and watch some reality TV. I can hardly say no to Cali on a regular day, but especially not today. We watched three episodes of a celebrity cooking competition, Cali and I tucked in under a blanket with Milo on top of it between us.

When Mickey came back, I took Milo for his nighttime walk and then took a long, hot shower. Fresh-faced and comfy in my pajamas, I went to the kitchen and poured myself a glass of my favorite soda. I would need the caffeine and sugar boost for the night.

Mickey and Cali were still watching TV, so I asked Cali if I could borrow her tablet on my way back to my room. Thinking nothing of it, Cali said, "sure, no problem." It was on the coffee table, so I picked it up as I said my thanks and goodnights.

Now, my soda has been drunk and I have only a few pages left to translate.

I had started with the part on Extensios. The term literally means extension. I would be creating an expansion of myself and my ability, specifically my telekinesis power.

The person has to be willing, I can't force anyone into becoming an Extensios. It's one of the many things that separates me from Darius.

"So who would I ask for help?" I say out loud. Milo shifts a little on the bed and raises his head to look at me. I drop my voice to be sure I'm not overheard by anyone possibly still awake in the apartment. "It would have to be someone I trust, right?

"Obviously, it would be someone I feel safe with. But that's a lot to ask of anyone. 'I need your help, so drop everything you're doing so I can give you a magical power and you can help me rid the world of its greatest evil.' God Milo, that even sounds crazy to me, and I know it's all entirely true.

"It would be amazing if you could learn how to speak right now and tell me what you think I should do." *Or I just use my powers to read your mind.*

Milo just yawns as a response.

I take off my glasses and drop my head into my hands. I rub my eyes with the heels of my palms, trying and failing to wipe away the heaviness and desire to close them. Milo's head snaps to my closed bedroom door and a second later I hear the creak of Cali's door opening followed shortly by a soft knock on mine.

"Yeah?" I say quietly but loudly enough to be heard.

The door opens and Cali pokes her head in. My brain is too sluggish to gather up the papers spread across my bed, so as Cali comes in and sits next to Milo, they're left exposed.

"What are you doing still up?" she asks.

"I, uh, I'm just—" I sputter trying to tell her anything but the truth. I realize the papers are still spread out in front of me and gather them into a pile and put them face down on top of the tablet.

"What's all this?" Cali's look of innocent curiosity and how much she's proven I can trust her almost makes me spill the beans.

"Oh, it's just some old papers I found. I must have lost track of time. What are you doing up?" I try to deflect the attention back to her.

"I can't sleep. Every time I close my eyes, I see those two guys," she says absentmindedly rubbing her arms where she was grabbed.

"I can't explain it, but I just got this feeling that they were..." She trails off. I know which word she's looking for, but I let her get to it on her own. I need her to get to it on her own.

"Evil," she finally says. "But not just that they were like bad news or anything like they were actually evil. Plus the way Milo reacted to them, nothing else makes sense. But even *this* doesn't make sense.

"I don't know," she shakes her head.

This is an opening, I think. *Talk to her about it, see if she's open to good and evil in the literal sense.*

"Do you believe in evil?" I ask gently.

Cali pets Milo, taking a minute before she answers.

"Yeah, I think I do," she says. "I mean, I know bad people exist, and there are some people who are only happy making others miserable. But, I don't know, I guess I also think that there is something worse out there?"

She sounds unsure, her expression matches her words. Cali looks from the papers on my bed to Milo before looking up at me.

"Go on," I nod my head to encourage her to continue.

"Yes," she says after a pause, looking me dead in the eye. "I believe that there is evil in the world that can't be explained in *natural* terms."

"So, you mean there is something out there that is *supe*rnatural." I carefully phrase my statement in a way that coaxes Cali to talk further about what she thinks.

"Yeah, I guess that's what I'm saying. Do you think there could be something like that in the world?"

My roommate doesn't know just how right she is. I take a deep breath before I answer her and heavily say, "Yes, I do."

Cali and I spend the next hour talking about what kind of beings we think are out there. I mean, I actually already know, but I phrase everything in an "I think" manner to test Cali's reaction to things. It's not every day you have this kind of conversation.

At 4:15 in the morning, I close the notebook with the papers tucked inside, and put it and Cali's tablet on my nightstand. I lay down on top of my comforter and Cali lays down next to me. We talk a little more, but before long my eyes are too heavy to keep open.

I've just closed my eyes when I hear Cali say, "Sometimes I think about what it would be like to have, like, powers or something of my own. It'd be so cool. Imagine all the good things I could do with them, you know?"

I don't answer her and stay completely still pretending to be asleep, allowing what Cali just said to sink in.

"Lex?" she asks, then whispers, "are you asleep?" I stay quiet and feel the bed shift as Cali settles herself closer to me. The last thing I hear before I actually do fall asleep is Cali say to herself, "I think it would be amazing."

• 3 7 •

My alarm goes off at seven playing the same popular radio morning show. The current segment's topic is about videos online posted by a dermatologist and whether the contents are gross or fascinating. Cali groans next to me and reaches over to turn it off. Her arm doesn't quite make it, and she ends up tapping me on the forehead a bunch of times. Through my groggy haze, I swat her away but leave the radio on so I don't fall back to sleep.

I want to get to the library early today and get a jump on the entries. If I can make five entries before lunch, then I'll have eight —hopefully uninterrupted — hours with *The Book*.

Cali, still mostly asleep, mumbles into the pillow next to me and her hand comes down on my forehead again. I huff and shake my head at my roommate and reach over to actually turn off my alarm. I roll out of bed and click my tongue for Milo to come with me.

I go right to the front door and pick up the leash and harness. Milo either senses my exhaustion, or he's just as tired as I am and lets me hook him in without a fuss. We leave the building and circle the block before making our daily stop at Roast.

The barista, Charlotte, gives me an amused smile as I come up to the counter. She looks me up and down then raises one eyebrow. I look at myself and see I'm still wearing my green plaid pajama pants and a heather gray pullover. I catch my distorted reflection in the vintage copper espresso machine. My hair looks like a nest, my glasses aren't on my face completely straight, and my eyes underneath are puffy slits. But at least I'm wearing shoes not slippers.

I shrug at my appearance, too tired this morning to really worry about it, and place my order through a large yawn.

"Two scrambled eggs with cheese on a multigrain bagel. Oh, and I know it's an unusual request Char, but could you put a double shot of espresso in my hot chocolate, please?" I hear a whine come from the area around my knee, so I quickly add, "Also a pup-cup for Milo."

Charlotte tells me my total and I open my wallet to pay. I'm running low on cash so I use my debit card. I haven't stopped at the ATM in a few days so that means I haven't added money to my box lately. It's not going to happen this morning with Cali sleeping in my bed right now, but I make a mental note to get some cash soon.

My name is called, so I take my order and walk over to a small table in the window. I sit down for a minute to give Milo a couple of licks of whipped cream. I feel my eyes starting to close so I quickly stand up, make sure I have everything, and head back to my apartment.

When I get home, I unhook Milo and give him food and water. I go through my usual routine and pour the hot chocolate into a travel container, rinse the top and cup, and put them both in the recycling bin. I push the bagel back out of Milo's reach and go toward my room.

The door to Cali's room is open so I peak in and see Mickey sprawled across the bed sound asleep. When I go through my own door, Cali is the mirror image of her girlfriend, except she's also snoring. I quietly grab my towel and clothes for the day, careful not to disturb my roommate.

In the bathroom, I put my hair up in a top knot to keep it dry and turn the shower on. When I see the steam curling over the curtain rod, I hop in to quickly rinse, then soap, then rinse myself. After I wash my face, I turn the knobs to shut off the hot water and leave the cold on. I let the water spray on my body as long as I can stand and then shut off the shower completely.

It's safe to say that stepping out onto the fluffy bath mat, I am finally one-hundred percent awake. I dry myself off and get dressed with measurably more energy than I've had since waking.

As quietly as possible I go back into my room to grab Cali's tablet and my notebook with the papers tucked inside it. I go back to the living room and see Mickey standing at the closed refrigerator drinking some orange juice straight from the carton.

"You're up early," I say. "I was just going to leave a note reminding Cali I'm working late."

Mickey wipes her mouth with her arm and says, "I'll tell her." She burps and her eyes widen before she laughs and says, "Excuse me."

I laugh with Mickey as I say, "I grew up with two brothers, trust me I've heard worse."

"Huh, I didn't know you had brothers."

Crap, I think. It's getting more difficult to remember what I've mentioned — or lied about — and what I haven't. Maybe I'm not as awake right now as I think I am.

"Mm-hmm," I walk past Mickey to get my leaded hot chocolate. I pop my bagel in the microwave for thirty seconds to reheat it.

"I have three," Mickey says. "All older. If they weren't messing with me, they were kicking the ass of whoever else was dumb enough to."

I turn around to face her and half her mouth is curled up in a smile. "That sounds familiar," I admit. The microwave beeps, so I take out my bagel and grab my travel mug.

"Hey, Mick?"

Mickey's in the middle of another swig of orange juice but is able to say through a swallow, "Hmm?"

"I was wondering if you had any tips for improving speed? My endurance has gotten really good, but I want to be faster."

"Faster? For what?"

"I don't know," I say trying to be as nonchalant as possible. "Just faster, I guess."

She folds her arms and leans against the fridge thinking. "Well, Jack does the sports specific training, so I'll ask him if there's something in particular. If you have the endurance, it could be that you just need to work on a more explosive start. But Jack would know for sure."

"Cool, thanks," I say as I gather my things for the day. Before picking up my bike helmet and leaving, I go over to the couch and give Milo a bunch of kisses and tell him to be good.

"Oh, by the way," I say straightening up. "Your girlfriend is drooling all over my pillows. You think you and Milo can take care of that for me?"

Mickey grins devilishly. "Oh yeah, I think so. Come on, Milo."

Mickey walks past me and puts down the orange juice carton on the coffee table. Milo hops off the couch to follow her. A few seconds pass between Mickey and my dog entering my bedroom and me hearing her gently call Cali's name.

Mickey's voice gradually gets louder and louder with no response from my roommate. There's a pause before I hear Mickey quietly count to three. Then Milo barks and Mickey yells "Cali!"

When I hear Cali scream followed by a thud which could only be her falling out of my bed, I open the door to my apartment and call out, "Thank you!" over my shoulder as I close the door behind me.

****

Because I'm not a coffee drinker, the few sips of my espresso charged hot chocolate goes right to my head. It takes me three tries to get the bike lock through the ends of the heavy chain, my fingers are trembling so much.

I take off my helmet and tuck it under my arm. I pull my lanyard with my ID out of my bag and walk up to the main door of the library. It isn't even 8:30, so not even Jeff should be here yet. If the magnetic strip on the back of my card does in fact open all the doors like it should, I will be the only person in the library for the next half hour.

I swipe my card through the reader with my left hand and take hold of the door handle with my right. The solid red light on the reader turns to green and I hear the familiar thunk as the lock is electrically turned. I step into the library and the door closes loudly behind me.

When the echo of the door fades, an uneasy silence fills its place. Libraries are inherently quiet but this feels different. I know I am completely alone in this well-over-a-century-old building, but it still feels like something's off.

I look around before moving from my spot. All the lights except the security ones are off, meaning nothing has tripped the motion sensors in at least fifteen minutes.

After a moment I understand what's off — everything. The normal sounds I'm used to hearing every day. There is no whirring from the fans in the computers; no buzzing from that one light above the counter that hasn't been fixed yet; no beep as books are scanned to be checked out, or being returned; no murmur of whispering voices.

I actually am completely alone in this building. But now I suddenly feel vulnerable and exposed.

You are a badass chick, and a powerful one to boot, I firmly remind myself. *You know how to defend yourself with or without magic. You are not in danger, you are dangerous.*

I nod a few times at my pep talk and begin walking toward the front counter behind which the employee lounge is located. The lights begin to flicker on as I move reassuring me I am in fact the only one here right now.

I sit down at the small table in the lounge and take out my breakfast. I search through my bag for my phone to send a text to Matt. As I eat, I type out that I'll be in the basement all morning but if he's free could we have lunch together at around one. Within seconds of sending it, Matt sends a reply.

MATT: definitely

My heartbeat quickens and I smile so wide that some of my food almost falls out of my mouth. I chalk that up to the foreign caffeine in my system rather than the fact that I have no chill.

I throw my garbage into the pail and write Jeff a note that I am here and already downstairs. I tape it to the monitor of the computer that only he uses. I would typically hang up my jacket and put my bag away, but today I bring both of them with me downstairs.

I have to use my card two more times just to get into the sub-basement. It's darker in here than upstairs, less security lighting, plus no windows to let the morning light in. As I step into the room of cubes and the door closes behind me, the motion lights blink to life and the space is illuminated.

I go straight to CCR1 to set up for the day. I put my bag down on top of the table next to the laptop, pull out Cali's tablet and my notebook. I tug on the white gloves and go to the shelf to pick up the next book. My hands are on the book ready to lift it when my whole body becomes momentarily immobile.

Cameras.

The word suddenly repeats in my head over and over again. My brain flashes back to the conversation I had with Jeff yesterday in this very room. I didn't think twice about it then but there are security cameras all throughout the library. That's how Matt and I were able to bring a thumb drive to the police station to assist in identifying the men who attacked Cali.

Are there cameras down here?! Have I been on video every time I've gone into room three?!

My voice is a panicked screech inside my head. I rip off the gloves and practically lunge toward my bag. I pull out my phone and making sure my lanyard is still around my neck with my ID, I open the door to the first cube and step outside of it.

I hold my phone up in the air and start to turn slowly in circles. If there is a camera in here, it would appear like I'm searching for a signal. In reality, I'm scanning the corners of the ceiling for a concealed red light, or a tinted glass dome, or an actual camera.

I'm standing in the center of the room and I don't see anything on the ceiling or in the corners. I walk down the makeshift hallway to the right of the cubes still holding my phone up to see if there is a camera inside the glass rooms. I don't see anything that looks like a camera anywhere.

I recheck the ceiling focusing this time on the air vents and the HVAC ducts that comes off the top of each cube. They are all uniform, no extra or misshapen pieces on the metal casings.

I scan the entire room again, making sure I absolutely have not missed a camera before I am satisfied. I drop my arms and return to CCR1. I put my phone back in my bag, pull on the gloves again, and pick up the book marked by the piece of paper stuck underneath it.

I get to work reminding myself that the more I get done before lunch, the more time I'll have later to do the real work.

• 3 8 •

"Hi, babe," I say as I come up to Matt outside the library near the bike rack. I lean in to give him a kiss on the cheek, but he turns his head so I get his lips instead. I smile before I pull back. His arms come around me and pull me in again for another long, lingering kiss.

I can't believe it's taken me this long to kiss him. Now that I have, I don't ever want to stop. I feel a stirring in my body and I want more. But I'm not the biggest fan of public displays of affection, so I put my hand on his chest and gently push him back a little.

"Babe?" he asks.

I think he's about to ask me something so I respond with, "Hmm?" When he just looks at me expectantly, I realize he was questioning the use of the term of endearment. "Oh. Is that not okay?"

"Actually, it's great," he says. I let out a small sigh of relief. "What do you want for lunch?"

"Honestly, I could go for a burger or something. What about you?"

Matt takes out his phone and starts tapping away. "Well, there are a couple of options close by."

He starts to turn his phone toward me but instead quickly spins me around, pulls my back to his front, and extends his arm out so we can both see the screen. It shows a map with a bunch of red pins and one blue one.

"You are here," he points at the blue pin. "The red pins are places with burgers nearby. Some are the food trucks up the block, some are sit down restaurants nearby. Any preference?"

"I want to say food truck, but that seems more like a sit-down-only option." I point up at the sky which is overcast with the clouds rapidly getting darker. "I'm regretting taking my bike today now."

Matt double-clicks the button on his phone and swipes through the open apps until he gets to a weather app.

"Zero percent chance of rain today, just cloudy. Your bike should be fine," Matt says. "So, do you want food truck or sit down."

"Well, in that case, food truck."

"Ah, excellent choice."

A couple of the food truck pins are around the block at the Shemanski Park Farmer's Market. But most are at the Food Truck Village on SW 10th. Matt takes my hand and spins me around again and we start walking toward our chosen lunch place. We head a few blocks straight up 10th. As soon as we pass the Galleria, I can see the brightly colored trucks set up in the parking lot.

A line is starting to form, so we jog over to the truck. When it's our turn, I step up to the open side and order the truck's version of a cheeseburger with avocado and a bag of kettle chips.

"Ooh, that sounds good," Matt says next to me. "I'll have the same, but with fries."

I take out my wallet to pay then feel Matt's hand gently cover my own. He shakes his head at me with a faux stern look on his face.

"It's on me," he says.

"Are you sure?" I ask. I don't ever make the assumption that someone will pay for me so I never have the expectation that they will.

"Yeah," he says. Then after a moment adds, "Babe."

Matt pays for our lunch and shortly after, we find ourselves sitting on a bench under some trees eating our burgers. It's quiet as we both chow down, the main sound being the rustling of the paper napkins as we grab from the mound between us.

"How's the project going?" Matt asks when he has only a few bites left.

"It's pretty cool actually," I say as I wipe my mouth. "So far today I've come across *The Federalist Papers* by Alexander Hamilton and *Twenty Thousand Leagues Under The Sea* by Jules Verne."

"That's one of my favorite books," Matt responds. "And I've always loved the smell that old books have, you know? It's like, dust and leather and paper and ink." He inhales deeply as if he could smell it right now.

"I know, I completely agree."

I finish my lunch at the same time Matt does. He leans back on the bench with his arm draped across the back. I angle myself so that when I lean back too, my back is resting more against him than the bench.

This is nice, I think. *It feels so normal. I'm just a regular twenty-something hanging out with a guy that I really like. A guy I have a date with in a couple days.*

"So about Saturday," I begin. I can feel Matt tense a little underneath me. I realize I sound like I'm trying to cancel.

"What do you have planned?" I ask. I turn slightly to look at him and continue, "You know, 'cause I have to know what I should wear and all."

"Oh," he relaxes with the sound. "Well, it's a two-parter. So maybe wear something you'd wear to one of Mickey's classes for part one. And then, I guess, bring something to change into that you'd normally wear when going out? Part two is pretty casual."

"Okay, well now I have more questions."

"You'll just have to wait until I pick you up to find out," he teases.

"Oh? And what time will that be?"

He purses his lips and looks up to the right as he calculates how much time each activity will take. "Four-thirty," he says finally and with conviction.

"Interesting," I say.

He chuckles at me and asks, "What?"

"Just that I can't quite figure out exactly what we'll be doing."

"And...?"

"And," I pause for a moment then answer truthfully. "I like it. It'll be a good surprise."

For the past five years, I've made every decision for myself. From the most significant choices all the way down to the mundane, I've never let anyone decide for me — I never could. So any surprise that came my way was never a welcome one.

It started out of necessity, and remains one: Do I stay in this place or do I move on and keep searching? Do I give up and let Darius win or do I fight him to the end? Do I trust this person or do I stay guarded?

It's nice for the first time in a long time to allow someone else to have a say on the small stuff. To relax and trust someone enough to let them take the reins for a bit.

Matt and I sit quietly for another ten minutes or so. He's stroking my arm lightly as we sit and people watch. There's a silence between us, but it's comfortable. It's as it the intimacy between us has been around for years rather than for a week.

I may appear serene on the outside, but my brain is never quiet for long. And it just kicked into overdrive analyzing everything about the man I'm resting against.

I obviously trust him enough to be beginning a... a what? A relationship with him? But, can I trust him with everything? I keep thinking in my head what I know about him, specifically about his friendship with Cali.

I've made the choice to trust Cali implicitly. I've put my faith in her and know she's someone I can count on. And Cali and Matt have been best friends since they were very young. So, if I can trust her doesn't that mean I can trust him too?

And I obviously feel comfortable with him. Each time I've kissed him, I'm left wanting something more. I'm sitting here leaning against him, and yeah maybe my mind won't shut up, but I'm also not itching to get away from him either.

I let out what I hope sounds like a sigh of contentment, rather than one of slight consternation just before the alarm I set on my phone goes off signaling that our lunch break is almost over.

"I guess we should get back," Matt says before I can. "You shouldn't be late from lunch two days in a row."

I nod and stand up first since I'm technically pinning Matt to the bench. I throw our garbage out in one of the many large pails placed throughout the park.

Matt wastes no time in reaching for hand and intertwining our fingers. We hold onto each other for the entirety of the short walk back to the library.

Rather than go in through the main entrance, we use my keycard to go in through a locked side door that leads to one of the stairways. From there I can go right down to the basement and Matt can go into the library.

It's a secluded spot, so before parting ways to go back to our respective areas, I pin Matt to the wall and kiss him until we are both left completely breathless. My second alarm goes off that it's really time to get back to work. I groan in frustration and take a step away. But Matt quickly pulls me back to him to kiss me again.

I finally pull completely away from him. I want to give him one more kiss but I know if I do, I won't be able to stop. I backpedal until my back touches the door that leads to the basement. Matt watches me with a look promising there is more to come. So much more.

• 3 9 •

Cali

She's sprawled across the covers of the bed, not quite asleep nor fully awake. The bed feels different though, smaller for some reason. Even the pillows and sheets don't smell like they usually do. There's a soft touch on her back. A hand rubbing gently up and down as she hears her favorite sound in the world.

Mickey's voice slowly worms through the warm fog in Cali's head. The sound is beckoning her to consciousness, but the heaviness of her eyes pulls her back toward her dreams.

"Cali... Caaal-lll... Baby..." Her girlfriend's soft voice sounds so far away that Cali easily starts to fall back into a deep sleep.

Suddenly a shout of, "Cali!" by Mickey and a loud bark from Milo sounds very close to her head.

The volume of it startles Cali out of any of her remaining grogginess. She yelps and rolls away from it taking the covers with her. Wrapped in a comforter burrito, she lands on the floor with a thud. Between the front door opening and closing she hears her roommate yell out a, "Thank you!"

"That was not nice," Cali grumbles while trying to disentangle herself from the down blanket surrounding her. She feels herself being lifted into the air bridal style, comforter and all. "Ooh, but this is."

Mickey sets her back onto the bed and moves the blankets to expose her girlfriend's face. She moves her face in close to give Cali a kiss but scrunches her nose and quickly pulls away.

"Jesus, baby," Mickey says making a face. "What did you eat last night?" Cali still wrapped up, just smirks at her. "Don't, it's too easy."

Cali raises an eyebrow at that. The brunette just rolls her eyes. Mickey helps the younger woman untangle herself and get out of bed.

"What were you doing in here anyway?" she asks as Cali heads to the bathroom to brush her teeth. Mickey crosses her arms and leans against the door jam.

"I couldn't sleep last night, so I got up I think around three. I saw that Lex's light was on and it sounded like she was talking to herself."

Cali puts some toothpaste on her brush and puts it in her mouth.

"I knocked on the door and she said come in. She was checking stuff online with my tablet and had a bunch of papers around her." She bends over the sink to spit and rinse. "She put them away quickly like she didn't want me to see. Then we started talking, and I must've fallen asleep in here."

Cali takes two steps to her left and finally gives Mickey a *good* good morning kiss. She presses into the taller woman and swipes her tongue across Mickey's lip. She opens her mouth and Cali deepens the kiss. She licks the roof of Mickey's mouth then rubs her tongue against the older woman's.

Mickey pushes her body against Cali's and maneuvers them so Cali's back is now flush against the other side of the door jam. As Mickey puts more of her body weight against her girlfriend and their kissing intensifies, she takes Cali's arms and pins them above her head.

As her hands hit the woodwork, Cali's brain flashes to yesterday. The sound of Milo's aggressive barks and the man's voice seeps into her brain. Her heartbeat picks up rapidly and not from having the body of her girlfriend so close.

"Stop," she says around Mickey's lips. "Stop, stop."

MY NAME IS NOT ALEXA PEARCE

Mickey immediately pulls back and looks in Cali's eyes. They're open wide, but with panic not desire. Mickey takes a step back and releases Cali completely. Her breathing is increasing rapidly and she's starting to hyperventilate.

"Oh my god, I'm so stupid," Mickey says. She doesn't move or touch Cali but continues talking to her. "I'm sorry, I wasn't thinking. I'm so sorry. Breathe baby, it's okay. You're safe, Cali. Everything's okay. Breathe with me."

Mickey starts taking slow deep breaths. Cali locks eyes with her girlfriend and mimics her breathing pattern. The older woman gradually increases the length of each inhale and exhale.

Milo who had gone back to lounge in the living room once Cali was up, comes trotting up to the couple now. He stops a few feet away and looks between the women, his head tilted in confusion. He tentatively takes the next few steps toward Cali and lets out a whiney whimper as he gently presses himself against her leg.

"I'm okay," Cali says. She pats Milo on the head. "I'm okay, Dog Man."

She puts her hands on her knees and takes one more deep breath. When she looks again at her girlfriend, Mickey's face is pale and her eyes are filled with worry and fear.

"Did I hurt you?" Mickey asks timidly.

"You didn't, no," Cali says shaking her head. "My brain just flashed back to yesterday."

"I'm so sorry Cali, I wasn't even thinking. Are you okay? I'm so stupid." The words tumble out of Mickey's mouth all rushed together.

"Stop," Cali says again. She moves to Mickey, Milo moving with her, and buries her face in the crook of her girlfriend's neck. "It's not your fault. I'm okay."

Mickey's arms circle the shorter woman and hold her tenderly. Her forehead is still creased with worry, she tilts her head so her cheek rests on the top of Cali's head. After a minute of them two holding each other, green eyes meet blue and the women share a soft kiss.

They part from their embrace and leave the bathroom. Cali plops onto the couch and turns on the TV. Mickey grabs her forgotten orange juice off the coffee table and goes to the kitchen. She takes down one of the boxes of cereal from above the fridge, grabs the biggest bowl from the cabinet, two spoons from a drawer, and the milk from inside.

Mickey takes out her phone and sends a text to Jack to cancel her appointments and classes for today and tomorrow. She waits for him to respond then puts her phone on the counter leaving it behind as she goes back to her girlfriend in the living room.

Mickey checks that Milo isn't on the couch before she plops down herself. He's curled up in a ball underneath Cali's feet that are perched on the table. Mickey pours the cereal, adds the milk, puts the box and carton on the coffee table, and hands Cali one of the spoons. They dig in together while watching a sitcom on a streaming service.

Cali pauses the episode and looks at Mickey without saying anything. Mickey's mouth curves up on one side as she looks back. She waits, letting the younger woman take her time. Cali's eyes travel all over Mickey's face, recording every inch.

When she returns her eyes to the blue ones staring back at her, Cali's eyes shine as they fill with tears. Mickey's face manages to soften and display concern at the same time. Still, she waits.

Cali clears her throat and nods her head sharply once. Mickey nods in return. Cali leans in and kisses her girlfriend on the lips. Everything she wants to say has already been communicated without words, but she says the words anyway to make herself doubly clear.

"I love you," she says.

"I know," Mickey says back in her soft, melodic voice. "I love you, too."

Mickey leans over to kiss the auburn hair of the woman next to her. Cali presses play on the remote and the sitcom on the screen in front of them continues.

The two women finish their shared bowl of cereal and the current episode. Leaving the cereal and empty bowl on the table, Mickey gets up to return the milk to the fridge so it doesn't spoil. She returns with two glasses of water. Cali has the next episode cued up and snuggles into her girlfriend as soon as she sits down. The couple spends the rest of the morning, and most of the afternoon, in that exact position watching successive episodes of the show.

Cali is uncharacteristically quiet, so Mickey is quiet too. She doesn't feel the need to fill the spaces with meaningless chatter. She knows Cali is still processing the last twenty-four hours and will give her the time to do so, she won't push her.

She'll be there whenever it is that Cali is ready to talk. Whether she wants to talk, or cry, or scream, or rage about yesterday, she's not going anywhere. Mickey will wait, and she will be here.

• 4 0 •

"ALEXA"

After peeling myself away from Matt, I go back to my cube. I got four books done this morning, so I get right back to translating *The Book.* I must've been more tired than I thought, because checking over what I did last night with the translator app on Cali's tablet, none of it makes sense.

I reenter the Latin into the app and what comes out is completely different than what I wrote down last night. Which means I'll have to redo everything I did last night.

I plan to start with the part on Victus and Extensios. If my gut feeling is right and Darius is a lot closer to finding me than I initially thought, it seems more and more likely that I'll need to make an Extensios or two.

I think Cali could handle it. Unless in my exhaustion last night I also imagined our conversation, she's open to the unknown of the supernatural world. Unknown to humans, that is. But changing Cali into an Extensios creates some challenges too, mainly Mickey and Matt.

Matt and I are just starting our relationship. I don't know if he can handle this, if *we* can handle this. I get a vivid image in my mind about me explaining to him or showing him my powers, his face contorting into *The Scream* by Edvard Munch, and then him literally running for the hills.

With Mickey, how could I ask Cali to leave her behind? They make me believe that people having soul mates is a real concept and not just a Hollywood fabrication. Their relationship is what I hope Matt and I are lucky enough to have — and work hard enough to achieve.

Telling Cali the entire truth, going through the process of becoming an Extensios, and then adding that there's a very real chance she may have to leave Mickey behind could immediately turn me into the bad guy.

If the roles were reversed I don't know if I could do it, so how can I ask Cali to give up the love of her life?

I don't even know how to make an Extensios yet! I grip my hair in frustration. I yell out loud at myself, "You're worrying about the wrong thing right now!"

I've been staring at my notebook for over half an hour, my mind circling. I haven't even begun the translations again. I'm thinking through scenarios in my head regarding Cali and Matt and Mickey; them as Extensios, them *not* as Extensios. Them helping me defeat Darius, or Darius getting *The Book...*

I'm going back and forth with if/thens over and over. I'm so lost in my head and my thoughts, that I don't hear the door to CCR1 open. I didn't expect anyone to come in so I don't have a book in front of me, not even *my* book, just my notebook.

"Alexa."

I gasp and nearly fall off the stool I'm perched on. *For someone with magically enhanced senses, you sure get snuck up on a lot, "Alexa."* I catch myself at the last possible moment and spin around to face my boss.

"Jeff!" I pant trying to slow my heartbeat. "You startled me." I put my hand over my heart before I say, "I'm sorry, I was just lost in my own thoughts for a moment."

"That's okay. I got your note that you were already here this morning," he says. "I just wanted to come down and check how things are going."

"Things are going well," I say. "I've gotten a few books done this morning before I went to lunch. I—"

"Wonderful," he cuts me off. "I would like to talk to you about payment for the extra time you'll be putting in on this project."

"Okay, sure."

"I've been able to get approval to pay you at your regular rate, plus time and a half for any time past your normal hours."

"Really? That's great. Thank you."

"Yes, however," he continues quickly with a slight huff, obviously impatient to just say what he has to say in full. "I could only get that approved for two days a week. So for this week, it will be today and tomorrow."

"Of course, I understand. Let me ask you something though," I say. "If I happen to stay later a few extra days, and I know I won't be paid past my normal hours, would that be okay to do?"

"You mean work without being paid?" he furrows his brow trying to understand what I mean.

"I mean, what if, for example, I'm in the middle of an entry for a book and it's six o'clock, and I stayed 'til seven or eight to finish it before going home, would that be acceptable?"

"I don't see why not. As long as you are aware that your wages would stop at the scheduled end of your shift?"

"I am."

"Then, yes that would be fine," he says. "Okay, well, I'll leave you to it then. I'll stop in again before I leave for the night."

"Sounds good, Jeff."

I get up and put the white gloves on, make my way to the shelves. Uncharacteristically, Jeff hangs around for a moment. He starts and stops a few times before fully expressing himself.

"How, um, ahem. How is your roommate?"

My eyebrows raise in surprise but I mask it with a smile. "She's okay... I think." My shoulders droop, "It's just, I still can't believe someone would grab onto her like that. It's just such a.... predatory kind of thing."

"Well," Jeff clears his throat again. "I hope that the footage you and Matt brought to the police station yesterday helps catch those men."

"Thank you, Jeff. I appreciate that. And I don't think I'll be able to thank you enough for thinking about the security footage. Hopefully it will help catch those creeps. I really think it will."

Jeff nods his head and takes a step backward in the direction of the door. Before he turns around I see a small, almost bashful smile on his face. He closes the door to CCR1 softly behind him and walks away after another quick look at me in the cube.

What was that look about? I ask myself.

Jeff's sudden unexpected expression of emotion, however subtle it may be, is one of the last things I need right now. I'm on a deadline of my own creation and cannot afford to miss it. To clear my mind of all the scenarios playing through it, I set myself up to do at least one more book before getting back to the decidedly more pressing issue.

I pull out the looseleaf marker and pick up the next book, *Ulysses* by James Joyce. I bring it over to the table and wake up the laptop. As I open the database and create a new entry, my eyes land on my open notebook and the thick line I've drawn between the word Extensios and Cali's circled name.

I hesitate and almost put *Ulysses* back on the shelf, my brain starting to circle through the if/thens again. *Stop,* I tell myself. *I need a reset, and it'll take less time to just do this entry now and then return to* The Book *rather than to keep waffling back and forth about it.*

As I flip through the first few pages taking photos and checking they upload clearly, I throw out a thank you to my previous years working in a library, my love of reading, and my advanced placement high school English classes. If I hadn't already read the majority of the books I've been cataloging, I'd have barely any time at all with *The Book*. I roll my eyes and think, *too bad I didn't take Latin in high school.*

I don't want to have to do the entry over so I slow down to type up the synopsis. I read over what I've written and then click save. I move the cursor across the screen to close the database and see that the entry I just made has a time stamp from a minute ago.

A light bulb goes off in my brain: if I make all the entries first thing, I can save them throughout the day which will make it appear as if the books I enter have taken me the whole day.

So if it takes me a half hour, maybe forty-five minutes at the most, to complete an entry, I'll leave it open for an extra ninety minutes before hitting save. I'll use that time to translate or study *The Book*.

I reopen the entry I did before lunch, before bringing *Ulysses* back to its shelf. I set a timer for ninety minutes on my phone to make a minor edit and save the entry.

Then I'll open and do the same with my entry for *Ulysses*, set the timer this time for two hours. When that's up, I'll take down the next book, which I see is *Moby Dick* by Herman Melville. *They really gotta work on the organization down here,* I can't help but think.

In the meantime, I have translations and studying to do. I stare at my notebook for another hour becoming more and more overwhelmed. A steel cage of doubt starts to encircle me as everything I don't know starts to add up on top of each other.

I've always been a pretty quick study. As a kid, after a couple of attempts or lessons at something new, I'd pretty much have it down. And that has relatively seamlessly translated to my adult life. So when I found *The Book* I figured I'd read it and study it and within a few days I'd know what to do.

I either severely underestimated my ancestors and my enemy, or I overestimated my quick study ability. Probably both.

Every time I open *The Book*, or my notes, I'm pulled in multiple directions. I have to have the purest of thoughts and intentions so that I don't give in to the temptation to just use my powers for whatever I want, good or bad. I have to translate the Latin that's written on the page simply to understand it. And, I have to make sure I don't recite a single thing out loud until I know what the words mean so I don't accidentally use my powers.

Plus, constantly swirling around my head, heart, and body are my growing feelings for Matt, my concern about Cali, my anxiety about being caught — by anybody — with *The Book*, the ache I have to see my family which I have to continually squash, and the as yet undecided way to explain all of this first to my roommate and then maybe to her girlfriend and best friend.

On top of all of that, I have this growing gut feeling that I'm in more danger now than I have ever been before. Even before Cali was attacked, basically as soon as I found *The Book*, I've felt like someone is looking over my shoulder, breathing down my neck.

And Victus being in Portland just confirms it: Darius knows where I am and could be here any minute.

I could find Darius right now and take the fight to him. But that would mean accessing powers that have been dormant for twenty-three years except for two times. And that was only to shield my family from my adversary and to get away from him myself.

I was told the story of the evil demon who is defeated by the good princess from the time I was born until the time I was told it wasn't just a story. So I know what powers I possess. But hearing about them in a story, or learning about them in a book, is completely different from internally connecting all the pieces of myself together to summon my powers to the surface to face someone who's had use of his powers for centuries.

Frankly, I don't know how to use my powers. I don't know how to control them once I access them. I don't know how to speak Latin properly. I don't know how to create an Extensios. I don't know. I don't know. I don't know!

I can feel the uneasiness starting to build in my chest. My palms are clammy and my vision is beginning to tunnel. I'm inches away from my first panic attack in almost two years.

I take ten deep, steadying breaths. Slowly in, hold, slowly out. I stop telling myself all the things I don't know and remember what I do.

The only thing I know with absolute certainty is that someone has to defeat Darius or it will be the end of the human world and the decimation of the good magical one too.

And by the ways of fate, the someone chosen to do it happens to be me.

After I count my breaths longe enough to return to normal, I make a mental hierarchy of the things I'll need to know and plan to tackle them one at a time. Because that's what I am going to do, what I *have* to do.

I am going to defeat Darius.

• 4 1 •

Darius

Damon and Julius returned to Atlanta three hours ago, and the black-haired man with tattooed hands has spent the last two and a half trying to convince Damon that joining him is something people simply don't say no to.

They're positioned at the back corner of the bar. Damon is sitting in a bar chair up against the wall, Darius seated in an identical chair facing him. His Victus flank him.

Now that he knows where the girl is with almost certainty, and why she must be where she is, Darius does not want to waste an extra day of recuperating from having to force Damon into becoming a Victus. He'd rather use the day to sneakily make his way out to the west coast, carefully flying under the girl's radar. But he'll do what he has to.

Damon is holding strong that he's not interested in whatever it is Darius and his little sidekicks are up to.

"I saw the look in your eyes when you spotted that blonde in here, little one," Darius says. He's switching between selling, intimidation, condescension, and baiting Damon that he's not "man enough" to join them. "You've got a vein of evil running through your body. I saw it as soon as you caught her in your crosshairs."

Darius leans in, invading Damon's personal space. "You are one of mine," he whispers.

Damon slowly shakes his head. He doesn't look at Darius, nor at Viribus or Julius. The demon sees light reflected in his eyes as the door to the bar opens and closes; Damon doesn't even squint.

"Need I remind you of the fate your buddies suffered because you were such a hard-headed piece of shit?"

That gets Damon's attention. His eyes harden with anger, and he finally levels his stony gaze at the thing in front of him. A tattooed hand comes up to rub a pale chin as the demon shakes his head dumbfounded.

"That's what gets you? That? I'm basically offering you free reign to do as you please... well as I please, really. Plus access to unlimited wealth. But crying over your useless, nothing friends is what gets a reaction from you?"

"I told you I'm not interested," Damon says through a clenched jaw. "I ain't no saint, but you guys are on a whole other level."

The man stands. The demon rises with him. The two are close in height, but Damon's muscular build outweighs Darius's lean frame by thirty pounds.

"I'm leaving now," Damon says.

"No," Darius sighs. "You're not."

The demon moves to the side allowing Viribus access to the man. Damon puts his hands up ready to fight his way out which causes the three in front of him to chuckle. When Damon drops his hands slightly, faltering at the trio's reaction, Viribus lunges.

The former tight end starts to struggle. It's been a while since Viribus has had anyone offer him an actual physical challenge, so rather than use his own power, he grapples with the man dragging him through the kitchen and out to the alleyway in back.

Damon yells for help the whole way, but as Darius rightly figured when he first set foot in this bar, you pay people enough and they become blind, deaf, and mute. Not a single patron or worker comes to Damon's aide.

Viribus slams Damon against the brick wall still sporting scorch marks from the last time Darius blew off some steam. Damon's breath audibly leaves him. He's held there but his body is slack, weakened by the lack of oxygen. He coughs and gasps trying to suck air into his starved lungs.

Darius takes off his jacket and throws it to Julius. He rolls the cuffs of his sleeves up three times on each arm. The tattoos on his hands continue up his forearms and disappear under his shirt. Viribus lets go of Damon but holds his arm up keeping the man in place with his power.

"No!" Damon cries. "Don't do this! Stop! No, no!"

Darius ignores the pleas and closes his eyes. He begins to recite in Latin:

Per vim, virtutem meam te esse maledicam.

By force, my power I curse to thee.

The demon brings his left hand up and says the spell two more times. The once pale hand turns as black as oil as the markings on it stretch and grow, encompassing the demon's skin. The hand hovers in the air an inch away from Damon's forehead. The blackness begins to creep up his arm, continuing up under the sleeve. Viribus flicks his arm, forcing Damon to his knees.

Darius sucks in an airy breath before continuing to speak.

"Corporalis motus animi." *Physical movement of the mind.* His voice sounds the same in pitch, but it echos as if there are one hundred of him speaking at the same time.

His hand extends, and just before it touches Damon, the demon opens his eyes. They are both bright red and as black as his hand at the same time.

"Don't —"

He reaches for Damon quickly and lays his hand on the man's head. The heel of his palm touching the forehead, the fingers stretching across the scalp.

Damon lets out an animalistic shriek of pain. The entirety of the blood vessels in his body slowly begins to turn black. From his head slinking down his neck and across his torso, to his arms down through his pelvis to his legs and toes. Each inch that the inky invader spreads evokes a roar of protest and torment.

With each howl of pain the man lets out, the demon holding onto him feels his own strength drain exponentially. Damon fights the transition the entire way, struggling against the grip on his head and the magic holding him in place.

Darius clenches on to Damon's head, chanting under his breath, "Ego ut malediceret tibi." *I curse to thee.*

He doesn't let go until he sees Damon's eyes become the same simultaneous red and black as his own. When they finally do, the demon releases his grip. Both demon and man fall to the ground, their energy depleted.

Julius and Viribus step into action now, both having been given explicit instructions before the plane even touched the tarmac. The plan is for Julius to hold the new Victus in place while Viribus gets their boss to safety. Then the two of them will teach Damon how to control himself before Viribus goes to stand guard over Darius.

The shorter of the two steps over and uses his power to keep Damon from moving from the ground while the giant scoops up the demon to carry him to safety.

Viribus cradles his boss gently as he moves back through the kitchen to the staircase leading to the room Darius has been using. He slowly lowers the comatose brute onto the mattress. After making sure he's as comfortable as can be, the Victus rushes back to the alley to check on his comrade and their new recruit.

When Viribus steps back into the dark alleyway, he sees Damon is writhing on the ground. Julius is trying to hold him in place, but now that they are equaled by having the same power, Damon's returning strength is slowly becoming enough to overpower the demon's number three.

Viribus puts his size-22 boot on Damon's chest. The footballer stares up through a creased brow, his fury clearly evident. His skin glistens with a sheen of sweat. His eyes have drained of the black that filled them but are still red, only now they're bloodshot as a result of his struggle.

"I said no!" Damon bellows. "I don't fucking want this!"

He thrashes his arms at the foot holding him down. Pieces of broken glass and splintered wood that litter the alley start flying through the air with Damon's movements. Julius counteracts any harm they could do by using his own power to swat the debris from the air.

When Damon sees what his arms are doing, he freezes. He looks down at his hands with his face slack. Julius and Viribus have seen this all before. They nod to each other and the giant Victus slowly removes the pressure of his foot on Damon's chest. Damon immediately tries to get up.

"Go slow," Viribus's baritone voice cautions.

The new Victus pays no mind choosing to stand up quickly. His vision swirls and he crashes back to his knees, then falls forward. His arms aren't quick enough to catch himself and he smacks his head on the pavement with a loud crack. He lifts his head slightly. Sporting a gash above his eye, he retches on Julius's shoes.

"Ah, come on you fucker," Julius whines shaking his foot out to the side. "Get your shit together, man."

Viribus helps the footballer get to his feet. He steadies him against the wall until Damon's eyes still enough to focus on him.

"Easy does it, little one," Viribus says. He lets go of Damon whose body is able to retake its own weight.

"Now, I have other things to do, so Julius is going to give you a crash course on what's going on inside you right now and your new job."

Damon's eyes zero in on Julius and narrow in anger. Viribus smacks him hard across the face to get the attention back on himself. Droplets of blood from the cut on his face are flung onto the bricks, splattering across the wall.

"You're new to this, moron, we aren't," he points between himself and the demon's number three, then shoves his finger in Damon's chest. "You do what we say.

"You need to control what's happening inside you right now, 'cause if you don't, you won't last long. Consider that lesson one."

He steps away from Damon and lets Julius take over.

"Lesson two," the short and wide Victus says jumping in. "You're on a short leash until you learn. A very. Short. Leash. And we control that leash."

Viribus raises one eyebrow to punctuate Julius's last statement.

• 236 •

"Lesson three," the giant says. "You're still technically human and we can and will easily kill you if you piss us off. So don't."

● 4 2 ●

"ALEXA"

I spent the rest of Thursday making a list and prioritizing the things on it. The most important items right now are my Extensios, how to make them and *who* to make (Cali? Matt? Mickey?); to tell Cali about who I really am, and deal with her reaction; and, figure out what to do with Darius — how was the curse put on him, and do I have to kill him or can I curse him again?

Translating and reading about Extensios took the majority of the rest of the day. I couldn't get my brain to concentrate for more than a few minutes at a time. Even when I tried to reset and enter a book into the database and then return to my notes, my brain just could not stay focused.

I went upstairs to get a candy bar from the vending machine hoping the sugar rush would rejuvenate me enough to get down to business. No dice.

Plus, I saw Matt as I walked out of the lounge area and, just like a movie, our eyes locked. He stared me down with a look filled with barely concealed lust and yearning. When I finally tore myself away to go back down to the sub-basement, I had to talk myself down from the arousal that was threatening to further derail my day.

I had just gotten down to work on *Moby Dick* when I got a text from Cali asking if I would be home for dinner. Then a quick text followed it saying that Mickey had just reminded her I was working late. Which then turned into a two-hour text conversation.

No matter what I tried, I got too easily overwhelmed and Thursday was a complete wash. I didn't get any further in understanding Extensios, or how to make one for that matter.

I left the library at 9 PM making sure each door locked securely behind me since I was alone in the building. Walking home I felt weighed down with guilt that I had essentially gotten nothing done, potentially putting myself and my friends in imminent danger.

****

The bad feeling that was filling my chest Thursday on my way home is still with me Friday morning when I wake up.

I didn't sleep well last night and I still haven't recovered from my previous late night. I wanted to get to the library early again today but barely make it on time. Thankfully Mickey is a morning person and after taking one look at me this morning, she took pity and offered to take Milo on his morning walk. If I had to walk him too, I definitely would've been late.

As I open the main door of the sub-basement, I rummage through my bag past my notebook, the tablet, my wallet, and keys, to find my phone. I send Matt a text that I'm sorry I didn't see him this morning but I was running late. He types back asking about lunch again today. I want to say both yes and no; I want to spend as much time with him as I can, but I also want to do as much work on *The Book* today as possible.

I text him back that I've fallen behind a little and I'm going to work through lunch. I grimace as I watch the three-dot text bubble appear, then disappear, then appear again. But the response I get from him quiets and calms my rising insecurity.

> **MATT:** ok no problem. maybe i'll you see you later?

> **LEX:** i'm working late again today, probably until about 9. but i'll definitely see you tomorrow

> **MATT:** ok i'll call you later babe

Even if I were using all of my powers right now, none of them would be strong enough to stop the fluttering of my heart. Dear lord! A cute boy pays attention to me and calls me babe, and I'm acting like the female lead in a sappy romance novel.

Umm, greatest evil to walk the earth? End of the human world, "Alexa"??

"Right," I say out loud agreeing with my inner monologue. "No messing around today."

I set myself up for the day: Laptop booted up and database open; notebook, tablet, and *The Book* close by but out of sight; phone on with the timer app cued up; white gloves on.

First book up for the day? *Crime and Punishment* by Dostoyevsky, which is thankfully another book I'm already familiar enough with. It takes me exactly twenty-seven minutes to finish the database entry. I hit save but don't start a new entry. Instead, I set my timer for ninety minutes and get to work on *The Book*.

I spend the time until my alarm blares re-translating everything that I got wrong during my sleep deprived delirium two nights ago making sure I've left nothing out and it all makes sense. I make some minor changes in the computer and hit save to update the timestamp and close the entry.

The next book on the shelf is *Madame Bovary* by Gustave Flaubert. Unfortunately, I haven't read it, so I actually spend the next two hours skimming through to be able to type up the synopsis.

I put the Madame back and take down the next which is *Hamlet* by Shakespeare. Easy peasy. It only takes me twenty minutes flat to complete the entry. I set my timer for two hours, take a deep, steadying breath and get ready to learn how to make an Extensios for myself.

If I'm understanding the translation correctly, I say a chant in Latin three times. After the third time, my hand will glow with a bright white light. I then say what the power is that I'm giving, and place my hand on top of the head of the person who has volunteered to become an Extensios.

Once my hand is on their head I say, "I gift to thee" in Latin. Everything is in Latin so I really have to get it right. I don't know what the consequences are if I mispronounce something or say it in the wrong order.

I also don't know yet if saying it out loud in English will set anything in motion, so I decide not to say anything until I know for sure.

I write down the order of what I say, first in English then in Latin, on a fresh page in my notebook. And then underneath that, I write Cali's name again and underline it.

I keep going back to Cali as the best choice. I take out my phone — I have less than forty-five minutes left on the timer — and I send a message to my roommate asking her what she's doing on Sunday. I get a quick response that Mickey has to work since she took off all day today, yesterday, and half of the day before, so Cali is entirely free. I suggest a roommate day of just the two of us, and Cali jumps at the idea.

Okay, good. Now all I have to do is figure out how to tell her exactly who I am in a way that doesn't convince her to have me committed. Great.

I go back to *The Book* to make sure I haven't missed anything on Extensios. It appears that I've translated everything I can. I turn to a fresh page again and flip to the next page in *The Book*. I'm hoping to find something about the powers I possess and how to use them.

My non-fluent eyes scan the page for the only word I know for sure in Latin: *imperium.* It means power. I don't see it on the page I'm on, or on the next page, or the next. *The Book* isn't very long, its depth more from the thickness of the sheets than the number of them. My stomach drops as I come to the back cover without seeing "power" anywhere.

I feel the panic rising within me and the blood rushes in my ears making me hear a loud, blaring sound. The noise gets louder and louder until I realize the noise is coming from my phone going off. I turn off the sound but it does nothing to abate my own alarm.

Of course, I know what powers I have. I've known since I was young because of the stories about the princess who is the only one able to defeat the demon. Granted, I didn't exactly know *I'm* the princess. But, the story never told me how to use my powers, just that I have them.

I put *Hamlet* back in its place, exchanging it for *Anna Karenina* by Tolstoy. As I put it down next to the laptop, the unease about not immediately finding something on my powers in *The Book* is replaced by a thunderous rumbling in my stomach. I guess only having a granola bar for breakfast wasn't the best idea. I quickly check the time on my phone screen and it's already 3:30 PM.

"No wonder I'm hungry," I say. "You're going to have to wait a minute, Anna."

I hide *The Book* so it's not immediately visible to anyone who could possibly come into CCR1 while I'm gone. I grab my wallet and my ID card and run up to the lounge behind the front desk to raid the vending machines. I get a blue sports-drink from one and two bags of chips from the other. I turn to leave, then think twice and get the same kind of candy bar as yesterday.

I stick my head out and check around to make sure I'm not going to run into Jeff or Matt, and scurry back to the door leading to the basements.

If I stay again until nine tonight, like I've been asked to, then I have five and a half more hours on the day. And unfortunately for me, I haven't read *Anna Karenina* or the next one on the shelf which is *Middlemarch* by George Eliot.

I eat one of the bags of chips and drink half the blue ade. Making sure my hands are clean, I pull on the white gloves and take the photos of Tolstoy's book. I go back and forth on whether or not to do a Google search instead of spending the time flipping through the pages when a lightbulb goes off in my brain.

"The movie!" I shout. I remember I'm in a library, so I quickly look around to see if I bothered anyone. *You're down here alone, "Alexa"... but it may be time for some human contact soon.*

Anyway, a few years ago *Anna Karenina* was made into a movie. While I don't know if it followed the book verbatim, I assume it followed closely enough that I could write a synopsis about it. I decide to just do that and give myself more time with *The Book*. I quickly type up the general arch of the storyline and then put it away.

After I set the timer, I start at the beginning to understand how my ancestors cursed Darius. I want to know exactly what they did and how. I want to know if I could just do that again or if the only way this story ends is with me truly ending Darius.

When my alarm goes off again bringing me back to my reality, I groan in frustration. It's such slow going to have to translate each page. I slam my hand down on the table in irritation. Try as I might, I cannot get rid of the bad feeling that is starting to overwhelm me again.

I know in the deepest center of myself that I am the closest I have ever come to finally winning this battle against Darius. But I also know that Darius is the closest *he's* ever come to reaching me. Still, the answers I've long sought which are finally right in front of me are, even now, just out of reach.

I wish I could just use my power of projection and give myself the ability to understand Latin. If I'm making wishes, then let's add every language while I'm at it, too. But that would be an unwarranted use of my powers for my own personal benefit, which even I know is a huge violation of my own abilities and responsibilities.

It's now just about the closing time of the library. I'm anticipating a stop in by Jeff any moment. But instead, I get a text from Matt saying Jeff had to leave and if I had any questions to write them down for Sam to ask him tomorrow. I throw up a thank you to the universal powers that be for one less distraction.

As I move the few paces to take *Middlemarch* from the shelves, I mentally go over the cliffs-notes of what I learned the last two hours from *The Book*:

1. Darius's entrance into this world created a giant scorched crack on the Earth's surface
2. He immediately began killing humans and magical creatures, causing pervasive evil to spread
3. His appearance caused the world to become a dark place as soon as he set foot on it, and that darkness lasted for another two-hundred years until he was cursed
4. The most powerful of each of the magical beings on earth came together to curse him. They pooled all of their collective magic to do so. The curse was able to stop Darius from fully opening the portal he created, thus preventing all of the demons of Darius's homeland from coming to earth
5. The curse will be broken only by the defeat of Darius's magical equal and him taking her powers to add to his own. Only then will he finally be able to set free his demon brothers and sisters on Earth

"The only way this ends," I say out loud realizing the full truth of the matter, "is with his death by my hands."

I put the book by George Eliot down next to the laptop and stay stock still.

"The only way this ends is with his death by my hands," I say again.

Hearing it in my own voice makes it more real, but somehow also less overwhelming. With a slightly calmer head, I open the front cover of *Middlemarch* and begin to catalog it.

When I'm finished with it, my day here is finished too. As I bring *The Book* back to it's resting place and slide it onto its shelf, I say out loud one more time, "The only way this ends is with his death by my hands."

I know that right now I can't defeat Darius without at least some help. I also know that Darius is coming for me. And that I won't be able to get back into this room and this very spot until Monday. Taking *The Book* with me right now seems more and more like my best option, but ultimately a simple realization dawns on me.

It's been here the whole time and he didn't know it.

If I steal *The Book* and Darius is somehow able to track it once it's taken out of what is basically a concrete bunker, then it will bring him straight to me. Which I am clearly not ready for. It's safer to leave it here camouflaged amongst the others and protected by the many walls around it.

I pack up my things and leave the library for the night telling myself the same thing about *The Book* as I do my family — *it's safe.*

For now.

• 4 3 •

Milo tries to wake me on Saturday morning with repeated, small whimpers. I grunt and roll away from the sound onto my stomach. That was apparently the wrong decision because next thing I know, the wind is knocked out of me by a sixty-five-pound dog landing hard on top of me.

I open my eyes and see the blurry outline of the clock on my nightstand. My eyes are still heavy with sleep so I can't even see what time it reads. I assume it's late enough that Milo is either hungry, thirsty, has to go out, or some combination of all three.

I turn my face stuffing it into my pillow and let out a muffled groan. Milo moves to the side of me and sticks his nose right under my ear. Then he starts sniffing. The quick little puffs of air from him breathing in and out start to tickle. I giggle which only spurs my pup on. He sniffs my messy bun and around the collar of my shirt.

When he pushes his face into my pillow and wedges his head between it and my own, I can't help but lift my head away from the soft, warm place it was resting. The movement gives Milo access to my face, and he starts licking it furiously.

"Okay, okay," I laugh. "I'm up!"

Milo stops licking but uses his body to nudge me until I'm up kneeling on my bed. I rub my eyes and face to wipe the sleep away. I open my mouth for a big yawn before stretching my arms above my head.

"Okay, one? You need a mint," I say to the big fur ball in front of me. "And two, what do you want first? A walk or food?"

Milo bounds off the bed and jumps at my closed bedroom door. When I open it for him after putting on my glasses, he trots past the front door of the apartment and goes right to the kitchen.

"Food it is," I say.

I go back into my bedroom and slide my feet into slippers and grab my phone off the charger. I walk into the kitchen and go through the motions of feeding Milo. My eyes are still heavy, and it isn't until I'm refilling his water bowl that I see the sticky note on the faucet.

On a run, back soon- M&C

I put Milo's bowl down and then decide what I want to make myself for breakfast. I take out the box of pancake mix, and after staring at it for a few minutes through heavy eyes, I choose frozen waffles instead because they're just easier.

Once the toaster pops, I drizzle my waffles with some syrup and strawberry jam. I make myself a glass of chocolate milk and bring my very adult breakfast to the couch in my living room. I turn on the TV and flip through until I find something that fits my meal: cartoons.

When my food is finished, I put my dishes in the sink and go back to my bedroom. I get dressed in comfy clothes and strip my bed. I put all of the sheets into one of the pillowcases and put my comforter and some of my laundry into a canvas laundry bag.

I run to the bathroom to brush my teeth, then strap Milo into his harness. I'm about to open the door when I remember quarters. And that I don't have any. I throw my head back, sigh, and drag my laundry back to my bedroom.

Milo trots after me panting heavily, all revved up to go for his walk. I can't tell him now that we're not going anywhere, so I decide to take him to the ATM and get some money to put into my box. I grab my phone and wallet, and tuck my keys into my pocket.

I open the door, and Milo and I step out. As I'm locking the door, I hear the door on the floor below open. Milo's chest rumbles as he lets out a low growl. He's on alert, ready to defend, but I give him a soft tug on the leash and hold a finger to my lips when he looks at me. *Be quiet.*

I peek over the railing of the stairs and see the top of Tyler's greasy head. He puts on bulky headphones and saunters down the stairs. I give him a solid minute head start to avoid running into him. I'm finally about to head down the stairs when I hear footsteps coming up from below me.

I give Milo the same signal to be quiet as we hear the footsteps get louder. I peek over the railing again and then the voice reaches me. Two of them actually. It's Cali and Mickey. Milo's tail starts whipping back and forth as he hears his friends coming.

"Hey!" I greet them meeting them on the landing outside of Tyler's apartment.

"Lex! Dog Man!" Cali squeals. Milo's body starts to vibrate as his tail wags faster and faster.

"You guys going for a walk?" Mickey asks.

"Yeah, not a very long one though."

"Well, don't take too long," Cali says. "You're being picked up in a couple hours."

"What?!" I check the time on my phone and it's already two in the afternoon. "The fuck? Where did the time go?"

"We knew you had a couple of long days," Cali starts.

"So we decided to let you sleep in," Mickey finishes. "We took Milo on a walk this morning."

"He was whining at your door though so we let him back in when we got back before."

"But, we were going to wake you up when we got back now if you weren't already up so you could get ready for your date with Matt."

"I have to say I'm very proud I haven't spilled the beans on what Moose has planned."

I'm getting whiplash looking back and forth between the couple. I shake my head and say, "Wait."

Cali and Mickey look at me expectantly. Even Milo is looking at me.

"What *does* he have planned?"

Cali opens her mouth but Mickey jumps in before she can say anything. "Nice try, Lex. You only have a couple more hours to wait and then you'll see yourself."

Cali points at me and narrows her eyes. "Oooh, you're a tricky one, Ms. Pearce."

I narrow my eyes right back at her and smile.

"Well, clearly you two have both talked to Matt about our date. So, since you know what the rest of my day looks like, will you help me get ready when Milo and I get back from our walk?"

Mickey and Cali look at each other with grins before they simultaneously say, "Definitely."

"Thank you," I nod to Cali then turn to nod at Mickey, "and thank you."

Cali tips an imaginary hat at me as Milo and I maneuver around the couple and continue down the stairs.

I walk Milo a few times through our neighborhood. I stop at the bank and check the balance of my account. There's almost $5,000 in this account.

Each of my identities has accounts set up with small amounts of money. But it becomes tricky to access those once the names fall out of use. And it creates a link between the identities if I transfer money from one account to another. So I try to keep the money in them low that way I don't leave much behind when I become someone new.

Since there's more evidence now than ever before that Darius is very close, I decide to take out almost all of what's in this account right now. I don't know when I'll next have the opportunity to. I can only take out $300 at a time from the ATM so I do thirteen transactions. I would just go inside the bank but one, it's already closed; and two, it's one of the only places Milo is absolutely *not* allowed in.

I check around me to make sure I'm not about to be robbed holding $3,900 in twenties. I give Milo his "casual" command as an extra precaution and after making sure I have all my cash and my ATM card tucked away in my wallet, my pup and I head home.

After I open my apartment door, I bend down to unhook Milo. When I stand, I look around my apartment but don't see Cali or Mickey. The TV is on in the living room with a reality show playing, but the only one on the couch watching it now is Milo. I move over to him and ruffle his fur before I take my bag into my bedroom to put the extra cash in my box.

When I step into my room, thankfully with my hand still hidden inside my bag, Cali and Mickey are standing side by side facing my closet in matching poses; eyes narrowed, one hand on the hip, fingers from the other drumming across the chin.

I stop short and look back and forth between them. I slowly remove my hand from my bag — sans cash — and adjust my glasses. When they still haven't noticed I'm standing there staring at them, I clear my throat. The couple startles as they finally see me.

"Oh good, you're back!" Cali sighs with relief.

"We need you to settle this for us," Mickey chimes in.

"Settle what?" I ask.

"What you should wear on your date. Duh." My roommate looks at me with a dumbfounded expression.

"I already know what I'm going to wear," I say as I walk past them and put my bag down on my bed. I turn back to face them, and I see two very expectant looks.

"Whatever Cali says—"

"Yes!" My roommate shouts. She turns to her girlfriend, "Ha! I win!"

"I'm not finished," I say.

Cali's triumphant expression drops. Mickey leans over slightly and goes, "Ha."

Cali grumbles a "whatever" in response and sticks her tongue out at both of us.

"I'm going to wear whatever Cali says for part two. And whatever Mickey says for part one."

"Interesting," Cali says, pondering my response.

"Diplomatic," Mickey adds.

"All I know is that it's two parts. And the two of you obviously know what both of them are, so it makes the most sense. I trust you."

"Well, that was easy," Mickey says. Cali nods along silently.

"Okay!" Cali says clapping her hands three times. "First things first, you go take a shower."

The couple leaves me in my bedroom to undress and get my things together for a shower. When Cali closes the door behind her, I dart over to extract the box hidden beneath my mattress. I use the key around my neck to unlock it and transfer ninety percent of the wad of cash from my bag to the box before returning it to its spot. I strip down and grab my towel and fresh underwear to take a shower.

I take my time in the shower making sure I'm thoroughly clean, that I'm smooth in the places I want smooth, and that I smell like green apple from head to toe. Laid out on my bed are the expertly picked outfits I'll wear tonight, both of which look like they were plucked from magazine spreads.

My roommate calls out to me asking if I'm dressed and ready for her to do my hair. I tell her I am and the next thing I know, both her and Mickey are in front of me pulling me back into the bathroom and plopping me down on the closed toilet.

When Matt knocks on the door at exactly 4:30, I'm in my bedroom gently packing the clothes I'll be changing into in my gym bag. Cali is flitting around me touching up my mascara, so Mickey opens the door. She lets Matt in and tells him that I'm almost ready.

Cali leaves my bedroom and greets her best friend. I take a steadying breath before exiting my room. When Matt sees me a big smile brightens his face. He's wearing dark gray athletic shorts and a plain white t-shirt with a black hoodie over it. It easily compliments my black capri leggings, dark gray tee and white thermal tied around my waist. I catch Mickey's eye. She looks at Cali first, then winks at me.

They obviously planned this.

"You ready to go?" Matt asks.

"Absolutely," I answer.

• 4 4 •

"Cali, I have to talk to you."

It's mid-morning on Sunday, the day after my date with Matt, and it's also the day I decide I'm going to tell her the truth.

"Before you say anything else," she responds. "I want to know every detail from your date with Moose."

I know she won't budge so rather than say I'll tell her later, it's easier to just get it out of the way and tell her now.

****

"You ready to go?" Matt asked.

"Absolutely," I said.

Matt took my bag for me and we left my apartment. When we walked out the main entrance of my building, I saw a navy blue coupe double parked in the street with its hazard lights on. Matt went over and opened the trunk putting my bag inside. Then he came and opened the front passenger door for me. I got in and Matt closed the door. He went around the front of the car and got into the driver's seat.

"So, where are we going?" I asked as I buckled my seat belt.

"You'll see," was all he said.

He started the car and went up Jefferson making a right onto SW Sixth Avenue. He drove seven blocks and made another right onto SW Alder Street which he followed onto and over the SE Morrison Bridge. Across the bridge, we got right on to SE Belmont Street. Matt followed that for a few miles until he made a final right onto SE 60th Avenue and then a left on SE Salmon Street. He parked the car and turned off the engine. It took us a half hour start to finish with the traffic.

I think Matt was getting a little flustered with the time, I tell Cali.

"You only need to bring your phone, I've got everything else," he said to me.

He got out and went around to the trunk. I got out also, and as I closed my door, he closed the trunk wearing a backpack. He took my hand and led me to the entrance of Mount Tabor Park.

"Okay, there are a few trails we can do. The soft surface is my personal favorite, but there are other ones." He looked at me for my input.

"Soft surface sounds good," I said. "As long as it has a peak to it."

"Soft surface it is," he said.

Matt started walking the closest trail very sure-footed. I followed him less sure. It's been a while since I've done any sort of hiking. He asked me about where I grew up if there were trails around there. I deflected as much as possible, but I don't tell Cali that.

We came down and went around what I thought was a lake, but Matt told me it's one of the city reservoirs. We loop back through the trees through a clearing passing the reservoir again. Then we started what felt like, and ended up being, a wide sloping loop that was the bulk of the hike.

We ended up at a clearing that was high enough to see a lot of the city. Matt took out two water bottles and granola bars from his backpack. We saw downtown to the west and Mount Hood way in the distance to the northeast. Matt pointed everything out to me, I'm not good with direction.

We stayed at the top long enough to see the sun start to set over the city. It got a bit chilly so I put my thermal on and Matt pulled me close. We took a picture with the city framed behind us and the sky a bunch of colors.

I show it to Cali and she tells me that we "look so good together".

Before it got too dark, we made our way back down stopping at the famous volcano "crater." We passed a playground and Matt pointed out Mount St. Helens in the background. I could just see it, but night was coming quick and it was almost too dark to tell.

When we got back to the car, it was almost completely dark. Matt put his backpack into the trunk and took out another bag as well as my own. He pointed out the restrooms, and we split up to changed.

I took my hair out of my ponytail and freshened up before putting on the clothes Cali had laid out for me beforehand: super tight, light wash jeans and a mocha colored sweater (that I again didn't know I had). She gave me a slouchy off-white scarf to use later if I got chilly. She had put a pair of Mickey's heels on the bed, but I nixed that so I put on a pair of slip-on Vans.

Matt was waiting for me outside when I finished dressing. He had on a chocolate brown button down, the perfect shade jeans that must have been tailored specifically for him, with a brown leather belt and brown shoes. He whistled as he got a full look at me and I told him he looked amazing.

"Not as good as you," he responded.

We looked like a couple. That's all I could think about as we got back into the car. I didn't pay attention to where he drove, I just couldn't stop looking at him.

We parked nearby at Wolverine Brewery and went in for dinner. Before our meals came, we did a tasting of all eight beers they make and each picked a favorite. Matt had me laughing so hard that the beer threatened to fly out of my nose. He filled me in on what I had missed the last few days being holed up in the basement.

I told him how sometimes it's pretty interesting down there, and other times it feels like my brain has gone numb. I left out what I've actually been doing down there and immediately felt guilty about it.

After we finished eating, I excused myself to the bathroom as the waiter cleared our plates. When I came back, Matt had three white roses in his hand. I don't know where he got them or how he knew, but white roses are my favorite flower. He handed them to me as the waiter came back with full mugs of each of our picks from the tasting.

The conversation was easy. It was funny, it was light, it was as if we'd been like this for years. I asked him to tell me more about what it was like growing up with Cali, he asked me my favorite story about my mother. We kept touching each other — light rubs of the arm, his hand at the small of my back guiding me, me holding his hand in the car, he took my hand at the table and brought it to his lips kissing the inside of my wrist.

He picked up the check and we walked back to the car hand in hand. When he was about to open the door for me, I stopped him and pushed him against the car. I had been holding myself back the entire night, but I just couldn't help it anymore. I kissed him with a salaciousness I didn't know I had.

When I say this to my roommate, she smacks my shoulder and says, "Damn, Lex!"

He flipped us around and pressed himself into me. I gripped the collar of his shirt in both of my hands pulling him closer to me. I swiped my tongue across his lip and he opened his mouth to me, he tasted like beer and barbecue sauce.

It was as if the dream I had had a week ago was coming true. His touch set my body on fire. I wanted all of him. One of his hands went around my waist, and then the other trailed down to my—

****

"Whoa! Whoa!" Cali cuts me off before I can give her any more juicy details. "Moose is like my brother, Lex. I don't really want to hear the naughty details."

"Okay," I laugh. "Well, then how about I just sum up the rest of the night?"

"Yes, I think that would be best."

"Well after an intense make-out that left both of us wanting more," I look at her with purpose. "I know because I could see and feel it."

Cali sticks her fingers in her ears and goes, "La-la-la-la-la."

I take her hands away from her head and say, "He dropped me off and we said goodnight."

"Sounds like it was a good time."

My face warms as I replay the entire night again in my head at warp speed. I can't deny anymore how much I like Matt, and it makes my whole body respond knowing that he likes me that much too.

"It was the best date I've ever been on."

"Oh my god, that's so cute!" my roommate teases me. She laughs at me a bit as I fan myself.

"So, what did you want to talk to me about?"

Oh, right. My light, bubbly mood changes quickly to a more serious, sober one.

"Right," I take a deep breath. "We've known each other a while now, right?" Cali nods.

"And I've told you before I'm slow to trust, and you respected that completely. But now you know that I trust you, right?"

"Right."

"Okay, so there is something I want to tell you, but I don't know how you'll respond to it, but I really want you to know because I trust you and I think you can handle it, and I could definitely use your help with it, but I also hope you won't hate me—"

"Lex, slow down," Cali interrupts me. She takes my hands in hers and holds tight. "Just tell me. Whatever it is, I promise I'll listen."

I open my mouth, but no sound comes outs. Now that the moment is here, it's harder than I thought it would be.

"I'mthereasonyougotattacked." I blurt it out all as one word and then I freeze and stare at my roommate.

Cali's brow is furrowed as she first tries to understand what I've said then what it means. "Wait, what?"

"I'm sorry, that's not what I meant to say."

"Okay, then try again. 'Cause I have no idea what you mean."

"Can I just talk and you wait until I'm done? I think that might make this easier."

"Yeah, sure."

"Okay," I exhale again. "Okay. I don't know specifically who the men are who attacked you, but I know why they were in Portland. They were here looking for me. The reason Milo reacted so strongly to them is because, in my world, they are what's called Victus. They are the soldiers of demons, actually of one in particular.

"Milo can sense evil and supernatural beings like a Victus because he has powers of his own, and has been trained to protect me, and the people I love, from them. He can also understand everything you, or I, or anyone says, on top of his enhanced abilities.

"So, the reason those guys were here for me is because I'm a witch. Well, I'm actually a descendant of multiple magical species, but witch is easiest to explain. Not which, like which one. But witch like pointy hat and broomstick. Not that I wear a pointy hat or fly on a broom."

Cali squeezes my hands which stops me from spiraling off topic. I take a deep breath before I continue.

"I, umm, I have powers, like magical ones. And I'm being pursued, well, hunted really, by a powerful demon named Darius who wants to kill me and take my powers so he can open the portal to his home world — a place that is literally worse than what we know as hell. And if that happens, it will be the end of the human world as we know it.

"I've been on the run for five years searching for the key to defeating Darius, and, I guess for lack of a better term, saving the world. And I have finally found it. It's a book literally called *The Book,* and it's been in the basement of the library for years. I don't know how it got there, but I guess that's not really important.

"*The Book* in Darius's hands would be very dangerous. It means the end of me, us, of all of this. And I think he somehow knows I found it, which is why those guys were here in Portland.

"Basically, I need your help, Cali. Now that I've found *The Book*, I can use it to stop Darius. But I can't do it alone."

Cali won't look directly at me. Her eyes move from her hands in mine, to Milo who is curled up at my feet, to the TV that is turned off. She slowly pulls her hands away and rests them in her lap. The rejection of her pulling away hurts so much more than I thought it would.

Finally, she looks me in the eye. "I don't even... I mean, what are..." Cali starts and stops, her words getting caught in her throat. "Lex..."

I wince and clear my throat before I say, "There's one more thing."

"My name is not Alexa Pearce."

PART THREE

• 4 5 •

Cali

"Wait, what?"

Alexa starts and stops multiple times but Cali jumps in again before she gets out a full thought.

"It sounded like you just said your name isn't your name."

Alexa looks down at her lap and quietly mumbles "It's not."

"Okay, then what exactly is your name?"

Her roommate won't look up. She starts scratching at a seam on her sleeve. "I, uh, I can't tell you that."

"You can't tell me that."

"No, not just yet."

Cali stands up from the couch and starts to pace in front of the TV. Milo sits up from his spot under Alexa's feet. He stays seated, but his head turns to follow Cali's movements back and forth. She runs her hands through her auburn hair. She looks up at the ceiling and lets out a long sigh.

"Okay, let's recap," she says. Alexa still won't look directly at her.

"Hey," Cali says waving her hands in front of her. "You trusted me enough to tell me all of this. Could you please look at me?"

Alexa finally looks up and makes eye contact with her roommate. "Okay, can you trust me now to just like, process all of this?"

Alexa nods.

"Alright, so let me see if I've got this right, and feel free to jump in if I get something wrong. You are not just a librarian, you are a witch who is on the run from a really old demon who wants to kill you, steal your powers, and use them to open the portal to his home which is very similar to what we know as hell, and that would be the end of the world."

"As we know it, yes."

Cali holds both index-fingers up and turns her head away. In a clipped tone she says, "Not done."

"Sorry."

Cali resumes her pacing. "So the demon sent his victors out here—"

"Victus."

"Victus out here to find you. And you're here because you've been search-ing for the very aptly and originally named, *The Book*."

"Which I've found."

"Which you've found. And this book will teach you everything you need to know about killing the demon, which will close the portal to his hell-like world that he created and therefore, prevent him and any other demons from destroying the earth.

"And as if that wasn't hard enough to believe — because trust me, it is — it's still not the hardest thing to wrap my head around. Not only is your name *not* Lex, but you can't even tell me what it really is? I mean, what the fuck dude?!"

Alexa bites her lip and flinches a little. Cali takes a deep, steadying breath.

"I'm sorry, I didn't mean to yell. But you can tell me all that other stuff, but not your real name? Why?"

Alexa sits quietly for a minute. She sucks in a long breath and explains, "I've had to use fake names since I was eighteen, Cali. For the entire time I've been searching for *The Book* and on the run from Darius. In that time I haven't told anyone my real name because there hasn't been anyone I could trust. Until now. Until you.

"I've tried to be as off the grid as possible. I don't know what kind of reach or network Darius has, and using fake identities was just another way of protecting me and my family. I didn't know if he could track debit cards, or job applications, or rent checks, or social media. If I had used my real name or told someone it then maybe he catches me a couple years ago when I was in Phoenix. That happens and you and I are not only not having this conversation right now, but most likely we are both dead.

"It's safer to keep using a fake name. It's safer for you not to know my real name, both for me and for you. Until I can tell Mickey and Matt the truth, it's just easier for you to keep calling me Lex."

"Well, now that I know it's not the truth, I don't know if it is easier."

"Cal," Alexa pleads.

"No, stop. Please, just give me a minute."

Cali turns perpendicular to her friend to stare at the living room windows. She stands still with her hands on her hips quietly thinking. She suddenly walks into the kitchen and opens the fridge to take out the water pitcher. Changing her mind, she closes the door, opens the freezer and grabs the bottle of vodka that is on its side next to the ice cube trays. She takes it out, unscrews the cap, and takes a long swig straight from the bottle.

She makes a face as she swallows then grabs two glasses and goes back to the couch plopping down next to her roommate. She pours two fingers of vodka into each glass and hands one to Alexa. She clinks the glasses together and downs hers in one gulp.

"Alright," she says holding her empty glass next to her cheek. "I've known you for a long enough time to know this isn't some joke you're playing on me. And as far as I know, you're not crazy."

She pours herself some more vodka and again swallows it all at once. "So I want to believe you, but I'm having a *very* hard time wrapping my brain around it."

"What if I could show you something that would help you know a little more? Help you understand."

Cali takes another sip of vodka. "Like what?"

Alexa gets up and goes into her bedroom. Cali looks at Milo thinking about what Alexa said, that he can sense evil. She thinks back to how protective he became the other day. How he was just waiting for the green light to attack those guys. And how he didn't calm down until he was told multiple times that everyone was okay. Cali reaches out to the dog to give him a grateful scratch behind his ears.

Alexa comes back holding a wooden box. She sits back down on the couch and hands it to her roommate. Cali runs her fingers over the beautifully carved top.

"Hope will heal the world," she says out loud, reading the shallow inscription that's been painted silver.

Alexa nods and removes a chain from around her neck. Hanging off of it is a key. She holds out her hand, silently asks Cali for the box back. She puts the key in its hole and turns, unlocking it. She opens it and the first thing Cali sees is a thick stack of twenties. Alexa moves them and sifts through until she pulls out a piece of paper.

"I'll explain everything that's in here after you read this."

Alexa hands the paper to Cali. When she unfolds it, she sees how fragile the page is — as if it has been unfolded and read thousands of times. Cali holds the paper carefully, paying extra attention not to rip it. When she's done, she folds the paper and hands it back to her roommate.

"Okay, I understand a little more," Cali says. "But tell me again slowly."

"Which part?"

Cali thinks it over. She wants to say "all of it" but instead says, "What if I just ask you specific questions about things?"

"Sure."

Cali looks at her roommate. She doesn't remember ever seeing Alexa this relaxed before. She's always been somewhat guarded, even when it was just the two of them. But now, she looks calm, peaceful, serene.

"Before I ask you anything, I just have to say one thing.

"It's just that, I could tell you've always been somewhat guarded, even when it was just us watching a movie or doing laundry. And this is like, the first time I've seen you totally relaxed. Like a big weight has been lifted from your shoulders."

"It has," Alexa sighs. A soft smile covers Alexa's face. She and Cali pause and just look at each other for a moment. Before speaking again, Cali squints as she thinks over everything she's just been told.

"Okay, I changed my mind. I only have a couple of questions for you."

"Whatever you want to know."

"You're the good one right?"

Alexa chuckles and answers, "Yes."

"And this guy...." she trails off.

"Demon. Darius," Alexa fills in.

"Darius. He sent those guys here looking for you?"

"Yes."

"And they are obviously bad. So you're going to what? Battle these guys to protect the portal and save the world?"

"It's a little more complicated than that, but basically in a nutshell, yeah."

"Okay, so I just have one more question. At least right now."

"Okay."

"What can I do to help?"

• 4 6 •

DARIUS

His strength is slow to return.

It takes the demon a full forty-eight hours to recover from a Victus transition when the person is willing. When Darius takes it upon himself to force a human into becoming one of his soldiers, it can take up to three days.

For the last seventy-two hours, Darius has been mostly comatose. The few moments that he was conscious were tainted by frightening hallucinations and spiking fevers. Demons are naturally cold-blooded to be able to withstand the scorching heat of their homeland so even the smallest of fevers can be life-threatening to an otherwise immortal being.

Viribus has never seen it take this long for Darius to recover from a Victus transition. Nor has he ever seen a recovery this violent before. He has spent the majority of the last three days soaking towels in ice water and draping them over his boss.

When Darius started convulsing at hour thirty, all Viribus could do was put Darius's leather belt in his mouth so he wouldn't break his teeth from his jaw clamping shut. When he started vomiting at hour fifty-seven, the giant turned him on his side so he wouldn't inhale any bile.

Now at hour seventy-seven, Darius opens his eyes. Gone are the milky irises that had clouded his vision for the last three and a half days, now replaced by shining onyx orbs. Gone are the rivers of sweat that poured off his body during his fevers. His pale skin glistens from the leftover salty residue.

"Viribus," the demon says. His throat is dry, and his voice is choked and tinny.

"I'm here, boss," the colossal man says. "What can I get you?"

"How long have I been out?"

"Just about three days."

"What?!" he attempts to shout. He growls in frustration and gives his Victus an order. "Help me stand."

Darius lifts his right arm. Viribus's large palm claps onto the raised one and he gently pulls his boss to an upright sitting position. Darius's eyes swim as the room spins in front of him.

"Maybe you should lay back down, boss."

"No!" the demon snarls. "It's been long enough. There's no more time to waste."

Viribus slowly lifts Darius. He holds on until the smaller man is steady on his feet. When he lets go the ancient brute starts to sway slightly. His Victus flicks two of his long fingers and the chair across the room skids over the floor just in time for Darius to collapse into it.

"Get me something to drink, would you?"

The soldier scurries from the room as quickly as his massive frame allows. He reappears a minute later with a pitcher of water and a glass beer mug filled to the brim with whiskey.

After downing both, Darius asks, "How's the little one coming along?"

Viribus hesitates before answering. "He's been a quick study but a royal, fucking pain."

Darius lets out a hoarse groan at his newest Victus.

"Boss, he's almost gotten into trouble a couple of times and is being very stupid about listening to our advice."

"What trouble?" the demon growls at the burden of breaking in a new recruit.

"He's just a real cocky son of a bitch. You know, hustling people playing pool by using his power, hitting on women and then throwing their boyfriends across the room when they step in."

Darius chuckles without any humor and then says, "Bring him to me."

Viribus disappears once more. Darius closes his eyes while he waits for his three Victus to appear. His eyes snap open as he hears a commotion outside the door. The noise from the hallway carries into the room as Damon is shoved through the door by Viribus who has a grip on his shirt collar, Julius close on his tail.

Damon yanks himself out of Viribus's grip and faces Darius who is still sitting. Darius doesn't stand or make a single move, his feet are flat on the floor, one hand on each knee. He stares down the young man until he looks away.

"So Damon," Darius says in a quiet voice. "I hear you're having a grand time in your Victus infancy."

"Yeah, well I figure why not?" With the tiniest flick of his wrist, Darius slams Damon into the wall behind him. From his spot pinned against the discolored plaster he yells, "You know, this getting-thrown-into-walls thing is getting really fucking old!"

"Is it? There's a real simple way for it to stop happening," Darius calmly says, standing up from his chair. "Stop acting like a goddamn fool you dumb fuck."

From his spot in the doorway, Julius smirks at the light end in response to his boss's words.

"You know Damon, I really don't know what your problem is. I mean, I hear you're hustling some people at pool and throwing others across the room. So while I'm up here regaining my strength, your stupid ass is downstairs exposing all of us time and time again."

"You think people don't know wh—"

Darius shuts up his new Victus with a forceful and humiliating slap across the man's face.

"I wasn't fucking finished," Darius says roughly. "What's wrong with this guy?"

Julius and Viribus shrug.

"I've been around for a long time, little one. A long time. And the reason I set up in rotten places like this one, instead of the lap of luxury is to stay anonymous. Because if humans become aware of me before I've killed the girl and opened the portal, then some pesky scientists or government agents could come along and become very annoying.

"So if you keep up with this shit you've been doing, then you're gonna attract attention that I don't want."

Darius's hand starts to glow as he gets ready to throw a ball of fire. Damon tries to move but he's riveted to the wall still. His head thrashes side to side, a vain attempt at moving his body out of Darius's path. Darius cocks his arm and launches the ball.

Damon shuts his eyes tightly, anticipating the moment he bursts into flames. But the moment never comes. He opens his eyes one at a time, and the ball is hovering right in front of his chest, rotating in place.

"See, here's the thing Damon, I need you but you don't need me, right? I need you to come with me to Portland, and I need you to help me finish what I have to do. You don't need me to be mad as fucking hell at you every goddamn second you're in my presence. You don't need me ready to rip you to shreds at any moment. And you don't need either one of these guys over here feeling the same way. Understand?"

Damon nods his head quickly. The man is terrified at being literal inches away from death. He's breathing heavily, his eyes never leaving the fiery orb in front of him. He's started to sweat through his shirt and perspiration is dripping from his temples down his face to his neck.

Darius comes over and clamps his hands together, extinguishing the flame. He blows the puff of smoke into Damon's face making his eyes water.

"Aw, don't cry now little one," Darius sneers. "You just stay out of the way and make sure you fucking behave."

Darius finally releases the young Victus and Damon falls to the floor physically and mentally exhausted. The demon turns to face his other soldiers.

"Where are the potions?"

"They'll be ready first thing tomorrow morning," Viribus says. He nods his head toward the table in the corner.

There are eight small glass jars the size of prescription bottles in the center of the table. The tops are fastened with black plastic caps. They're filled with a clear liquid. Darius picks one up in his hand and holds it up to the single bulb lighting the room.

"They aren't black."

"Not yet, boss," Julius answers. "But they should turn in a few hours and be ready for use tomorrow morning."

"Why are there eight potions, Viribus?" There's a distinct edge to Darius's voice. He believes his number two has disobeyed him.

"Two extras just in case they are needed, boss," Viribus answers. His voice shakes slightly under the demon's scrutiny. "There's enough for two more potions still brewing. I'll be here waiting for word to meet you at the portal, sir."

Darius sits down on the dirty mattress. He lays flat and speaks at the ceiling.

"Book a flight for tomorrow to Seattle. I want to save those potions to get us right into Portland unannounced. We take her out and head to the portal. Clear?"

Three voices chorus "yes, boss" back at him.

"Good. Now get out, all of you."

Darius closes his eyes and dismisses his Victus with a non-magical wave of his hand. He needs to recuperate a little more before taking on the girl. He wants to make sure there aren't any surprises.

On the table in the corner, the liquid in the eight bottles has turned a faint gray, almost milky liquid. Another step closer to being ready to use.

• 4 7 •

"ALEXA"

I launch myself at Cali. I can't believe that she not only believes me but that she's willing to help. It's what I was hoping for, but until the words came out of her mouth, I wasn't sure exactly how she was going to react.

"You believe me?" I feel like crying, I'm so relieved. I latch on to her and hug her tighter than I ever have before.

"It's pretty unbelievable, but yeah, I do."

"Oh, thank god! I was so nervous you were going to think I was crazy and have me committed or something."

I finally let her go and lean back, wiping the tears from my eyes.

"So, what can I do, *Lex*?" Cali winks at me as she says my name.

"Umm, well that's the tricky part," I say hesitantly. "Have you ever imagined having a power of your own?"

"Intriguing."

"Indeed," I say getting up from the couch. I put my mother's letter and my money safely back into the box, lock it and replace the chain with the key around my neck. I gesture for Cali to follow me to my bedroom. She gets up, Milo close on her heels.

We sit on my bed, and I hand her the red leather notebook and sheets of paper with the translated parts of *The Book*. She flips through them quickly before looking up at me with a confused look on her face.

"What's all this?" she asks.

"It's parts of *The Book* that I used your tablet to translate. The whole thing is in Latin, it's taking me forever."

I take the notebook from her and flip back through it to the pages I wrote about Darius and the princess when Cali and I were at the laundromat.

"When you were a kid, were you ever told the story of Sleeping Beauty?"

"No," Cali says. "But I saw the animated feature film."

"Okay, good. So the story goes that the princess is tricked by the evil queen and pricks her finger and falls into a deep sleep. Then the prince battles those crazy vines and the dragon to save her. He finds Sleeping Beauty and kisses her. She wakes up so it's no longer necrophilia, but a romantic love story with a happily ever after. Right?"

"What a way to put it, but right."

"Well, when I was a kid, I was told stories where the princess was the one who did all the saving."

I hand her back the notebook and point out what I'm talking about.

"Both the princess and Darius had magical powers. They also had armies with their own soldiers. His were called Victus... like the guys that grabbed you, and it means "the defeated" in Latin. Her's were called Extensios, which means "extension." Both armies were given the power to move things with their mind."

Now I hand her the translated page from *The Book* with what I learned about Extensios.

"The difference between my army and Darius's army is that all of my soldiers have to volunteer. But Darius can force humans to become Victus. If what I was told as a kid is true, then when someone becomes a forced Victus, it drains Darius's energy so much that he has to rest for a few days to recover. So he can have more people in his army, but it costs him more. Plus if I die, my Extensios go back to being normal people. But if he dies, except for the Forced, his Victus die too.

"On this planet, Darius has had a twelve hundred year head start on me. I've only used my powers twice in my life. He, I'm sure, uses them probably every day."

I pause. "Cali, I can't defeat him on my own. So if you really want to help me, then the way to do it would be for you to become an Extensios."

Cali stares at me while she processes everything. Milo is sitting on the floor next to the bed. He's been looking back and forth between us as I've been talking and handing stuff to Cali. He shifts a little and nudges Cali's hand. She startles and then starts petting him.

"What happens when I become an Extensios?"

"You'll get the power of telekinesis, so you can move things with your mind."

"That's pretty awesome."

"Yeah, but there's a major downside, too."

"Yeah that whole demon thing."

"No, it's not just that."

I bite my lip. This is the part I've dreaded the most. How can I tell Cali that becoming my Extensios means leaving Mickey behind if I have to hide again, or travel somewhere else? She's waiting for me to explain, but I'm still struggling to find the right way to tell her that the love of her life doesn't get to come too. At least not right now.

"Umm, if you became an Extensios, and I had to leave here and go somewhere new, you'd have to drop everything and come with me. Sever ties, take nothing, and no *one,* with you."

Cali's brow scrunches together. "I don't understand."

A bead of sweat is running down my back between my shoulder blades. I can hear my heart pounding and the blood rushing through my ears. My breathing is shallow. I'm on the verge of a panic attack. *I can't do it*, I think. *Cali deserves better than this.*

"You know what? I can't ask you to do this. Let's find some other way you can help besides the Extensios thing."

I stand up and try to walk away but Cali grabs my hand, stopping me. She tugs on my arm making me sit back down on my bed.

"What is it? Tell me."

Please don't hate me, I silently plead.

"It's just that if you become an Extensios, it means you would essentially have to pick me over every other person in your life. Forever."

• 4 8 •

Cali stares at me as though I've just spoken German. I watch her as she sifts through everything I've told her. I can see on her face the exact moment she understands what I'm saying. She blinks rapidly as if clearing tears from her eyes. She looks hurt. Her grasp on my hand loosens.

"I still don't think I'm fully getting this," Cali says.

I know she is, but I'll tell her again anyway. I squeeze her hand a couple of times and wait until she looks me in the eye again before I speak.

"It means that if you are my Extensios, and I have to leave here, you would come with me and leave everything behind. The apartment, your clothes, your friends, Matt.... and Mickey."

Cali's face shows betrayal. I just became the bad guy. I knew this would be her reaction. Even though I tried to prepare myself for it, it doesn't change the spear of pain that goes through my chest. Her eyes are wet and unfocused, she's looking through me, not at me.

"Cali, look at me please," I say. Her gaze recenters on mine.

"This is why I can't ask you to do this. Why I won't let you do this. You and Mickey are made for each other, you're soulmates. And I can't ask you to leave her. I won't."

I wait for my roommate to say something. I'm expecting her to say she's sorry but she can't, how dare I make her choose me over Mickey, that I can just get out right now. I see her mouth begin to open, I steel myself anticipating the worst.

We're both startled when my phone rings before Cali can say anything. I take it off of my nightstand and see Matt's face lighting up the screen. I turn it so Cali can see and she gives me a signal to answer it. I swipe the screen and tap on it to turn on speaker phone.

"Hello?"

"Hey, it's me."

"Hey, what are you up to?" I can't help the smile that spreads across my face at hearing his voice, the warmth that fills my chest.

"I'm running some errands, and I was thinking of you. I had a really great time yesterday."

"Yeah, me too." I feel heat rush to my cheeks as I flush remembering my night with Matt. I bite my lip to stop my smile from getting bigger. I'm conscious of Cali sitting next to me and the conversation we were just having.

"So, um, I was thinking maybe tomorrow after work we could get some dinner? Are you free?"

I look at my roommate and don't know what to say. We had just been talking about her possibly having to leave her girlfriend, and her best friend calls to ask me out again.

"Lex? You there?"

"Yeah, yes I'm here. Actually, tomorrow I was going to hang out with Cali." I look at my roommate with purpose and mouth, "What do I do?"

"Yeah, Moose," Cali chimes in saving me. "And right now you are interrupting our roommate day. Rude."

"Begging your pardon, Captain Squirrel," Matt deadpans. "I forgot about that sorry, sir. Um, permission to request a call back at a later time. Sir!"

"Granted, Major Moose. At ease, ten-four. Over and out."

Matt laughs, "Aye-aye Captain. Call me later, Lex. Bye guys."

"Bye," we both say before Cali ends the call.

She stands to put the phone back on my nightstand and begins pacing at the foot of my bed. She runs her hands through her auburn hair again. The atmosphere in the room immediately changes from the light-hearted banter between friends back to the serious, life-altering one from before.

"Can I see the box again?" Cali asks.

I take the key from around my neck, unlock the box, replace the key under my shirt and hand the open box to Cali. She takes out the money and puts it on the bed. Then she takes the letter from my mother and places it next to the stack of bills. Next, she takes out and lines up my previous identities: Janice Laurels from Cincinnati, Ohio; Christie Fields from Mesa, Arizona; and, Frankie Rolland from Boise, Idaho. She puts each ID on the bed spaced out evenly.

Thankfully, she doesn't realize that there is a false bottom to the box. I'm still hiding things from her, and I don't know if she would view that as another betrayal or another bombshell she has to try and wrap her head around. I don't even know if *I'm* willing to find out the answer to that just yet.

"Okay, let's do this bit by bit," she says.

"Okay."

"What is the money for?"

"Every time I go to the ATM, I take out another twenty or forty bucks and put it in the box. Or I'll throw in the change from a trip to Roast. It's my "just in case money." If I have to take off quickly, it's so that I would have at least some cash with me.

"Last time I went to the ATM though, I took out almost all of what's in my account because I know Darius is closer to finding me than ever before. I don't know when he'll get here, but it'll be soon. And if I can't beat him this time, I'm going to have to leave again or else risk putting everyone I care about in danger."

"Okay, that I understand." Cali takes the money and puts all of it back in the box. She points now to the fake IDs.

"Why so many?"

I take a deep breath before I answer her, "For the last five years, Milo and I have traveled the country searching for the right place, for the location of *The Book*. I've used different identities in each place. I rotated those three for a long time and only started using the Alexa identity when I got here.

"As soon as I got here and I saw the library, I knew this was the place that my mother was talking about in her letter. She had to be both detailed and vague in case it was stolen or somehow ended up in Darius's hands. But I knew."

"So the fake identities were so that Darius wouldn't know where you were or when that was?"

"Right."

"But you said you and him are connected."

"We are, but only when I actively use my powers. Before I turned eighteen, my powers were bound, hidden by a potion and spell. Since then I've had to use every ounce of self-control to make sure I don't accidentally use my powers."

Cali looks at me unsure.

"I guess I'm not explaining it right. It's like a signal flare. Whenever I use my powers, we connect and he knows where I am, and I know where he is. Like for example, my transport power. If I held your hand and Milo's collar and transported us to a certain place, he'd get a blip like on a radar map of where I left from and where I showed up. The connection is lost once either of us goes dark, or stops using our powers."

"So when you "power down," so to speak, neither of you can sense each other. But when you're both active, you can?"

"Basically. I mean, I think so. I've only ever used my powers twice in my life, so this is all still new to me too."

Cali puts the IDs back in the box and gently places my mother's letter on top. She closes the box and runs her fingers over the inscription.

"Hope will heal the world," she says again. Her face brightens as if a light bulb just turned on in her brain. Instead of addressing her possible realization, she hands me back the box and says, "Let's talk some more about Extensios."

Cali resumes her pacing as I lock the box and tuck the key under my shirt. I don't know exactly what my roommate is going to say, so I wait and let her take the lead.

"So if I go with you, it would really be only until Darius is dead, right?"

"Uhh, yeah," I say before quietly mumbling, "or I'm dead."

"That's not going to happen, Lex. If I go with you, I'd do everything I could so that he wouldn't win."

"But Cali, it could be weeks, months, or even years that you'd be away. You don—"

"I could help you save the world."

I stop and watch her as she grasps what she just said.

"People do things every day that they hope will save the world. They recycle, they ride a bike or take public transit instead of driving, they sponsor charities that provide clean drinking water, whatever. How many times does someone actually get to do something that they *know* will save the world?"

"Not that often, I guess," I shrug trying not to influence Cali's decision. I am not Darius, I will not force her.

"But, just because Darius, his Victus, and demons would be gone from the earth, it doesn't mean that bad things would just stop happening. Cali, people did bad things long before Darius got here, and they've done bad things while he's been here without an ounce of his influence."

I'm literally playing devil's advocate right now, I think.

"Saving the world from Darius doesn't just fix everything that's going wrong right now, Cal. It gives everyone else the *chance* to."

• 4 9 •

Our back and forth about Cali becoming an Extensios is interrupted again by a phone ringing. This time it's Mickey checking in with Cali in between sessions. My roommate steps into the hall to talk privately with her girl-friend. I catch snippets of the conversation, but I do hear her ask if the tall brunette would be staying over tonight.

"Good, then I'll see you later baby. I love you," Cali says coming back into my bedroom. She ends the call and tucks the phone into the waistband of her sweats.

"She'll be done in about three hours. She said she's going to stop at her place and then come here."

I'm sitting on my bed. Cali comes over and steps right up to me. Her green eyes bore into my own hazel ones. She puts her hands on my shoulders.

"*Lex*," she says purposely. "I want to help you. Let me help you. I under-stand what I'm saying and what it means, but I can't let you do this alone. We're in this together."

"Cali, how can I let you do this though? You could die. And it would be my fault. I couldn't live with that."

She spins away frustrated.

"Ugh! Everyone is going to die someday, Lex! And if I do, it'll be no one's fault other than that fucking demon!"

She lets out a deep exhale and comes back to put her hands back on my shoulders. When she speaks, her voice is calmer, almost pleading.

"I understand the desire you have to try and keep me safe, to keep everyone safe. I really do. You said you've been doing it every day for the last five years. But I respectfully decline your protection and request to be right there beside you kicking some major magical ass!"

I don't know what to say. I know that I can't do this alone. But allowing Cali to put herself in danger like this goes against every rule I've put in place for the people I love. My mind is warring with itself. I put my head in my hands and try to massage the tension out of my temples.

"Are you sure? Like really sure that you're okay with what it means to be my Extensios and everything it entails?"

"Yes, I am. But I have two conditions."

Crap. I was worried about something like this. That I might be viewed like a genie and can give Cali the permanent ability to fly or something.

"Okaaay...." I say hesitantly. "What are they?"

"You have to tell Moose."

That's not what I was expecting. "*What?*"

"He has to know. You guys are starting a relationship, he's head over heels for you, Lex. He deserves to know. Especially if you think we'll have to leave here soon."

"He's head over heels? Really?"

"Oh my god, yes. And obviously, you are too. So you have to tell him."

"Okay." I bookmark the fact that Matt is falling for me to think about later.

"The other condition is I have to tell Mickey." I open my mouth ready to protest but Cali holds her hand up stopping me. "That is non-negotiable. I'm not saying I have to tell her right now, but just like Moose, she deserves to know."

"You're right, you're right." I stand up and start to pace around my room. "This is getting complicated."

"I know. So. When are we gonna do this?"

"Do what?"

Cali looks at me like I'm an idiot.

"Umm, what we've just been talking about for the last few hours?"

"I don't know. Tomorrow? I work until eight tomorrow night, so maybe we can sneak back in and go to the climate-controlled storage after the library closes? I want to have *The Book* right in front of me so I don't accidentally turn you into a lizard or something."

"Yeah, please don't turn me into a lizard," she deadpans. "I mean, if you're going to turn me into anything, make it an elephant or a honey badger, you know? Something formidable."

It's not that funny of a joke, but Cali's delivery is the levity that the moment needs.

"Tomorrow," Cali says. "Okay. Personally, I think you should make Moose into an Extensios too, but that's up to him. He should at least be there with us tomorrow night."

"I think we're getting ahead of ourselves. The most important thing we have to remember is this: as soon as I use my powers, Darius will know exactly where we are. Like latitude and longitude GPS coordinates exactly."

"Right, but at that point, you'll know exactly where he is too. Right?"

"As long as everything I've been told proves true, yes."

Cali picks up the pages I ripped from Sam's notepad. She reads the Extensios columns through start to finish. She puts the pages back down on the bed then walks out of my bedroom.

"Where are you going?" I call after her.

"I need more room," she answers.

Milo and I leave my bedroom to find Cali in the living room pushing the couch and coffee table from the middle of the room up against a wall. She goes into her bedroom and comes out a moment later. In her hands are a plastic case and giant pad of sketch paper that would look more at home on a kindergarten teacher's easel. She plops the pad down, tosses me the case, and goes into my room to get my notebook and papers.

I open the plastic case and it is full of oversized permanent markers. Cali crouches on the floor and opens to a fresh page on the oversized pad.

"Red," she says looking down at the paper and holding one hand in the air. I search through the markers and hand her the red one. When she uncaps it, I expect the telltale pungent smell of permanent ink but am met with a pleasant synthetic strawberry smell instead.

"Scented?" I ask as I sit down facing my roommate, a few feet between us. I hold up a blue which I hope is blueberry.

Cali mindlessly, "Mm-hms" as she writes something on the pad. She turns the pad around and has written DARIUS in all capital letters at the top and underlined it. She tears off the sheet and puts it in front of her on the left.

"Green," she says, hand out again. Mint. I hand her the green marker. She turns the pad around and writes ALEXA at the top, underlines it and tears off the page putting it on the right.

"Yellow." Lemon. A sheet with EXTENSIOS written across it lands in front of me.

"Black." Licorice.

The pad flops to the floor in front of Cali, blank. The uncapped black marker in her left hand perched above it ready to go.

"Actually we don't need this yet." Cali covers the marker and tosses it back to me. She puts the ALEXA paper on top on the pad and grabs the green marker from the floor.

"Okay. We have a couple of hours until Mickey gets here. Let's spell everything out and make a plan for tomorrow. Yeah?"

"Yeah."

"Okay, tell me your powers."

I tell Cali and she writes all seven of them down with bullet points. She switches out the sheets and places down DARIUS, exchanges the green marker for the red.

"His powers?"

"That's where it gets a little murky. I'm pretty sure he doesn't have projection or super senses, and I know he doesn't have transport. But other than that I don't know."

Cali writes all of that down. She tosses it on top of my sheet. Next up is EX-TENSIOS in yellow.

"Now, we'll do all of this in English, just to be safe," Cali smirks at me. I roll my eyes in response.

"So what do you do to make me an Extensios?"

"I close my eyes and chant three times 'By choice, my power I gift to thee.' Then I say something about what powers I'm giving you. After that I reach out and touch your head, and say again 'I gift to thee,' Your body will glow... I think."

She glances up from the paper to give me an incredulous look. I throw my hands up in the air. "I don't know! I've never done it before!"

"Okay, take a breath. So... I glow, then what?"

"Then I let go of you," I shrug. "And when you stop glowing, you're an Ex-tensios."

"And I'll be able to move things with my mind?"

"Telekinesis, yeah."

Cali writes all of this down on the EXTENSIOS sheet and then lays it on top of the other two. Then she returns back to the black marker and picks up the blank pad. She puts in her lap.

Uncapping the licorice-scented marker she asks, "And how do I do that?"

"Do what?"

"Telekinesis."

I think of the instructions my grandfather gave me when he whisked me away from Darius's first attacked five years ago.

"You clear your mind, and all you think about is the thing you want your power to do. So, like, if you wanted to deflect something, you'd hold your hand up and think of whatever's coming at you going in the opposite direction."

"What would I be deflecting?"

Balls of fire, or just things that could generally kill you. But we can save that for tomorrow.

"Umm, you know, just things," I look around for something that to use as an example. "Oh! Or say, you wanted Milo's leash from the hook, right? Then all you would think about would be Milo's leash coming over to you."

"Do I say anything? Like 'Milo's leash, I command you!' Like that?" I stare at Cali like she's got three heads. "Okay, that's a no."

"Your power is controlled through your hands, so you don't have to say anything. You think and point."

"Think and point." Cali squints intensely at Milo's leash, points at it, then flings her arm across her body.

Nothing happens.

"Oh man, how cool would that have been if it had actually moved?"

• 5 0 •

DARIUS

After his three day absence, he's perched in his usual place at the back corner of the bar. He's still not feeling fully like himself, but what Darius does feel is triumphant. He *knows* he's close to finding the girl, he feels as if he's inches away. And soon he will be.

Darius lets his eyes slowly navigate the entirety of the bar and its patrons. The room is only about half full, it is pretty late on a Sunday night in the south after all. He can't hide the sneer on his face as he thinks about seeing his demonic clan soon.

"These little rodents have no idea what's coming," he chuckles quietly into his tumbler of whiskey.

"You say something, boss?" Julius asks wiping off the beer foam on his lip with his sleeve.

Darius makes a face of disgust at Julius's characteristically human lack of refinement. "No," he says not wanting to repeat himself to the messy, over-weight man.

He shifts his gaze to his newest Victus. Now that the demon has regained enough of his strength to be a physical presence, the former footballer isn't as reckless as he was the past few days. He's shown nothing short of model behavior since Darius less than gently put him in his place a short time ago.

He watches Damon's eye dart to the door every time it opens. What he's looking for, Darius doesn't know. The demon is curious, so he asks.

"What are you watching for, little one?"

Damon ignores him, still sour over being thrown around like a rag doll earlier. He also makes a point of not answering to the ridiculous nickname the demon has given him. He lifts his beer to take a long, surly, swallow when Julius smacks him on the back of the head hard enough that the glass bangs against his front teeth, catching his lip in between.

"When he asks you a question, you answer."

The bald man puts his glass down and checks his mouth for blood. When his hand comes away red, he spins on his stool and wipes it across Julius's fat, wide face. The heavyset Victus bristles, ready to take a swing at the larger man.

Damon taps his own cheek and says, "Make it count, sweetheart. 'Cause I'm only letting you get in one."

"Now, now, children. That's enough," Darius cuts in. When the two don't back up from their face-off, Darius yells, "I said, enough!

In his normal voice, he continues, "We're flying under the radar tonight. And me yelling at you two fucking idiots to knock it off is the opposite of that. So no fights, no games, no bets. No attention. Just drink your drinks until it's time for our flight. Understand?"

Damon swings his stool back and stares at himself in the mirror behind the bar. Julius just glares at the newest addition. Darius slams his whiskey onto the bar shattering the glass tumbler.

"Understand?!"

"Yes, boss," Julius mumbles.

Damon grits his teeth making his jaw muscles flare. "Yes," he grumbles.

"Yes, what?" Darius prods.

"Yes, *boss*," the youngest begrudgingly says.

"That's right, little one," Darius points a finger at himself. "Boss."

Darius turns to signal to the bartender for a replacement, but there's already a freshly filled glass in front of him. The pieces of his previous drink have already been swept away. He raises his glass to the man who's looking older and older each time he serves the demon.

Darius is in the midst of tipping his glass to drain it when Viribus enters the bar. Julius springs off his stool to intercept the biggest Victus.

"Finally. What the fuck took you so long?"

"The goddamn computer froze so I had to make the flight reservation over the phone," the giant answers in his deep voice. "Then I had to wait for the email confirmation to print."

He hands the sheet of paper concealed in his baseball mitt-sized hands to the demon in front of him.

"Unfortunately the next flight out is a red-eye that leaves Atlanta at 11:30 Monday night. I asked if there was anything earlier, but all direct flights before that are booked across the board. I asked about one- and two-stop flights, but they all end up arriving at SEATAC at the same time. So, I figured you'd rather take a direct flight, boss, and I booked the next available."

"Good job, Viribus," Darius praises. "Julius, go upstairs and check the potions. Barkeep! How about a beer for my friend here?"

In a rare moment of what passes for kindness by a demon but is closer to thinly veiled contempt in human terms, Darius has been favoring Viribus all day knowing the behemoth is irked at the fact he will be left behind. Viribus sits in Julius's vacated seat and gets a big clap on the back from the demon.

The short Victus returns to the trio at the bar reporting the potions are now dark gray. That means only a few more hours until they're ready. Darius looks at his watch before indicating to the bartender to serve another round.

"A toast gentlemen," the demon announces holding up his whiskey neat. "After waiting over a thousand years and millions of hours, we're just over a day from finally ending this. We are moments away from making this decrepit, nothing world finally mirror the fiery depths of home. To home!"

"To home!" Julius and Viribus chorus each taking a swig of their drinks. Damon just raises his glass silently.

"And to the girl," Darius adds wickedly. "May she lose well, and may she die a slow and incredibly painful death."

• 5 1 •

Cali

After putting away the large pad and the markers, Cali is anxiously awaiting her girlfriend's return. "Lex" had folded the torn-off sheets and put them in her room with the notebook and box. When she comes back and sits down on the couch, Cali reaches for her hand and squeezes it.

They hold hands comfortably until they hear Mickey's keys jingle in the lock. Alexa squeezes Cali's hand again and says quietly, "You don't have to do this. I know what I'm asking of you, and you can still say no."

Cali feels her nose tingle as tears threaten to form, but she swallows hard and just as Mickey comes into the apartment whispers back, "No. I've made up my mind."

"Hey guys," Mickey says dropping her bags to pet Milo who is sitting there waiting for her. Her long hair is back in a low messy bun and she's wearing a puffy blue jacket zipped all the way, jogging shorts over compression shorts, and gray sneakers with neon green accents.

"Whew! What a day! It was so busy at the studio today that I had to create a waiting list for some of the classes. And every class was completely full."

Mickey takes off her jacket and hangs it up. She comes over to the couch and leans over to kiss her girlfriend hello. Cali grabs the back of her head before the brunette can pull away, holding her tightly in place and deepening the kiss.

"What was that for?" Mickey asks breathlessly.

"Nothing. I'm just happy you're home. What's all this?" Cali asks pointing to the apartment door that is still ajar, blocked by a bunch of reusable grocery bags.

"Oh," Mickey says hanging up her coat. "I stopped at the little corner store and got some things. I had this hankering for sesame chicken all day. So I looked up some recipes on my way home and found one I want to try."

"That sounds delicious, but you can count me out," Alexa chimes in. "I'm going to take Milo for a nice walk and then go get in a workout myself."

Cali watches her roommate go to the door and pick up Milo's leash. Like Cali, the dog has followed Mickey into the kitchen to watch her unload the bags of food. Lex snaps her fingers and points to her foot and Milo obeys immediately.

"Good boy. Alright, I'll see you guys in a little."

As soon as the door closes, Cali has Mickey pinned to the fridge and is attacking her neck. She finds the spot that makes her girlfriend's knees weak and positions her thigh in between Mickey's legs just before sucking on it. When the brunette's legs give a little, she lands on Cali's thigh which provides the slightest bit of pressure to her core. Just enough to get her girlfriend's heart going.

Cali's hands waste no time in grabbing her girlfriend's ass and pushing down to increase the pleasant pressure. She physically moves Mickey's hips back and forth to get her going even more.

The shorter woman's mouth moves across Mickey's neck, under her jaw, and up to her earlobe. Cali sticks the tip of her tongue just for a second into the trainer's ear, causing the brunette to gasp and grind herself down on Cali's thigh.

When Cali moves her mouth again, this time capturing Mickey's mouth in a feverish kiss, the taller woman puts her hands on Cali's shoulders and lightly pushes her away. They are both gasping for air; their eyes dark, pupils blown wide with want. The brunette drops her head panting into Cali's shoulder.

"Damn, you really are happy I'm home," Mickey says placing a small kiss on her girlfriend's collar bone. "But I spent the entire day in these clothes at the studio. I need to take a shower."

Cali presses her thigh up into Mickey before slowly dragging it free. "Okay," she says with a wolfish grin. "Let's go shower."

They close the bathroom door and turn on the tap. Mickey sticks her hand in to check the temperature. When she turns around to undress, Cali is already naked. She takes Mickey's hands and gently raises them into the air. She pushes up the tank top Mickey is wearing and pulls it over her head.

Cali runs her hands down the woman's sides to her waistband. She pulls everything, including Mickey's underwear, down kissing one thigh as she bends and the other as she stands. She pulls off the tight sports bra and captures one breast in her mouth before the bra even hits the floor.

The room has filled with steam, both of their naked bodies are glistening from the humidity. Cali pulls away from Mickey's chest, takes her hand, and steps backward into the shower.

As soon as Mickey is under the stream of water, Cali grabs the bar of soap and begins lathering it up. She washes her girlfriend, kissing every inch of skin before covering it with soap suds. Before Mickey can do the same to Cali, the auburn-haired woman is on her knees.

She kisses the apex of Mickey's hipbone then drags her tongue along the vee of the muscles downward. She kisses and sucks across the clean-shaven mound and drags her tongue up to the other hip.

Mickey runs her hands through Cali's hair. She puts her fingers under Cali's chin and tilts the younger woman's head back. She gently pulls up making Cali stand. Mickey kisses her softly, tenderly.

"You don't have to do that, baby," Mickey says. "I don't want you to think you have to do anything. I know that it's only been a few days and you're still processing what happened on Wednesday and—"

"Shhh," Cali cuts her off. "I'm okay, baby. I want you so much right now that it hurts. There are so many things I want to do to you. Just touching you already has me right at the edge."

She starts punctuating her sentence by kissing Mickey's plump, red lips. "I love you so much, and I want to show how much over and over until you can't take it anymore."

As the last word comes out of her mouth, Cali enters her girlfriend with two fingers. She curls them and drags them out making sure to rub the soft, sensitive bundle of nerves inside. Mickey moans loudly. Cali captures it with a hard kiss and forces Mickey's mouth open with her tongue. She takes control of the kiss, her hand never stopping its movements. When she moves her thumb to Mickey's clit and grabs her breast, the brunette's head snaps back in pleasure.

With her eyes shut tight, she doesn't see Cali moving down. The contact from her thumb stops only to be replaced in seconds by her tongue. Mickey cries out even louder at Cali's dexterous mouth. She loves the brunette's taste and can't help but moan too.

It doesn't take long for Mickey to come with a shout but Cali doesn't stop. She doubles her efforts and brings Mickey to a second, stronger climax then slowly brings Mickey down from her orgasm. It's only when Mickey whimpers and gently swats Cali's face away, that the shorter woman completely stops her ministrations.

Cali kisses her way back up to Mickey's lips and the two share a languid kiss. Mickey's eyes are hooded with satisfaction. The two finish their shower and go to Cali's room to get dressed.

The moment Mickey drapes her damp towel over a chair to put on clothes, Cali is on top of her again. Cali's momentum makes them fall onto the bed. They land with Cali on top. Mickey has recovered enough from her strong double orgasm to take the upper hand this time. She bucks her hips up and rolls to pin the younger woman beneath her.

Cali's eyes widen in pleasant surprise at the show of strength. But the only thing she wants tonight is to make sure Mickey knows how much she loves her and wants to be with her forever. So she smirks and maneuvers them back to how they landed. She puts her thigh in between Mickey's legs and presses up as she bites down on her girlfriend's bottom lip. Mickey hisses at the sting of the bite before devouring Cali's mouth with her own.

Cali reaches over to her nightstand and opens the drawer. The color of what she pulls out tells Mickey that Cali is taking charge tonight.

They forget all about the groceries and the sesame chicken. They don't hear Alexa come back from Milo's walk, then leave to go to the gym and come back again.

Cali doesn't know when she'll be able to be with Mickey again. She wants to make sure there is no doubt in the brunette's mind how desperately in love with her Cali is.

The only thing in the world right now is the two of them. Their hearts pounding in sync, their breath heaving and ragged, their bodies wrapped together pulsing with desire for each other.

The couple spends the rest of the night making love to each other. Sometimes gently, sometimes rushed and hard, but always listening to and giving each other what they need.

****

In the morning, the bedroom is softly lit with the gray light of a rainy day. Cali watches Mickey sleep. They are both laying on their sides facing one another. Cali hears the multiple plinks of heavy raindrops hitting the window. The older woman's face is peaceful, framed by her dark hair. Her olive skin flawless. Her lips plump from the previous night's activities.

Cali lightly runs her finger along the chiseled jawline causing Mickey to stir. Her eyes slowly flutter open. The blue irises sparkle, even in the dim light from the half-open blinds. Cali leans in and places a soft kiss on Mickey's lips.

"You're beautiful," she says propping herself up on an elbow to look Mickey over again. "I could look at you forever and still be amazed at how perfect you are."

Mickey blushes and ducks her face into the pillow slightly. She looks back at Cali with one eye, smiling. Cali moves over to position herself right next to Mickey, their bodies flush. She looks over her face one more time, runs her fingertip along her jaw again, trying to memorize every single detail. When she kisses her this time, all she wants is to let Mickey know once more how much she loves her.

In case the kiss doesn't say everything for her, Cali adds, "I love you so much. I care for you more than I've ever cared for someone. You are the best thing that's ever happened to me."

"I feel exactly the same way, baby. You're everything to me, Cali."

Cali kisses her again and then pulls Mickey so she's half on top of her. The brunette quickly falls back to sleep in warm arms and listening to her girl-friend's heartbeat. They lay like that, with Cali awake listening to the rain, for a long time. She hears Alexa get up and take Milo out. She shuts off her first alarm when it blares from her phone.

Cali has fully expressed herself to Mickey. She's shown her everything she needs to show, and said everything she needs to say, except the one word she just couldn't bear to speak.

Goodbye.

• 5 2 •

"ALEXA"

I haven't been able to concentrate for more than five minutes at a time all day.

I've holed myself up down in the sub-basement with *The Book*. I haven't even tried to keep up the charade of entering books into the library's database. Instead, I've been frantically trying to copy the entire contents of *The Book* into my notebook. I don't know when Darius will be arriving, but I figure it's better to have a backup in case something happens to the real one.

After every few lines that I write, I'm up and pacing around CCR3. I have the translator app on my phone cued up with the saved Latin chants I'll need to say to transform Cali into an Extensios. I listen to the words a few times with headphones on before sitting down to write down more of *The Book*. I mouth them as I listen, but I don't dare say them out loud.

My nerves and my adrenaline are sky high by four o'clock, and I'm only halfway through my day. I need a change of scenery to clear my head. I tuck *The Book* back into its place on the shelf, grab my phone and notebook, and clear out of cube three. I use my keycard to bypass security locks and doors and quickly find myself up on the roof.

I've never been up here before. I've only gone up to the roof of my apart-ment building. It's not that quiet up here since the library isn't all that tall. I can still hear the sounds of traffic below and periodic shrieks as people get sprayed by or step into one of the puddles left over from this morning's heavy downpour. I put my phone in my back pocket and clutch the notebook to my chest.

"Mom," I say out loud.

I've found a way to talk to her over the last three years without risking her safety. I couldn't do it right away, the ache for her was too fresh. It's just as strong now, but I've learned to live with it, to work around it.

I talk out loud as if she's right in front of me. But I don't picture her in my mind. And I don't ask questions, unless rhetorical. I don't open myself to wishing for her presence in any way. If that happens I shut it down. Like on the stairs ten days ago, I'll remind myself that she's safe and they're all okay.

I start it the same every time: "I know you can't hear me, but I just need to talk to you for a minute."

I don't know if saying that has become something of a ritual at this point, but it helps. I say that first and then tell her what's bothering me.

"I'm scared. I'm honestly really scared. I know he's close, that he's coming. I don't need to use my powers to know, I can feel it, Mom. More than ever, I know Darius is coming for me.

"But that's not what I'm afraid of. I am terrified of Cali getting hurt or even killed. She said that it won't be my fault if it happens, but I know it will be. She's become my best friend, and I don't know how I'd be able to go on liv-ing if her death is added to the list of ones I've caused.

"I know what you're going to say, that I haven't caused anyone's death. But me hearing that doesn't make me feel any less responsible."

I stop. I take a moment to reset myself before continuing.

"And she wants me to tell Matt. She thinks he'll fight for me, that he'll join me. But I'm falling for him, Mom. *Hard*. I've never felt this way about any-one. And now I have to tell him, 'Hey, I know we've been on like, one official date, but would you mind leaving your family and everything you know behind to help me battle a demon which could very well get you killed? Cool? Thanks.'

"Then there's Mickey! If Matt and Cali help me, and then the three of us have to flee, we'd have to leave her behind. At least for now. So I make Cali choose between me or her soulmate, but then I get to take the guy I'm fall-ing for with me. How is that at all fair?"

I start pacing around the roof, zig-zagging around the HVAC stacks and small patches of standing water.

"I don't know what to do, Mom. I can't do any of this alone and I know I have to ask for help, but I can't get past that I'll be ruining three people's lives in the process. I know what you would say to me right now. You'd say 'make good choices,' and I think, so far, I have. But that still doesn't change how much guilt I'm feeling right now about the possible outcomes of all of them."

I sigh and drop my hands to my sides. I haven't done this in a while, haven't been on the apartment roof in months. But every time I do I always feel bet-ter. Except, this time I'm left with just as much uncertainty as before. I shiver as a cold, damp breeze sweeps across the roof.

I go back inside the building, making my way down to the employee lounge. I'm hoping to not run into anybody and finally a small stroke of luck lands in my favor. I buy a bottle of soda from the vending machine and sneak back down to the climate-controlled sub-basement.

I finish copying the rest of *The Book* — including a second, different inscrip-tion on the back cover — into my notebook and tuck it into my bag so I don't accidentally leave it here. I have a couple more hours here before I go home to get Cali and Milo. *I might as well do some actual work,* I think.

I'm closing the door to CCR3 to go to CCR1 when I get a text from Cali. She says she talked to Matt and got him to agree to meet us later outside the library. I don't ask what she told him, although I imagine it must've been something extravagant.

I can't think about tonight anymore. I'm spinning myself in circles as it is. Before I pick up where Sam left off on Sunday, I decide to listen a few more times to the saved chants in Latin in the translator app. I mouth them again a few more times to be as familiar as I can be with the words for later.

After I finish entering the next two books, I have less than half an hour left, so I pack up all my things and leave cube one. I walk the carpeted walkway to two cubes down. I move around to the side and stare through the glass wall at the corner *The Book* is in.

I feel completely unprepared for what's about to happen tonight. But for now, I've done all I can.

• 5 3 •

When I get home, Milo meets me at the door. I feel the familiar pressure as he sticks his head between my knees. Instead of the calm that usually washes over me, it's replaced by something that's not quite dread but pretty close to it. I hang up my coat and plop onto the couch a tight ball of tension.

"Oh, good. You're home." Cali comes out of her room with a large duffle bag. She puts it on the coffee table and unzips it. "Okay, I went to the drug store today and got a bunch of stuff we might need."

She starts removing items from the duffle, naming them as she goes. "Dry shampoo, water bottles with a filter in the straw, heavy duty garbage bags, glow sticks—"

"Cali, you don't have to take everything out."

"—the biggest resealable plastic bags they had."

"Okay, I guess you do."

"Sunscreen, gloves, those things you stick in shoes to warm your toes, deodorant, a sudoku book, gummy vitamins, a Swiss army knife, matches, trail mix, bug spray, protein bars, bars of soap, four travel size toothpaste because they were on sale, band-aids, allergy medicine, anti-itch cream, tampons, baby wipes, and of course, chapstick."

She reaches all the way into the bag and comes out with three multipack boxes, each a different flavor, and puts them at the top of the mound of items on the coffee table.

"Where exactly do you think we'll have to go?" I ask her. "Camping in the Grand Canyon?"

"I have no freakin' idea, Lex. So I tried to plan for anything." Cali starts putting the things back into the duffle bag. Once the bag is full and zipped closed, she says, "Oh, and I went to the bank and took out some money too."

I wince from my spot on the couch as it becomes more and more clear what Cali is giving up to help me. Not only is she choosing to come with me and leave the love of her life behind, but she's leaving the apartment that her grandmother — the only family she had — willed to her. My debt to Cali keeps getting bigger. I don't know if I'll ever be able to repay her.

"I also went to the post office and had our mail forwarded to Mom starting tomorrow."

I'm confused until I remember that when she says Mom, she means Matt's mother. *Oh my god, Matt has a mom and a brother.* My eyes well with tears, the emotion surprising even myself. I drop my head into my heads. Cali sits down beside me and gently puts her hand on my back.

"What's wrong?"

"Matt has a mother and a brother. You have Mickey and this apartment." My voice is thick with emotion, heavy tears fill my eyes. A few overflow, tracing a line down my cheeks, dripping off my chin onto my sweater. I wipe my tears harshly off of my face and look away. I don't have the courage right now to look Cali in the eye.

"I can't let either of you give up so much when I can't guarantee I'll be able to give it back to you somehow."

"Alexa, stop it."

My head snaps around. She's never called me Alexa, not even when we first met.

"That's right, I said Alexa, so you listen good. I'm not choosing you over Mickey. I'm choosing my future with Mickey over some dickless, demonic bastard who wants to destroy the world and take that future away from me."

She puts her arm around my shoulders and pulls me in so our foreheads are touching. "And I know that when we tell Moose all of this tonight, he's going to make the same choice. For his future with you."

I nod. My forehead still touching hers. *Okay,* I think. *She's really in this.*

"Are you—"

"Oh my *god*, Lex," she says pulling away and standing up exasperated. "If you ask me if I'm sure one more time I'm going to punch you."

I hold my hands up. "Whoa! Okay, wow. One, violence."

Cali chuckles and relaxes her weight onto one leg. She crosses her arms and stares me down.

"And two," I continue. "I was going to ask are you done packing a bag of clothes? If I had known the reaction I was going to get, I'd have said forget it and just let you fight Darius and his Victus naked."

"That's an option?" she deadpans. "Sign me up!"

She spins around and leaves the living room going to her bedroom again. She returns this time with a large backpack. Sliding the large duffle bag over, she starts laying out her clothes: three pairs of shoes — two sneakers and one pair of hiking boots, seven or eight pairs of socks, underwear and bras, a blanket, a sweatshirt, three pairs of jeans, two sweatpants, a couple pairs of shorts, five t-shirts, two long sleeved shirts, a towel, a small toiletry bag, and a pajama set with squirrels and acorns on it.

"Good," I say checking my watch. "It's just after nine, we have to go soon. I'm going to go pack for myself and Milo."

Cali nods at me, already repacking her bag. I go into my bedroom thinking about all of the things Cali did today.

In my bedroom, I take out the essentials and sort them on my bed. I grab clothes from my closet similar to what Cali has packed, minus the squirrel pajamas, and plus an additional blanket and sweatshirt. I pack all of that in the only bag I own that's large enough: my canvas laundry bag.

I have room left so I add Milo's towel, shampoo, and his brush. I dart into the bathroom for my own toiletries and wrap them in a clean bath towel.

The wooden box goes into my purse which already holds my red notebook. I throw in my glasses case and my phone charger.

I change out of the flats I'm wearing and put on fresh socks and my hiking boots. I leave on the faded black, skinny cargo pants and red and gray striped sweater I wore to work today.

I've learned, having moved around so much, that what I have now is really all I need. There's enough money in my box to replace whatever I've left behind. The only things I absolutely can't replace are Milo and the box with all of its contents. And now, of course. Cali and, hopefully, Matt. Anything else I need along the way, I can figure it out then.

I scan the room and see nothing else I absolutely have to or want to take. I throw the laundry bag over one shoulder and hang my purse on the other. I leave my bedroom and close the door behind me.

I drop my two bags by the front door and go into the kitchen. I get a plastic bag from under the sink and open the cabinet with Milo's treats. He's there in a second waiting for his cookie. I can't deny him one when he's looking up at me with his expectant eyes and puppy-like face.

"Alright, Milo. Just a small piece." I put the rest into the bag. I add his collapsible bowl, a couple of his toys, and every tennis ball I can find.

Cali opens the apartment door and puts her bags in the hall. I follow suit then bring my bike in and rest it against the back of the couch. I strap Milo into his harness and hand his leash to Cali while I take out my keys.

"Are you ready?" I ask her. She takes one more look around the living room before hesitantly stepping into the hall with me. I decide to give her another chance at an out. "Cali, you can still stay. I understand."

"No," she answers without pause. "I'm ready. I'm coming with you."

I slide my key in and close the door. As the latch catches and the lock slides into place with a final click, I know in my gut I will never see this place again. But I hope more than anything that Cali will.

It's familiar to me by now, leaving. It has happened time and time again. But this time it's not just another place along the way. I've made a life here, a home. And leaving it is just another tally added to the long list of things Darius has robbed from me.

• 5 4 •

Rather than carry the three large and two small bags between us all the way to the library, Cali calls for a cab that's pet-friendly. We have the driver drop us and our luggage at the church around the corner from the library on SW Taylor Street.

Matt calls as we are getting out of the car and Cali tells him we'll be right there. We pay the cabbie and wait for him to drive away before we head down the block and make a left toward the library. Matt is there waiting, looking around, with his own duffle bag hanging on his shoulder.

Cali must have told him something that was convincing enough for him to be not only here, but also packed, I think.

"Hey," he says greeting us. He and Cali hug, and he gives me an unhurried, relaxed kiss. He releases me and crosses his arms. "So, anyone want to tell me exactly what's going on?"

"Well, um, what exactly did Cali tell you?"

"That I should pack some clothes and essentials, and meet the both of you here tonight. She said you need our help with something but wouldn't tell me what."

I open my mouth to explain to him why he's here, why we're all here, but no coherent words come out. I look to Cali with pleading eyes hoping that she'll jump in and say something. She does, it's just not what I expect to hear.

"Lex is a witch."

Matt looks confused for a moment and then cracks up laughing. My jaw drops at her brashness.

"Cali! Let's not talk about this out here. Please."

"What?" Cali asks innocently. "I thought a direct approach was best."

Matt's smile slowly fades from his face. He looks back and forth between us. Then cracks up again as if he was suddenly let in on the joke. He chuckles a few more times, but when neither of us laughs with him, his face falls again.

"Wait... what?" He looks between the two of us. His eyes even drop to Milo who's sitting patiently between Cali and I. "What the hell are you talking about?"

"We should really go inside, Cali. I don't want to talk about this out here."

I take my bags and Milo's things, along with Milo, and head around to the side entrance Matt and I used after our food truck lunch a few days ago. Before swiping my card through, I look behind me and see Cali pulling Matt with her. I unlock the door and hold it open with my foot for them.

We gently close the door behind us and make our way over to the next door that leads to the basement and sub-basement. I swipe my card again and this door opens onto a stairwell. At the bottom are two metal doors, one leads to a second stairwell, the other into the regular basement.

At the base of the stairs, I swipe my card again and we go down the last set of stairs to the sub-basement. I'm about to slide my keycard through the last electric lock when I freeze. My lungs feel like they're about to collapse and my heart like it has stopped all together.

"It's okay, Lex," I hear Cali say behind me. She puts a hand on my back in between my shoulders and says, "We're here. We're with you."

I exhale, unlock, and open the sub-basement door. I step in and let Milo, Cali, and Matt come in after me. I close the door and wait to hear the click that the door is secure. The security lights cast an ominous glow throughout the room. Only the outlines of the first two cubes are visible in the low light. I unhook Milo and put his leash in my bag, and take three steps into the room — just far enough to activate the motion sensor. The room floods with light.

"Wow," Cali breathes out.

"I had no idea this was even down here let alone how huge it is," Matt says dropping his bag at the door and walking over to the first cube to peer inside it. As the novelty of the space wears off, he turns around and stares Cali and me down. "Alright, we're here, we're inside. Now tell me, really. What is going on?"

"I told you, Moose. Lex is a witch."

"Cali," I start. "I don't know if—"

"Actually, she's not just a witch. She's a descendant of multiple magical creatures, but witch is the easiest to explain. Right?"

She turns to me expectantly. I sigh resignedly and say, "Yes."

"So there you go, Moose."

"Okay, Squirrel. You've obviously been eating too many nuts lately and it's starting to affect your brain. Because you sound completely crazy right now."

Neither of us says anything. He starts laughing again but with more nerves and less humor. "Okay, someone explain. Because what you said just isn't possible."

"Actually," I say nervously. "It is."

"Okay, sure. Yup. You're both insane. My best friend and my girlfriend: insane!"

"We're not ins— wait, girlfriend?" Cali asks. "Really?"

"Really?" I ask.

"Damn, Moose. You do have it bad."

"Cali now is not the time for this! I mean, let's put a pin in the word 'girl-friend' and definitely come back to it later and all, please. But right now, I have to get Matt on board before Darius shows up and kills us all!"

"You're right, you're right. Okay," she says sitting down on top of the large duffle bag with the supplies in it. "You've got the con."

"Lex?" Matt looks at me shocked and terrified. His face bears the expression I imagine someone would have after being told that not only is Santa real, but the heat his sleigh generates traveling around the world is the actual cause of global warming.

I take a deep breath and decide to just dive in head first. "Matt, I'm a witch."

"Stop," he puts both hands up angrily. "What is this? Some kind of sick joke?"

"No, Matt. We're telling the truth. *I'm* telling you the truth."

His mouth turns down in hurt and disgust. He turns away from me.

"Matt, please," I say. My voice is heavy with emotion, about to break under it all. *I can't lose him now too.*

He heads to the door, aiming to leave, but Cali blocks him.

"Hear her out, Matt. I'm not above playing jokes, but this is serious. She's telling the truth. And she needs our help."

Just like Cali has never called me "Alexa," I've never heard her address Matt as anything other than Moose. When he hears that, he rears back as if she's slapped him.

"I don't understand." His eyes dart between the two of us.

"Matt," Cali says again, he turns to face her completely. "When Lex first told me everything, I needed five or six shots of vodka to process it. You don't have that luxury, and we don't have that kind of time."

He looks at me over his shoulder as Cali continues.

"The Cliff-notes version is this: Your girl here is crazy powerful, like with actual magical powers. And there is a demon, Darius, after her who wants to kill her, steal her powers and use them to literally burn the world to the ground. Plus, Milo over there? Dude can sense evil. That's why he was so wound up when those guys grabbed me. They were demons—"

"Victus," I correct.

"Right, Victus, which is just a fancy name for the demon's soldiers. The guy coming for her has a literal army at his disposal. But what does she have? Us. You and me." She points to herself and then to him to emphasize her statement. "And she was actually going to face this guy alone. I had to basically convince her to let me help. And I told her that you would help too, because you love her, Matt. You're in love with her."

"Dude!" he exclaims in embarrassment.

"Now ain't the time to be modest, man.

"Look, she told me what the deal is if we help her: that we'd have to go with her if she has to leave, thus the packed bags. She told me that we'll have to leave everything and everyone behind for an unknown length of time, possibly forever. Hence, this."

She pulls on an envelope from the pocket of her jacket. I don't need to see it up close to know that it's addressed to Mickey.

"I'm choosing to help her, Matt. If you don't want to help, I understand and I'm sure Lex will too. I just hope that you can at least understand why I have to. I'm going to tell you the same thing this letter will tell Mickey, and what I said to Lex back at our apartment: the only thing I'm choosing is my chance at a future with the blue-eyed, brunette, good-souled, gorgeous love of my life. And I'll be damned if I let some douche-bag demon destroy it.

"Oh, and one more thing. Her name isn't Alexa, but that's like, the least important of all the things I've told you."

Matt runs his hands through his hair, very similarly to how Cali did when she first heard all of this. Hearing Cali stand her ground and defend her choice to help me, I expected to be weighed down with guilt again. Instead, I feel like my energy has been renewed, and it's made me more determined than ever to fight back and give Darius the biggest surprise of the millennia that he's spent on earth.

"Cali," I say, my voice strong and steady. "Give him a moment."

I pick up the duffle bag, my laundry bag, and my purse and start walking into the room, down the faux hallway to the side of the cubes. I whistle over my shoulder and Milo, who's been patiently observing this entire time, jumps to his feet and trots after me. I hear Cali lift her own bag and the scuff of her shoes on the thick carpet as she catches up to me.

I go around behind the last cube so the only thing behind me is a cinderblock wall. I drop the bags in the corner and kneel down to rummage through for the plastic bag with the tennis balls. I talk to Cali over my shoulder.

"Okay, here's the plan," I say taking the tennis balls out and putting them on the floor one at a time. "We'll leave the bags here that way they're out of sight. We should come up with a code word for when it's time to go. I can transport us out of here, but I have to be touching you. Milo won't be a problem, he'll be by my side the whole time. And we can use telekinesis to grab the bags if we have to.

"Also, I'm not going to call you Cali, from here on out you are only Squirrel. We shouldn't risk Darius hearing your name. Just so that we have another way of keeping everyone else safe."

I let a heavy silence settle between us. I wait for Cali to understand that everyone else means Mickey. I watch her gulp and nod as she gets it.

"Okay, so what do I call you?"

I can't help but smile softly before I answer her. "Royal." She cocks her head, silently asking why. "It's what my brothers called me when I was little."

"You have brothers?"

I nod. "Two. They're both older so I was always tagging along with them. Whenever I would annoy them, which was a lot, they would tell me I was being a royal pain in the ass. Eventually, to avoid getting in trouble, they shortened it to them just saying to me, 'You're being a real royal right now.' So I would knock off whatever I was doing.

"Huh," I shake my head and snicker. "I hated that nickname as a kid, but now I miss hearing it."

"Royal," she says. "That works. What's the safe word? Mine is Strawberry Fields Forever."

"I don't kn—"

Before I can answer her completely, I feel someone pull me into a standing position and whip me around. I get a whiff of laundry detergent, Old Spice, and peppermint before I feel Matt's lips cover my own. He kisses me more passionately than ever before. I don't hesitate for a second before I'm responding in kind wrapping my arms around him.

After a few good and hot seconds, Matt slows down and kisses me sweetly and tenderly. When he pulls away from me, he tucks his head into my neck and hugs me tightly.

"I love you," he says releasing me. "That Squirrel is right, I keep forgetting she's smarter than she looks."

"I take offense to that," Cali lazily offers from her spot a few feet away.

"I've loved you from the moment I saw you. I fell in love with you the first time we talked. When you kissed me last week, I nearly died right then and there from happiness. I don't want you to say it back, I don't need to hear it back right now.

"I just want to tell you that I'm choosing the same thing that Cali is: I'm choosing my future with you over some..." He stops, searching for the right word, "...*thing* that thinks he can take it away from me."

The blood is pumping so hard through my body right now that I'm sure he can hear it along with the pounding of my heart. I kiss him one more time and caress his stubble covered cheek. I could get lost in this moment with Matt, but thankfully Cali speaks up before I do.

"Well, then I guess there's only one more thing to do before we get this party started," she says.

"And what exactly is that?" Matt asks.

The smile Cali gives him is one of badass determination. "We join *her* army."

• 5 5 •

DARIUS

The demon and his three Victus are driving on Interstate 85 on their way to Atlanta International Airport. It's just before 10 P.M. and the drive is smooth with very little traffic. Viribus is behind the wheel of one of Darius's many luxury SUVs.

"Go over it one more time," Darius instructs from the back seat next to Damon. He has his window cracked slightly to allow the smoke from his cigarette to escape.

"I drop you three off at the airport, go back to the bar, and wait for your call," Viribus answers obediently.

"I handle our bags and print out the tickets from the kiosk," Julius chimes in from the front passenger seat.

Darius swings his head around to face his newest soldier.

"I stay out of the way and do what I'm told," Damon says in a monotone.

"Excellent," he praises. "Then what?"

"We land in Seattle, and use the potions to transport to Portland," Julius says first. "We start at the library to search for any leads. From there, we find the girl and kill her. Then, we use the potions to head to the portal."

Viribus's baritone continues, "Once you get to the portal, you let me know and I will meet you there transporting from the bar."

Again the demon turns his head to the man sitting next to him. Damon grits his teeth and adds his role in a tight voice. "I stay out of the way and do what I'm told."

"Very good, children," the demon purrs.

Viribus takes the exit off of I-85 onto Camp Creek Parkway. He follows the signs for departure, pulling up in front of the terminal and shutting off the engine. The three Victus get out of the car, but Darius hangs back a moment. He finishes his cigarette, throws the butt out the window.

"Watch out girl," he says to the empty car. "Here I come."

****

The three had no issues getting through the airport and onto the plane. They are seated in business class. Darius has a single window seat on the left side of the cabin, Damon and Julius are across the aisle in the middle of the plane in a pair of double seats. On the other side of Julius are a second aisle and an empty single window seat. They're settling themselves in when a male flight attendant comes by and asks if he can get them anything.

"I'll have a whiskey neat, three fingers," Darius answers quickly. "And keep them coming."

"I'll take a Sprite now," Julius says. "But right before we land, I'll take a very strong coffee."

"I'll just have a water," Damon answers last. He's also the only one to add a "thank you" before the flight attendant moves down the aisle to the galley to prepare their drinks.

A few minutes later, a female attendant brings the drinks back to the men. Damon perks up and starts talking to the woman.

"Hey there, sugar. I'm Damon. What's your name?"

• 313 •

"I'm Elaine. Here are your drinks gentlemen," she says handing out the liquor, soda, and water. "Please fasten your seat belts, we'll be taking off shortly."

Damon's eyes follow Elaine as she gets ready to demo the safety instructions. Darius looks around to make sure no one is looking before he reaches across to Damon and punches him in the middle of his chest. The blow lands right on his sternum. The bald man grunts in pain and doubles over as the air escapes his lungs.

"Tell me, Julius," Darius says in a hushed voice. "Am I asking for a lot?"

"No, boss."

"You hear that, shit head? I'm not asking for a lot. I'm asking for you to just sit in that fucking seat, watch some cartoons for the next few hours, and attract as little attention as possible. And what's the first thing you do? Creep out the fucking flight attendant! Is that what I asked for Julius?"

"No, it's not, boss."

Damon coughs trying to replenish some oxygen to his burning chest. He takes a long gulp from his bottle of water. He looks at Darius with unadulterated rage on his face.

"Save it, little one," Darius scolds before dropping his voice to almost a whisper. "Because if you do anything else besides say 'yes, no, please, and thank you' to anyone on this flight, I'll kill you myself before we even land. Got it?"

Damon puts his head back on the oversized chair and stares at the ceiling of the plane. He doesn't answer, just closes his eyes and nods.

"Good. Jesus Christ, Julius! You think this kid has a problem with authority or what?"

Julius chuckles along with the demon.

"Don't let go of that attitude completely, little one," the demon says. "But you'd best drop it entirely when it's my orders in question."

The bald man keeps his eyes closed and his head back. He doesn't open them when Elaine, the female flight attendant, stands at the front of the plane and begins performing the standard safety guidelines. He keeps his eyes closed as the plane taxis to the runway. He doesn't open them as the plane speeds up and takes off. The repetitive clench of his jaw is the only indication that he hasn't fallen asleep.

Darius doesn't have his usual perch to people watch the morons who frequent that cruddy little bar, so he does the next best thing: scan the channels for a reality TV competition. Once he sees people with bandanas, backpacks, and maps on the screen trying to communicate unsuccessfully with each other, he leaves the channel on. He doesn't put on headphones, he prefers to just watch.

There isn't enough time for Darius to go into a deep meditation, so he's effectively stuck in limbo. Reduced once more to waiting.

He hits the call button in the bulkhead above him, and when the flight attendant comes over, he orders another whiskey. As he sips the last of the tepid liquid before his fresh one arrives, he imagines everything he'll do after killing the girl and stripping her of her powers. The first of which will be to find her family and murder them while he makes that meddling old man watch.

The demon opens the shade of the small window all the way and looks out. His own reflection in the plexiglass catches his eye. He flashes a conniving smile at his image knowing that pretty soon all of this goddamn waiting will finally be over.

• 5 6 •

"ALEXA"

As I lead Matt and Cali over to the third cube in the row, I hear Cali behind me giving Matt another crash course. This time the topic is Extensios.

"So, basically, she's going to say some stuff in Latin, and then her hand will glow, and she'll touch us, and then BAM! We are her Extensios and can move stuff with our minds."

"This is all still really unbelievable, you know?"

"I know, Moose. But how fucking cool is it at the same time though?"

"Alright, it's pretty fucking cool."

"Right?!"

I slightly shake my head and smile to myself at their antics and swipe my card through the lock on CCR3. I hold open the door for the two of them to come in with me. Milo is already inside, he's been at my knee since I gave him the "side" command minutes ago.

"Wait here," I say to Cali and Matt as I put the tennis balls down on the small, empty table.

I make my way across the cube to the last shelf where I know *The Book* is. As I pick it up, I remind myself this is right and that hopefully after tonight this will all be over. I bring it back over to where Cali and Matt are waiting, and gently set it down on the table.

"Wow," my roommate says. "This is it?"

"Yeah. This is what I've been searching the past five years for."

I open *The Book* and flip to the pages on Extensios that I went over and over earlier today.

"Okay," I take a deep breath. "As soon as I use magic, Darius is going to have a bead on where we are. He and I are linked, and the only reason he hasn't already found me is because I have been meticulous about not using my powers.

"I don't know where he is, or how long it'll take him to get here, but I'm going to try and spy on him a little once the connection is made."

"Spy?" Matt asks.

"She can read minds, Moose. She's going to try and figure out his plan without him knowing."

"You can read minds?"

"Yes."

A look of realization brightens his face. "So when you told that little boy that you could read minds, you actually meant it?"

"What?" For a moment I have no idea what he's talking about. "Oh, that! I really said it just to help the mom out."

"But It's true. You can."

"It's one of my powers, yes."

"See? Isn't that *awesome*?" Cali asks excitedly. Matt nods his head with a literal look of awe on his face.

"I have one more question before we get started here," Cali says raising her hand and waiting to be called on.

"Yes? The squirrel in the front," I say playing along.

"What are the tennis balls for?"

"Practice. When Darius gets here, I'm going off an assumption of course, but I'm guessing he won't show up alone. His Victus will have the same powers as you, telekinesis, but they'll have had them longer. They could pick up stuff and launch it at you. And if Darius has similar powers to me, then he probably will throw fire.

"Regardless of what's coming at you, you have to know how to deflect it away first without it hitting you, and second without it hitting the other two of us."

"How do we do that?" Matt asks.

I have honestly no idea, I've never used my telekinesis power, is what I want to say. Instead, I confidently reply, "I'll teach you."

I look back and forth between my best friend and my boyfriend — still can't get over that word, but now is not the time. I feel the need to ask them one more time. "Are you both sure you're ready to do this? Really think before you answer. You can still say no."

"I'm staying," Cali immediately answers.

Matt is quiet for a long minute before her answers. His face softens, and with a smile, he says, "I'm not leaving, either."

I return his smile. I don't realize that we're staring at each other until Cali clears her throat and says, "Umm, still here guys."

"Right!" I shake my head quickly and return to the task at hand. "From here on until we're safely out of here, you guys are only Moose and Squirrel, and I am Royal. Got it?"

"Yes," they answer together.

"Good." I kneel down and pet Milo and tell him the same thing. "Now, who's Squirrel?"

Milo gets up and takes the few steps over to Cali pressing himself against her leg. "Good boy, Milo. Go to Royal." He comes back to me. "Now, Moose." He presses himself against Matt.

"Way to go, Dog Man." Cali holds out her fist for a bump, which Milo dutifully gives her with his nose.

"Okay," I say. "I guess let's do this."

I look over the page of *The Book* one more time. I position myself in front of Cali and Matt, close enough to touch them, and close my eyes. I clear my mind of everything except the words in Latin that I have to recite out loud. I tell myself I can do this, that I am the most powerful magical creature on this planet.

I feel something opening within my chest. It's as if a small part of myself that was wrapped up in chains is being freed link by link. I take three deep breaths.

"Elegit ex mea potestate te i donum."

By choice, my power I gift to thee.

I keep my eyes closed and feel my hands start to warm up. There is a tingling sensation that goes up both of my arms into my chest. I say the chant two more times.

"Elegit ex mea potestate te i donum. Elegit ex mea potestate te i donum."

When I open my eyes, both of my hands are glowing with a blinding, pure white light. Cali's and Matt's eyes are the size of dinner plates, but as I reach for their heads, they both close their eyes and bow. As my hands hover over each of their heads, I say the next part.

"Corporalis motus animi."

Physical movement of the mind.

I lay my hands on their scalps. I see them start to glow, the light travels the inner map of their blood vessels from their temples to their necks and branching out. The light spreads until every vessel in their bodies is bursting with bright, white light. I hold on to them and say the final words that will transform my friends into my Extensios.

"Ego donum tibi."

I gift to thee.

I don't remove my hands until the light retraces its path and lands in their eyes. Both Cali and Matt open their eyes at the same time to reveal glowing orbs that slowly fade back to their normal green and light brown colors.

I drop my hands to my sides, they've stopped glowing. I watch Matt and Cali with sharp eyes to gauge how they are feeling. The two best friends look at each and start laughing.

"How do you feel?" I nervously ask them.

"I don't know about her," Matt says. "But I feel pretty much the same, except also maybe a little lighter and stronger at the same time?"

"Yeah," Cali agrees. "When it was happening, my whole body was tingling which felt weird. But then I kinda liked it, if you know what I mean."

"Jeez, Squirrel," Matt groans.

Right then my whole body jolts as if I've been electrocuted and becomes rigid. My vision fades to white and then materializes again with a new scene in front of me. I'm on a plane. There are three men seated around me, one by himself with multiple tattoos on his pale hands.

Darius. I instinctively know that it's him.

My vision dissolves again. When it clears this time, I'm back in CCR3 in the library. Matt and Cali are looking at me both frightened and concerned.

I don't waste a second before telling them. "I saw him. He's coming."

• 5 7 •

DARIUS

Seven miles up in the airspace above Fort Collins, Colorado, Flight 156 is cruising along with clear skies ahead all the way to Seattle, Washington. In the business class section, Darius sits in his comfortable chair with his eyes closed, biding his time.

They suddenly snap open, entirely white as if clouded over. His hands grip the armrests as his muscles tense. A snapshot materializes in front of him. He sees the girl and two other people, along with the black dog, in what looks like a glass cube. They are surrounded by books. One in particular, is laying open on a table next to them.

As his eyes clear, the cabin of the plane refocuses around him.

"Looks like someone is gearing up for a fight," he says aloud. "That'll make killing her that much more satisfying."

He looks across the small aisle at his Victus in the double seats. Damon's jaw is slack, Julius's chin is resting on his chest. They've both fallen asleep. Darius flicks his fingers in the air and both men's heads simultaneously get knocked to the side waking them.

Julius and Damon both wipe their eyes and look around dazed, until they see Darius waiting impatiently on their left. The two awaken fully then.

"Sorry, boss," Julius says, adjusting himself in his seat. "Must've dozed off."

"Never mind that, I know where she is," the demon says in a quick, hushed whisper. "She's in that library, and she's got some friends with her. Probably made them into Extensios. Plus that damn dog."

"So what's the plan, boss? We can't transport from the plane."

"I know," Darius replies angrily. "It'll force too much attention on us. We have to wait until we land in Seattle. We'll use the potions to transport right from the nearest terminal bathroom. We get into the library, kill her and her little toy soldiers, then go right to the portal."

"Alright, sounds good to us, boss."

Julius pushes the call button above him and asks for the strongest coffee they have for both himself and Damon. When the flight attendant asks if the men need anything else, Darius answers.

"Yes, I'll take another whiskey, make it a double. And how much longer until we land?"

"Just over two hours, sir. And that's a whiskey neat, correct?"

Darius nods and the male flight attendant turns around and goes back to the galley. He brings the three men their drinks shortly. While Damon and Julius are stirring sugar into their coffees, the demon returns his attention to the window. His only movement comes from his arm bringing his drink back and forth from his armrest to his mouth.

"A couple more hours," he says to himself with a sinister smile.

• 5 8 •

Cali

Cali watches as her roommate's eyes go completely white. She goes to grab her hand but Matt holds her back. When Alexa's eyes clear completely, she says something that Cali didn't realize she wasn't exactly ready to hear.

"I saw him. He's coming."

"Oh, shit."

"Okay, okay," Matt says trying to stay calm. "What do we do?"

"Two things," Alexa answers. "First I try my hand at espionage to see what his plan is. Then, we practice using your new power."

"Right, okay." Cali feels her palms start to sweat and her mouth goes dry. "Wow, I'm more nervous than I thought I would be. So how do we spy?"

"*We* don't," Alexa says pointing between the three of them. "I have an idea."

She sits down cross-legged on the floor and calls Milo over. The dog lays down in front of her and puts his head on top of one knee.

"What are you gonna do, Lex?" Cali asks. "Jesus! I mean, Royal."

"I'm going to try and let my mind go to Darius using Milo as an anchor."

"I don't understand," Matt says. He's sat down next to Alexa, close but not touching.

"I don't either, really, but in theory I should be able to just pop in and pop back. And hopefully, he won't know I'm doing it if I don't stay too long.

"*Squirrel*," she says purposely. "Don't let me go too long. Give me a shake if it's past sixty seconds."

Cali watches as her roommate closes her eyes. She puts one hand on top of her dog's head, the other on the floor. When she opens her eyes, they are completely white again and slightly glowing. Cali lifts her arm to watch the time.

At the forty-ninth second, Alexa blinks a few times and her eyes return to their normal hazel.

"What'd you see?" Matt asks quickly. He takes her hand in his.

"He's on a plane. He's with two men. A short, fat white guy, and a tall, bald black man." She drops her head to her chest and grits her teeth. "I fucking knew it."

"Hey, hey," Cali says squatting down next to Alexa. "It's not your fault. You are not the reason they hurt me. Those guys being predators is separate from them being Victus. That guy didn't grab me because I'm your friend, he would've grabbed anybody who bumped into him. It's okay, and I'm okay."

Alexa still won't look her in the eye. "Look at me, Royal." She waits until her friend looks up. "Okay?"

"Okay," Alexa nods, regaining her composure. "I don't know exactly how long is left in their flight, but they are going to transport right to here once they land.

"I'm thinking less than a couple of hours until they get here, a full two at the most." Alexa takes out her phone and sets a timer for ninety minutes.

"Then we'd better get started," Matt says standing up. He's still holding Alexa's hand and pulls her up with him.

"Right, okay."

Alexa closes *The Book* and moves it to the side of the table. She takes three of the tennis balls and lines them up in the middle. Then she takes three steps backward and raises her right hand, palm up. She slowly curls four fingers back and forth. The tennis ball all the way to the right starts to float up and down in the air in tandem with the movement of her fingers.

"So, I'm focusing on the ball and imagining the movement I want it to make. Then I channel that into my hand."

She stops the movement of her hand, and the ball hovers in the air. She points at the ball and quickly flicks her wrist toward Cali. The ball flies through the air and Cali catches it. Alexa bends two fingers toward herself, and the ball zooms back into her hand.

"Now, you try."

Matt and Cali adjust themselves so they are standing on either side of Alexa.

"Does it matter which hand we use?" Matt asks.

Alexa shrugs. "I don't think so, but maybe your dominant one because it has more coordination."

Matt raises his right arm, Cali her left.

"Go slow," her roommate tells them. "Nice and easy, smooth movements."

Matt bends his fingers and nothing happens. He's staring with creepy intensity at the tennis ball.

"Relax," Alexa advises.

Cali bends the fingers on her left hand, but instead of slowly, she makes a quick fist. The tennis ball hurtles off the table and beelines right for her forehead.

It stops inches before it can smack into her face. It came at her so fast that Cali didn't have time to flinch until the ball froze. She clamps both of her eyes shut anticipating the sting of the tennis ball bouncing off her face, but when nothing comes, she opens her eyes.

Matt is staring slack-jawed at Cali and the tennis ball, Alexa has her hand up. When she lowers her hand, the tennis ball falls to the floor, bouncing a few times.

"I saw that happening before it even did," Alexa says. "Whether that was a premonition, or I just know you really well, I'm not sure."

"I should take offense to that," Cali says making a face. "But my dignity thanks you."

She bows slightly to Alexa making her roommate laugh lightly. Alexa picks up the tennis ball and puts it back on the table.

"Okay, let's try again."

• 5 9 •

"ALEXA"

I'm watching Cali and Matt learning how to channel their power and move the tennis balls when an image flashes in my head. It's like a stop-motion movie. I see Cali's tennis ball come straight at her and bounce off of her head. My ears ring as the image disappears.

Holy shit. Was that my first premonition?

I can't be entirely sure having never had one before, but I ready myself to stop Cali's ball anyway. Seconds later there is a blur of bright yellow streaking through the air. I raise my arm and am able to stop the ball inches before it hits her.

I let the ball drop to the ground before I say, "I saw that happening before it even did. Whether that was a premonition, or I just know you really well, I'm not sure."

Cali thanks me and bows. I pick up her tennis ball and put it back on the table. I tell her and Matt to try again.

After a few more tries, the tennis balls are easily floating up and down in place above the table. Next, I tell them to lift the ball at one end of the table, move it across, and set it down at the other end.

Predictably, each of their first tries bounce off the glass wall of the cube and roll into the row of shelves. The second and third attempts get there but aren't graceful, but after that, they start to get the hang of it.

"Good," I say putting the tennis balls back in the bag.

"That's it?" Matt asks me. I can tell he's a little disappointed.

"No, I just want to put *The Book* on its shelf so that it's safe."

Cali frowns and asks, "Wouldn't it be safer to put it with our bags behind the last cube?"

"I'm not sure, but I don't think so. It's been here for so long and Darius hasn't found it so there must be a reason right? Maybe it's safer to keep it camouflaged with the rest of the books."

I gently replace *The Book* back to its spot and making sure I have my key-card, I take the bag of tennis balls and leave the cube. Matt and Cali follow me without my having to ask them to. The minute my feet are outside the cube, Milo is in his place at my knee.

I face my best friend and boyfriend and tell them what I'm going to do next as I take big steps backward in the direction of the entrance to the sub-basement.

"I'm going to throw the balls at you now, and I want you to deflect them. If you can, send them right back at me or to either side. Imagine when the ball comes at you that it suddenly goes the opposite direction. Then channel it like before."

I show them how by putting my arm out straight in front of me, palm forward and perpendicular to the floor. I look as if I'm telling a car to stop.

"Ready?"

"Yes," Cali answers. Matt just nods.

I tell Milo to stay before I throw the first ball in Cali's direction, more a light toss than anything. She puts her hand up to deflect and... nothing happens. The ball lands behind her and bounces away. She turns to run after it.

"No, leave it Squirrel. Okay, Milo, go get it!" My dog takes off in a mad dash after the tennis ball. He pounces on it and trots it back, tail wagging happily.

"Thank you, pup," I say taking the ball from him. "Stay."

I throw the ball now to Matt. Same as Cali, his arm comes up to deflect. The ball stops and reverses its trajectory, but instead of coming straight back to me, it travels about eight feet then falls to the ground bouncing the rest of the way back.

Cali scoffs at her place next to him and grumbles, "Teacher's pet."

He smirks at her and taunts, "Beat that, Squirrel."

"I will! Come on, Royal. Give me your best shot."

Cali gets in the ready position: feet spread, knees and elbows bent. I throw the ball at her, harder than before. Palm out, her arm straightens. The little neon sphere deflects but veers off to the right and lands on top of the first cube.

"Well, that's umm, better I guess." I shrug and flick my wrist so the ball comes off the glass ceiling. I catch it, ready to throw at Matt again.

"In your face, Moose," I hear Cali mumble without any glory.

Just like inside CCR3 before, it only takes a few more tries before both Matt and Cali have the hang of things. I make my throws harder and harder until eventually I'm using my power to fling the tennis ball. The learning curve steepens at that point but quickly smooths out.

Milo is behaving so well, staying put as tennis balls fly through the air. But I can tell he's getting wound up because, while he's staying seated next to me, his front paws are stomping lightly. I can also tell that Cali and Matt could use a break, so I ruffle the fur by his collar and tell him to get ready.

I toss a tennis ball in the air a couple of times. When it lands in my hand the second time, I squeeze it making the thing squeak loudly. The high-pitched noise echos throughout the room. I use my power to hurl the ball to the opposite end.

Milo takes off in an instant, disappearing down the giant room. Having been down here so much recently, I've forgotten how big the place actually is. The jingle of Milo's tags fades out the further he runs.

It's silent for a full five seconds as Milo searches for the ball. I feel myself get nervous that maybe someone snuck in without us aware and that someone's got him. I let out a huge sigh of relief as I hear him coming back. The squeaker in the tennis ball is going nuts as Milo repeatedly bites down while he trots back to me.

He drops the ball in front of me and puts his chest on the ground ready to go again. I pick it up and throw it this time, so he doesn't have to go as far away from me.

I toss another ball to Matt, an idea blooming. "How many times do you think you guys can go back and forth without dropping it?"

"More times than him!" Cali immediately yells.

"In your dreams, Squirrel!" Matt fires back.

I've easily goaded them into a competition, but it's for a good reason. I need them as prepared as possible.

Cali and Matt are yelling and taunting each other as the tennis ball zooms back and forth between them. I have my arm cocked ready to throw the ball for Milo for the sixth time when the light mood is abruptly interrupted as the alarm on my phone goes off.

Has it really been ninety minutes already? I look at my friends, my Extensios and think, *Are they ready? Am I?*

My roommate catches instead of deflects the tennis ball. I look at the time on my phone, it's 12:45 A.M. Darius could be here any minute.

"So," she says. "What's the plan now?"

I have no idea what to say to her or Matt. So I don't say anything.

• 6 0 •

I motion for the two of them to follow me, and I walk the length of the room to where we've left our bags behind the very last glass cube. I rummage through the large duffle bag that Cali filled with supplies until I find three protein bars.

The water bottles with the filter straws were left empty to keep the bag as light as possible, so there is nothing for us to drink. I could risk running up the stairs and through the library to the vending machine in the employee lounge, but it would leave all of us vulnerable.

I'm battling internally if I should run upstairs, transport there, or use my projection power and make three bottles of water appear. Milo's heavy panting beside me makes the decision for me.

"Wait here," I say moving a few feet away. Milo comes with me but I tell him no.

"Where are you going?" Matt asks me.

"To get something for us to drink."

I picture the employee lounge in my head, the vending machine specifically. The only other time I did this, all I did was think of a beach and say, "Florida." This time I'm recreating as much detail as possible so I go exactly where I want.

I close my eyes and say, "Upstairs."

I feel my body get lighter for a second. It's similar to when an elevator initially starts to descend. The sensation is gone in less than a second.

When I open my eyes, I'm standing in front of the vending machines. The room is dark, only lit by the internal light from the snack machine. There are no motion sensors in here for lights, so the room stays dark. I'm exactly where I want to be. I can't help the pride I feel and the satisfied smile that spreads across my face.

I reach into my pocket and take out the change from the cab ride earlier. I put the singles into the machine and get three bottles of water. It occurs to me that I could just use my powers instead, but that would be taking advantage and it's not my style.

I peek my head out of the door to make sure all is still quiet up here. The lights are still off, meaning no one has moved around up here for at least fifteen minutes.

I quietly close the door and picture the sub-basement. I see Cali and Matt and Milo at the back of the room where I left them. I close my eyes again trying to paint as much detail as possible into the snapshot.

"Milo," I say knowing I will be taken to wherever my pup is. After I feel that elevator sensation and I open my eyes again, I'm standing in front of Cali and Matt who have giant smiles on their faces.

"That was so fucking cool!!" Cali exclaims "It's one thing to be told you have magical powers, but it is so much cooler when you actually see it!".

I don't say anything but toss a water bottle to each of them with a grin. I pick up Milo's collapsable bowl, pop it into shape, and pour half of my bottle in. My dog dives in lapping up the cold water.

"So which power was that? Transporting?" Matt asks. I frown at him confused. I don't remember telling him just what my powers are. "Squirrel told me when you disappeared into thin air."

"He looked a little panicked, so I had to calm him down," Cali says after a long drink.

"Did not," Matt pouts.

"Did too," she shoots back.

I sit down on the floor next to Milo, across from Cali and Matt. My back is up against the cool glass of CCR6.

"What do we do now?" Matt asks.

"We wait, I guess," I say unsurely. "I don't know when he'll be here, but I've left him enough bread crumbs for him to know this is where I am."

"Bread crumbs?"

"He can track her," Cali explains. "Remember? Every time she uses her powers, he gets like a radar blip or something. But now that you're using your powers shouldn't you get your own blip when he does something?"

"In theory," I shrug. "I'm still getting the hang of all of this."

I eat my bar to be able to have a moment to myself. Cali already knows we're more likely than not going to have to leave here. But does Matt know? I could read his mind, but that's an invasion of privacy I don't want to be a part of.

It's quiet for a moment before Cali asks, "Where do we go from here?"

"What do you mean?"

"Like, Darius is coming here, right? And the reason you made us Extensios and taught us how to use the power that comes with it is to protect ourselves and to help you. But how are we getting out of here? And where do we go?"

"There was an inscription at the back of *The Book*. If we have to, we'll go where it said to."

"What do we do when Darius gets here?"

"We fight. He's going to throw something a lot more dangerous than tennis balls. All you have to do is deflect them. Just not at each other, or me and Milo.

"He has two Victus with him, and they have the same power you do. So watch out that they don't redirect your deflections."

"What are you going to do?" Matt looks at me nervously.

"I'm going to protect you both, and give him a taste of his own medicine."

I leave it vague intentionally. Because I have no idea what the hell I'm going to do. I sit there quietly while Matt and Cali continue talking.

"Uhh, Moose? Maybe you should write a letter or something to Mom. Explain all of this in a way that... I don't know, explains all of this?"

"I will," he says. "When the three of us get out of here, I will."

"Good," Cali says softly.

"Okay, I sort of have a plan," I tell them. "There is only one way in or out of here. I don't think Darius will know we're down here, just that we're in the library somewhere. Milo will know when they get here, he'll be able to sense it. I will too."

"Why don't we just leave when he gets here? Grab *The Book* and go," Matt suggests.

"He'll follow us," I say. "At least here we have the upper hand. It's better to fight and wound him or something so we can get away safe."

The hair on the back of my neck stands on end just as Milo starts to growl. I feel my eyes begin to cloud, but I shake it off. I don't need to see the scene to know Darius just used magic of some kind.

"Listen, we'll hide behind the cubes. He's going to try and draw us out, maybe with some big show of power or taunts."

Milo starts to pace, becoming more and more agitated. He's alternating whining and growling.

"If you have to move, do it quickly and stay low." I'm speaking as fast as I can."If Milo brushes against you, go with him. Keep your head moving and don't turn your back on anyone. Okay?"

Cali and Matt nod. I can see on their faces that things just got very real for them.

"Stay together. Where one goes, you both go. Got it?

They both nod at me in understanding. They look terrified, they've both started to sweat, and they are pale from fear. But neither of them have wavered, not even for a minute, on staying here with me.

I know right now at this second that everything that has happened the last five years has been leading me to this moment, leading me to Matt and Cali. And I swear to myself that I will do everything I can to win this for them. I will exhaust every single one of my powers if it means all of us coming out alive from this.

"Okay. Get into position."

"Now?" Cali asks.

"Now," I say, my eyes drifting up to look at the ceiling. "He's here."

• 6 1 •

DARIUS

Darius's leg is bouncing impatiently as Flight 156 makes its final approach into Seattle-Tacoma Airport. Each time the girl has used her powers over the last one hundred or so minutes, he's become more and more agitated. If it weren't such an unnecessary risk to his future plans, he would've transported mid-flight. But it wouldn't be smart to attract that kind of attention when he's so close to finally getting his way.

The plane bounces a few times as the wheels make contact with the runway. The announcement is made with the time and temperature, and to wait until the aircraft has reached the terminal before unbuckling seat belts and turning on phones.

Damon and Julius ignore the voice over the speaker system and stand up to remove their overnight bags from the overhead bin. Darius swallows the last of his whiskey before standing also. He takes down his own bag and adjusts his tailored suit jacket.

The plane docks with the airway and the door is opened. Julius exits first, followed quickly by Damon. Neither responds to the well wishes or good-byes from the flight attendants. Darius asks where the closest men's room is as he makes his way off the plane.

"There will be one directly to the right once you enter the terminal," the male flight attendant answer.

"Good," Darius replies. As he walks away, he doesn't see the male and female flight attendants share a relieved look at finally being rid of the three rude, demanding, and creepy men.

The demon's long strides allow him to quickly catch up with Damon and Julius, and to take the lead. The Victus follow him into the nearest bathroom which is exactly where the flight attendant said. It's just about 1:30 in the morning, so the airport is all but deserted.

The three of them head for the last stall in the bathroom, making sure the rest are empty as they go. Each of them takes out one of the two potions from their bags and open it. Darius keeps the two "just in case" extras in his outer right jacket pocket.

Damon clears his throat before asking, "How exactly does this work?"

"We drink the potion, I touch each of you, and I say where we have to go."

"Simple enough," Damon shrugs. He's learned quickly to just agree with whatever he's told.

"Should be as long as it was made right," Darius growls. He turns to Julius and asks, "What's the name of this place again?"

Julius removes a piece of paper from his pocket and reads off, "Multnomah County Central Library, Portland, Oregon."

"That's a goddamn mouthful," the demon says annoyed.

He picks up his bag and throws it across his shoulder, his Victus mirror his actions. Each of them bring the small vials to their mouths and drain it of the black liquid inside. Darius grabs onto the shoulder of each man and grips firmly. He closes his eyes and takes a deep breath.

"Multnomah County Central Library, Portland, Oregon."

All three men feel a sudden strong tug on their bodies, similar to the initial burst of speed on the straight vertical of a roller coaster. The pull gets more and more intense until finally, it feels like they'll all be split in two when suddenly it stops.

Darius lets go of Damon and Julius. He spins in a slow circle taking in his surroundings. They are on the first floor of the library, near the main entrance. Their arrival triggered the motion sensors, and the large room is bathed in bright, fluorescent light. The demon takes another look around. As he scans the room, he sees an elevator to one side, a staircase to the other, and a door marked Employees Only.

This is the right location, he can tell from all the blips she sent out, but it doesn't look anything like what he saw. He sucks in a breath to think for a minute. When he lets it out, it sounds like half sigh and half growl.

"She's here," he says. "But she's not *here*. There has to be another floor or a basement." He thinks for a minute then says, "Definitely basement. Prey always foolishly think underground is safer."

The three men drop their bags where they stand and move as a group first toward the elevator. Darius hits the call button, and when the doors open he peeks his head inside. There are three buttons for floors: a B with a keycard slot next to it, an L with an asterisk, and a 2 for the second floor.

"B must mean basement," Julius offers. "But taking the elevator down is too risky, gives away any element of surprise, boss. Plus we'd be packed in tight. One shot and she could get all three of us."

Darius narrows his eyes and nods. They move through the shelves of books across the library to a large, ornate staircase. In the wall directly behind it is a metal door with another Employees Only plaque on it.

The men go through the metal door and find themselves in a closed in stairwell. There is another door directly in front of them, and one to the left a little ways away with a red light and a card slot. Darius walks right up to it and throws his arms across his body to use his power to rip the door from its hinges. It shifts slightly but stays put.

The demon growls audibly. He holds his hand out to the side and it starts to glow.

"Are you sure she's down there, boss?"

"Yes, I'm fucking sure." Julius ducks his head and backs away from the riled demon.

"So much for a stealthy arrival," he says as his hand brightens more. The light is eventually replaced by a ball of fire in his palm. He pulls his arm back and heaves the orb of fire forward as hard as he can.

The electronic lock explodes on contact sending pieces and sparks across the floor. The door swings inward with a hard bang revealing another staircase. The demon and Victus don't hesitate to head down it. At the bottom are two more doors, one in front and one to the right. Both have a card slot with a red light over it.

Darius pauses, studying each door. He smells the air before turning his body to face the door on the right. He sniffs again and turns back to the other door.

The men are in a much more enclosed area, so when Darius cocks his arm, his palm already full of fire, Damon and Julius backtrack up the stairs to avoid being hit by any of the debris. The demon lets the ball fly, and again the door lock explodes. The boom is considerably louder in such a smaller space. Unfazed by the concussive sound or the smoke and bits of plastic raining down, he pushes the door hanging cockeyed on its hinges. A third staircase is revealed, but this time with only one door at the bottom.

With a lascivious smile, Darius heads down the stairs with a cocky swagger. He's followed his instinct and knows it's about to pay off. He gets to the bottom of the stairs and waits for a beat before pulling his arm back ready to fire again.

"Time's up, girl," he says with a sneer.

• 6 2 •

"ALEXA"

Just as Cali, Matt, and I are getting into position — the two of them behind cube three, myself and Milo behind cube four — we hear a loud explosion come from above us near the door to the room. I see Cali pop her head around CCR3 searching for me.

"What the fuck was that?" she whisper-yells.

"It's Darius. Stay down!" I whisper back at her. I kneel down and grip onto Milo's collar. His chest rumbles as he starts to growl but I silence him with a finger to my lips.

Another explosion goes off, this time louder and closer. Not even thirty seconds pass before the door to the sub-basement is blown open. I peak out to get a better look. There is a large gaping hole where the electric lock and keycard slot have been demolished. I see a dark figure come through the smoke and pull my head back behind the cube before the smoke fully clears.

I hear someone take in a long, deep breath through their nose then let it out with a loud sigh.

"Come out, come out, wherever you are," a vicious voice sings.

Darius. His voice is strong and clear with no trace of an accent. I hear him take a few steps into the room. Something skids across the floor into one of the concrete walls, probably a piece of the door. Two pairs of footsteps enter behind him and move off to his side.

"Listen, girl," Darius calls out. "I know you're here and I know you aren't alone. Come out now, and I won't kill your little friends."

He pauses waiting for me to respond. I don't, I stay completely silent and still. Milo, beside me, doing the same. Darius apparently isn't satisfied by that because the next thing I know, there is a quick *whoosh* followed by a deafening boom.

I cover my ears and poke my head up slightly. What I see doesn't make any sense to me. The first cube is practically completely gone.

Left in its place are small fires made up of shredded books and shelves reduced to kindling. Surrounding that is the metal frame curled in an unnatural twist, the shattered glass panels litter the floor. The larger ladder and the track it was on are nowhere to be seen. The ducts above are swinging slightly from side to side. Live-wires spark every time the ductwork makes contact with them.

"Come on, now. I haven't got all day!" the demon yells to me again. "Show yourself, or I'll blow up all of these boxes one by one until there is nothing left. I'll make you watch as I torture and kill your friends! When I'm through with you, you'll beg me for death!!"

I've found an angle that allows me to watch from my place hidden behind CCR4. Darius looks crazed. His eyes glow, reflecting the light of the fires where cube one used to be. His Victus, the short, fat man and tall, bald man, are off to his left watching, waiting for an order.

I watch Darius's hand glow, getting brighter and brighter until a flaming ball appears in his palm. My mouth hangs open as I see Darius pull his arm back and launch the ball of fire straight into CCR2. I hear the same boom as before, but this time I see the impact. The cube bursts apart, showering glass, splinters of wood, and pieces of metal down onto the third cube. Right where Matt and Cali are.

I stand and move over so that my voice can carry to my friends. I cup my hands around my mouth and yell as loud as I can.

"Squirrel! Moose! Move now!!"

KERRI MCLOONE

Matt and Cali dart out from behind CCR3 and run toward me. I see the moment that Darius sees them. His eyes light up, and a sinister smile whips across his face. He pulls his arm back, his palm already reloaded with fire. He directs his throw toward the two of them.

"Watch out!" I yell.

Matt spins around and deflects the ball of fire just in time. It sails back across the room to our right and hits the shoulder of the shorter Victus. He's launched into the air, spinning in a tight spiral. He smacks into the wall with a thud and slides to the ground.

"Good catch," Cali says to Matt as they sprint past me and duck behind the fifth cube.

Seeing my friends in such dire, direct danger, makes me angry. I feel it settle like a boulder in my stomach. This creature has taken enough from me, he's not taking them too. My mouth turns downward and my features set as my fury grows.

I imagine myself returning fire. I look down at my hand still flesh colored and imagine a ball of fire in it. I feel a brief warming sensation before Darius gets my attention again.

"Still nothing? You're going to leave your friends to fight your battle for you? Just like you left your brother, and I think we both remember how that turned out, don't we girl."

I grit my teeth and clench my fist to stop myself from reacting emotionally, but I can't let that barb about my brother go. I step out from behind CCR4, Milo glued to my side.

"Ahhh, there she is," Darius says when he sees me. "So, I see, your friends do mean more to you than your brother."

He's trying to goad me into reacting, but I won't let it work. I concentrate on channeling my emotions into my powers. I get a quick flash in my brain of what Darius is going to do next. He's going to fake like he's throwing a ball of fire at me, but use his telekinesis to slam me into the wall on my left.

My ears are still ringing from my premonition when I see Darius pull his arm back as if to throw again. Knowing what's coming next, I don't hesitate to whip my arm out to use my own power and throw Darius. I see a look of shock on his face before he slams into the wall, his head cracking against the concrete.

The tall, bald Victus is the only one left on his feet at the moment. He's the one who grabbed Cali. He's the one who hurt her.

He uses his power to pick up a piece of twisted metal and heave it toward me. I easily deflect it back into the pile of rubble that used to be CCR2. *You will not hurt her again!* my mind yells. I clench my jaw and let all of the anger I feel show on my face.

I glare at him through furrowed eyebrows and silently dare him to try again. He bares his teeth at me and picks up another, even bigger piece. My attention is on him, so I don't see Darius move up onto one knee.

At the last second, I see the flames coming toward me. My only option to force the ball up into the ceiling. A section of the maze of ductwork above me falls onto the top CCR3. The glass splinters under the weight and impact.

This all distracts me long enough to allow the tall Victus to launch the piece of metal at me. I duck out of the way, but the metal still slices my left arm as it goes by, the momentum of the steel spins me around. I grab the cut, searing pain runs down to my fingertips. It's deep. I can already feel the blood seeping into the sleeve of my sweater. I pull my hand away, and it's completely covered, dripping red.

"Royal, watch out!!" Cali's voice comes from behind me.

I spin back around to see another two orbs of fire flying toward me. I deflect again, one right back to Darius catching him on his left side just below his armpit. He grasps his body and falls to his knees. Darius had moved in front of the bald Victus to launch the fire at me, and after nicking the demon, the ball of fire catches the soldier directly in the chest.

The other unfortunately goes right into CCR3. The blast is so close to me that I'm launched through the air backward.

I land on something soft which is unexpected. I roll off of it and see I've landed on Cali. She's not moving, her eyes are closed, and has a jagged cut that's bleeding beneath one eye. I panic not knowing how badly she's been hurt, or if she's even alive. I call out her nickname a few times with no response.

I check for her pulse and when I find it I jump to my feet in relief and drag her with my one good arm out of harm's way. Once Cali is safe with Matt, I duck down low and poke my head out to observe the damage.

The third cube, like the first two, is completely gone. Not one shelf is left standing. Pieces of paper from the destroyed books flutter through the air. More fires and smoke heats the air of the room.

My stomach drops like a rock as I remember that *The Book* was in cube three.

"No!" I scream. "NO! Oh my god, no."

What have I done?!

I dive into the debris to see if there is a chance it survived. Ignoring the pain in my left arm, I sift through the charred books on the floor burning my hands on the fires around me. I'm losing hope by the second that *The Book* is still intact.

There's nothing here, nothing salvageable anyway. It's all gone.

The Book is gone. And it's all my fault.

• 6 3 •

I step out of the rubble of cube three and see Darius down on the ground. The short, Victus is just getting back to his feet from the earlier hit to his shoulder. Behind Darius, I see a large pile of ash. It must be the other Victus.

I feel sick to my stomach looking at the ash. That was a person just a minute ago. He was a Victus and came here to kill me, but he was still a person at one time. And now he's dead, and it's again my fault.

No, I think. *All of this is Darius's fault.*

My hatred for the demon grows in my chest until it is hard and burning. I feel a warmth in my hand, stronger than before. It gets hotter and hotter until my skin is glowing. With a small hiss, a floating orb of fire appears in my hand. It amazes me that even though I can feel the increasing heat from the fires around the room and my hands sting from pawing through the ash to find the remains of *The Book,* the ball of flames doesn't burn me while still in my control.

I imagine the ball getting bigger and bigger, growing to the size of a basketball. In my palm, the fire starts to grow. I look at Darius still on the ground, his hand pressed against the burn on his side.

I look at him and then the fire in my hand. I've never wanted to kill someone before. But this demon has taken so much from me. I've had to leave my family and my home behind, he's ripped that away from me. He's taken the life I knew from me. He's hurt people I love before, and he'll do it again.

My attention is focused solely on Darius, so I don't see that the remaining Victus has his feet firmly underneath him again. I hear a guttural yell from Matt come from behind me.

"NO!"

The next thing I know, the Victus is throwing multiple pieces of metal and large shards of glass in my direction. Matt is able to deflect the majority of them, but not the largest piece of glass. It keeps coming at me, fast. There is a blur in the corner of my eye as Matt tackles me to the ground, my fire-ball gets extinguished in the process.

Matt lands on top of me hard and I get the wind knocked out of me. I choke and cough trying to bring my breath back. Matt is gasping and hissing in pain on top me. He slides off and I can see the glass is sticking out of his thigh. It's wedged so deep that it must have pierced the bone.

"Milo!" I call out when I can breathe again. My dog is in front of me in an instant. He's covered in dust and bits of paper, his black fur tinted gray. "Get Moose to safety with Squirrel."

Milo grabs the collar of Matt's shirt and begins tugging him backward toward where Cali is behind CCR5. Matt grits his teeth uses both hands to hold his right leg the entire time. Blood is quickly soaking his pants, and he's got his hand over the glass ready to yank on it.

"Don't pull it out!" I yell to Matt as Milo drags him out of sight behind the glass cube.

I get back to my feet ready to take on the Victus, but he's no longer a threat. One of the pieces of metal that Matt deflected from reaching me is sticking out the side of his neck. His black shirt is shiny, obviously drenched in blood. He's slumped against the wall, his eyes are open but completely lifeless.

Darius is the only one left. He's looking at me and laughing. I'm in shock, I'm terrified, I feel sick at the amount of blood that's been shed in this room — my own continues to drip from the fingers of my left hand. The room is bright, lit by the fires everywhere that are constantly threatening to spread and engulf us all at any minute. I don't find any of this funny.

I stare at him, another fireball at the ready, prickling beneath the skin of my right hand.

"Well, well, well girl," he says with a tight voice.

The burn on his side must be causing him a lot of pain. Every movement causes him to grimace and grunt. *Good,* I think.

"You think you've won, have you?" He's stepping gingerly toward me, slowly. "You think because you killed my Victus it's over? I have thousands more where they came from. And what do you have? Nothing!"

He throws a fireball at me quicker than I thought he could in his current state. I deflect it up into the ceiling. Chunks of concrete and more sections of ductwork fall around us. Darius takes another slow step toward me while I stay silent not saying anything.

"I'm going to burn this whole place down with your friends in it. I'm going to bury your family! I'm going to skin that mutt and roast him on a spit."

Every word that comes out of Darius's mouth is making me even angrier. Both of my hands are searing ready to launch ball after ball of fire at the demon in front of me.

The fires around us are getting hotter. I can see the heat dancing off of the glass of CCR4. I take a few steps backward toward the fifth cube that Matt and Cali are tucked behind. Just as I hoped, my movement draws Darius further into the room with me.

I feel a pressure on the side of my knee, and without looking down, I know that Milo is next to me. He would only return to me if both Cali and Matt were safe enough for him to do so.

Darius's eyes light up seeing my dog next to me. His next throw, the fire angles downward toward Milo. I use my telekinesis power to sweep the ball back toward Darius. It crashes into the wall behind him next to the door leaving a large crater in the cinderblock.

I take another step backward, trying to draw Darius to me. He's so focused on me that he doesn't realize that he's walking into my trap. I want to get him right next to CCR4. When he throws his next ball, I'm going to deflect it into the cube which would explode right next to him. The blast will knock him off of his feet and then I could finish him off.

But the next thing Darius does surprises me. He claps both of his hands together in front of his chest then slowly pulls them apart. The empty space between his hands is filled by a growing fireball. I mirror him clapping my hands together and pulling them apart to produce my own giant, flaming orb. Quickly, an image flashes in my mind. I know what's going to happen.

"Milo, go to Moose and Squirrel." He presses himself into my leg once more and then darts away.

"I've had just about enough of you, girl," Darius growls at me lifting his fireball above his head. "I admit I didn't think you'd put up this much of a fight. But now, playtime is done. And so are you."

I lift my arms above my head and Darius and I launch the flames at the same time.

The two orbs meet midair melting into each other. A strong pressure wave sends both myself and Darius flying backward through the air. I land hard on the carpeted pathway between cubes five and six with Milo, Matt, and Cali directly to my right.

The right side of my body screams with pain. My right pant leg and arm are on fire, my skin is burning, but I roll around to snuff the flames out. I have a long gash across my right shoulder from debris hitting me as I spun through the air.

I force myself to get back up. *I have to make sure we get out of here.*

I look up in time to see the swirling flames smash into the ceiling causing a giant eruption on contact. Fire spreads the length of the room, shooting down the ductwork into cubes four, five, and six. The books and shelves inside catch the blaze and ignite.

I scramble to my feet. The first step sends a shot of pain through the badly burnt skin of my right leg. I limp over to my friends and dog in the space between the cubes. I grab Matt's arm and drape it over my shoulders lifting him to his feet.

"Come on!" I shout. He rests most of his weight on me and I drag him out to the walkway. I ignore the signals my nerves are sending to my brain from the pain that encompasses my body. I pull him with me and go around cube six to where our bags are. He grunts with every limp as he moves his injured leg. I drop him a little less than gently and go back to get Cali.

Milo has stayed with her as a guard. I do the same thing, lift her up and put her arm around my shoulders. She's lighter than Matt, so I get her behind cube six quicker and set her down beside Matt.

The room shudders, large sections of the ceiling start to fall. One lands on top of cube four crushing it. As the fire inside the cube meets the oxygen outside of it, there is a large whoosh, and the flames shoot out causing a wall of fire to divide the room.

Sparks start to fly throughout the air as electrical wiring is exposed to the growing flames. Acrid smoke is filling the room and blocking me from seeing clearly. It's getting harder to breathe and the heat in the room is beginning to singe my clothing.

I suddenly hear Darius screaming in pain. I look where I heard the sound come from through the flames and I see his left arm is severely burned. The skin is red and bleeding, his shirt sleeve and the left side of his jacket completely burnt away.

He's hurt, I think. *I can finish this.*

He clutches his arm to his chest before reaching into his pocket with his right hand. I have my arm cocked ready to throw a ball of fire at him. My hand is starting to tingle with warmth when I see Darius pull out a small glass bottle. He drinks whatever is inside it, then yells something I can't fully hear. He instantly disappears. My hand falls to my side, the warmth dissipating.

Large pieces of concrete slabs, beams, and ducting falls from the ceiling and begins to pile up where Darius was just sitting. The room is starting to cave in. Above me, I hear the building groan as its foundation is compromised.

I get back to where Matt, Cali, and Milo are. My boyfriend is looking at me with pure terror. Cali's eyes are open but hooded, and can't focus on any one thing but at least she's awake. Both of their faces are stained with soot, their clothes are ripped and dirty, both of them have everything from minor scratches to major injuries.

"It's okay," I tell them. "We're getting out of here right now."

I grab the bags from their pile and hand one to each of them. I put the strap of the large duffle across my shoulders. I wince as the gash in my shoulder tears open further from the contact.

There is another groan and crash as more of the room collapses behind us. I crouch down and grab onto Milo's collar and tell Cali and Matt to do the same. I don't have time to paint a vivid enough image in my head. I picture the outside of the library, the main entrance, the benches, the corner across the street with the crosswalk I use every morning.

"Outside," I say.

The sound of the roaring fires and the crumbling concrete is immediately replaced by silence. I open my eyes and the three of us, Milo, and our bags are outside the library. We're in the same position, huddled together on the ground.

The street lights reflect off of the shiny asphalt. It must have rained again while we were inside. I don't see anyone else around, the street looks deserted. I think we're finally safe until I see a blinding flash and hear a thunderous boom.

• 6 4 •

I throw myself on top of everyone to protect them. I raise my head to figure out what the hell just happened and I don't fully believe what I see.

The library is engulfed in a consuming blaze. Every window has been blown out, and flames are billowing straight up from where the roof used to be. The mortar around the brick face of the building starts to crack. Bricks loosen and rain down, shattering on the sidewalk.

Suddenly, another bright flash comes from inside the library and lights up the whole street. That is followed quickly by three of the loudest eruptions I've ever heard. A giant mushroom cloud of fire shoots into the air above the roofless building. The walls teeter faintly before they collapse inwards.

The library implodes on itself.

A giant dust cloud is kicked up and flies across the street engulfing us. The ground shakes as the building falls into the crater left by the destroyed sub-basement.

Once the dust clears, the three of us cough trying to catch our breath. Milo stands up and shakes from nose to tail. There is so much dirt in his coat that his shaking covers us in another cloud.

The scrapes and cuts on Cali and Matt are now caked with the ash from the building. Their clothes are ruined even more, and their hair is a dirty gray color. I'm sure I don't look much better.

Milo's ears prick to attention and a moment later I hear the whirl of multiple sirens closing in.

I stand and look around for a place we can all get to before the Portland Fire and Police Departments show up. There's nothing close enough that any of us can get to in our current condition.

I can't transport us back to the apartment, Darius will track it. I can't go to Mickey's or Matt's for the same reason. There's only one place I can think of that we can get cleaned and patched up that won't put anyone else on the demon's radar.

The sirens are getting closer, we're running out of time. Ignoring the pain that screams throughout my body with every movement, I squat down and grab Milo's collar again.

"Hold on!" I wait until they both grab on and say, "Mount Tabor Park."

Instantly the sirens are gone. We're just inside the main entrance to the park where Matt and I came the other night for our date. We're off to the side of the path on a patch of grass. I do a quick visual search around and determine, based on what I see that we're alone.

"Milo, casual," I command. Milo begins a short patrol of the immediate area around us. He comes back tail wagging, and I'm satisfied that we are definitely the only ones here.

"Okay, now what hurts?" I ask both Matt and Cali.

"My leg the most," Matt says through gritted teeth. The shard of glass is still sticking out of it.

"What else?"

"A couple cuts and bruises, but my leg is really bad."

"Okay, okay," I rub my hands together getting ready to try something I've never done before, but that's been the status quo tonight. "I think I can heal you."

"You think?" Cali asks groggily.

"I've never done it before but I can try. The princess in the story could, and I'm supposedly her and able to do everything else in the story so why not this too, right?"

They both look at me unconvinced.

"Trust me," I beg. "Give me your hands."

Matt holds out his hands for me to take. I grasp them tightly and look him in the eye. He nods slightly, his face pale and still tight with pain.

I take a long deep breath. I close my eyes and picture Matt as he was earlier tonight when he and Cali where deflecting tennis balls back and forth. There were no scratches on his face, no glass in his leg. He hadn't been pummeled by explosions, thrown around like a rag doll.

Matt squeezes my hands tightly and begins to grunt in pain. I keep picturing in my head what Matt looked like before, how he was uninjured. I wish for him to be that way again.

My whole body starts to vibrate as I use my projection power for the first time. I open my eyes and lock them onto Matt's. The scratches and nicks start to disappear. His face begins to loosen as his pain lessens. I look down at his leg and see the glass has been pushed out and is laying next to him on the grass. Its jagged edge still dripping with his blood. Matt relaxes with a final sigh.

"How do you feel? Are you okay?" I ask.

"I feel fine," he says. "I feel like nothing even happened."

I let out a massive sigh of relief that it worked then turn to Cali. I reach out, and she removes her hands from her head and grabs mine immediately. I repeat everything I did with Matt — I visualize her how she was earlier and wish for her to be that way again.

The gash on Cali's cheek is the first thing to heal, it leaves the faintest of scars. Just like Matt, the tight grimace on her face loosens until she is relaxed.

"How does your head feel?"

"Much better," she says rubbing it. "The ringing is gone, and I don't see double anymore." I go to let go of her hands, but she doesn't release mine. "Okay, Lex. Now you."

"No, I have to check Milo first."

I whistle for him and he comes over. I look him over from head to toe and thankfully, maybe even miraculously, he doesn't seem to have a scratch on him. Just to be safe, I put one hand on his head and the other under his chin. I use projection to heal anything I can't see or feel.

"Good boy, Milo," I say.

Only then do I inventory what hurts on me and where. My whole body feels like it's been put through a meat grinder. The spots causing the most problems are the gashes on my shoulder and my left arm, and the bad burns on my arm and leg.

With a grunt of pain, I cross my arms in an X across my chest and put each hand on the opposite shoulder. I wish for those injuries to heal.

It feels like I'm being wrapped up in a warm hug. My body vibrates again, and I feel the warmth change to a high heat. It starts at my toes and as it climbs up my body, the aches and pains begin to lessen. I feel the burnt flesh on my leg cover over with new, unblemished skin.

The feeling continues up my chest and down my arms. The gash on my left arm feels like it draws back in all the blood that left it. My right shoulder loosens as if a giant knot has been released from the muscle as the edges of the long cut come back together.

"Okay," I sigh when I finally feel back to normal. "We can't stay here long. We have to keep moving."

I stand up and help Matt and Cali to their feet. I drape the supply duffle across my back and toss my laundry bag over one shoulder. They each pick up a bag, and the two of them look at me for direction.

"Ready?"

After looking silently at each other, they both nod at me.

"Okay, let's go. Milo, side," I command as I head off to my left, back toward the main entrance of the park.

EPILOGUE

VIRIBUS

The giant Victus is waiting at the bar like he was instructed. The room is empty, it's just the bartender and him. In one hand, he's holding a thick glass beer mug, the other holds his phone waiting for the boss's call. He raises the glass for a swig, but it never makes it to his lips. He's interrupted by Darius appearing in the middle of the bar looking worse than the giant has ever seen him.

The demon's clothes are destroyed. His jacket is missing the left sleeve, exposing burnt and blistered skin from shoulder to fingertips. There is blood dripping down his side, staining his shirt. His pants are ripped and covered in dirt and dust.

"Viribus," the demon croaks out.

"Boss! What the fuck?"

"That little bitch," Darius grunts, clutching his injured arm. He groans in pain before continuing. "Ahhh... she... she wasn't... ah, shit!

"That fucking bitch!" the demon roars.

The demon's legs give out, and Viribus catches him. The demon screams as the touch of his Victus sends another wave of pain through his body.

Viribus sets Darius down on the ground gently, his back up against the bar in a sitting position. With his long arms, the Victus reaches over the bar and grabs the nearest bottle of whiskey.

"Get out of here," he directs the bartender. The old man doesn't think twice before he turns tail and leaves.

Viribus bends down and pours a drink down the fiend's throat. Darius coughs at first, some of the whiskey spilling from his mouth. Once he gets a clean swallow, he closes his lips around the bottle and sucks all of it down.

"Where are Julius and Damon?" Viribus asks.

"Dead!" Darius yells grasping the behemoth's clothing and pulling him in close. "They're both dead! She had help and fought back. She won this time, Viribus, but she won't next time."

"What?" the giant scratches his head. "What are you talking about, boss?"

"*The Book*," the demon sneers. "The magical tome her ancestors used to curse me. It's been destroyed. She's on her own now."

"How do you know?"

"She yelled and ran into the flames after I blew up one of the rooms."

The Victus is confused but is more concerned with the state his boss is in. Darius drops the empty whiskey bottle from his hand. Viribus hands the demon a second bottle of liquor. His skin is clammy to the touch, and his eyes flutter. He's on the verge of passing out.

"I need to rest," the demon says. "For next time."

The mammoth Victus lifts the black-haired man into the air and carries him through the bar toward the kitchen.

"Next time we bring more, Viribus," the demon says again, fighting to keep his eyes open. "Next time her life will be mine! And I will fucking take it!"

The demon passes out limp in his Victus's arms, his strength completely exhausted. The giant cradles his boss close and brings him upstairs to the small room with the stained mattress. He closes the door with his foot and lays the demon down gently. He peels off what's left of Darius's torn jacket and shirt leaving him bare-chested on the bed.

Viribus steps backward until his back hits the wall. He slides down it and sits with his legs straight out. He watches Darius's chest go up and down, the demon comatose on the bed.

The Victus uses this opportunity to examine the demon from afar, see just how much damage the witch was able to do. As Viribus looks his boss over, he sees the skin on the demon's arm start to bubble as it begins to heal itself. The gash on his side has stopped bleeding but still looks bad.

He has no idea how long it will take the demon to be fully healed. If the witch was able to take on Darius and two Victus soldiers, then next time they should send at least ten after her.

Viribus feels fierce anger settle in his chest. He doesn't mourn the loss of his Victus brothers. He seethes thinking about the girl who took their lives. He pulls out his phone and searches through his contacts for a number. He presses send and puts it to his ear listening for the call to connect.

"Hello?" a tired voice on the other end of the line answers.

"It's me," Viribus says. "I need a favor."

"ALEXA"

The mound of paper towels and baby wipes next to the sink in the park bathroom is quickly growing as Cali and I clean ourselves up. We change out of our dirty clothes and clean up every bit of dirt we can see. *Unbelievable*, I think. *Except for a couple small scratches, my glasses are pretty much intact.*

I turn around to check myself over in the mirror. The deep gash that was on my shoulder has healed to a long, jagged scar. There is another line that bisects my left arm between the shoulder and elbow. Both are bright white and stand out in stark contrast to my mocha skin tone. The burnt skin thankfully left no scar behind when it healed. Other than that, there are no bruises or blemishes on myself or Cali.

I pick out whatever is on the top of my bag — an oversized, long-sleeved gray shirt and another pair of skinny cargo pants, olive colored. The clothes I was wearing are completely ruined, so I wrap them up into a ball and shove it as far down in the garbage as I can.

I take out Milo's brush from the bag of his things. I brush him out as much as I can, throwing away clumps of the shed dirty fur. I splash some water on him and use some paper towels to try and get as much dirt off of him as possible. I brush him again, and when I'm done his coat is at least black again. Whether or not he's entirely clean, I'd lean toward no.

Next to Milo and I, Cali puts on a teal v-neck tee, a navy hooded sweatshirt, and jeans. She throws all the clothes she had on in the library into the garbage, then tosses the pile of paper towels on top.

I pick up my canvas laundry bag, stuff Milo's bag inside it, then I grab the supply duffle and throw it over my shoulder. The three of us exit the bathroom making sure we haven't left anything behind. I use my telekinesis to re-lock the bathroom door. I take in a deep breath of the fresh night air and blow it out with puffed cheeks.

Matt comes out of the men's room shortly after. He has a red sweatshirt on with a yellow shirt poking out from underneath and jeans. He's washed up like we have, and has his bag slung over his shoulder.

I know this is not the time for it, but I can't help but swoon at the sight of him. Facing death is known to be an aphrodisiac and I imagine if I weren't so exhausted, I would jump him right here and now. I tilt my head to the side as I enjoy the thought for a minute.

Cali breathes deeply and sighs. She crosses her arms then asks, "So where to now?"

"What?" I reply, my brow furrows in confusion as I'm knocked out of my fantasy.

"Where to?" Matt asks.

"Are you guys still sure about this? I mean, you saw what just happened. It'll only get worse from here."

I know I wouldn't have gotten out of the library alive without them. But how can I expect them to come with me again after all that happened tonight?

"You still have to ask us that?"

"I will always ask you that."

"Lex, we're coming, or at least I am."

"I'm with the Squirrel," Matt adds. "And with you."

"You're both sure?" They nod in sync. "Like really, really sure?"

"Yes," Cali says. "So, now that the library is gone, does that mean *The Book* is gone too?"

"Well, yes that one is, but *The Book* itself isn't technically gone," I say off-handedly.

"What?" Matt asks. "I saw the third cube blow up. And the whole library is gone. Did you take it out somehow?"

"No."

"Then how is it not gone?" Cali.

"It has a twin."

"A twin?" they ask at the same time.

"Yup," I say popping the P.

"So that's where we're going?" Cali.

"That's right."

"And where is that?" Matt.

"The twin is in the Eternal City. The place where all roads lead."

Acknowledgements

There are an abundant amount of people who are responsible for this book. However, it would be incredibly boring and indulgent to list everyone, so I'll just hit the main bullet points.

To my mother, Marguerita, for listening to the ever-changing plot until I landed somewhere that made sense: thank you for never discouraging my wild ideas and reading draft after draft without complaint. Thank you for being there regardless of the situation, or your level of irritation with me. Thank you for showing me the type of person I want and strive to be.

To my father, Dan, for helping me out of a jam or two (or three or four): thank you for giving me a little more freedom to pursue this than I probably would have had.

To my sisters, Meghan and Kaitlin, who set the bar really high in life: thank you for always pushing me to rise to your level, telling me like it is to toughen me up, trusting your baby sister to give you advice, and always, always, always providing me with unwavering support.

To my nieces and nephew: thank you for reawakening my imagination and creativity.

To Amanda, Brittany, Erica, Kristen, Meryl, and Phil (you're listed alphabetically, not in any order!): thank you for keeping me laughing when the days were dark and seemingly endless, for thrilling game nights no matter how many times I lost, meals filled with genuine excitement over this project, and text messages of constant love and encouragement.

To the rest of my family, far and wide, extended and near: you are all very dear to me, and I love you wholeheartedly.

To Ms. Donna B, who gave me the final push to ultimately start all of this: thank you for keeping tabs on my progress and proofreading. You are one of the best teachers I have ever had.

To the magical medical professionals — SD, DM, KA, and everyone at NY Orthopedics and Lenox Hill; JD, and everyone at NY Pain and Spine; and EK, JD, and everyone at Burke Rehab: thank you for returning me to being a functioning human again, for reminding me to trust that the day would come when I would be back to myself again. Once my spine healed because of your multiple combined efforts, my mind was finally clear enough to be able to write this book. I am eternally grateful to you all and forever in your debt.

To my pups, Corie and Jax, who were meshed together to create Milo: you are both very good dogs. However, one more so than the other.

To Joey, the love of my life: thank you, quite honestly, for everything. There are not enough words to describe what you mean to and what you've done for me in our time together. I am my best self with you. If I had nothing else in the world but you, I'd still have everything I've ever wanted.

And finally, to you, the reader: thank you for taking the time out of your life — from whatever schedules, appointments, play dates, chores, errands, or any of the other tasks that endlessly fill all of our days — to read this book. Our time on this earth is limited, and that you spent a little piece of it with the words I've written fills me with a gratitude I'm not sure I could ever completely express.

ABOUT THE AUTHOR

Kerri McLoone has worked as a camp counselor, an administrative as-
sistant, and plenty of jobs in between. She first came up with the character
of Alexa Pearce when she was a college student. In 2009, Kerri graduated
from the Conservatory of Music at Purchase College. A few years later, she
was inspired to go back to school and pursue an area that had always
been of interest to her. She received her Master's Degree in Marriage and
Family Therapy from Long Island University in 2015.

Only a couple short months later, she suffered an accident at work that left
her in constant debilitating pain, severe physical limitations, and resulted in
two major back surgeries before her thirtieth birthday.

Recovering her health allowed her the time she had not previously had to
explore the story of Alexa and finally, after many long years, see it put
down in tangible form.

She currently resides just outside of New York City with her dog, Jax.

This is her first novel.

Email: KerriMcLooneBooks@gmail.com

Follow Kerri McLoone on Social Media:

 @KerriMcLooneBooks   @_kmbooks_   @_kmbooks_